HIS DARKEST DESIRE

THE CURSED ONES 2

TIFFANY ROBERTS

Copyright © 2023 by Tiffany Freund and Robert Freund Jr.

All Rights Reserved. No part of this publication may be used or reproduced, distributed, or transmitted in any form by any means, including scanning, photocopying, uploading, and distribution of this book via any other electronic means without the permission of the author and is illegal, except in the case of brief quotations embodied in critical reviews and certain other noncommercial uses permitted by copyright law. For permission requests, contact the publishers at the address below.

This book was not created with AI, and we do not give permission for our work to be trained for AI.

Tiffany Roberts

authortiffanyroberts@gmail.com

This book is a work of fiction. Names, characters, places, and incidents are products of the author's imagination or are used fictitiously and are not to be construed as real. Any resemblance to actual events, locales, organizations, or people, living or dead, is entirely coincidental.

Cover Illustration by Linda Noeran

Vex & Kinsley Art by IF.Art

Tree of Life Art by Anna Spies

❀ Created with Vellum

HIS DARKEST DESIRE

A cursed goblin sorcerer. The human female he's waited an eternity for. A secret that could tear them apart.

A quaint cottage in a Scottish forest seemed the perfect place for Kinsley to start anew. But when a tragic accident leaves her isolated and dying, her new life is over before ever beginning.

Until a dark, mysterious being emerges from the night gloom and offers to save her—for a price.

With no other choice but death, she accepts. She awakens to find herself bound to an ancient, powerful goblin who is equally terrifying and intriguing. He's terse, demanding, brooding.

Despite that, Kinsley is drawn to him, captivated by his sinful crimson eyes, craving his every wicked touch.

But what will happen when he discovers the truth? What will happen when he learns that Kinsley cannot fulfill their pact?

What will happen if she lets this goblin claim her heart along with her freedom?

Check author's website for detailed content warnings.

To everyone with wonder in their eyes and magic in their hearts.

CHAPTER ONE

As a child, Kinsley had held such simple views of the seasons. Spring had meant picking wildflowers and helping her mum in the garden. Summer meant no school, long adventures in the woods, and swimming. Fall had been about the beautiful colors on the trees and Halloween, which she'd loved even though she was so easy to scare. Winter had been all hot chocolate, warm fires, Christmas, and the near-mythical snow day.

Sitting here on a blanket in the back of her SUV with rain pattering on the raised hatch, she longed for that childhood simplicity. But the innocent mindset of her youth could not be restored by the soothing rain or the tasty ham and cheese sandwich her aunt had packed for her, and the landscape surrounding her, for all its wonder and newness, refused to let Kinsley hide from the fact that her perspective had forever been altered.

Gray clouds loomed over the dark, restless waters of the loch beside which she'd parked, contrasted by the nearby vegetation. Some green lingered, but yellow, orange, red, and brown dominated the Scottish Highlands. It wasn't just the trees and undergrowth—the ground itself had ceded to autumn.

Her marriage had ended during the fall three years ago, just before the lush Oregon woodlands had started changing color. Kinsley's view of the season hadn't been the same since.

Autumn, a time of decay and decline. A time of growing darkness, of day giving a little more of itself to night with every cycle.

And here, now, five thousand miles away from the place she'd called home, she understood that autumn meant change. Wasn't that what she'd been searching for?

Kinsley took another bite of her sandwich. All things changed with time, and change wasn't inherently bad. The fallen leaves would fuel new growth in spring. Life would slow down, but it would not end. The plants and animals that would sleep through the winter would awaken to a world reborn.

Didn't that make autumn a season of hope? Of harvesting and reflection, of...healing?

She swallowed and glanced down at her half-eaten sandwich with a smile. Perhaps everything else had changed, but Aunt Cece's sandwiches were just as delicious now as they'd been during the holidays Kinsley had spent in England throughout her childhood.

How could ham, cheese, mustard, and mayo—arguably the most basic of sandwich ingredients apart from peanut butter and jelly—be so *good*?

Was it simply that taste of the old and familiar amidst all this change? All this...

She sighed and returned her gaze to the loch.

What is this?

"It's an adventure, Kinsley. You're going to explore the ancient forests of Europe like you always wanted to do."

At least that was what she'd been telling herself, though she knew it was only partly true.

I'm running.

Ding! Ding! Ding! We have a winner!

Kinsley scrunched her nose and lowered the sandwich to her lap. "I'm not running."

But saying those words out loud didn't change the truth.

And yet being here felt...right. All her life, she'd always had this vague sense of an invisible tether tugging her in this direction, leading her to these ancient lands. Now that she was no longer resisting that call, it was like...

Like she was meant to be here.

"One day at a time, Kinsley. One day at a time."

She lifted the sandwich to her mouth. Before she could eat any more, her phone rang, disturbing the peaceful ambience that had allowed her thoughts to wander where they shouldn't have. Grabbing the phone from the blanket beside her, she turned it over and smiled at the name on the screen. She accepted the call.

"Hey mum."

"Hello love!" came Emily's cheerful voice. "Are you in your new place?"

Kinsley took another bite of the sandwich. "Not yet."

"Dear, don't talk with your mouth full."

Kinsley chuckled. "Sorry."

It didn't matter that Kinsley was a twenty-eight-year-old woman, her mother would always scold her for her manners as though she were still a rambunctious five-year-old opening her mouth to gross out her older sister with a clump of chewed up food.

"When are you due to arrive?" Emily asked.

Kinsley hurriedly chewed and swallowed. "I still have a couple more hours of driving to go."

Emily sighed. "I just don't see why you couldn't stay with Cecelia. There are so many more opportunities for you in London, and so much more to see and do. You'd be with family, and you know she loves having you there. There's no reason for you to live alone somewhere so remote."

"Mum, I live alone when I'm on the road."

"Living in your car, I know. But it's so…so dangerous!"

"It's basically camping, but I'm in my car instead of a tent. If you think about it, that's way safer, right?"

"Kinsley…"

"I'm fine, mum, really. You don't need to worry so much."

"I'm your mother. I will never stop worrying about my daughters. I love you."

"And I love you. But I… I just need a place of my own and some time to myself. Time to think, to clear my head."

To heal.

"I know, love," Emily said softly. "I know."

"And," Kinsley said with a grin, "as much as I love Aunt Cece, we both know she *hovers*."

Emily laughed. "She does, but she's like me. She's worried about you."

Kinsley sobered. "I know, but I'll be fine. I promise. And this place is beautiful, nestled against the forest like an old, fairytale cottage. I'll be able to work right in the garden."

Her mother chuckled. "Well, you always did love nature. You were always running out into the woods barefoot, talking to fairies, making them little houses, and bringing them gifts and sweets. You were my little fairy child. You still are. We miss you, Kinsley."

With her chest constricting and tears stinging her eyes, Kinsley looked up and watched the raindrops falling upon the windshield. "I miss you guys, too. How are you and Dad and Maddy?"

"Your father and I are doing well. We're treating ourselves to dinner out tonight once he's home from work. Oh! Did Madison tell you her good news?"

"What news?"

"She finally found a space in town to open up her bakery!"

"Oh my gosh, that's so exciting! I'm so happy for her. Tell her she better send me some of her lemon bars. I have a sudden craving, and she knows how much I love them."

They continued chatting as Kinsley finished her sandwich. The rain grew heavier, the wind picked up, carrying an icy bite, and thunder rolled somewhere beyond the glen.

"Is it storming there?" Emily asked.

"It's been raining, but it looks like it's getting worse. I'm going to get going. I want to make it to the rental before it gets dark so I don't get lost."

"Kinsley!"

"I'm kidding! Well, not really. But worst-case scenario—"

"Kin—"

"Which isn't bad at all," Kinsley hurriedly said, "is that I sleep in my car till morning."

"I swear all of my gray hairs come from you."

Kinsley snickered. "That's cause I'm your favorite."

"I don't play favorites."

"It's okay. You don't have to admit it to Maddy. It's our secret, mum."

"Three more gray hairs, Kinsley. You just gave me *three* more."

"And you look gorgeous with those grays."

Kinsley could practically hear her mother's eyes roll.

"You know we're all here for you if you need us, right?" Emily said.

Kinsley tightened her hold on her phone and closed her eyes. "I know, mum. I love you."

She ended the call after saying goodbye and lowered the phone, staring at the home screen. Kinsley had always been close to her family. Her mother, despite having grown up in a house that she and Cece described as stuffy and proper, had always tried to be open and honest with her daughters. Kinsley and Madison could go to her for anything, no matter how uncertain or uncomfortable, knowing they wouldn't be judged. Their father, Aiden, had always been a hands-on dad, and was just as supportive as their mum.

Aunt Cece had been wonderful too. She'd welcomed Kinsley into her home, and her warmth and kindness—including an offer to *give that knobhead a proper thrashing*—had made the process of Kinsley establishing her life in the United Kingdom far smoother than it should've been.

But in this…Kinsley needed to find her own way. She needed to find her own peace.

Before she even realized what she was doing, she tapped on one of her social media apps. There were multiple notifications awaiting her. Smiling, she browsed the comments on her videos and pictures, replying to several and even laughing out loud at a few.

Kinsley loved that her adventures in the wilderness brought so much joy and entertainment to others. She loved sharing the wonderment she experienced out in nature with her audience. Even her scrapbooking and journaling videos provided inspiration and escape to people, if only for a short while. Kinsley had been scrapbooking since she was a child, and the hobby had evolved over the years into not just a fun activity, but a way to decompress.

Switching to her camera, she raised the phone and grinned before taking a selfie.

Almost there! I can't wait to take you all on this new adventure, she added to the photo's caption before posting it to her profile.

She swiped through her feed, liking her mutuals' pictures and laughing at a video of Madison's husky howling like a banshee with a sore throat. They'd always joked that the dog was broken. That was followed by a picture from one of her friends showing off new rims on his car, after which was an inspirational quote, and then a sponsored ad for a fancy tent.

Yeah, they're totally not listening to every word, right?

She scrolled to the next post. Her heart clenched, and her smile fell. It was a photo with a very familiar face. A *painfully* familiar face.

Liam. Kinsley's ex-husband.

But he wasn't alone in the picture. His wife was beside him, smiling brightly and holding their baby boy.

Kinsley's chest flooded with raw, jagged emotions, making it impossible to breathe.

How many times over the last couple years had she told herself to remove Liam from her socials? How many times had she happened across a picture of him and his new wife, his new life, and felt that deep, potent sting? How many times had she poised her finger over the unfriend button only to stop herself?

She'd always told herself that she would just…get over it one day. When Kinsley first moved to the United States at eight years old, Liam had been her first friend. They'd been inseparable. At sixteen, they'd started dating, and they'd married not long after high school. Unfriending him after what was on the surface an amicable divorce had always felt wrong. Petty. They were still friends who cared for one another.

But seeing him now with his newborn baby, with this sweet, adorable little life he'd made with someone else…

It was too much.

Kinsley closed the app and clutched her phone to her chest. She took a deep breath and slowly, shakily, released it as she forced her teary eyes up to the stormy sky.

"Everything may seem dark and scary," she whispered, "and you may not always be able to see the sun, but it is there."

CHAPTER TWO

FROWNING, Kinsley leaned forward and squinted at what little of the winding road she could see through the windshield. The wipers could barely keep up with the downpour, and the rain drumming atop the car nearly drowned out the music playing on the stereo.

She huffed. "So much for getting there before dark."

The main road had been blocked by a fallen tree, resulting in a detour that had added an hour to her drive. According to the car's navigation system, it'd still be another ten minutes before she reached her destination.

Now, it was pitch-black outside, and the relentless rain and walls of trees to either side of the roadway only further reduced visibility. Were it not for the blue blob on the car's map screen, she would never have known there was a huge loch nearby.

"In half a mile, turn left," the navigation guide said, cutting through the music.

Another car rounded the bend ahead, its blinding headlights made more intense by the reflections from the water pooled on the narrow road. Kinsley winced and shifted her vehicle aside to make room for the car to pass. Thankfully, there'd been little traffic on these backroads, so such encounters had been rare—though that didn't make it suck any less.

"Almost there," she said.

Static crackled through the stereo, warping the singer's voice into something otherworldly. Though the static cleared quickly, Kinsley's frown deepened.

She was listening to music through a Bluetooth connection. How was that getting interference? There'd been thunder and lightning, but the storm wasn't that bad, was it?

"Turn left," said the guide.

Flicking on the turn signal, Kinsley slowed the car and peered through the darkness until she spotted where the trees opened on a narrow dirt road—or rather, a narrow mud road. She switched into all-wheel drive and turned onto the path.

"Continue straight."

Clutching the steering wheel, Kinsley followed the bumpy path. "Please, oh please don't get stuck."

As she continued onward, the music once more grew distorted, and now the instrument panel and dashboard screen dimmed and flickered along with it.

She reached out and thumped on the dashboard. "What is going on?"

Kinsley stopped the car and put it in park. Reaching into her purse, which lay on the seat beside her, she retrieved her phone and unlocked it. She tapped on the map; it came up with a *No Connection* page. Her gaze darted to the upper right corner of the screen.

No signal.

"Damn it."

Closing her music app, she tossed the phone back into her purse and lifted her gaze. The cottage awaited somewhere ahead. She just needed to take it slow and steady while keeping an eye out for the place.

"People survived without wi-fi and GPS for most of human history. This shouldn't be that hard."

She shifted the car into gear and continued onward, leaning closer to the windshield to better focus on the road. The headlights made little difference in the rain and gloom. On one side, tall, densely packed trees marched up a rugged incline, their tops shrouded by the night. On the other, the ground dropped away so abruptly that she could just make out the tops of some of those trees.

Kinsley couldn't be certain whether it was a sheer drop or a steep hillside, but it didn't matter. Going down it would've been bad either way.

According to the map on the dashboard screen, that downward slope led to the loch, from which she was separated by only a few dozen yards of land.

Her hands tightened on the steering wheel as a bend in the road ahead came into view. During the day, she might've seen the waters of the loch through the trees there, but now that space was filled only with impossible, impenetrable black.

Slow and steady.

A warning chime sounded, but nothing on the instrument panel indicated an open door, unbuckled seatbelt, or engine problem. Pixelized artifacts spread across the display screen, making the map unreadable. The headlights dimmed and flashed erratically. Sound buzzed from the speakers—not just static but strange, high-pitched warbling noises, like an old radio being tuned, run through by what she swore were…whispers.

She tapped the screen. Her touch only caused new glitches to blossom on the display.

In any other place, at any other time, all this would've just been a terrible annoyance. But here in this dark, stormy, secluded bit of the Highlands, miles away from the nearest town…

All at once, everything went out—the instrument panel, the screen and dashboard lights, the headlights. Thick, cloying darkness invaded the vehicle. The static ceased, but the whispers persisted. Kinsley's skin broke out in goosebumps, and the hairs on her arms rose.

"What's happ—" Her breath caught in her throat and her eyes widened as she looked ahead.

A bright blue orb floated in front of the car. A light adrift on a sea of utter, unforgiving black.

Kinsley did not understand what she was seeing. Part of her mind insisted that this…this apparition wasn't real, that it couldn't be. Some other part, smaller, quieter, insisted that she should've checked whether the cottage was in a haunted forest before signing the paperwork.

She barely noticed that the SUV was still moving forward.

The orb brightened, and the whispers grew louder. Though she couldn't make out the words, they were melodic, hypnotic, beckoning her closer.

Just as the voices reached a crescendo, they fell silent. The car's lights, both interior and exterior, flared on.

The blue orb vanished in the cones of illumination cast by the headlights, which fell on the golden leafed boughs of a tree that was much too close to the road.

Kinsley's heart leapt into her throat as she realized that she'd reached the bend.

But she hadn't turned.

The front wheels hit a bump, jolting her. She slammed both feet on the brake pedal. Her body shifted forward, and the seatbelt dug into her chest as the SUV slid on the muddy road.

The vehicle pitched downward.

She must've gasped, or screamed, or cursed, but she didn't hear whatever sound emerged. Only the sight before her held her attention—the steep downward slope riddled with trees, undergrowth, boulders, and logs, all lit starkly by the headlights.

Her stomach lurched as gravity overrode the brakes, dragging the SUV fully off the road.

Chaos swallowed Kinsley. The vehicle bounced violently down the hillside, jostled by the many obstacles. The noise was deafening, the jerky movements of the headlights were disorienting, and the punishment on her body was immediate as she was thrashed from side to side and up and down mercilessly. Even the seatbelt couldn't keep her fully in her seat.

The car halted with an immense crash. Something hard and very, very heavy crushed her midsection back against the seat even as her head snapped forward and struck the steering wheel.

Darkness enveloped her vision, deepened by the wave of agony washing over her.

From somewhere far off, she tasted iron, smelled rain and dirt, and heard faint whispers drawing closer over the rush of the storm.

Blue light tinged the black behind her eyelids, but she could not open them.

Unconsciousness sank its claws into Kinsley, dragging her down, down, down. She didn't fight.

Then she didn't see, hear, smell, or feel anything at all.

A CRACK of thunder jolted Kinsley awake. Her eyes flashed open. Bright, ethereal blue luminescence filled her vision. The orb came into focus before her, flitting from side to side before drawing closer. Kinsley slowly blinked, struggling to clear the blurriness from her vision.

Sound rushed back into her awareness. Heavy raindrops striking the car and nearby foliage; wind whipping through leaves and branches; creaking metal; the drawn-out echoes of the thunder that had roused her.

And whispers. Not from the speakers anymore, but from the floating orb. They were softer now, almost soothing, coaxing her to wakefulness.

The scents of rain, wet earth, wood, and decay filled her nose, as well as that of acrid smoke. A tang of bitter iron remained on her tongue. She swallowed, but it did not rid her of the taste. Was that…blood? Her body trembled, but it wasn't simply the air from outside making her shiver. It was a deep-rooted cold chilling her from within.

She raised her throbbing head. The orb's light revealed the shattered windshield and crumpled dashboard, the broken window and its bent frame, and the rear-view mirror dangling by a frayed wire.

Kinsley attempted to sit back, but she cried out as agony ripped through her middle. She looked down.

Her gaze fell on something protruding from the instrument panel—a tree branch. It had run through a gap in the steering wheel and was…was…

A nightmare. I'm stuck in a nightmare.

This…this can't be real.

She drew in one ragged breath after another as she lifted her quivering fingers to the branch. The bark was rough and solid. As though in a dream, she trailed her fingers along the branch to the place where it impaled her belly. They came away wet and sticky with blood.

"Oh God," she rasped, the words sending another wave of pain through her. "Oh God, oh God, oh God..." Every breath she took was fresh agony, building and building. She screamed.

The sound tapered into sobs and a soft, pitiful whine as Kinsley closed her eyes and weakly clutched the branch. "This can't be happening..."

Tears streamed down her cheeks. She was all alone, in the middle of nowhere, run through and pinned in place by a branch.

She was going to die here.

My phone!

She opened her eyes and looked at the passenger seat. Her purse was gone, replaced by broken safety glass, forest debris, and gathering fog. She swung her gaze to the floor. Just visible in the shadows there was her overturned purse. With fumbling fingers, she unlatched her seatbelt. The branch prevented it from fully retracting, but it left her shoulder unrestricted.

Kinsley reached for her purse, and a cry spilled from her lips as her body shifted on the branch. Warm liquid ran down her belly.

You're not supposed to move!

But what choice did she have? She had no other means of calling for help.

With harsh breaths, Kinsley searched her surroundings for anything of use, anything at all.

Movement to her right drew her attention to the driver's window. Only jagged fragments of cracked glass remained around its edges. The glowing blue orb circled a small, thin stick dangling just outside.

Was it...helping her?

She reached through the opening, grasped the stick, and broke it free. Drawing it into the vehicle, she turned back toward her purse, extending her arm as far as she could. But the stick wasn't long enough.

Gritting her teeth, she leaned a little farther. Searing pain engulfed her as the branch resisted her movement. It stole her breath, and black spots danced in her vision, nearly causing her to lose hold of the stick in her battle to remain conscious. She let out an anguished growl and forced herself to shift upon the branch just a little more.

The stick hooked under the strap of her bag, and Kinsley released a sob as she carefully drew it toward herself.

But as soon as the bag's weight pulled the strap taut, the stick bent with tension.

"Please... Don't..."

It snapped. Kinsley's heart ceased beating, and time froze.

"No! No, no, no, no!" She threw the broken stick and grasped the branch impaling her with both hands. Nails digging into the wood, she attempted to pull it out while simultaneously pushing back against the seat. Her tormented wail overpowered the pelting rain. A dizzying wave of agony ripped through her, and a gush of hot blood spilled from her belly as her body slid back along the branch.

But the limb itself did not budge, and she was only doing more damage to herself.

She was speeding the inevitable.

Stop, stop, stop!

Defeated, Kinsley let her hands fall away and dropped her head against the headrest. Tears ran down her cheeks as her shoulders quaked with her painful cries. But her pain was lost to the storm. She was trapped, and no one was coming. There would be no help.

And she was dying.

The orb of light drew closer to her. It dimmed, and its indecipherable whispers took on an undeniably sorrowful tone. Even this close, she couldn't tell what it was, couldn't tell if there was something casting the light, or if it *was* the light. Regardless, it was all she had. Her last hope.

"Please," she whispered. "Help me."

It zipped away, leaving Kinsley alone in the darkness.

She closed her eyes. "I don't want to die."

More tears fell, trickling down her cheeks and chin. She thought of her family, of how distressed they would be when they couldn't reach her, of their devastation when they would eventually discover what had happened. She thought of the places she still longed to see, the things she still wanted to do. She thought of Liam and the life of which they'd dreamed. Of the life they'd tried to make.

She thought of the life that had been taken from her again and again and again.

She thought of the life she would never have.

Ice spread within Kinsley, creeping through every vein, seizing every muscle, pervading every bone. It chased away all memories of warmth and comfort. The time between each thumping beat of her heart stretched, pushing toward eternity. She felt herself fading. Felt herself falling into the darkness that enveloped her.

The sound of the rain dulled as though it too were being swallowed up in that darkness.

"You spoke true," someone said from just outside the vehicle in a deep, velvety, masculine voice. Something warm touched her cheek, firmly but gently, and turned her face toward the window.

That voice wound around Kinsley, halting her descent, and that touch instilled her with just enough warmth to fight.

"This cannot be," the stranger rasped. "*She* cannot be."

"Please," Kinsley begged, struggling to open her eyes. "Help me."

Her plea was answered by a chorus of whispers that blended with the rustling of leaves and pattering of rain.

"Silence," the man commanded, and the whispers ceased.

Her eyelids finally fluttered open. A large, dark figure stood outside the SUV, silhouetted by the glow of not one but three orbs of light hovering behind him. Her eyes battled to find something to focus upon, but she could discern none of the man's features—he was blacker than the nothingness threatening to devour her.

"I can heal this mortal flesh." The man's hold on Kinsley's cheeks tightened as he leaned closer, his form blotting out more of the light. "But my aid comes at a price."

Kinsley's next inhalation was colored by a new scent, nuanced, layered, and alluring. It was earthy and spicy, masculine but warm. Oakmoss and amber.

A shiver stole through her, renewing her pain and deepening the chill. "Anything."

"What is your name?"

"Kinsley."

"Your *true* name," he demanded.

It was growing harder and harder for her to focus, to think, to breathe, to keep her eyes open. Everything felt numb, and she was tired. So, so tired. The way he spoke, the way he'd worded that, it was wrong, but she couldn't understand why.

And right now, she didn't care.

"Kinsley...Wynter...Delaney," she whispered as her eyelids fell shut.

"In exchange for your life, Kinsley Wynter Delaney, you will be bound to me. You will be my mate, and you will take my seed into your body until it bears fruit. Do you swear it?"

She nodded, though she wasn't sure whether her head moved at all.

The man grasped her wrist and lifted it, holding it securely. He growled. "Do you swear it upon your true name, mortal?"

"Yes," she breathed as the endless, insatiable void yawned around her.

The warmth of his grip intensified, coalescing into a searing heat around her wrist that made the ice in the rest of her body even more terrible in contrast.

Just before she slipped away, his voice flowed into her, resonating right to her heart, where it embedded itself.

"You are *mine*."

CHAPTER THREE

Kinsley's eyes snapped open, and she bolted upright with a gasp. Bending over her raised knees with her hair falling to the sides of her face, she drew in one deep, ragged breath after another, but she couldn't fill her lungs with enough air. Her chest felt constricted, and her heart raced.

She pressed a hand to her belly. There was no branch impaling her, no blood, no pain. Only soft, unbroken flesh, the hard press of her navel piercing, and the haunting memory.

It was a dream. Just a dream.

Kinsley squeezed her eyes shut, slowed her breathing, and willed herself to calm.

More like a nightmare, but not real all the same. You're okay, Kinsley.

What she'd experienced had been no different than a dream of falling from a high place and jolting awake just before striking the ground. Except this had felt so *real*.

Once she'd finally calmed, Kinsley opened her eyes and lifted her head. Her brow creased as she looked around the unfamiliar room.

"I...am not at Aunt Cece's..."

She wasn't in the back of her car either, and this certainly didn't look anything like the pictures of the rental.

Not that she could remember getting to the rental to begin with.

This place... It was straight out of a fairytale.

Kinsley sat at the center of a huge four-poster bed. Vines of lush ivy spiraled up the posts and ran across the cloth and carved wood of the canopy. More ivy clung to the stone walls, dangled from the ceiling, and crawled up pieces of furniture. Flashes of color stood out amidst the vines—bright mushrooms, delicate flowers, and raw quartz crystals growing from the walls. Those crystals emitted their own faint light.

Directly ahead stood a wide fireplace made of rough-hewn stone that tapered to the chimney. The thick wood plank serving as the mantle was laden with baubles, bottles, jars, and ancient-looking, leather-bound books, as were the shelves carved into the walls all around. A lone chair was positioned before the hearth, its wood detailed with intricate carvings.

There were two wooden doors on the left wall. Both were adorned with ironwork in swirling, leafy patterns that stretched across their faces from the hinges. Their handles were metal rings.

A tall, wide wardrobe stood to one side of the bed, its doors and drawers also decorated with elaborate carvings. On the opposite side was a desk with a low-backed chair, its surface cluttered with sheafs of parchment, jars of ink, feather quills, and more old books in haphazard stacks.

Somehow, even the more refined pieces of furniture blended well with the natural aesthetic of the walls and ceiling, which made her question whether she was in a house or a cave. The dim light of the crystals would've reinforced the impression of being underground were it not for the main source of light—daylight streamed into the room from behind Kinsley, muted but far brighter than the crystals' glow.

She twisted and looked back to find a large circular window on the wall behind her. Ivy and thick, dangling moss grew around the base of the frame. The window was dominated by a carved tree, its branches spreading to connect to the frame all around, reminiscent of the tree of life. The trunk and boughs were so detailed that she was left to wonder whether it had been made or had just...grown that way. Beyond the glass, she spied a green, thriving forest. A forest without a hint of autumn color in sight.

This room was right out of her cottage-core-loving dreams.

Maybe...maybe she *had* been in a crash, but it wasn't as bad as she remembered. Maybe she'd hit her head, and someone had found her while she was unconscious and brought her here?

Kinsley reached up to touch her forehead. There was no bump, no tenderness, no broken skin, no bandage. In fact, no part of her body hurt at all.

Judging by the hollow ache in her stomach, however, she was starving.

She drew the blanket aside only to pause.

Whoever had found her must've changed her clothes, because what she was wearing definitely wasn't hers. Instead of jeans and a T-shirt, she was dressed in a long white nightgown, something straight out of a Jane Austen novel. There were ruffles on the low-cut bodice and short sleeves, and lace trim on the hem. The fabric itself was so delicate that she could nearly see through it. Worse, she wasn't wearing anything beneath it. No bra, no underwear. Nothing.

Kinsley wrinkled her nose and clutched the blanket. "Okay… That's not totally freaking creepy. Not at all."

Where were her clothes?

She shoved aside the thought of someone undressing her. She just…couldn't spend time thinking about it when she had far more pressing concerns, first and foremost of them being, *Where the heck am I?*

Scooting toward the edge of the bed, she stood, and the skirt of her nightgown fell to brush her ankles. Her feet touched down on something soft. Looking down, she spotted clumps of green moss growing on the floorboards. She wiggled her toes.

"This is just getting stranger and stranger."

It was like this room was a living, breathing part of the forest.

And while nature was literally claiming this room, it didn't look at all like it had been abandoned. Everything was clean, free of dust and cobwebs, and lived in.

She glanced around, searching for her things, but they were nowhere to be seen. Moving to the wardrobe, she reached for it and hesitated. It was intrusive to go through a stranger's belongings.

Isn't it also intrusive to undress an unconscious person?

Maybe there were exceptions to be made, given the circumstances?

She opened the wardrobe.

The aroma of oakmoss and amber filled her senses. Her eyes fluttered shut, and she leaned forward to take that fragrance in deeper. It was sensual and heady, and so...familiar. Heat stirred in her core, her nipples tightened, and her sex clenched.

"Oh..." Kinsley gripped the wardrobe door and curled her toes. Why was she reacting so strongly to a smell?

Get a hold of yourself, Kinsley! You're sniffing a stranger's clothing.

She jolted back and forced her eyes open.

Now who's being creepy?

"Apparently me," she muttered as she scanned the contents of the wardrobe. The dark clothing hanging within looked like something out of a renaissance faire costume collection. Long tunics with intricate embroidered patterns, refined poet shirts, and even a few hooded cloaks. Most of the color came from sashes folded over hangers.

If any of her things had been inside, they would've stood out like a sore thumb.

Closing the wardrobe, she walked to the desk, where she sought her purse and clothing amongst the clutter. But her belongings weren't there either.

Kinsley ran her fingers along the spine of one of the books, studying the writing upon it. The same writing was on the other books and the loose papers—strange runes which held no meaning for her. But something itched at the back of her mind all the same.

When she and Liam had been in school, they'd sometimes written notes to each other in elven runes, which they would decipher using a guide they'd copied from a fantasy book. These symbols were nothing like those, but they still seemed familiar all the same. Like she'd known them once, long ago, but had somehow forgotten them.

Just your imagination, Kinsley.

Yet the thought remained, a little unsettling, a little intriguing.

Turning away from the desk, she moved to the nearest door and pushed. It swung open to reveal a bathroom.

A magical, breathtaking bathroom.

Looking around in awe, Kinsley slowly stepped inside.

Like the bedroom, ivy, moss, and crystals abounded here. Trees grew from the stone floor on either side of the room. Their branches spread across the ceiling, twining with each other to create a beautiful, interwoven pattern too perfect to be real. Tall windows with branchlike adornments across their glass dominated the far wall, looking out into dense woodland.

The shelves built into the stone walls held stacks of towels and all sorts of colorful bottles and jars.

But what truly caught her attention was the huge bathtub at the center of the room. It was crafted of rose quartz, its outside raw and irregular, its inside smooth, and was filled with steaming, spice scented water. The tub emitted a gentle pink glow that was contrasted by the thick green moss blanketing the stone floor around it. More little jars and bottles stood on the rim near the old-fashioned faucet.

"This is unreal," Kinsley said as she moved toward the bathtub. The moss was cool beneath her feet.

She skimmed her hand along the smooth rim, unable to detect even the slightest imperfection in the quartz.

Either an insanely rich, eccentric hermit or an elf lived here, both of which seemed equally absurd and equally likely.

What she didn't see right away was a toilet. After some searching, she located a small room tucked in one corner, its door nearly hidden amidst the wall's stonework. The simple chamber featured a bench with a hole cut out. It reminded Kinsley of an outhouse, though it lacked the smell usually associated with such places. Bravely—or foolishly—she peered into the hole. It looked…bottomless.

"I half expected a crystal toilet, but I suppose this fits."

She'd used plenty of outhouses in her life, and she'd had to go full-blown mountain woman many times during hikes and camping trips. This hole was the pinnacle of luxury compared to some places.

She didn't see any toilet paper, but there was a spigot built into the wall that she assumed was a bidet. There was also a shallow basin carved in the stone nearby with water trickling into it as though from a spring, likely meant for washing hands.

Lifting the hem of the nightgown, she hurriedly used the toilet and cleaned herself up.

"Now to find my host." Returning to the bedroom, she strode to the only other door, grasped the iron handle, and tugged it open.

"Oh wow," Kinsley breathed as she crossed the threshold into a large, circular chamber.

The trunk of a ginormous tree stood in the center of the space. The ceiling closed around the trunk overhead. At its base, the tree spread into numerous thick roots, all of which disappeared beneath the floorboards. Moss and mushrooms clung to the bark in places, and shards of crystal on the walls cast it in a multihued glow.

Tentatively, Kinsley stepped closer to the tree. There were tiny markings carved in the bare bark—runes like she'd seen in the bedroom. She traced one of the symbols with her fingertips. It thrummed beneath her touch. She jerked her hand back, rubbing her fingers and thumb together as her brow furrowed.

Odd.

If it weren't for the gnawing hunger in her belly, Kinsley would've been certain she was still dreaming. How could any of this be real? Why did it feel like there was something more powerful at play here?

"Hello?" she called.

She swept her gaze around the chamber. There was a closed door to her right and an open door to her left; she followed the curving wall to the latter. When she reached the open archway, she descended the steps beyond into a room with a cold stone floor.

A huge fireplace with iron fixtures for hanging cooking pots dominated one wall. Bundles of dried herbs dangled from the ceiling, pots and pans hung from a metal rack, and the wooden shelves bore neatly stacked plates and bowls, sealed clay and glass jars, and baskets, which were filled with various fruits and vegetables. Water burbled into a large basin carved in the wall, from which wood slab counters ran to either side. Light from another large window that looked out at the forest brightened the room.

There were no electrical appliances, no power outlets, no phones, no wires, not even an old-fashioned wall clock. Not a single sign of modernity.

To Kinsley's right was an open space with a dining table and two chairs. Upon the table stood a cloth covered basket, a plate with cheese, slices of roasted ham, and fruit, and a pitcher of water with a cup beside it.

Frowning, Kinsley called out again, louder this time. "Hello? Is anyone here?"

The only answer she received was the trickling of water in the sink.

Kinsley's hunger deepened as she stared at the tempting spread.

Biting her lip, she glanced back toward the kitchen's entrance. Had the person who saved her set out this food? If so, where were they?

She approached the table. The aroma of freshly baked bread coaxed her closer. She folded back the cloth atop the basket and touched the loaf of bread within; it was still warm. That had to mean whoever lived here had set this up recently, right? Had Kinsley just missed them?

Plucking up a cube of cheese, she brought it to her mouth, but paused to examine it.

What if this is some kind of Goldilocks situation and I'm about to eat the bears' lunch?

What if it's poisoned?

Everything about this place, about this situation, seemed so...off.

"You're just being paranoid, Kinsley. Why would someone poison you after going through the trouble of saving you?"

Kinsley popped the cheese into her mouth. She closed her eyes and hummed as she chewed, savoring the creamy, sharp, nutty flavor. Her stomach chose that moment to growl. Before she knew it, she had devoured the strawberries, melon, grapes, ham, and cheese, had eaten nearly half the loaf of bread, and had chugged two full cups of water. It was like she hadn't eaten in weeks.

Rather than feeling bloated and lethargic, she felt relieved. Energized.

Kinsley returned to the circular chamber and continued clockwise, soon encountering a pair of staircases that followed the curve of the wall up to another floor. Two open archways stood between the stairs, leading down into a foyer, where daylight flowed in through the windows flanking a closed door.

She walked to the door, grasped the handle, and pulled it open.

"Oh wow," she repeated as she stepped outside.

The surrounding land was exactly what she'd hoped to explore when she'd left her aunt's house—Celtic rainforest. The trees and stones were thick with moss, ferns with featherlike leaves sprouted from the ground, and mushrooms clung to anywhere they could get a foothold. And it was all so, so green.

How was that possible in the autumn? All the trees between London and Inverness had been turning.

She swept her gaze around the little path leading away from the door. Low stone walls served as borders for tiered gardens on either side, which were filled with herbs and flowers in full bloom. Standing stones with more of those strange runes carved onto them were scattered about the grounds. The moss clinging to those stones grew around the carvings but never within the grooves.

Once Kinsley was several paces away from the building, she turned to look at it, and her eyes widened.

Fuzzy moss grew on the roof and ivy clung to the stone walls. The center of the two-story cottage was a wide turret, from the roof of which jutted the tree. That mighty trunk split into countless branches that stretched out in all directions, so bountiful with leaves that they served as an immense umbrella that afforded not even the slightest glimpse of the sky.

The cottage was straight out of a fantasy world.

Once Kinsley was able to pick her jaw up off the ground, she again called out. "Hello? Is anyone here?"

The only sounds to follow her voice were the distant songs of birds and the rustling of leaves overhead.

"Where are they?" she asked quietly.

Grasping the skirt of the nightgown, she lifted it and followed the stone path into the forest before circling around the building. Damp leaves squished beneath her feet as she picked a careful route, avoiding stones and sticks.

There was no sign of a road, no tire tracks worn through the vegetation. She saw no cars or bicycles, no power lines, no telephone poles.

The hairs on the back of her neck rose, and a shiver ran down her spine.

"Hello?" she called again, her voice echoing through the forest.

Listening, she searched the cottage windows and the spaces between the trees. No response came, and no one showed themselves.

But she sensed someone there. She could almost feel their eyes upon her in a heavy, intense gaze...

"Okay, this is just weird," she muttered, turning toward the forest. There had to be a path leading back to the road somewhere nearby. How else could whoever lived here have found her? Once she reached the road she could locate her car, her clothes, and most importantly, her phone.

Kinsley took a step forward, hesitating as she glanced at the cottage over her shoulder.

"I just need to find my things and call a tow truck. I can come back and thank them afterwards."

And she was sure her mother was worried sick.

But she was also barefoot in a thin nightgown in a completely unfamiliar place. No map, no phone, no means of discerning direction. If she was still near the loch, she could follow the downward slope to the water and potentially find her way from there, but there was a chance that this wasn't anywhere near where she'd crashed. There was a chance she would walk and walk and only end up terribly lost.

Well, more lost than she already was.

Kinsley squeezed the fabric of the nightgown in her fists and released a frustrated huff, blowing a loose strand of hair out of her face. "I guess I'm waiting."

Returning to the cottage, she sat on one of the chairs in the kitchen, where she passed the time by absently walking her fingers across the tabletop, nibbling on the remaining food, sipping the water, and staring out the window.

Still, there was no sign of anyone inside or out.

There was, however, that persistent sense of being watched. It was so strong that it was almost tangible, and it made her increasingly uneasy—yet oddly intrigued—as the day began to darken and the glow of the crystals on the walls became the main source of light.

Against her better judgment, Kinsley found herself longing for the unseen presence to reveal itself, and that longing triggered an inexplicable spark of excitement and anticipation in her.

Kinsley scrunched her nose.

What is wrong with me?

With an elbow propped on the table and her jaw cupped in her hand, Kinsley drummed her fingers against her cheek. "Why would someone leave a stranger unattended in their home?"

When her eyelids started to droop, and she couldn't bear to wait any longer, she rose and walked back toward the stairs, meaning to return to the bedroom. She paused as she passed one of the shelves, noticing the rolling pin rack mounted at its edge.

She grabbed one of the rolling pins and tapped it against her palm. The wood was solid and weighty. "Savior or not, this is freaking weird."

Rolling pin firmly in hand, she returned to the room in which she'd awoken. It had also darkened considerably, with the gently glowing crystals acting as mystical nightlights.

She closed the door and took a step back from it. Without a key in the keyhole, there was no way to engage the lock. Whoever lived here could simply walk right in. Regardless of it being their house, Kinsley wasn't comfortable with that notion, especially while she was vulnerable in sleep.

They already undressed me.

Creeeeeepy.

Pursing her lips to the side in thought, she scanned the room. Her gaze fell upon the desk chair.

Kinsley grabbed it, carried it to the entrance, and jammed it snuggly against the door. She wasn't sure how well it would hold, but it'd at least make enough noise to alert her if someone tried to get in.

Tucking the rolling pin beneath the pillow, she crawled onto the bed, slipped her legs under the covers, and lay on her side, staring at the shadows gathering in the room as the last of the daylight faded.

Maybe tomorrow her host would deign to show themselves.

CHAPTER FOUR

The slide of the blanket down Kinsley's body roused her from a deep slumber. She shivered as the comfortable warmth she'd enjoyed was replaced by the night's chill. Groaning, she rolled onto her back and reached for the covers, but her hand fell limp as sleep reclaimed her.

She stirred again when the mattress dipped near the foot of the bed, grogginess compounding her confusion. Before she could wrap her sleep-addled mind around what was happening, big, warm hands settled on her legs.

Kinsley remained still as the hands slid up her thighs, raising the hem of her nightgown. Her skin prickled in awareness. As those hands glided higher, her awareness focused on that touch, and heat bloomed low in her belly.

A thousand thoughts raced through her head, but not a single one was coherent enough to understand. This was a dream, wasn't it? A fantasy? A mysterious lover coming to her in the dark of night?

But something didn't feel right. This felt...real. The hands upon her felt real.

She forced her eyes open.

The room was darker than before, and the glowing crystals somehow only deepened the darkness. Her memories flooded back. She was in a strange cottage, on a bed with a vine-wrapped canopy.

And someone was touching her legs.

Those hands spread her thighs apart, and the stranger shifted closer to her.

Kinsley looked down. A pair of glowing red eyes stared at her from within a mass of impossibly thick shadows.

She started, yanked her legs away from the intruder, and screamed as she kicked and scrambled up against the headboard. Her hand delved beneath the pillow to grasp the rolling pin, which she dragged out and swung at those unnatural eyes.

The rolling pin halted abruptly before it could reach its target, striking something so solid and unyielding that the impact jolted her arm. Her eyes widened, and her breath hitched as the improvised weapon was wrenched from her grasp, nearly dragging her along with it. She jumped as it clattered on the floorboards and rolled across the room.

"What is the meaning of this?" the red-eyed visitor demanded in a harsh, deep voice. "I have healed you, clothed you, sheltered and fed you, yet this is the welcome I receive?"

Kinsley had heard that voice before. She couldn't recall where or when, but it was achingly familiar, and she *knew* she'd heard it.

"Who are you?" she asked as she drew her knees up and pressed her body against the headboard. "What are you doing?"

"I have come to sow my seed."

To sow his seed?

"What the hell does that mean?"

"Be not obtuse, human." He grasped her ankle, and though she could not see them in the dark, she felt his long, strong fingers and the pricks of...claws?

She tugged her foot back and swatted at his hand. "Don't touch me!"

He caught her wrist with a growl and surged forward, slamming his other hand against the wall and caging her in with his body. Kinsley squeaked and pressed herself back, trying to make herself as small as possible. With him so close, she could see nothing but darkness and those glowing crimson eyes, could breathe in nothing but his dominating scent. Oakmoss, amber, and musk. It was heady, masculine. It was pure seduction.

And his *heat*. After the chill that had crept across her skin, his body heat scalded Kinsley right down to her center. Her nipples tightened and tingled beneath her nightgown, and a familiar shiver of awareness swept through her.

"You will not make demands of me," he said, voice low and brimming with power, danger, and fury. "We have an accord, and you shall fulfill your obligations to me."

"Obligations? Wh-what obligations?"

"Are mortal minds truly so fragile, or do you believe me easily deceived?" His hold on her wrist strengthened. Though it didn't hurt, the potential for that grip to become crushing was quite apparent. "Feigning ignorance will not release you from our agreement."

Mortal?

"I don't understand. I...I don't remember," Kinsley said, trying hard to keep her voice from quaking.

He caught her jaw with his other hand and tipped her head back so she was staring directly into his inhuman eyes with their slit pupils. "In exchange for saving your life, you must bear my child."

"What?"

Oh no. This...this can't be happening. This isn't real, it's a dream, a nightmare.

Her heart quickened. She had to be dreaming, because this...

Wake up, Kinsley!

His grasp eased slightly, and his eyes narrowed. When he spoke again, his words were more measured, though they lacked any of the compassion they might initially have implied. "You've endured much since trespassing in my realm. For that reason alone, I will grant you a reprieve this night. But be not mistaken, Kinsley Wynter Delaney—by your oath, you are bound to me, and you shall fulfill your duty. Upon my return on the morrow, you *will* be welcoming. You will be grateful."

He leaned closer, close enough that she felt his heated breath on her lips. "For without my intervention, you'd be naught but food for maggots and crows."

All at once, he released Kinsley and withdrew, moving so quickly that the breath fled her lungs in his wake. Were it not for the support of the headboard, she was certain she would've collapsed right there.

Somehow, her gaze landed upon him—he was the deeper shadows amidst the darkness as he strode away from the bed.

Kinsley drew in a shaky breath. "Who are—"

"Sleep," he said, turning his head so his eyes blazed at her. "I would have you adequately rested for tomorrow."

Her brows fell. "I don't want to sleep, I want an—"

"*Sleep.*" His voice rippled with undefinable power, with irresistible compulsion.

Kinsley's eyelids fluttered. She had just enough time to wonder what the hell he'd done to her before she slumped to the side and oblivion reclaimed her.

CHAPTER FIVE

THOUGH SHE FELT like her eyes had just closed, Kinsley awoke to dim daylight streaming in through the window.

In exchange for saving your life, you must bear my child.

She blinked.

Upon my return on the morrow, you will be welcoming. You will be grateful.

"Oh, fuck that shit." Kinsley shoved herself up onto her knees, fists raised and muscles tense, ready to fight as she scanned the room. There was no shadowy man with bright red eyes anywhere to be seen. Even the rolling pin he had tossed aside was gone.

Had it been a dream?

No. It'd been real. He was real. However dreamlike everything had seemed since the accident, it was all somehow very, very real.

"Come out!"

Only silence replied to her demand.

Keeping her hands up, Kinsley crept off the bed and backed toward the exit. "I said come out!"

When she reached the door, she grasped the handle and tugged. She nearly sagged in relief when it opened. Poking her head out into the chamber beyond, she glanced to either side, finding it as quiet and deserted as before.

Kinsley stepped out of the bedroom and eased the door closed behind her, trying to make as little noise as possible. She cringed when the wood scraped the frame.

It's not like you weren't just yelling a second ago, Kinsley.

After ensuring the silence continued, she took a few deep, fortifying breaths and moved forward. Her eyes swept her surroundings ceaselessly as she padded around the tree, past the closed door to the right, and finally down the steps into the foyer. All the while, her brain insisted that some shadow monster was lurking around the next corner or sneaking along right behind her.

The fact that there was nothing there every time she glanced back offered her no comfort.

Nor did she take comfort in the sense that someone—or something—was watching her.

Adrenaline made her hand tremble when she reached for the front door handle, but she didn't hesitate. She yanked it open and bolted out of the cottage. Kinsley didn't dare look back as she followed the path deeper into the forest.

Her breath sawed in and out of her, her arms pumped hard and fast, and her feet pounded the ground. She barely registered the pain of sharp pebbles and sticks digging into her soles. She was driven by the need to run, to escape. To survive.

It didn't matter that she had no idea where she was or where she was going. Anywhere was better than...than this fucked up scenario.

She rounded trees and boulders and climbed over twisted, moss-covered roots and fallen logs. Branches caught at her long hair and nightgown. Her thighs burned, her breasts bounced painfully, and her side ached with exertion, but she kept going. If she continued downhill, she'd eventually reach either the loch or the river connected to it. From there, she could follow the water until she spotted a road, or another house, or any sign of civilization besides the nightmare cottage.

Kinsley darted between a pair of wide trees.

"No," she rasped, her knees nearly giving out as she came to a halt. Her chest heaved with her desperate, ragged breaths. "No, this can't be right. I... *No.*"

The cottage stood before her.

Kinsley shook her head and looked at the forest around her. She hadn't veered off her path; she'd been going straight. And yet the trees she'd just passed, those huge, side-by-side trunks, were gone. How was that possible? Trees didn't just…disappear!

No, not going to think about it.

Turning, she ran back into the forest.

Her chest constricted, the twinge in her side sharpened, and sweat trickled between her breasts and down her back and temples. Still, she forced her legs to keep moving.

For all her endurance while hiking, she wasn't a runner—especially not across such uneven terrain, and especially not barefoot. Exhaustion set in quickly, making her limbs heavy and her movements increasingly sluggish. So when she didn't lift her foot quite high enough to clear a raised root, it snagged, and she found herself rushing to meet the ground.

Kinsley cried out and threw her hands forward to catch herself. They took the brunt of the impact before she rolled to her back. Rocks, roots, and sticks dug into her body, and her palms and knees stung.

"Damn it!" she bit out, squeezing her eyes shut and clutching her hands to her chest.

Get up, Kinsley. Keep going.

Opening her eyes, she stared at the canopy overhead. Teases of the dreary gray sky were visible through the leaves, which swayed in a gentle breeze that did not reach the forest floor.

She groaned as she sat up. Every part of her body hurt, but she turned her attention to her hands first. Her palms were red and dirty, and her skin had been broken by a twig in one place, but they were otherwise fine. She could feel leaves and debris caught in her hair, and her feet, arms, legs, and nightgown were smeared with mud. She wiped her hands on a clean bit of fabric, adding a smear of crimson to it.

Kinsley turned onto her hands and knees to push herself to her feet but froze.

The cottage stood before her once again.

"No!" she screamed, slamming her fist on the ground. "No, no, no! Fuck!"

Panting, she dug her fingers into the earth and glared at the cottage. What the hell was happening? Had she…had she somehow ingested hallucinogenic mushrooms? Was she losing her damn mind?

Haunting whispers reminiscent of leaves falling in the autumn drifted to Kinsley on the wind, tickling her ears. She snapped her face toward the sound. Her breath caught, and her eyes widened.

An ethereal orb of blue light, perhaps eight inches in diameter, hovered in the air beside her. Though it was diminished by the daylight, it was the same orb she'd seen the night of the accident. The reason Kinsley had veered off the road.

Only then did the old legends occur to her—this was a will-o'-the-wisp. A ghost light. Said to mislead travelers at night, drawing them on chases into the wilds that left them hopelessly lost.

She narrowed her eyes. "You... This is your fault!"

The wisp flickered and shrank back even as more of those indecipherable whispers sounded. Those whispers were coming from the wisp; it was struggling to communicate with her.

Kinsley's anger swiftly faded. She sat back, drew her knees up in front of her, and propped her elbows on them. With a sigh, she combed her fingers into her hair and grasped her head, closing her eyes. "I'm sorry. It's not your fault. Not...not really. I just don't know where I am or what's going on." Tears stung her eyes. "I just feel so lost and scared."

Something brushed her forearm. It was a strange sensation—feathery and airy, somehow both solid and insubstantial, so gentle that she wondered if she'd imagined it. She opened her eyes to find the wisp directly before her, and only this close did she realize it wasn't really an orb at all.

It flickered like a flame, though there was a quality to its light more reminiscent of the aurora borealis than fire. Despite the malleability of its form, it bore a distinct little head and body, with two tendrils trailing off like tiny arms, one of which was touching Kinsley.

The wisp was comforting her.

"So you are real," Kinsley said softly.

The wisp brightened and made its strange whispers. Understanding teased at the back of Kinsley's mind, but whatever words the little creature was speaking—and she was certain there were words—remained unknown to her.

She frowned. "I'm sorry. I don't know what you're saying."

As the wisp backed away from her, its touch lingered, tugging gently upon Kinsley's arm before letting go. That ghostly limb beckoned her.

"You want me to follow you?" Kinsley asked.

The wisp bobbed up and down.

She turned her head and cast it a sidelong glance. "You're not going to lead me somewhere dangerous, are you?"

Its posture sagged. How could something so incorporeal, so inhuman, seem so sad?

"Don't do that! Okay, okay." Kinsley pushed herself to her feet, wincing at the tenderness of her soles. "I'll follow."

Perking up instantly, the wisp led on. Kinsley walked behind it, mindful of her footing and using patches of moss to cushion her poor feet whenever possible. When she wasn't watching the ground in front of her, she watched the wisp, noting the way it bobbed as it floated, almost dancing, the way its body, though amorphous, maintained the same basic shape.

She also noted that it avoided the beams of sunlight breaking through the forest canopy.

I'm willingly following a will-o'-the-wisp through a cursed forest.

And somehow that didn't feel like the weirdest part of the last couple days.

No, the weirdest—and scariest—part had been last night.

Do not think of him, Kinsley. Just don't. Not now. Focus on getting out of here.

The wisp's path wound between trees and crossed over stones, roots, and logs. At any moment, Kinsley expected she'd look up and find the cottage in front of her again. She had no way of knowing just how far she'd traveled in her prior attempts to leave this place, but that cutoff had to be fast approaching.

Yet as they continued onward, the only thing that came into sight was a gradually thickening fog. The wisp grew brighter in the deepening gloom. When they reached the side of a steep hill, the wisp led her along the base. The many rocks and jutting roots forced Kinsley's attention downward again. The last thing she needed to do was roll an ankle out here.

New sounds drifted to her from afar. At first, she thought they were more whispers from her ghostly guide, but it quickly became clear that they were different.

They were voices. Human voices. Men calling out to each other, their words muffled and made unintelligible by the fog.

Heart speeding, she lifted her head, meaning to cry out for help. Her voice died before reaching her lips, and her steps faltered.

The wisp had stopped before a large object wedged against a tree. Vines and moss clung to it, but they weren't enough to obscure the shape and silver paint of her SUV. The passenger side of the vehicle was utterly consumed by the fog, which was so thick from that point onward that she couldn't see into it at all.

Body numb, mind blank, Kinsley staggered forward. "This...this can't be right. *How?*"

She reached out and brushed her fingers over the thick moss growing on the roof of the SUV. It looked like the forest was consuming her car. But...it had only been two days since the accident.

Hadn't it?

Kinsley trailed her hand down the vines hanging over the driver's side window and drew them aside. The fog had invaded the cab, shrouding the passenger seat, but it didn't hide the driver's seat at all. It didn't hide the shattered glass, the cracked windshield, the torn-up dashboard.

It didn't hide the thick branch that had pierced the instrument panel or the dried blood clinging to the bark and pooled on the seat. The end of the branch was snapped off not far past the steering wheel, but when she followed the trajectory it would've taken, it led to a hole punched through the back of the seat. The surrounding leather was also dark with blood.

Kinsley brought her hands to her belly. "Oh God."

Her breath quickened, and her heart raced as memories surged to the forefront of her mind.

She remembered the storm. Remembered feeling thunder rumble through her body, remembered the smell of rain, of the forest, of decay and stinging smoke. She remembered being trapped. Pinned in place. Remembered being impaled. She remembered calling for help, pleading for it, remembered how desperately she hadn't wanted to die...

And she remembered a dark figure. Remembered his scent, his voice.

"It was real. Oh God, that wasn't a dream... It was real." Kinsley clutched her stomach. There was no wound, no scar, but the echoes of that pain pulsed beneath her fingertips.

Why was there no wound? How was she alive? Was she...

Dead?

Kinsley frantically shook her head. "No. No, I'm not dead."

Somehow, that dark stranger had saved her. Had *healed* her.

The muffled voices, so much closer now, broke through her rising panic.

"Hello?" she called, striding around the car toward the fog. "I'm here! Please help me!"

The wisp flew in front of her, stopping Kinsley short. It shook its tiny head.

"There are people there," she said. "They can help me."

It spoke, its whispers almost frantic as its body flickered.

"I need to get help." She stepped past the wisp and plunged into the fog. "I'm here!"

Warmth blossomed on her right wrist, but she barely noticed it. She needed to get home, needed to tell her family that she was all right. The air was so heavy and thick that she couldn't see, and she could barely breathe. It felt like the fog itself was fighting to bar her passage. She raised her hands in front of her to feel for obstacles in her path.

The warmth on her wrist grew into searing heat, sending waves of pain up her arm. Kinsley hissed and clamped her other hand around the spot, squeezing, seeking some relief even as she pushed onward.

Those voices only sounded farther away.

She called out again, begged for help, for acknowledgement, for anything, and the pain in her arm became so great that she stumbled. Somehow, she remained upright. Somehow, she kept moving.

The wisp's indecipherable pleas intensified along with her pain. Kinsley clenched her teeth. Fire blazed through her veins, raced along her spine, and flooded her head, sinking scorching claws into every corner of her mind. A scream welled in her throat. It built with explosive pressure, burning almost as much as the pain, but it wouldn't come out.

Not until the pain drove her down onto her knees. The world spun dizzyingly around her. Kinsley squeezed her eyes shut and bent forward, pressing her forehead on her arms as every muscle tensed against the agony.

Everything stopped. The press of the fog ceased, and the voices gave way to a silence so total that it was deafening.

Hesitantly, Kinsley opened her eyes and lifted her head. There was a glowing green, tattoo-like band of ivy and thorns circling her wrist. Its light faded, and with it, so did the pain, leaving only a throbbing memory in its wake. She brushed her thumb over her skin.

The mark was gone.

What is happening to me?

Brow furrowed, she slowly shifted to sit back on her heels as she gazed around her.

She was no longer in the fog. She wasn't even in the forest.

Kinsley was upon a bed of moss in the center of a small depression, surrounded by a circle of standing stones, each of which was around five feet tall. The runes carved into their faces were varied and intricate, and they emitted their own ethereal green light that dimly illuminated the chamber. Thick, gnarled tree roots came down from overhead, splitting and delving into the ground all around the circle without a single offshoot crossing into it.

Beyond those roots she could just make out walls of stone, some of it shaped, some of it natural, with clusters of faintly glowing crystals embedded in them.

The tree.

She was beneath the tree that stood at the center of the cottage.

A scream burst from Kinsley as she dug her fingers into her thighs. It was powered by anger and frustration, by helplessness and fear.

When that scream faded, she clenched the fabric of her nightgown in her fists and growled.

"You are a persistent creature," said her host, his deep, cold voice echoing off the stone and layering upon itself. "But here, your stubbornness will bring only suffering."

CHAPTER SIX

Kinsley shoved herself to her feet and spun around, searching the shadows for those glowing red eyes, but they were nowhere to be seen. "Who are you? *What* are you?"

"You've dragged filth into my home, human." His reply came from all around her, impossible to pinpoint because of the echo. "You will bathe. Then we shall attend to the fulfillment of our contract."

Fulfillment of their contract, which stated she was supposed to have his baby?

Despair pierced her heart.

"No," she said.

Some of the darkness shifted beyond the roots, but she lost track of the movement too quickly.

He growled. "I can take your life as swiftly as I restored it. You will do as I command."

Heart hammering, Kinsley turned in place, still searching for him. "I didn't ask for this! I didn't ask to be trapped here as your… your…broodmare!"

"No, you asked to *live*, and I offered it for price. A life for your life. I saved you, and you shall bear my child in exchange."

You are mine.

She grasped her right wrist, the wrist he'd held that night, and shook her head. "I was under duress! I...I was dying. I would have said anything."

"And you said yes." His voice suddenly came from behind her. "Your words led you here. You have spoken, now you must act."

Kinsley curled her fingers tightly and whirled toward him, swinging her fist. "No!"

Her attack met only empty air.

A strong arm banded around her middle from behind, crushing her against a tall, hard body, and a long-fingered hand closed around her wrist where she'd been branded.

"You swore by your true name," he said against her ear, the feel of his warm breath upon her skin making her shiver.

She tried to wrench herself out of his grasp. "Let me go!"

Despite her struggles, he easily turned her around to face him. Her gaze met his an instant before his hand wrapped around her throat and he forced her backward.

Kinsley gasped, eyes flaring as she gripped his forearm. She came to a halt only when her back struck one of the rough, cold standing stones. Energy buzzed along her spine.

His head dipped closer to hers, and he growled, "You'll not escape our pact, Kinsley Wynter Delaney."

What breath remained in her lungs was stolen by the sight of his face in the otherworldly light of the runes. Those demonic red eyes with their slit pupils were narrowed in a glare. They were red on black, no whites to be seen, and were framed by thick, dark lashes and arched brows. A pair of small, curling scar patterns, with two dots beneath them, extended from the outside corner of each eye. He had long, curved, pointed ears, high cheekbones, and sculpted lips that were drawn back to reveal fangs on top and bottom. His features, framed by long, raven hair, were sharp and elfin but for the bump on his otherwise straight nose.

As though all that weren't enough, his skin was green.

"Wh-what are you?" Kinsley asked, running her gaze over his terrifyingly beautiful face.

"Your master."

Before she could voice any of her many, many objections to that, his hands dropped to her waist, claws pricking her flesh, and he lifted her like she weighed nothing. Kinsley cried out as he draped her unceremoniously over his shoulder. Her breasts squished against his back and pressed against her chin, and her hair fell around her.

She fought his hold, flattening her palms on his back and kicking her legs. "Stop! Let me down!"

Undeterred, he clamped an arm around her thighs while planting his other hand on her ass, trapping her in place as he strode forward. Only when she flicked her hair out of her face and looked down did she realize just how high she was. This man—this *thing*—was tall. Six and a half feet, at least. And it was a long way down.

"It is degrading enough to have made a bargain with you," he said as he stooped down to pass between two of the roots and exit the standing circle. "I shan't debase myself further by yielding to the demands of a human."

Clenching the fabric of his shirt and loose strands of his waist-length hair in her fists, Kinsley pushed herself up and twisted as much as his hold allowed to glare at him. "Debase yourself? You're holding me captive!"

Ahead, she glimpsed a pair of large doors at the top of a set of low, crude stone steps. The doors' wood was etched with runes and tree patterns. She'd seen them from the other side yesterday, in the foyer.

He didn't slow as he approached the doors, which swung open before he was even close enough to touch them. "I am holding you to the terms to which you agreed."

"I-Isn't there some rule about contracts being made under duress not being valid?" she asked, panic creeping into her voice despite her attempts at remaining calm.

How the hell can you expect yourself to be calm, Kinsley? You're being carried off by some unknown creature that wants you to have his baby!

He ascended the stairs, his every step making his shoulder dig into her diaphragm and forcing a grunt out of her. "Should your oath be so devoid of meaning, I will return you to your carriage. The bough that ran you through may easily be replaced."

Had he just threatened to impale her?

Apparently he intends to, one way or another.

They entered the foyer, and he swiftly followed the steps up into the round central room. Pressing her lips together, Kinsley grasped a handful of his hair and yanked.

"Damn you!" he snarled as his head was wrenched to the side, throwing him off balance. Kinsley nearly struck the wall before he recovered his footing.

Straightening, he lifted his hand from her ass, only to bring it down again with a sharp slap.

Kinsley's breath hitched as the sting radiated through her, but what shocked her more than the pain was the surge of arousal it triggered.

What. The. Fuck?

"Did you... Did you just *spank* me?" she asked, aghast.

"Mind yourself, human, for this is the most lenient punishment you will receive."

"Mind myself? Let me go, asshole!" She renewed her struggles, pushing, wriggling, and kicking, doing everything she could to escape. But he only held her more firmly, his claws pressing into her skin.

She heard the bedroom door open and slam against the wall, and she saw it shut on its own after he carried her through. He didn't stop until they'd reached the bathroom. The air was warm and humid, perfumed with spice and a floral hint, a welcome change from the coolness of the forest and fog.

Without warning, he hefted Kinsley off his shoulder and dropped her—nightgown and all—into the tub's steaming water.

She slipped, head going under. Thrashing, sputtering, and coughing, Kinsley sat up, splashing water over the sides. She swiftly wiped her wet hair out of her eyes, blinking them open.

Firm fingers caught her chin and turned her head, forcing her gaze to meet his. He towered over her. In this lighting, he didn't look any less imposing, nor did he look any less beautiful. A glint on his ears drew her attention to the intricate silver cuffs at their helixes.

"Wash yourself," he commanded, his gaze dipping, "or I shall do so for you."

Kinsley jerked her chin out of his grasp and scooted away from him. Water sloshed over the tub walls. His eyes lowered further, and a fire sparked in their crimson depths.

She glanced down and hurriedly crossed her arms over her breasts, which were completely exposed in the clinging, now transparent nightgown. She flushed.

"Where are my clothes?" Kinsley asked.

"I have disposed of those blood-soaked rags."

"Well, is there anything I can wear that's not see-through?"

"Be grateful I have provided garments of any sort. Our accord does not obligate me to clothe you."

Kinsley glared at him. "Oh, you mean the accord that was pressed on me while I was *dying*? You know, you could have just saved me out of the goodness of your shriveled heart."

He leaned close enough that his nose nearly touched hers, his inhuman countenance filling her vision. Long strands of his hair fell into the water. She shied away from him.

He halted her retreat by grasping her jaw.

"I have had a great many years to deepen my well of patience, Kinsley. Yet you are fast draining it. Wash yourself. I will await you in the bedchamber."

Kinsley whipped her head to the side, yanking her face out of his grasp. "Screw—"

The bathroom door slammed shut, startling her. When she looked back, he was gone.

She blinked. "...you?"

CHAPTER SEVEN

Glaring at the door, Kinsley growled through bared teeth, raised her arms, and slammed them down in frustration—splashing water in her own face. That only angered her further. She grasped the hem of the nightgown and wriggled as she peeled it up over her head. Once it was off, she wadded it into a ball and rose onto her knees.

"Asshole!" She hurled the nightgown across the room.

It struck the door with a splat before plopping onto the floor.

With a huff, Kinsley sat back down, closed her eyes, and tipped her head back. Water lapped against the tub walls and spilled over them to patter on the moss below. She didn't know whether to be relieved or angrier that the door didn't crash open so her inhuman host could storm in and admonish her for her tantrum.

Calm down, Kinsley. You'll gain nothing by being angry.

But what the heck was she supposed to do?

Everything she knew about the world, about reality itself, told her this had to be a dream. Magic and monsters weren't real. People couldn't...couldn't get impaled by tree branches and wake up totally fine the next day. You couldn't just reappear at the place you had started from regardless of what direction you'd walked in.

And she couldn't...

Her hand dropped to settle low on her belly. Over her...her womb.

The one thing this monster wanted was the one thing she could not give him.

Anguish lanced her. Tears pricked her eyes, and her lower lip trembled. She pressed her fingers against her belly and bowed her head until her nose almost touched the steaming water. A quiet sob escaped her.

What if she hadn't survived the accident? What if she had died, and this was some sort of purgatory? The forest had overgrown her car like it had been there for months, and the voices she'd heard in the fog had been people, she knew it. But she hadn't been able to understand them, hadn't been able to reach them. And the deeper she'd delved into the mist, the more it had hurt.

Tears slid down her nose to drip into the water below.

What was she going to do? Running didn't work. Every time she'd tried, she was transported back to this damned cottage. Whether she was dead or alive, there was nowhere for her to go. She was…trapped.

Kinsley sniffled and opened her eyes. Deep down, she knew she wasn't dead, knew this wasn't a dream. It was all very real, but the rules of her world didn't apply here.

And the only way she would get answers…was from *him*.

Releasing a shuddering breath, she closed her eyes once more and splashed her face, washing away her tears. She needed to be strong.

Kinsley sat up and peeked at the door. Still closed. Yet she could sense him waiting on the other side.

"You got this, Kinsley," she said quietly.

Picking up one of the bottles from the side of the tub, she removed the lid and gave it a tentative sniff. It smelled of musk and amber, spicy and sensual.

It smelled like him.

She replaced the lid and set the bottle down a little more roughly than she'd intended.

Okay, so maybe it *had been* intentional…

She picked up another bottle and tested its scent. This one was fresher, reminiscent of rain. Much better.

Using the soap, Kinsley scrubbed away the mud and green stains from her skin and washed the dirt and debris from her hair.

Tiny twigs and bits of leaves soon floated atop the water. When she was done, she rose and carefully climbed out of the tub, stepping onto the wet, soft moss. She grabbed a towel from the shelf, dried herself, and wrapped it around her body.

She stared at the door, chewing her bottom lip, as she considered her predicament. Was she just supposed to parade on out of the bathroom in a towel?

Remember, Kinsley? You don't need clothing for what he has planned for you.

She clutched the towel against her breast. "Be brave. You can do this."

Saying those words didn't ease the anxiety roiling within her belly.

She approached the door and grasped the handle, pausing to take another steadying breath before opening it. A wave of warmth greeted her. Kinsley stepped into the bedroom.

With night approaching, the window over the bed was already dark. A low fire blazed within the hearth, its light mingling with the faint luminescence of the crystals to cast a gentle glow on the room that belied what was meant to happen here.

And there he was, seated in the lone chair before the fireplace, his eyes more hellish than the flames. He did not look at her when he said, "Get onto the bed and present yourself, human."

Kinsley narrowed her eyes and wrinkled her nose. *"Present myself?"*

He turned his face toward her, tapping a finger on the armrest of his chair. The skin of his hands was as black as his claws, as were the tips of his long, tapered ears. "Lie down and spread your thighs that you may receive me."

"Absolutely not."

He bared his fangs. "Now."

Kinsley leaned forward, keeping her eyes locked with his as she firmly said, "No."

Grasping the armrests, he thrust himself to his feet, making the movement look so graceful and yet so powerful and intimidating. Two strides brought his tall, lean body up to her. "You are fortunate that I chose you, female."

She tilted her head back but didn't retreat. "Why? Do you get many candidates through here?"

The room dimmed, and shadows coalesced over the monster's features, making the glow of his eyes brighter in contrast. "I will not tolerate this impertinence, especially not from a human."

She didn't look away from him, couldn't look away. At the corners of her vision, everything…warped. The walls, ceiling, and floor were drifting farther away even as the shadows darkened. And he towered over her more than seemed possible.

It was disorienting and frightening on a primal level. It felt like he was larger, but also that she was somehow smaller.

This can't be real.

The darkness became so complete that all she could see were his eyes, a pair of crimson flames in the night.

"But I should tolerate it from you?" she asked despite the dryness of her mouth.

With a snarl, he clamped a hand around her throat. She was aware of movement, aware of her feet leaving the floor and the towel being ripped away, but everything happened so suddenly that her mind could not comprehend what was occurring until her bare back came down atop the bed. Though the room remained dim, the shadows had thinned just enough for her to see her host, her captor, to see the fury in his eyes. To see their lack of pity and compassion.

Keeping hold of her throat, the creature lodged his hips between her thighs and dropped his other hand to open the lacings of his pants. Kinsley's eyes widened, and she clutched his forearm and squirmed beneath him, trying to free herself. But he held her in place.

"You made a pact with me," he gritted through his teeth, "and you shall honor it."

Fear both deathly cold and witheringly hot coursed beneath Kinsley's skin as he tugged out his cock. It was long and thick, with prominent ridges running along the top and underside of its shaft, which tapered into a point at the head. At its base, the skin was black, but it faded to the same green as his face toward the tip.

And to her further horror, the sight sparked a hint of desire deep in her core.

As he grasped the thick shaft, Kinsley knew his strength was too great for her to resist. She knew that no matter how hard she fought, she wouldn't be able to stop this...this *thing* from happening.

The physical pain she knew he would inflict blended with the pain in her heart and soul, with her fear and humiliation, with all her confusion and dashed hopes, all of it coming out in a strained cry.

Kinsley struck his chest with a fist as tears filled her eyes. "Fine. Rape me, you fucking monster!"

He froze. His fingers flexed, pressing his claws into the tender flesh of her neck. He lowered his gaze, dragging it from her eyes and down her body to her parted sex, where his cock was poised.

A slow, harsh breath escaped him, and the muscles of his jaw bulged as he clenched his teeth. Kinsley dared not so much as breathe as she stared at him.

His chest rumbled with a low, ragged growl that escalated into a bestial roar so powerful and furious that the building trembled around him. Huge wings unfurled from his back, batlike and leathery, stretching out past the sides of the bed.

A demon. She was in the clutches of a demon, and it was about to devour her, body and soul.

This is the end.

Kinsley squeezed her eyes shut, awaiting the killing blow.

His hand tore away from her throat, claws grazing her skin, and the bed shook as he shoved himself away. The flames in the fireplace sputtered as though disturbed by a strong wind just before the bedroom door slammed shut.

She jolted, opened her eyes, and sought him out. But he was gone, and she was alone.

A cry broke past her lips as she snapped her thighs together and curled up into a ball on her side, letting the tears flow.

CHAPTER EIGHT

Vex threw open the ritual chamber doors with a blast of magic. They pounded against the stone walls and bounced off, vibrating with the impact. He stormed through, boots thumping on the worn stone steps, and thrust his hands backward to release another violent arcane burst.

The heavy oak doors barely had time to groan on their ancient hinges before slamming shut. The sound reverberated through the chamber like thunder across the heavens.

Echo, Flare, and Shade whispered amongst themselves behind him.

"Silence," he commanded.

Their words ceased. Vex stalked along the centuries-old groove he'd worn into the ground around the standing stone circle.

Tension, fury, and magic crackled through his being, more volatile than any storm. Raw mana buzzed up his legs each time he crossed one of the ley lines that converged beneath the tree. Those tastes of magic only exacerbated his frustration. Virtually limitless power, and yet he could not use it to accomplish his singular goal.

"Freedom dangles before me," he growled, lifting a hand with fingers curled, "and I cannot grasp it. This human knows not her place. She needs but submit, and our suffering will end. I demand nothing more than that to which she has agreed!"

His wings drew in tight against his back, thrumming with tension.

She is my mate.

Kinsley carried a piece of his soul within herself, and it had meant *nothing*. She'd disobeyed him. She'd rejected him. She'd looked upon him like he was a monster.

The wisps drifted closer, casting their soft glows over his shoulders. He should have bidden them to watch the human. Kinsley was no more capable of escaping these woods than Vex, not while she was bound by their pact, but she was human. She was vulnerable to all manner of threats, from the overt, like the dangerous, unnatural creatures that sometimes stumbled into his realm, to the mundane, like a raised root in the forest or a bramble patch. Above all, she was vulnerable to her own stubbornness and folly. The lifeforce he'd shared with her had certainly enhanced her survivability, but he doubted it had pushed her limits particularly far.

She was too fragile and too important to be left unattended.

By root and thorn, the memory of her feel lingered at the forefront of his mind. That soft, supple skin beneath his hand, those yielding thighs, her heat. The ghost of her scent remained in his nose, a fragrance that had haunted him since the night he'd found her—orange blossom, honey, and fresh rain. She smelled of foreign lands, and yet her scent was somehow familiar.

But in her defiance, she'd spoken those damned words.

Rape me, you fucking monster!

Roaring, he halted and hammered a fist into the wall, wings extending to lend momentum to the blow. Stone cracked and crumbled around his hand. "What could a human know about monsters?"

"No less than you have shown her, magus," Flare responded in their raspy voice.

Vex tore his hand free from the wall with a growl, sending more debris to the chamber floor. "I commanded sile—"

The word caught in his throat as he beheld the sight before him. His shadow was cast large upon the wall by the light of the runestones in the circle, but the flickering glow of the wisps made it amorphous, unstable. He stared at that unpredictable, insatiable mass of darkness. Yet regardless of its imposing presence, it was ultimately empty. Impotent. Powerless.

A shadow...or a reflection?

"You knew well the answer already," Echo whispered, "else you would not have stopped yourself."

Vex lowered his gaze to his hands. Hands that had grasped the human's throat, that had been about to guide his cock into her heat. Hands that had acted despite her protests.

He'd been about to take Kinsley against her will.

A shudder coursed through his wings, which reflexively folded against his back.

"We have a pact," he said, voice low. "She swore by her true name."

"Did you not do the same, all those years ago?" asked Flare, their light brightening to diminish Vex's shadow.

Vex balled his fists, digging his claws into his palms. "It is *not* the same."

Kinsley was his mate. It could not be the same, was never meant to be the same.

"It is, magus," said Echo, their intensifying glow further dwindling the shadow.

Nostrils flaring with a harsh exhalation, Vex turned on his heel and resumed pacing. "Insolence at every turn, and in my own home. Am I not master here?"

The wisps fluttered behind him, making the shadows dance.

"You are, magus," Echo and Flare replied in unison.

"And what have you to say, Shade?" Vex glared over his shoulder at the third wisp, who lingered behind their fellows.

"You have ever been master here," Shade said in their haunting, gentle voice. "Master of illusion foremost. Thus, this one trusts that you have not fallen prey to your own deception."

Vex halted. Echo and Flare brushed against his shoulders before they stopped, their light sputtering as they backed away. Fury swelled inside him, a firestorm with intensity enough to swallow the heavens and sear away the stars, but it was not a new fury. It had not been spawned by Shade, nor by Flare and Echo.

Neither was Kinsley Wynter Delaney its source.

This rage was much older than the human. It was older than

this cottage, than this tree and the runic standing stones, older even than the pact he'd made with the fae queen all those centuries ago.

The pact that had destroyed his life and everything for which he'd worked, everything for which he'd hoped.

"Have I truly become no better than *her?*" he rasped.

Shade drifted closer. "When that question ceases to weigh upon you, magus, you will have your answer."

Vex strode forward, ignoring the heat roiling beneath his skin and the flickers of magic flowing into him through the ground. What was done was done—Kinsley was bound to him. Her opinion of him mattered not.

He spread his wings, stretching the heavy limbs, before willing them to dissipate to nothingness. Cool air brushed his back through the slits in his tunic before the fabric settled. "Self-reflection aside, the situation remains unchanged. A child birthed of my seed is the only means by which to obtain our freedom, and as Kinsley guessed, we've a dearth of females. And now that I've instilled my lifeforce in her... There is no other way. She must conceive."

And yet he could not force himself upon her. Even if she was no longer mortal, she was a human, little more than an insect to a being such as himself. But even had they not been bound, he could not have brought himself to cross that line. He could not do to Kinsley what the queen had done to him.

How infuriating to have the key in his hands but not the will to insert it in the lock.

"Centuries have passed, magus," Echo said, "and in all this time, she is the first. Does that not signify something more meaningful?"

"Indeed," Vex snapped. "It signifies that she is likely a fae-touched mortal with a realmswalker in her ancestry, who happened to tap into the latent power of her bloodline in her desperation."

"Mayhap. Yet for her to cross into your realm at that moment, magus, out of all the places she might have been, might have gone..."

"You would imply her arrival is fated. I contend it is merely fortunate."

"Are not fate and fortune oft intertwined?" asked Shade.

Vex clenched his teeth. "I've no desire to discuss this further."

Fate had no hand in this. The pull he'd felt toward Kinsley, even before the wisps had informed him of her presence, had been the siren's call of opportunity. He'd not been fated to take this human as his mate. He'd chosen her.

Those thoughts were oddly unsettling. They'd burrowed into his mind like insidious vermin, diseased, *wrong*. Somehow, he shoved aside the discomfort, the imbalance. Somehow, he silenced the part of himself that sought to refute his assertions.

But he could not deny the blossoming longing within him. He wanted to feel Kinsley's smooth, soft skin under his hands. Wanted to breathe in air perfumed by her scent, to sink into her heat and stare into those entrancing periwinkle eyes, which held such unexpected depth.

Vex growled and stepped between a pair of roots to enter the stone circle. Magic thrummed all around him, a ceaseless rumbling caused by the meeting of four ley lines. "She is the vessel by which we will break this curse. She is our freedom. Naught more, naught less."

"She is a gentle soul, strong but lost in suffering," said Shade.

Even before he spoke his next words, shame crawled beneath Vex's skin. "Shall I compare her suffering to my own? Shall I weigh our pain upon the scales and determine whether hers is of greater worth than mine? She must fulfill her oath. She will have to learn to set aside her pain."

Flare flitted in front of Vex, their blue ghostfire swirling into a little inferno. "Unless you mean to emulate the queen, magus, you must find another way."

"So what, then?" Vex demanded. "What would you demand of me?"

"Would it be so terrible an inconvenience to show kindness?" asked Echo, who moved into place beside Flare.

Kindness... What role did kindness play in any of this? The world, life, fate; it was all cruel. Kindness was the greatest illusion of all.

Yes, Kinsley had awoken a...carnal hunger within Vex. Was that not to be expected after so many years without companionship? She was a lovely creature, especially for a human. But his longing for her body, for her feel, her taste, was not so simple. It was underlaid by a want for something more. A craving far deeper than it had any right to be.

He yearned for *her* desire. He wanted her to welcome him, to reach for him, to beg for him. Wanted her to be wet and ready for him. Wanted to hear her moans of pleasure and her cries for more as he thrust into that lush body.

But most of all, he yearned to protect and care for his mate.

His brows fell, and the corners of his mouth ticked down. "You suggest I demean myself further by...*wooing* a human?"

Shade floated over to their companions. "You wield power over her, magus, and your use of that power will define you."

Vex pressed his lips into a tight line and dragged his gaze around the circle. He'd placed the standing stones himself, had carved the runes and cast the enchantments. They'd never been meant to serve as a prison. Once—long, long ago—they had meant freedom. Once, they had been an unspoken promise to his people. He'd turned all his power toward fulfilling that promise.

And he had failed.

His pact with Kinsley was more binding still. He'd agreed to save her life, and he had done so by the only means available to him —he'd woven his lifeforce into her. Such a thing was only done between mates. But the sharing of his immortal soul had been the only way to stave off her death.

She was his mate and his debtor. He'd fulfilled his end of their bargain, but that did not mean he had to make her existence unpleasant while she worked toward completing hers.

"I shall take your counsel into consideration." Vex strode forward.

The wisps parted to clear his path.

"Go," he said with a wave. "I weary of company, and it is well past time I attended my own thoughts. Keep watch over our guest."

With acquiescent whispers, the wisps took their leave.

Vex stopped at the center of the circle. Ancient, unimaginable power coursed beneath him. It rushed up through the mighty roots of the tree he had fostered, flowed through the stones and wood of the cottage he'd erected with his bare hands and raw arcane energies, and filled the air with a tingling charge.

He'd been master of this realm since he'd been banished here, and everything had bent to his will. Apart from the wisps, Kinsley was the one thing in this place he could not control.

Not without killing the last shred of what set him apart from the queen.

"It is for me to decide the price I will pay for my freedom… Just as *she* intended."

CHAPTER NINE

BETWEEN THE FEAR of her captor returning to finish what he'd started and the hunger twisting in her stomach, Kinsley's sleep was fitful. Each time exhaustion claimed her, some unfamiliar sound, or a flicker of ghostly light—whether real or imagined—startled her to wakefulness.

But her captor hadn't returned by the time the dreary gray light of dawn spilled in through the window.

And she was so damn tired.

Kinsley drew the covers over her head to block out the light and hide from the world. To hide from him, the nightmare made flesh who kept her here. She told herself that she'd be okay, that he wouldn't come, she tried to settle her thoughts and clear her mind, but sleep remained elusive.

With a sigh, Kinsley rolled onto her back and scrubbed her hands over her face before letting them fall to her sides. She stared up at the bed's canopy.

What am I going to do?
You could tell him the truth.

Kinsley crinkled her nose. "Yeah, because he totally wouldn't kill me for that."

Hadn't he already threatened to return her to where he'd found her? *Exactly* as he'd found her?

She was stuck here until she could find a way to escape, and so far, every attempt had led her back to this cottage. That last time, when she'd plunged into the fog...

Frowning, she lifted her hand and studied her wrist, tracing a finger over the skin where that strange mark had glowed. It had been the source of her pain when she'd been in the fog.

He'd placed some sort of spell upon her.

Or a curse.

There was so much wrong here, so many things that didn't make sense, that shouldn't have been possible. But if this place really was filled with magic, it had to have its own rules. Just because she wasn't familiar with them didn't mean they didn't exist. And somewhere in those rules was her way out.

If that's what you need to tell yourself to carry on, Kinsley.

Well, what else am I supposed to do?

A hint of blue light spread across the canopy. Brow creasing, she turned her head. A wisp was hovering beside the bed.

Kinsley started, then narrowed her eyes. The sounds last night, the glimpses of light from the corner of her eye, they hadn't been imagined. She hadn't been alone.

"You're his spy, aren't you?" she asked.

Shifting its arms behind its back, the wisp bowed its head.

"Well"—Kinsley sat up and scooted toward the edge of the bed, keeping the blanket tucked around her chest—"you can go tell him I said to jump in a loch. And stay down there. Deep, deep down."

The wisp shook its head and pointed at her, its soft, unintelligible whispers tickling her ears.

Kinsley touched her hand to her chest. "Oh, I should tell him, should I?" She rose, wrapping the blanket around her body as she padded to the wardrobe. "I'm sure I can find a way to let him know the next time I see him."

She opened the doors. That spicy, woodsy scent wafted out, flooding her senses and igniting an unexpected, unwanted heat in her core.

No, damn it!

It was bad enough that his scent had enveloped her all night, coming from every thread of the bedding. For her body to respond to it with anything other than revulsion was a betrayal.

Scowling, she took out a tunic and looked it over. It was

elegant and archaic, made with soft, pristine fabric. She might've questioned the pair of vertical slits on its back had she not seen those large, powerful wings spreading out behind him the night before.

Don't go there, Kinsley.

She wrinkled her nose and held the tunic up. Her captor might've been tall and broad shouldered, but he was lean, and there was no way her boobs would fit in this garment. She might've been able to get it on if she sucked everything in, but she'd only end up popping the buttons with her next breath.

Kinsley tossed the tunic away over her shoulder.

She removed another garment, and another, throwing each onto the floor to join the first, along with the sashes. When nothing remained hanging, she tugged open the drawers and surveyed the neatly folded pants within.

A blue light caught her attention. She glanced over to find the wisp looking back and forth between her and the pile of clothing.

"What?" Kinsley asked. "Do you think it'll bother him?"

Though she couldn't be sure given its flickering, flamelike form, she swore the wisp's shoulders were shaking, and its whispers had become a light, tinkling sound. Laughter.

Kinsley smiled and, with immense satisfaction, added the pants one by one to the growing heap on the floor, followed by the boots that had been tucked at the wardrobe's base, until nothing was left to remove.

She turned around to survey the mess. It wasn't enough. Whipping the bottom of the blanket aside, she drew her foot back and kicked the pile, scattering the clothing farther. The boots thumped on the floor as they fell.

"Asshole," she muttered, wishing her act of rebellion could've accomplished more than this fleeting, hollow sense of triumph. She walked into the bathroom, spun around, and thrust a finger at the wisp, who had been right behind her.

The wisp jerked back.

"You stay," Kinsley said. "This space is private."

She closed the door before the wisp could respond and leaned against the wood.

The nightgown was still on the floor, having been swept aside by the door. She crouched and picked it up. It was still dripping wet.

"Damn it." She released the nightgown, and it plopped on the floor stones. "Blanket toga it is."

Though the water inside the bathtub was the same she had bathed in, with dirt settled on the bottom and leaves and twigs floating on top, it was still steaming and fragrant. She turned on the faucet and cupped her hands beneath it, gathering cold water in her palms. She drank deeply.

It did nothing to appease her hunger.

She hadn't eaten anything since she'd woken here after the accident. Just the thought of that cheese, fresh fruit, and warm bread made her stomach clench.

Pushing away from the tub, she rifled through the jars and bottles on the shelves and counters. She discovered another depression within the wall where water ceaselessly flowed into a basin. A carved comb, a small wooden toothbrush, and a little clay jar lay upon a recessed shelf beside it. She picked up the jar, removed the lid, and sniffed its contents, which had a light, minty scent.

"Toothpaste?"

Somehow, the thought of a creature like her captor standing here, brushing his teeth, was just...comical.

"I mean, he has teeth, so I guess it makes sense, but..."

Shaking her head, she dipped her finger into the jar, gathered some of the contents, and scrubbed her teeth. As she did so, her eyes kept returning to the toothbrush. A thought began forming. By the time she'd finished washing her mouth out, the idea had taken full shape.

With a grin, she plucked up the toothbrush and made her way to the lavatory. Kinsley leaned over that deep, dark hole, dangling the toothbrush above it. "Would be *such* a pity..."

She released her hold.

"Whoops."

She listened, but never heard it strike the bottom.

Just how far down does that hole go?

After using the toilet and securing the blanket around her chest, she returned to the bedroom, where the wisp was waiting for her, its little arms bent like it had its hands on its hips.

Kinsley smiled as she walked to the desk. "I didn't do anything."

She sat down and looked over the clutter atop the surface. Picking up a piece of parchment covered with runic symbols, she turned it toward the wisp. "What even is this? A spell? A curse? A letter to his mother?"

The wisp remained silent.

"Right. As if you'd tell me, even if I could understand you." Kinsley sighed and pursed her lips to the side as she stared at the parchment. "Is it important?"

The wisp flared briefly.

"Must not be if it's just strewn about like this." She flung the parchment aside, watching as it fluttered to the floor. The rest of the loose sheets quickly followed until she came across a blank paper.

"Hmm..." She grabbed a feather quill and examined it, from the slightly frayed barbs on one end to the ink-stained tip at the other. She'd never used a quill before.

A brief search turned up a small glass inkwell, which she opened. Kinsley tapped the feather against her chin and looked at the wisp. "What should I draw?"

The wisp floated closer until it was hovering over the desk. It looked from her down to the paper.

"Shall I draw you?" she asked.

It brightened and whispered excitedly, bouncing in the air.

Kinsley chuckled as she dipped the quill into the inkwell. "I take it you like that idea. Okay, let's see what I can do."

Leaning over the desk, she set the quill to the paper and drew. It wasn't easy; she left several thick splotches of ink and had to dip the quill multiple times, but she soon got the hang of it. She sketched the wisp's body, creating its ghost-like tail, two little arms, and round head, all with flowing, flamelike strokes. Thin lines spreading outward served as the wisp's radiance.

Kinsley sat back, wiping her ink-stained fingers on the blanket, and looked up at the wisp. "What do you think?"

The wisp drifted closer to the parchment, head down as it silently studied her drawing. It glowed brighter with each passing moment, giving away its delight. Returning to Kinsley's eye level, the little creature shifted its ethereal body, mimicking the pose in which she'd depicted it.

Kinsley squinted against the light and laughed. "You do shine pretty bright."

She was about to dip the quill into the ink again when her stomach cramped and let out a long, loud growl. A wave of nausea and lightheadedness struck her, forcing her to set down the quill and press a hand on her belly.

Squeezing her eyes shut, she took deep, measured breaths, waiting out the dizziness.

When the sensation passed and she opened her eyes, the wisp had drawn closer. It touched her hand, making her skin tingle, and whispered.

"I'm okay," Kinsley said. "Just hungry."

The wisp gave her hand a gentle tug before drifting toward the door.

Kinsley lowered her hand to her lap and shook her head. "Nope. I'm not going out there."

Those whispers grew more urgent as the wisp pointed toward her belly. It waved for her to follow as it backed away, but she didn't move.

"Is he out there?"

Hesitantly, the wisp nodded.

"Then I'm not leaving this room."

Those ethereal little flames sagged. The wisp turned, glancing around the room, and floated to the door. It passed through the wood just like a ghost in a movie, leaving only fleeting hints of glittering light in its wake.

Kinsley sighed.

Stubborn to a fault. That was how Kinsley's father had once described her, and maybe it was true sometimes. But she had to work with what she knew. She knew her captor had stopped himself even though she clearly wouldn't have been able to resist. She knew he wanted a child from her. So, that meant he needed her healthy, right? That she had *some* leverage, however small?

Still, it didn't mean he would stop himself next time.

And when he came... Kinsley would be ready to fight him.

CHAPTER TEN

When Flare entered the chamber, Vex did not look up from his work. With a steady hand, he poured the vial's contents into the bottle, watching the ingredients collide. A sweet, floral fragrance filled his nose.

Flare hovered over his shoulder, their light flickering either in excitement or agitation. Sometimes it seemed there was little difference between the two for the wisp.

Setting aside the now empty vial, Vex rolled his wrist, swirling the bottle to mix the ingredients.

"Whether by strength, magic, or alchemy, magus, it is still forcing her," Flare said, their glow intensifying.

"This"—Vex placed the bottle atop the worktable and inserted the stopper—"is oil. Lavender, rosemary, and peppermint. For the bath."

The wisp dimmed. "Apologies, magus."

Vex stepped to the wash basin to clean his hands. "I've already brewed tinctures to induce sleep, compliance, and lust."

"This one believed you had chosen a different course."

"I have. The human's behavior will determine whether those potions are necessary. Now…" He turned to face the little wisp, folding his arms across his chest. "I trust you've good reason to abandon your watch?"

Ghostfire flaring, the wisp raised their head. "She refuses to leave the bedchamber."

"Which should make your task quite easy to fulfill. And yet here you are."

"She has not eaten, magus," Flare replied. "Not in two days."

Vex drummed his fingers on his biceps. "And?"

"Mortals require food." Flare's flames grew as the wisp drew closer to Vex. "Without it, they weaken and die."

"She is mortal no longer."

"Yet immortal is not undying."

Vex could not deny the truth of those words. He'd learned that lesson much too harshly, at much too young an age.

A scowl pulled down his lips. Most fae creatures could survive without food, though they would be diminished and gravely weakened. Would his lifeforce be enough to sustain Kinsley through starvation, or would her human blood make her susceptible to it?

He knew only one thing—everything hinged upon her, no matter how much he wished otherwise. He could not afford to risk her safety. He could not afford to ignore any threats to her wellbeing, no matter how inconsequential they seemed.

And part of him insisted he protect her regardless of their pact, regardless of the curse. It insisted he protect her because she was his mate. It was his duty to safeguard her, to provide for her, and should she starve or come to harm because of his indifference, because of his carelessness...

"Unacceptable," he snarled, crossing the workshop. He ascended the steps, strode around the tree in the central chamber, and threw open the bedchamber door with his magic.

Vex stalked inside, fists clenched. The female leapt up from his desk, her eyes wide and her long, wavy, honey brown hair tumbling around her bare shoulders as she faced him.

"Human, I've not saved your life only to have you sta—"

Kinsley glared at him, her periwinkle eyes flashing. "Go away!"

He halted, spreading his arms to the sides. "This is my bedchamber. I'll not be cast out of it."

"Since I'm being forced to stay here, it's *my* room now. And I said to go away."

Vex growled, stepping toward her. "Do not presume to command me in my own home. I am master here."

Kinsley slapped a hand onto the books stacked atop the desk, snatched one up, and drew her arm back. "Don't come any closer."

He paused, brows falling. "Put that down."

Kinsley cocked her head and wiggled the book. "This? Would be a shame for it to be damaged."

A different approach. Why had he taken the counsel of wisps into consideration?

Clenching his teeth, Vex leveled a finger at her. "Return it to its place, human. I shan't tell you again."

Pressing her lips together, she hurled the book at him.

It sailed across the room, pages flapping. A book that had survived untold years was now threatened by a mortal who'd lived for the span of a single breath. He shifted aside, head narrowly avoiding the tome, and his hand darted up to catch it.

Vex glared back at the human and snapped the book shut. The sound was thunderous in the otherwise silent room. "You threw a book at me."

"Oh, so you *are* the master of something. The obvious."

"I care not for your tone."

"And I don't care for your face!" The female grabbed another book and threw it at him, followed by another, and another.

He caught the second book, and the third, if only barely. By the fourth, he knew he wouldn't be able to keep up with only two hands.

Why had he let this escalate? Why was he allowing a human to wreak havoc in his home, to threaten him and his belongings? He advanced toward her, dropping the books onto the bed, just as she hefted a rune-craved crystal pillar.

It was a spell focus, and it happened to be both pointy enough and heavy enough to hurt even Vex.

She threw it without hesitation.

"Enough!" Vex extended an arm, projecting his magic in the shape of a hand. Its translucent green fingers wrapped around the crystal, halting it in midair.

Kinsley stared, wide-eyed, as the hand swept past her and returned the crystal to the desk.

Nostrils flaring with a heavy exhalation, he dispelled the hand. He kept his eyes on the human until he was sure she wouldn't reach for anything else before surveying the chamber. His eyebrows sank lower with each piece of clothing or sheet of parchment he spied upon the floor.

"Were you trying to destroy my bedchamber, human?"

"Most recently, I was trying to destroy your head."

"I have killed for less."

She spread her arms and gestured to herself. "Yet here I stand."

Despite his irritation, Vex found himself battling back a smile. This defiance, this confidence, this...*liveliness*, it all seemed so out of place here. And from a human of all things. A human who was utterly powerless here and should have been begging his forgiveness, who should have been cowering in fear.

He'd seen Kinsley many times since removing her from her strange carriage and delivering her from the brink of death. He'd watched, cloaked in magic, as she'd wandered his home, as she'd eaten in his kitchen, as she'd desperately sought a way out of the woods. He'd seen her confusion and frustration as his illusions had repeatedly warped her path and guided her back to the cottage. He'd witnessed her tenacity when she'd trudged into the fog and fought through her pain, only to be returned here by the curse.

And he'd glimpsed her naked form when she'd been beneath him.

Yet this was the first time he'd truly seen her.

Her body was soft and sensuous, with ample curves and yielding flesh. Her pale skin had an appealing pinkness to it, complemented by another color that was a whisper of something forever unattainable to Vex—the kiss of the sun. Though she stood a head shorter than him and was dressed only in a blanket, her feet were planted firmly, and her stance was solid. She was unwilling to back down despite knowing she was outmatched.

And her face... It was heart shaped and gentle, so far removed from the angular perfection of the fae. But there was strength there. It lay in the firmness of her full, pink lips, in the set of her dark, elegant eyebrows, and in the light of her blue-violet eyes, which were framed by lush black lashes.

Kinsley was human. A newly immortal being bearing all those mortal imperfections. Inferior to him in every way.

And yet he was drawn to her. She kindled a heat in his core unlike anything he'd ever felt, already intense enough that he feared it would consume him if its flames were fanned.

Behind him, the wisps drifted into the room. They lingered near the threshold, speaking to each other in hushed tones.

Kinsley looked past him and gasped. "There's three of them?"

"Indeed," he replied, glaring at the wisps over his shoulder, "making them thrice as unreliable. I bade you watch her."

Flare inflated their flames and moved forward. "This one did, magus."

"So, you watched as she tore my bedchamber apart?"

"This one's duty was to watch." Flare lifted their tendrils in a tiny, nonchalant shrug. "This one was not told to intervene."

"Have I expected too much by assuming you would report to me were she being destructive?" Vex demanded.

"It's not their fault," Kinsley said. "If you're going to blame anyone, blame me."

Vex returned his attention to the human to find her glaring at him again. He strode toward her. She held his gaze, giving not an inch against his advance, until he was directly before her.

"Though it should come as no comfort, human," he said, "know that I hold you entirely responsible for this mess."

She crossed her arms beneath her breasts, which pushed those soft mounds of flesh up and together. His gaze dropped to them, and his cock twitched in response, hardening. The blanket she'd wrapped around herself betrayed only a hint of the body beneath. That such a hint should stir any reaction in him at all...

Vex clenched his jaw. She was here for one reason—to give birth to his child. That required no attraction. He possessed tonics to induce his own arousal, were it necessary. This was a bargain, a transaction. He should not have felt *anything* for this human.

But his fingers flexed with the urge to reach out and touch her, to divest her of her covering, to draw her closer so he could feel that body against his.

Shadows guard my breath, what has overcome me?

Vex forced his gaze back to hers. "What are you wearing?"

She gave him a droll look. "A blanket."

He matched her expression. "Why are you clad in my bedding?"

Kinsley rolled her eyes. "It's not like I have anything else to wear. Oh, but wait, I don't *need* clothes for what you intend, do I?"

Gritting his teeth, Vex hooked his fingers beneath the top of the blanket, between her breasts. His knuckles pressed against her soft skin. Her breath hitched, and her glare faltered.

"No, you do not," he said.

She caught his wrist.

He dipped his head closer to hers. "You prefer to remain covered, then?"

"I would prefer that you don't touch me at all."

Her words struck him with a weight and a sting far greater than should've been possible. He had endured hatred for much of his life before his imprisonment, had taken it in stride so many times, had never allowed himself to be brought low by it. But coming from her…

She is no one. Her words are unimportant but for the word that bound her to me—Yes.

Yet he wanted to touch her. Wanted to feel her. More, he wanted her to crave his touch. Why? Why was he being plagued by such desires? Why should he have wanted anything more from her than the offspring that would set him free?

Why did his every interaction with this female make the wisps' advice ring truer?

Exhaling slowly, he released the blanket and withdrew his hand. His skin was immediately cold with want for her heat. "It has been brought to my attention that you've not eaten in some time. This must be remedied immediately. Come."

Kinsley frowned. "I'm not going anywhere with you."

Vex closed his eyes and pinched the bridge of his nose. "Have I failed to make clear how little I enjoy repeating myself, human?"

"Do you think I enjoy repeating *myself*?"

He dropped his hand and narrowed his eyes. "You must eat. Now."

"Just go away and leave me alone."

He growled as he lunged at Kinsley, snatched her off her feet, and threw her over his shoulder. Locking her in place with an arm around her thighs and a hand planted securely on her round backside, he turned and walked toward the door.

"You asshole!" she shrieked.

She writhed and struggled, striking his back and voicing her protests at excessive volume directly in his ear, but he found himself able to focus only upon how her body felt, her enticing scent, and the excitement coursing through him.

Without the aid of any tonic, his cock grew erect, straining against the confines of his trousers.

As though dealing with her wasn't difficult enough.

He sensed the wisps following as he carried Kinsley to the kitchen. They spread around him, their voices silent but their gazes heavy, when he deposited her onto one of the chairs at the table.

She immediately moved to get up.

Vex jabbed a finger at her, baring his fangs. "I will bind you to that chair."

His gaze dipped, and his eyes widened. One of her breasts had come free of the blanket, its soft flesh and rosy nipple bared to him, beckoning him.

With a glare, she tugged the blanket up, plopped back down, and crossed her arms over her chest. Her bottom lip stuck out in a pout, tempting Vex to lean closer and nip it with a fang, to draw it into his mouth and suck.

That desire, however small and seemingly innocuous, unsettled him. He'd never been one to harbor such desires. Even before the queen, he'd been focused solely on his work. His rare dalliances had been brief and unsatisfying, and he'd ultimately considered them wastes of time. They'd been moments of weakness. Itches he'd needed to scratch.

Whatever she'd stirred in him was more potent than anything before. It was beyond his control. Where there had only been a void, there now existed blossoming desire. And he *wanted* to feel that desire.

Satisfied that Kinsley would not attempt another escape, Vex turned his attention to the table. Though starvation could not kill him, it would weaken him over time, and he'd not eaten in some time either. He'd been too…preoccupied.

Though the ley lines offered an unending stream of mana from which to draw, conjuring aught from nothingness required concentration and strength of will, and oft proved taxing. Yet in this instance, the use of energy was justified.

And he wanted to provide for his human. Through their pact—and his lifeforce—she was his mate, but this went beyond their agreement. It was almost...instinctual. His female hungered, and it was his duty to feed her. She was his ward, his charge, his future, his—

Enough. I must concentrate on the task at hand.

Trusting the wisps to maintain their vigilance, Vex bent his will toward the act of shaping, toward wrestling physical form from the ether. Tendrils of green magic swirled outward along the table, with more flowing behind him to form sets of hands that floated off to gather plates and utensils from the cupboards.

Food coalesced before Kinsley. Roasted tubers and carrots, fresh bread, butter, a large wedge of cheese, soup with leeks, onions, and kale, and a roasted pheasant.

Eyes rounded and jaw agape, Kinsley watched the meal materialize.

Vex smirked. "While your mouth is hanging open, mortal, *eat.*"

CHAPTER ELEVEN

DESPITE EVERYTHING KINSLEY had experienced over the last couple of days, she couldn't believe what she'd just witnessed. The food before her looked real enough to touch, real enough that she could smell it—the sweet, yeasty fragrance of freshly baked bread, the spices on the potatoes and carrots, and the savory aroma of juicy meat.

Yet the way it had appeared... It reminded her of a movie she'd seen as a kid, *Hook*, where the Lost Boys literally imagined their food into existence.

"This is all real?" Kinsley asked, touching the breast of the roasted bird. She'd half expected her finger to pass through the pheasant, like it was a hologram or a mirage, but it didn't. The bird was solid and hot.

Her captor let out a soft sigh. "I was under the impression that eating involved putting food into your mouth, not letting words spill out of it."

She looked up at him. "You just conjured a whole meal out of thin air."

His brows ticked down toward the bridge of his nose. "I will forgive that gross oversimplification if you cease your questions and *eat*."

She leaned back as a pair of ghostly hands floated in front of her and set down a plate, a bowl, and utensils before her. Another pair brought a pitcher of water and two wooden cups.

Kinsley blinked at it all. "You're so bossy."

"And you are quite human." He gestured at the food with a long-fingered hand before tugging out the other chair, sweeping back the bottom of his tunic, and sitting down.

Choosing not to respond to the way he'd said *human* as an insult, Kinsley eyed him warily. "So you're staying."

He tore off a chunk of bread, drawing her attention to the claws on the ends of his fingers. "I produced this fare. Is it not my right to partake of it?"

"I didn't say you couldn't. I guess I just figured you wouldn't want to sit and eat with a lowly mortal."

Plucking a knife from the table, he scooped up a pat of butter and spread it on the bread, his movements as graceful as they were aggressive. "I do not. Yet unpleasantness is oft unavoidable."

He extended his arm and dropped the buttered bread onto her plate. "Eat."

"If you tell me to eat one more time, I'm going to—"

Those crimson eyes narrowed in a glare, daring her to finish her threat.

Wrinkling her nose, Kinsley picked up the bread and took a bite. The creamy butter melting atop the warm, soft bread was heaven in her mouth. She took another bite before she'd even swallowed the first.

"Don't expect me to say thank you," she said around the mouthful of food.

Her captor rolled his eyes as he tore off another piece of bread. "From what I've come to know of you, human, gratitude is the last thing I'd expect."

"You don't know anything about me."

"The only thing I need know of you is that you agree—"

The wisps flared, fluttering to either side of him. Their haunting whispers filled Kinsley's ears as her captor glared at the little creatures, his mouth twisting into a scowl. He buttered his bread, this time with far more aggression than grace, and tore into it with his fangs.

He looked like a child who'd just been scolded.

Kinsley watched him, amused. "Were you going to finish your thought, or…"

He turned his scowl toward her. "Have you finished eating?"

She stared at him as she slipped the last bite of the bread he'd given her into her open mouth with deliberate slowness. "Nope."

One of the wisps moved to his ear and spoke to him, its voice barely audible to Kinsley.

"So you can understand them?" she asked.

Without looking at her, he ripped off one of the pheasant's legs and placed it on her plate. "Unfortunately, I do."

"Do they have names?"

The wisps turned toward her.

Her captor added some roasted vegetables to her plate. "Yes."

"And they are…?"

Picking up a knife, he cut a thick slice of cheese from the wedge and dropped it beside the vegetables before gesturing to the brightest of the three wisps. "Flare."

That was the one who'd been in the bedroom earlier. The one she'd drawn.

He pointed to the next. "Echo. And Shade."

The last wisp, Shade, was a little less intense than the others, a little more incorporeal. And their core was just a smidge darker.

"Nice to meet you, Flare, Echo, and Shade," Kinsley said.

Flare sketched a tiny bow that was mimicked by Echo. Shade dipped their head.

Kinsley picked up the pheasant leg and looked at her captor. "And do *you* have a name?"

"You may refer to me as your—"

She thrust the drumstick at him. "I am not calling you master, so you can just forget it."

His features darkened, and briefly, it seemed as though the room had darkened with them. "My name is of no concern to you."

"Lord Asshole it is then." She took a bite out of the leg.

That light, tinkly sound came from all three wisps. Their laughter.

He growled, flattening a hand on the table. "My heart swells with gladness at seeing the four of you amuse each other so."

Kinsley widened her eyes in mock surprise as she pressed her fingers to her chest. "You have a heart? Who would have thought?"

"Vex."

"What?"

"Vex," he repeated through clenched fangs. "It is both what you do to me, human, and what you may call me."

She smirked, taking pride in his irritation. "Vex. Now was that truly so hard?"

"In my limited experience, naught is easy with you."

"Yeah, well, as nice as it is to meet the wisps—they are will-o'-the-wisps, aren't they?—I can't say it's nice to meet you, Vex."

The wisps laughed again.

Vex shot them a look before staring at Kinsley, drumming his claws atop the table. "You are exhausting."

Kinsley shrugged and set the drumstick on the plate before ladling some soup into her bowl. "My mum and dad have said the same thing."

"So there is yet wisdom to be found amongst mortals."

Keeping her eyes on her bowl, she ate a couple spoonfuls of soup, fully aware of Vex's gaze upon her the entire time. She glanced at him.

He'd leaned back in his chair, arms upon the armrests and legs spread. His long, black hair hung over his shoulders. A few thin braids, all adorned with tiny bands of silver, were tucked behind his pointed ears, which were tipped with those elegant silver cuffs. Between his stance and his formal attire, he looked like an agitated prince.

An agitated, strikingly attractive prince.

No, Kinsley. You are not going to think that way about your captor. You've heard of Stockholm syndrome, haven't you?

Doesn't change the fact that he's beautiful.

Shush.

"So...what are you?" Kinsley asked, stirring the soup in her bowl.

"A deceptively simple question without a simple answer." He tilted his head, narrowing his eyes as he regarded her. "What would you say, were I to ask you the same?"

"I would say I'm a human."

"Ah. So, your entire being may be reduced to your humanity."

"A human is what I am, not who I am."

Vex continued studying her, scrutinizing her, until he finally nodded and said, "I am a goblin."

"A goblin?" Kinsley's brow furrowed. That…couldn't be right.

His head tipped in the other direction. "Are you displeased with my answer?"

"No, it's just… Goblins are always depicted as small, evil, ugly creatures, and you're…"

Keeping his elbow on the armrest, he lifted a hand and gestured with an upturned palm. "Please. Do go on."

"Well, you're just not," she said quickly, turning back to her bowl. Her hair fell forward. She hoped it would hide the blush on her cheeks as she ate another spoonful of soup.

You just admitted to your captor that he's hot.

No, I just said he wasn't ugly. There's a difference.

"So, it is unpleasant to meet me," he said, a note of amusement in his voice, "but it is pleasing to look upon me?"

"I'm just saying you don't fit how goblins are described in stories." Smiling, she peeked up at him. "You are green though, so there's that."

"Then I am not evil?"

"That remains to be seen."

Vex fell silent, and Kinsley chanced another look at him. He was still watching her, his dark scowl replaced by a contemplative frown.

She cut off a piece of cheese from the slice on her plate, slipped it into her mouth, and nearly hummed as she savored the creamy texture. God, it had to be the best cheese she'd ever tasted.

"Where are your…wings?" she asked.

"Away."

Kinsley stared at him blankly. "Away."

Vex arched a dark eyebrow. "You understand the word, do you not?"

Flare brightened, making a curt gesture at the goblin. Vex glanced at the wisp and grunted.

"Of course I do," Kinsley said. "But I don't understand it as your answer. I don't see wings bulging under your clothes. Are they detachable? Can you just set them aside? Are they magic? Do you understand how *away*" —she raised her hands to mimic quotation marks—"doesn't quite answer my question?"

"If you desire specific answers," he said, grasping the arms of the chair and sitting forward, "perhaps you'd be better served by asking more specific questions. My wings manifest when I have need of them. If you wish to see it as magic, you are most welcome to do so."

"Were you born with them?"

His jaw muscles ticked. "Yes."

"Then they're not really magic."

"Yet magic is woven in the very fibers of my being," he grated.

"Do all goblins have wings?"

"No."

"Can I see them again?"

"Finish your meal."

"Is it true goblins like to scare and threaten to eat children?"

He dragged his hand down his face before returning it to the armrest. "Would that it were. Mayhap then I'd have been spared such questions."

"Are there faeries?"

"*Eat.*"

Kinsley huffed, picked up a wooden fork, and looked back down at her food. "Can't help that I'm curious."

"But I would have thought you more than capable of helping the words that come out of your mouth."

"So I'm not allowed to talk?"

A low growl rumbled from Vex. "However appealing a notion that might be, I have said no such thing."

"No, you didn't. But you'd rather I close my mouth and open my legs, right?"

"It would certainly expedite our dealings."

The wisps flickered and spoke quickly, their voices swirling through the air like phantom calls carried upon the breeze.

Kinsley glared at Vex. "You're an asshole."

His fingers bent, pressing his claws into the chair's arms. He must've heard the wisps, must've seen them, but he spared them not a shred of attention. "Is the food to your liking, human? Has my bed been comfortable?"

Tossing the fork onto the plate, Kinsley stood and faced him, waving at the table. "Do you think food and a soft bed makes it all okay? You are my *captor*. My jailer. You can decorate the cell however you like, but that doesn't change what it is or what you are."

He leaned back in his chair, and the tension that had been in his posture shifted into something more aloof. "You are but a means to an end, Kinsley Wynter Delaney, and you are bound by your word to serve that role."

She threw her hands out. "And that justifies everything? That justifies what you were about to do to me? That you were about to—"

His fist came down on the table hard enough to rattle everything atop it, startling Kinsley, and he shoved himself to his feet.

"It does not," he growled, shadows coalescing around his face and turning his eyes into a pair of glowing, hellish coals. "The depravity I nearly visited upon you is inexcusable. Yet neither my mistake nor my admission of it can change our reality. I've no desire to play keeper to a human, no more than you desire to be kept. But we are *bound*."

The room darkened around them, shadows swallowing even the light of the wisps.

"You need not spend your time here in suffering, Kinsley," he continued as those eyes—all she could see of him—drew nearer. His strong, hard fingers caught her chin, tipping her head back. "I have eternity, human. How many years are you willing to spend trapped in this place?"

Kinsley pressed her lips firmly together to keep them from trembling as anger roiled within her and tears of frustration filled her eyes. "People are looking for me."

He brushed his thumb along her jaw. His voice was low and not without a hint of sorrow when he said, "They will not find you, Kinsley."

As she searched his gaze, tears trickled down her cheeks. She knew he was right. Kinsley had heard those voices in the forest, but they had all been like ghosts calling from another realm, always out of sight, always far away.

"I'm not hungry anymore," she said quietly. "I'd like to go back to the room."

"Escort her," Vex said to the wisps, though he did not break eye contact with Kinsley. "Let her not stray from your sight."

His red gaze lingered on her before his eyes faded into the darkness. He withdrew his hand, the pads of his fingers stroking her skin, the tips of his claws grazing it, and then the shadows dissipated.

And he was gone.

Kinsley's chin dipped, and she wiped the moisture from her cheeks. Anger, helplessness, regret, and pain whirled in a maelstrom inside her, looking for a way out, but she held it all in. Just as she had for so many years.

Without waiting for the wisps, she stepped out of the kitchen and made her way back to the bedchamber. They lit her way all the same, whispering amongst themselves behind her.

When she entered the bedroom, it was clean. The books and papers were stacked on the desk much more neatly than before, the bed was made with a different blanket, and Vex's clothes had been returned to the wardrobe, which stood open. His garments had been shifted to one side, making space for several colorful dresses.

The wisps flitted into the room, but Kinsley paid them no attention. Her gaze was caught on the new white nightgown lying atop the bed.

Pushing the door closed behind her, she approached the bed. She ran her fingers over the soft, unblemished fabric before clenching it in her fist. Kinsley threw the garment across the room and screamed, crumpling to the floor as she let out all her anguish, pain, and loneliness, all those emotions she'd thought she had put to rest. Eyes closed, head down, and fingers clawing at the floorboards, she let that raw scream continue, let the tears that accompanied it spill freely.

The scream faded, leaving a pulsing ache in her throat exasperated by her sobs.

Soothing whispers caressed her ears, accompanied by gentle,

barely perceptible touches—ghostly limbs stroking her hair, her back, her cheek.

Her sobs faded as time passed. She didn't open her eyes, didn't get up, didn't move at all as her breath slowly evened and the tears finally ceased.

Kinsley couldn't know if it was real or imagined, but the comforting touches of the wisps had a subtle warmth to them. And that was enough for now.

It had to be.

Because the truth of this place, of her situation—that she would never escape—was simply too much to bear.

CHAPTER TWELVE

Beneath moon and stars, the mist looked every bit like the impenetrable barrier it was. It greedily drank all the silvery light, leaving nothing for the dark swath of woodland it encircled.

An entire world lay outside that shroud. A world that had for so long been beyond Vex's reach and hidden from his sight, no more real to him than the illusions he created. A world that had existed only in his memory.

With hands clasped behind his back, Vex stared at the ivy and moss laden conveyance resting at the mist's edge. It was a piece of that unreachable world, but it wasn't an echo or a memory. It was tangible. And it had delivered Vex's only hope of returning to that realm.

An infuriating, unpredictable, beautiful human.

Kinsley.

For all his knowledge and experience, for all the power he'd once wielded, he could not comprehend the convoluted twists of fate that had brought her to him. After untold years of nothingness, suddenly there'd been her.

He'd suspected she was fae-touched, and he believed it still. One of her ancestors must've been fae, and they must've possessed the rare and coveted ability to cross between realms of existence without the need for conduits or portals. It was the only explanation that made sense.

Yet the confluence of circumstances that had brought Kinsley here were far more difficult to explain. She seemed to know nothing of her own power, nothing of magic, and little of the fae. For her to have drawn upon such a potent ability just as she'd crossed the border of his realm; for it to have brought her *here*, into this in-between world, rather than any one of the countless planes layered through existence; for Vex to reach her just before she would've perished...

What else but fate could've orchestrated everything so perfectly?

So why did he seem destined to squander the only opportunity that had been presented to him since he'd been cursed?

It is not a question of destiny. It is my own hubris that threatens everything.

Flickers of magic teased at his senses. He recognized them— Flare and Shade were approaching.

Vex growled. "Were my instructions unclear?"

"Echo holds vigil over her slumber," replied Shade.

The wisps' light bathed Kinsley's ruined carriage as they neared Vex, making hints of its strange metal gleam through the vegetation.

He stepped closer to the conveyance, extended his arm, and caught a vine between two fingers. "You know full well that my command was not for Echo alone."

"If you are displeased, compel us to obey," Flare said with a little growl of their own.

Slowly, Vex pulled the vine off the carriage. The tendrils holding it in place gave way one by one. "I find myself sorely tempted to do so."

"And yet you never have, magus." Shade floated just behind Vex's left shoulder. "Not once in all the years since these three found you."

Flare moved into place over Vex's other shoulder, their light brighter but more erratic than Shade's.

Night sounds padded the ensuing silence. Boughs creaked and leaves whispered in the breeze, insects made their music, and the waters of the loch lapped against the tiny strand that fell within the realm's borders. No fell monsters brayed at the moon. No ghostly mortal voices drifted from beyond the mist.

No female voice, sweet and warm and passionate, spoke to him.

"You did not seek me out to hover at my back in silence." Vex released the vine. "Speak."

Flare obeyed without hesitation. "Your behavior toward Kinsley has been abhorrent."

Keeping his gaze on the carriage, Vex again clutched his hands behind his back.

"You had shame enough to reel when she called you monster, magus," Flare continued, "and yet you seem to have gone to great lengths to ensure she may perceive you in no other fashion!"

"What goodwill you may have garnered you have swiftly undone," said Shade. The continued calm and neutrality in their tone stung more than Flare's indignance. "And you have inflicted more damage beyond that."

Vex drew in a slow breath, dipping his chin. "How does she fare?"

"She is stricken with sorrow, anger, and anguish," replied Flare, emphasizing their words with sparks of ghostfire.

"She sleeps now only due to exhaustion," added Shade. "Her tears fell freely until slumber claimed her."

Vex felt like a huge hand wrapped around him and squeezed his chest, constricting his lungs and heart. He brushed Flare aside with one hand and took a step along the length of Kinsley's conveyance, pressing his other hand to his chest to rub at the deep, pervasive ache.

Rather than fade, the discomfort only spread, tightening his throat.

"You claimed she was strong," he said, voice ragged. "She will endure this. Words shan't be her undoing."

Softly, Shade asked, "Are not words the very thing that wove this curse?"

The queen's voice arose in Vex's memory, beautiful, terrifying, sultry, melodic, powerful. He forced it back into the depths, back into silence. This place was reminder enough of her. He would not allow her words to haunt him any further.

"A single word may uplift a soul…" Shade floated closer still.

"Or crush it," said Vex.

"Just so, magus."

"The way you spoke to her has done the human harm," Flare said, "and it sits not well with these three."

Vex's fingers flexed, and his claws pricked his skin through his tunic. "Nor with me."

Kinsley had pushed him, no one could deny that. She had tried his patience at every opportunity, had antagonized and insulted him. She had hurled objects at his head and made a mess of his bedchamber.

But she had also teased him with surprising warmth and good nature. She had smiled, and he'd glimpsed amusement twinkling in her lovely eyes. She had asked questions of him with genuine curiosity, and her interest in his answers had not been feigned.

And he'd rewarded her with evasiveness and aggression.

Despite himself, Vex had been enjoying her company during their meal. And he hadn't missed the blush staining her cheeks when she'd favorably remarked upon his appearance.

Flattening his hand, he smoothed the front of his tunic. Her desire to learn more about him and the wisps could've been used to his advantage. He could have answered her honestly, without giving away information that could harm him, all while earning her trust. Humoring Kinsley would've been only to his benefit.

"A true effort must be made, magus," said Flare, hovering at Vex's shoulder again.

"In this, be not guided by your fury." Shade's phantom touch trailed across Vex's upper arm. "You are much more than the pain bequeathed to you by the queen."

Drawing in another breath of cool night air, Vex glanced skyward and fixed his gaze upon the moon, which was just visible through the trees. "What further counsel would you offer? What would you have me do?"

Flare's ghostfire swirled. "Kind words bolstered by kind deeds."

"Has it truly been so simple all along?"

Gentle laughter sounded from Shade. "Indeed, magus. You have ever been the complicating factor."

Vex huffed, turning his head to glare at the wisp. "Your cleverness is ever the greatest threat to you."

"Would that this one had been clever enough to spare you from all you've been made to suffer, magus."

At that, Vex turned to face Flare and Shade fully. He lifted his hands, cupping one beneath each wisp, and brushed their ghostfire. Faint ripples of arcane energy flowed into his fingers.

"The choices that led me here were my own, my friends," he said. "You three are all that have sustained me through this curse."

Both wisps rubbed against his hands. Their touches were warm and tingling, familiar and comforting.

"These two shall share your words with Echo, magus," said Shade.

Flare laughed. "Echo would not believe those words, even had that one been here to hear them."

"First"—Vex lowered his hands—"I must request your aid. Kinsley has asked after her belongings."

As the wisps returned to their usual places over his shoulders, Vex faced the wrecked carriage. He visualized his hands as extensions of his magic, sending out countless invisible tendrils to latch onto the plants growing over the conveyance. When he swept his hands to the sides, those magic tethers tore away the vines and moss, revealing the silver metal and broken glass hidden beneath.

Vex's eyes did not need his companions' glow to cut through the darkness inside the conveyance, to see the dried blood on the broken branch, the chair, the floor.

His dealings with humans had been infrequent, limited to instances through which he'd been able to procure greater power or new knowledge. Their lives held no importance to him. He'd not spent a moment of his existence worrying over a mortal.

So why did the memory of Kinsley impaled, bleeding, dying, cause that tightness in his chest to resurge?

Growling, he braced a hand on the carriage's roof and leaned down to look through the broken window. The mist cut the vehicle in half lengthwise, so thick that only the very edge of the secondary seat was visible.

"A strange conveyance indeed," he muttered. Apart from the leather of the seats, the materials used to craft the carriage were unfamiliar. The metal bits looked much too polished yet somehow brittle. Not even the glass was right, with much of it having broken into tiny fragments rather than shards.

"No reins, but a wheel like a ship's," he continued. "I saw neither rudder nor sails."

"It is called a *car*, magus," said Flare. "It moves without the aid of wind or beast."

"Even before I was cursed, mankind had been losing its command of magic. How could they have crafted a carriage that moves itself without potent enchantments?"

"A great many years to experiment and innovate, magus," Shade replied. "It is not magic, but machinery."

"A great many years…" Vex had felt every day of his curse. They'd fallen upon him like stones piled atop a cairn, each heavier than the last. Yet he could not guess how long he'd been here.

An eternity, by the feel. Mayhap two.

This…*car* had come through with Kinsley. Her power, raw and untrained, had wrenched both her body and her vehicle into this space between worlds. Now the car stood as proof that the world beyond the mist, the world in Vex's memories, was truly unreachable for him.

Because that world no longer existed. Not as he'd known it.

Purpose, people, time…all the things he'd lost… But had he not been the one to risk everything to begin with? Had he not overestimated his capabilities when it mattered most?

Vex shoved those thoughts aside. "Where would a human store their belongings in such a carriage?"

Shade and Flare floated through the window. With their light cast upon its interior, the car looked even stranger to Vex, and the mist within only looked more solid.

"She had a bag." Shade drifted into the mist over the other seat, their light becoming a muted, indistinct blue glow. "It fell onto the floor beyond her reach, where it yet lies."

Releasing a harsh breath through his nostrils, Vex stepped back. He swept his gaze over the side of the car. Considering the broken glass that had been around the window frame, it seemed unlikely that passengers were meant to climb in and out through the windows—though that was how he'd removed Kinsley from within.

His gaze fell to a handle on the side of the car. Grasping it, he tugged. The door barely moved before catching with a metal scrape. It had been bent out of shape by the impact, apparently. He grasped the window frame with his other hand and pulled harder.

The door groaned open, swinging wide, and bits of debris tumbled from within the car to land on the forest floor.

Using Shade's glow as a guide, Vex leaned into the conveyance and reached into the mist pooled on the floor of its far side. The sting immediately escalated into a burn where the mist touched him. He lowered his hand. It came down on something lumpy with a texture reminiscent of canvas.

The pain was already coursing up his arm and echoing at his core. It was not as intense as that caused by direct sunlight, but it would not take long for it to rival that agony.

Vex snatched his arm back, pulling the bag out of the mist. He dropped it onto the seat, atop dried blood and bits of broken glass, and shook away the lingering sting.

Shade emerged from the mist, joining Flare to hover close to Vex, their ghostfire flickering uncertainly.

"Your concern is better turned elsewhere," Vex said with a frown.

He opened the bag, and the wisps repositioned themselves to cast their light into it. Vex's brow furrowed as he examined the eclectic contents, withdrawing items one by one for closer examination.

There were several small, narrow things wrapped in what had appeared to be paper, though its texture was decidedly unlike paper. Curious, he tore one open. Inside was a hard cylinder, wider on one half, with a string hanging from the narrow end. Placing those aside, he took hold of a white cord that had been tangled with several other items in the bag, laboriously pulling it free. It ended in a little box with metal prongs on one end.

He found a relatively thin, rectangular object that rested neatly along his hand. Its face was black and reflective, like obsidian polished to glasslike perfection, but it was encased in a hard shell made from a different material.

"Quite an impractical hand mirror." Vex turned it over to find a trio of tiny glass eyes staring up at him and a painting in soft colors of several elegant, winged beings reclining on the stems of flowers.

"Are those meant to be faeries?" Flare asked.

"Is this truly how humans see them? Fair and playful?" Vex grunted, shaking his head. "It is a wonder mankind has survived."

From the mirror, he moved on to a folding leather container. The inside was separated into several sleeves. The largest sleeve was filled with strange paper notes bearing the likeness of an unfamiliar human queen. The smaller sleeves held little cards, all of which were similar in size. Some of the cards were made of thick paper, others from a harder, though still flexible substance. Most had numbers written across them.

Vex removed a card that caught his eye—a *driving licence*. On the side was a tiny painting of Kinsley, stunningly detailed and realistic despite its size and lack of color. She was smiling softly, staring straight ahead.

Staring at him.

He craved that smile. Longed to have it directed at him, only at him.

He brushed his thumb across the bottom edge of the painting. It was perfectly smooth. He might have thought it was protected by a thin sheet of glass, but the card was not entirely rigid, flexing slightly when he gently bent it.

Most bewildering of all was the writing at the top. *Delaney, Kinsley Wynter*. Her true name.

Susceptible as they were to enchantments and charms of all sorts, humans were surprisingly resistant to compulsion through their true names. They were far less vulnerable than fae in that respect, even when they bore traces of fae blood in their veins.

Yet that did not make Kinsley's true name any less precious a thing. It had its own sort of power, and there were ways it could be used—such as the pact Vex had made with her. Beings more powerful and knowledgeable than him could use it in potentially more sinister fashions.

Carrying this easily stolen card, with her true name plain for all to see upon its face, was foolish at best.

Magic crackled across his palm and to the tips of his fingers.

The card vanished, willed away to safety behind the arcane wards in his laboratory.

Flare flickered with uncertainty, but voiced no question, leaving Vex to continue his perusal of the bag. There were tools for grooming, like the pair of tweezers in their small pink sheath, and other tools for which Vex had no name but might well have been diminutive torture devices with their curved cutting edges and hooked files. A few of the items were clearly for beautification.

Many of the objects were either made from or enclosed in that strange material he'd only encountered in this car. It was light but solid, some of it pliable, some of it rigid. Not metal, wood, or glass, not clay or crystal. An unfamiliar substance from an unfamiliar world.

He returned the items to the bag and was about to exit the car when he glimpsed something behind the seat. Grasping the headrest, he leaned farther in.

A translucent white box lay tucked on the floor behind Kinsley's seat. He reached down and grasped the handle, shimmying the box to work it free from where it had been wedged. Stepping back so he could stand upright, he examined the new find.

The container was made of that mysterious material, though this was like fogged glass. Despite a prominent crack running down one side, it was intact and secure. Through the lid, he could see numerous compartments containing a variety of items—colorful papers, twine, thread, ribbons, pressed flowers, buttons, and more items that Vex couldn't identify.

Flare dipped to peer into the box. "Are those butterflies real?"

"Are they dead?" Shade asked.

Vex laid the container atop the car, released the latches, and lifted the lid. Flare and Shade eased back as though expecting the tiny cluster of butterflies to suddenly take flight, but the vibrant creatures did not move.

Gently, Vex plucked one of the butterflies from its place. His brow furrowed as he gently rubbed the wing between forefinger and thumb and raised it closer to his eyes. "Parchment."

The details were impressive. Human artistry and craftsmanship had certainly improved while he'd been imprisoned.

As he replaced the paper butterfly, his eye was drawn to another item. A leather-bound book with a tree etched on its front. Vex brushed his fingertips over the tree. There was power in this book, he could feel it, but it had naught to do with magic.

He opened the cover and slowly turned the pages. Items just like those in the clear box—and a great deal else—were present within in bursts of controlled chaos. Images, some of which were so crisp, clear, and vibrant that they were like gazing through a tiny window, mingled with bits of cloth and paper, with leaves and patches of moss, with dried flowers and lace and seals pressed into colorful wax.

There were pages about nature, about forests, plants, and animals, pages about the sun, moon, and stars. And some, which made him smirk, were about *fairies*, filled with dubious information and speculations about the fae folk.

But as he neared the center of the book, he reached a pair of pages that made his hand still and his breath catch. They were different than all the rest; they were the source of the vague power he'd sensed.

Both pages were covered almost completely in scribbled black lines, many of which had been made with force enough to leave grooves in the paper. A painted silver cage spanned the pages in the center. Two halves of a broken, blood-red heart lay in the cage.

Words penned in flowing, elegant script, contrasting the rest of the imagery, ran beneath the cage, white ink against solid black.

All the world will look upon you and never know the crushing weight of your broken heart.

His chest ached, and his throat tightened. He felt more than the raw emotion these pages conveyed—he felt the raw emotion with which they'd been made. The overwhelming sorrow, the grief, the anger.

The soul-deep pain.

Vex had spent his life in pursuit of his goals, driven to protect what was his, and he'd afforded little time to the emotions of others. The rage smoldering in his heart had been enough to fuel him. Never had he felt the anguish of another person so clearly as he did now. Never had he longed with such vehemence to take another soul's pain away.

He recalled Shade's words.

She is a gentle soul, strong but lost in suffering.

"You three see the world with clearer eyes than I," Vex rasped.

"These ones see not more clearly, magus," Shade said softly. "Merely differently."

Flare ran a ghostfire tendril along the page. "You may yet ease her suffering, magus. And if you allow it...she may ease your own."

Vex stared at the book as those words settled upon him with all their weight. Had he not lost enough to recognize the pain she'd expressed here? Had he not longed for respite from his pain even as he'd used it to push himself onward?

"Freedom will ease my suffering," he said, but he did not believe himself.

Gently, he closed the book, returned it to its place, and sealed the box. The blood on the seat beneath it caught his eye as he lifted the container by its handle. Magic again thrummed through his free hand. Flakes of dried crimson rose from the leather seat. They liquefied and coalesced in the air, forming a small sphere of glistening blood which, in a green flash, disappeared.

It would await him in his laboratory. A few simple tests on it would offer some insight into her ancestry, and mayhap her latent abilities.

Vex stepped back and shoved the car door closed with his boot.

"Magus," Shade intoned, their ghostfire pulsing with sadness.

"Survey our borders," Vex commanded as his wings took shape at his back. He stretched them wide. "Alert me of any breaches."

He sensed unspoken words from both wisps; the air crackled with them. But he leapt off the ground before they could say anything more, crashing through the boughs until he finally escaped the canopy.

But even the clear night sky could not comfort him this night. Why, just as he'd found what he'd needed for all these years, was he plagued by doubts? Why was he fraught with indecision when the key to his freedom was *right there?*

Why was Kinsley's pain still throbbing in his chest as though it were his own?

Vex swiftly returned to his home. His wings dissipated immediately after he landed, and his legs carried him inside and to his bedchamber before he'd even made the conscious decision to go. Quietly, he opened the door and stepped inside.

Kinsley lay on her side upon the floor, several paces away from the bed. Her hair was mussed and spread out upon the floorboards, the flesh around her eyes was pink and swollen, and she remained clad in only a blanket. She had one arm beneath her head, with her other hand tucked beneath her chin.

Echo, who was hovering over her, turned to look at Vex, flaring with surprise.

Vex clenched his teeth. The sight of her upon the cold, hard floor, where she'd cried until she had succumbed to exhaustion, made something icy coil around his heart and squeeze it.

My mate.

This was wrong. His mate should not have been made to suffer such indignity, such discomfort, such distress.

And it was his doing.

Sighing, Vex strode across the chamber, feeling the wisp's gaze upon him the entire way. He placed Kinsley's things on the desk before moving to stand over her.

She looked so peaceful now despite the circumstances. In her slumber, she was freed from the troubles of her waking life. She was freed from Vex and his cruelty.

I need not be so cruel.

How fulfilling would it be to make her smile? To hear her laugh?

He waved Echo away with a gesture. The wisp hesitated, head bobbing as they looked back and forth between Vex and Kinsley. Again, Vex gritted his teeth, but he did not argue. Instead, he knelt and, with as much care as he could muster, slipped his arms under Kinsley and drew her against his chest. She stirred, turning her face against him and wrapping an arm around his neck.

Vex stilled. For a long while, the only sounds in the room were the thunderous beating of his heart and her slow, steady breathing. Her scent enveloped him, so sweet, so natural, so perfect, and her body was warm and soft.

An ache spawned low in his belly, and his cock throbbed, pressure building in it with each pulse.

He craved the feeling of her hands on his flesh. He longed to explore her, to soothe all her worries and fears with his touch, to bring her pleasure.

He yearned to continue holding her, to continue being held by her just like this.

Somehow, he stood. Somehow, he carried her to the bed, with Echo trailing behind him. Somehow, he summoned enough magic to peel back the bedding. And somehow, though it was more difficult than anything in recent memory, he laid Kinsley down. Though he was loath to withdraw from her, he slipped his arms free, tucked the bedding over her, and took a single step back from the bed.

Something in his chest warmed and melted, spreading its heat throughout his body even as everything constricted again. Kinsley in his bed, warm and serene...*this* seemed right.

She was human, unfamiliar with his kind, with his world. And she was, at times, maddening. But would it be so terrible to have her companionship? Would it be so terrible to...

To what?

To be *with* her.

To want her.

To make her his mate in truth.

CHAPTER THIRTEEN

The sweet aroma of cinnamon and honey coaxed Kinsley from her slumber. She smiled. When she was little, she'd often awoken to her grandmother making breakfast. The house would be filled with voices and laughter as everyone gathered around the table, which would be laden with bacon, beans, tomatoes, sausage, fried eggs, and fruit. But that cinnamon and honey smell was Kinsley's favorite, because it was the scent of her grandmother's porridge.

Was Aunt Cece making breakfast this morning?

Kinsley opened her eyes. Dull, gray morning light spilled through the window, leaving the bed's canopy shrouded in shadows but for the highlights along the edges of the ivy leaves. She lay atop the soft mattress with a warm blanket draped over her. Strange. Aunt Cece didn't have any four-poster beds at her house...

Kinsley's brow creased in confusion before reality came crashing down on her.

The cottage.

Vex.

A pang of homesickness struck her heart. Yes, she'd chosen to move up to the Highlands, she'd chosen to live on her own for a while, but she'd never gone more than a day or two without at least talking to her mother on the phone. Her family had to be worried sick.

Should I be worried sick too? Being held prisoner by a goblin, sleeping in his—

In his bed. She was in Vex's bed, but she didn't recall climbing into it last night. Had...had Vex...

Kinsley sat up. The blanket fell to her lap, baring her breasts. She quickly tugged it up to cover herself as she looked around the room. He wasn't there.

But there was a wooden standing tray beside the bed holding a bowl of steaming porridge topped with cinnamon, honey, and nuts, a plate of fruit, and a cup with a pitcher of water.

One of the wisps hovered near the utensils. This one had a darker core and dimmer flame than the others.

"Good morning, Shade," Kinsley said.

The wisp offered her a shallow bow and whispered what sounded very much like a greeting.

"Have you...been here all night?"

Shade shook their head.

"Do wisps sleep?"

Another head shake.

Kinsley smiled. "You must get pretty bored, especially having to babysit me."

Shade's armlike tendrils curled and rose in what could only have been a shrug.

Clutching the blanket to her breasts, Kinsley scooted toward the edge of the bed and swung her legs over it to sit with feet dangling. The blanket she'd worn the day before must've worked loose while she'd slept, as it was now bunched beneath the current bedding.

She picked up the wooden spoon. "Did you bring me breakfast?"

Again, Shade shook their head, floating to the other side of the tray.

Dipping the spoon into the porridge, she mixed in the sugar, honey, and nuts. "So Lord Asshole brought me breakfast then?"

Light laughter sounded from the wisp, who nodded.

"At least he remembered to feed the lowly human this time." She took a bite, and her whole world quaked.

This...this was better than her grandmother's porridge.

No way. Doesn't count. He used magic, and that gives him an unfair advantage.

Heck, who's to say if this even counts as food at all?
You're tasting it, aren't you?
Kinsley wrinkled her nose.
Nan's is still the best.
"What's the point of a kitchen if he can just magic food into existence?" Kinsley asked as she ate.

Shade simply watched, their silence confirming what she'd already known—if she wanted an answer to that, she'd have to ask *him*.

Kinsley sighed. She was torn in so many directions when it came to Vex. Though he'd been unkind and sometimes downright mean, he hadn't been cruel. He'd manhandled her and bossed her around, but he hadn't truly hurt her. And beneath that hard exterior, she'd sometimes glimpsed someone...good.

She understood what he wanted from her, but she didn't understand *why*. Why did he want her to have his baby? Why did he want one so badly that he'd somehow bound Kinsley to himself and had nearly done the unforgivable to her?

Just as she didn't understand his motivations, he didn't seem to understand her reluctance. Kinsley didn't believe he was some cold, inhuman creature, detached from emotion. No, there was a desperation underlying his interactions with her. She just didn't know why.

Kinsley poured water into the cup and took a drink before looking at Shade. "Where is he?"

The wisp offered a shrug and an indecipherable whisper.

"Guess I should stick to yes or no questions, huh? I wish I understood you."

Shade glided closer, brushing an arm over the back of her hand. They spoke again, the words so, so close to something she could figure out. Every time the wisps talked, it was like a tickle in her brain. A build-up on the cusp of understanding, on the edge of a payoff, but the payoff never came. It was the same feeling she had while looking at the writing in Vex's books—a feeling that if she just concentrated hard enough, it would suddenly make sense.

"My parents live in a house next to the woods," Kinsley said as she ate. "It was a giant, mysterious, magical forest to me as a little girl, right in our back garden. I'd venture out there almost every day thinking it was filled with little forest faeries and imps. I'd make homes for them out of milk cartons or boxes that I'd decorate with things I found in the woods, plant flowers for them, and bring them food. Every day when I went back, the food would be gone."

Kinsley glanced up at Shade with a smirk. "I'm sure it was just animals eating it, but to a little girl, what else could it have been but faeries?"

Shade tilted their head, easing closer.

"As I got older, I stopped visiting the faeries, but I don't think I ever stopped believing in them." She stirred the remainder of the porridge. "Every time I hike through a forest, I always feel like there's some kind of…magic around me. I've always felt more at home out in nature than I ever did in my house."

She chuckled and sat up, letting go of the spoon. "If I were talking to anyone else, they'd think I was crazy. But here I am, talking to a will-o'-the-wisp and being held captive by a goblin sorcerer. How's that for magic?"

The wisp swelled, their flame brightening as though in pride.

Kinsley moved the tray aside and slipped off the bed, catching the blanket and wrapping it around her body as she dragged it off the mattress. She looked to where she'd thrown the nightgown, but it was gone. Her eyes caught on something familiar atop the desk as she lifted her gaze toward the wardrobe.

No… Is that…?

She hurried to the desk and reached for her purse. To her surprise, it was really there, not an illusion or a figment of her imagination at all.

"Oh my God."

Hope sparked in her chest. Kinsley opened the bag and rummaged through its contents until she found her phone. She yanked it out, turned it toward her, and tapped the screen.

Nothing.

She pressed the power button, pressed it again, held it down. The screen remained black. It was dead.

"No…" she whispered, clutching the phone in both hands.

Just as swiftly as her hope had flared, it fled.

She closed her eyes against gathering tears of frustration and let her head drop back.

Kinsley was trapped here. There was no way to leave this place, no way to call for help. Though she'd agreed to Vex's terms in desperation, she was bound by her oath. Even if the terms could not be fulfilled.

She was here to stay.

You need not spend your time here in suffering, Kinsley.

Though Vex wasn't here, she could still smell him, could still feel the warmth of his fingers as he'd held her chin while speaking those words, could still feel the gentle brush of his thumb as he'd looked into her eyes, could still see the hint of sorrow in his red gaze.

No, she did not need to suffer while she was here. Apart from the stipulation about being stuck until she had Vex's baby, wasn't this exactly what she'd always dreamed of? A beautiful, magical cottage in the forest where faeries, goblins, and will-o'-the-wisps were real?

If only she had been able to tell her family that she was alive. That she was…safe.

Releasing a slow, calming breath, Kinsley opened her eyes and lifted her head. She could explore and learn, could make the most of this. She didn't have to isolate herself in this bedroom. Vex hadn't locked her in; she was free to roam. While she was restricted by the mystical fog, she wasn't sealed in a dank prison cell.

It's still a prison, Kinsley.

Yes, it was, but…

She didn't need to treat it as such.

As she dropped her phone back into her purse, something else caught her eye. Kinsley lifted her bag off the clear container upon which it had been set. Her chest constricted. Vex had brought her scrapbooking supplies. She ran her finger over the crack in the plastic lid.

He hadn't been obligated to bring any of her things, but he'd done so regardless. Maybe that was minimal effort on his part, but it was effort. It was more than she'd expected.

Having these things wouldn't enable her to make her escape. Apart from a few items in her purse, they weren't necessities. But having some of her belongings was a comfort she could not deny.

She'd left the States to start over, to figure out how to move on with her life. To...escape. What better place to do all that than a slice of magical woodland?

A woodland ruled over by a broody yet beautiful goblin.

But if she was going to embrace this place, if she was going to accept this latest twist of fate, she would do so on her own terms. She would not merely exist, she would *live*.

Kinsley walked to the wardrobe and studied the clothes Vex had provided her. She pinched the skirt of one of the dresses and lifted it. The sheer violet material was delicate, light, and so, so soft.

She opened the drawer beneath to find feminine underwear within. She plucked one out and let it dangle on her finger. Skimpy, lacey underwear.

Kinsley arched a brow. "So this is what he'd have me dressed in?"

Was this sort of clothing normal for goblins or fae?

If not, it's definitely baby-making clothing.

She quickly rejected the idea of wearing anything so revealing. She wasn't ashamed of her body and the extra cushion it carried, but she'd never worn anything like this before. Had never worn something so beautiful. And yet...

And yet, she wanted to. Kinsley had noticed the way Vex looked at her, had seen the heat in his eyes. What would it be like to have him want her for more than a baby?

What would it be like for him to crave *her*?

With a grin, she glanced at Shade, who hovered beside her. "Guess I should make myself at home."

CHAPTER FOURTEEN

Kinsley stepped out of the bedroom and ran her clammy palms over the gossamer skirt, which flowed around her legs as she walked. She'd brushed her hair, which now hung in soft waves down her back, applied a little makeup after washing her face, and had finally put on the dress.

It fit perfectly. The diaphanous fabric was thicker at the bodice, concealing and supporting her breasts, but the rest left little to the imagination. Thankfully, the underwear covered her sex and ass—if only barely. The loose short sleeves fluttered against her arms, leaving her shoulders bare.

Confidence had come easily while she was locked away in the bedroom by herself, but now that she'd left that relatively safe space, she couldn't deny the truth. She was nervous about seeing Vex.

She was nervous to be seen by him.

Their relationship hadn't exactly started off in a great place, and their every interaction had felt like they were walking a tightrope from opposite ends, disrupting each other's balance more and more the closer they came.

But Kinsley sensed his loneliness. More than that, she sensed in Vex the same deep desire she harbored—to make a true connection with someone. She'd thought she'd had one for so long, yet in the end, it just...hadn't been enough.

She hadn't been enough.

So Kinsley would do what she did best—she would make the most of this. She was going to ask Vex every question that came to mind, was going to examine every interesting, mysterious object he owned, was going to talk to him no matter how rudely or dismissively he responded. She would wear him down until he accepted her as she was, as a presence in his life.

He had, after all, chosen her for this. He had proposed this deal.

And if this cottage was to be her home, she wanted to be familiar with it. There were parts she hadn't yet seen. She knew the kitchen lay to the left, but what was behind the closed door on the right?

Destination decided, she walked around the mighty tree trunk. Shade followed her, their luminescence adding to the glow of the crystals, making the space just as wondrous as it had been the first time Kinsley had seen it.

When she reached the door, she paused and sniffed the air. There was a faint smell here. No, not a single smell, but a collection of scents that was not unpleasant despite the hint of a sting it bore. It was like incense, potpourri, and pipe smoke. The designs carved into the wood were different than those on the bedroom door. These weren't patterns mimicking vines, leaves, and trees, but deliberate symbols laced with tiny, precise runes.

It was the sort of door behind which dark secrets or terrible monsters hid, the sort of door that one should never try to open.

The sort of door Kinsley couldn't resist.

She pushed on the door. It didn't budge. She grasped the metal ring handle and tugged, but the door remained unmoving.

Kinsley glanced at Shade. "Guess I'm not allowed in there?"

The wisp shook their head.

Her eyes widened. "What dark, dirty secrets is he keeping in there? Is it a family of elves he enslaved to tailor his clothes? A secret collection of human memorabilia he's stolen from passing hikers?" She covered her mouth in mock shock. "Or is it the ritual chamber where he inserts an enchanted stick into his ass every morning?"

Shade's flame pulsed with laughter, but the wisp made no gesture to either confirm or deny her speculations.

"Guess I'll have to revisit this room another time," she said, stepping away from the door to continue toward the front of the chamber. "Maybe I'll even teach myself to pick a lock. I have plenty of time, right?"

Rather than take the steps down into the foyer, Kinsley grasped the sides of her long skirt and followed a curving staircase up to the next floor.

At the top was a large, arched door adorned with intricate, abstract carvings. The door opened easily when she pushed on it. She walked through to find herself in a library—the most fantastical library she'd ever seen.

Sconces standing on the floor and mounted on the walls throughout bore luminescent crystals, which put out orange and yellow light like that of a fire, bathing the space in warm radiance. There were countless shelves built into the walls, some sections tall enough to have rolling ladders standing against them. All of them were filled with books and scrolls.

Branches and vines snaked along and between the shelves, their lush leaves making the place feel alive, but nowhere did they seem to actually touch the books. On the far wall, several of those branches twisted together to frame a large, circular alcove across which spanned a cushioned bench with several plush pillows set upon it.

Kinsley walked the length of the library, which curved around the cottage's central chamber in either direction. Her path led her back to the entrance after she'd beheld what must've been thousands of books and scrolls. She ran her fingers over the spines. Like the books in Vex's bedroom, these were old-fashioned but in excellent condition, and most were marked with symbols Kinsley could not read.

She stopped and withdrew a blue leather-bound book with silver adornments and writing on its cover. Opening it, she flipped through the pages one by one. While she couldn't understand the writing, the drawings inside transcended language—charts of stars and constellations filled many of the pages, some accompanied by drawings of creatures both mundane and mythical. There were also charts dedicated to the moon and its phases.

"Should I be concerned that there is a book in your hand, mortal?"

Kinsley shrieked, jumping reflexively and losing her grip on the book. She scrambled to catch it but wasn't fast enough. It struck the floor with a thump, landing open with its pages down.

Vex stepped in front of her, his crimson eyes glowing as he sank into an easy crouch and plucked the book off the floor. "Safer for myself, but no less ideal for the tome."

She stepped back and pointed at him. "That was your fault for startling me."

"Oh?" He held the book upon one large hand, using a finger from the other to leisurely turn a few pages before gently closing it. Then he offered it back to her. "Then I shall be sure not to startle you again, for the sake of my library."

Kinsley took the book and returned it to the shelf, glancing at Shade. "Someone could have at least warned me I wasn't alone."

With another of those little shrugs, Shade whispered.

"What'd they say?" Kinsley asked.

"That their current duty is to watch you, Kinsley," Vex replied. "Not me."

"So they are spying for you."

"Spying?" Vex eased closer to her.

She instinctively retreated a step, unable to look away as his eyes devoured her. "Yes."

"They are watching, mortal. Listening. To protect you."

"To protect me? From what? You're the only dangerous thing here."

"Would that your words were true. You are by far the fairest creature to enter my realm, and also the most vulnerable."

"Unless I have a book in my hand."

The corner of Vex's mouth quirked. "Indeed."

When he moved closer again, she held her ground, catching the sides of her skirt and clutching them.

His eyes dipped, and heat sparked in his gaze. "You've donned one of the dresses I left for you."

Had his voice grown a bit deeper just then?

"Well, it was either this or the blanket," she said.

He extended a hand and trailed his fingers down Kinsley's arm.

A shiver stole through her. She shouldn't have stood there and allowed it, but she was unable to move, spellbound by his touch.

His hand paused at her elbow, and he curled his fingers around it loosely to brush his thumb over her sleeve. His claws pressed into Kinsley's skin just enough to make her aware of their wicked points.

Her body's response was immediate—her nipples hardened; her heart quickened. She was ashamed that she couldn't tell whether it was from fear...or arousal.

A low hum sounded in his chest as his gaze flicked back up to hers. "You are beautiful in either."

Kinsley flushed not only due to his words, but the intensity of his stare.

This was different. He was different. She wasn't used to...to *this* Vex. He was so much calmer, so much more collected. And somehow, that made him seem more powerful, more intimidating.

She backed away, withdrawing from his touch, and turned to walk around the library. Though she couldn't see him, she felt his gaze upon her, which reminded her just how revealing this dress was.

Is he staring at my ass?

She looked at him over her shoulder.

He is definitely staring at my ass.

The heat on her skin deepened, pooling low in her belly.

Kinsley cleared her throat. "So were you locked away in that room downstairs, brooding?"

"I was within that chamber," he replied as he lifted his gaze and fell into step behind her, "but I was not brooding."

"Sulking, then?"

"No. Nor was I overseeing the elvish slaves who tailor my clothing, as they do not exist." He locked his hands behind his back. "And while I indeed possess several enchanted sticks, not a one has ever been or will ever be—what were your words?—shoved up my ass."

Kinsley faced forward and bit down on her lips to keep her laughter from bursting out, but she couldn't stop the muffled sound from escaping. "You heard that, huh?"

Shade laughed quietly from beside Vex.

"It's not as though you made any attempt to speak softly, human," Vex replied.

"I wasn't exactly yelling either." Kinsley trailed her fingers over the ivy growing on the shelves. "What is that room?"

"My workshop. Or mayhap…laboratory is more accurate."

"A lab?" She stopped and turned to face Vex, her nose crinkling. "So do you have human body parts floating around in jars down there, waiting to be sewn together?"

Vex's brow furrowed. He was studying her again, scrutinizing her, but somehow, there was no judgment in his gaze. "You've a rich imagination, haven't you?"

"Considering what I've seen and experienced here, it's not all that farfetched. And there are sick people who do that sort of thing, you know."

"I am well aware."

"So what's down there then?"

The muscles of his jaw ticked. Just when she was sure he wouldn't answer, he said, "Potions, salves, tinctures, and a myriad of reagents and arcane items that are both powerful and dangerous, especially for a mortal. Hence the locked door—which shall remain so."

"Aww. I don't get to see your dungeon?" Kinsley stuck out her lower lip in a pout.

His eyes fixed upon her lip, and heat again swirled in their crimson depths. Distractedly, he replied, "It is not a dungeon, as I've already stated, and you shall not see it. I would not risk undue harm to you."

Of course. He couldn't let anything happen to his baby maker.

Kinsley swept her hand out. "What are all these books?"

Vex finally looked away from her, turning his head to survey the room. He moved closer to a set of shelves, running his fingertips across the books upon it. "They contain all manner of knowledge. Herbology, cartography, metallurgy, linguistics… A great many subjects, though most pertain to arcane and mystical arts."

Shade drifted in the wake of Vex's hand, casting a ghostly glow on the books.

"Are any of them books that you'd read for fun?" Kinsley asked.

Vex looked back at Kinsley, his brow furrowing. "For *fun*?"

"Guess I shouldn't be surprised that Mr. Stick-Up-His-Butt is confused by the concept, but yes, for fun. You know, reading because you like to. Reading books with adventure, excitement, romance and tragedy, books with gripping stories."

"Treatises detailing the alchemical properties of madame's cup lichen fail to rouse excitement in you?"

"Potentially interesting, but very, very far from exciting."

"How unfortunate." Vex stepped back and swept his gaze across the shelves. He kept one hand raised, marking the progress of his eyes with an extended finger until, finally, that finger stopped. "There."

Shade floated up to the high shelf Vex had indicated, illuminating the books there.

"Fae histories," Vex said, "brimming with tales of love, ambition, and betrayal. The deeds described within would seem as myths to a human."

Kinsley crossed her arms over her chest. "All right. History isn't what I expected, but that sounds promising."

"I've a few volumes and scrolls of poetry, as well, though some of the poems are fragmented." He slowly lowered his hand. "There were once many more books in my collection that might've satisfied your criteria, but that library is long since lost."

"What do you mean lost?"

Vex clasped his hands behind his back and walked along the shelves, leaving Kinsley to follow him. There was a wistful light in his eyes as he perused the books and scrolls.

"Long ago there stood a tower on this very spot, taller than the tree that is the heart of this building. My tower. From its pinnacle, I could gaze across my lands in their totality. I could watch the moonlight dance upon the loch, observe the gathering storm clouds race along the glen. The uppermost levels served as my library, which contained more books than could be counted.

"It was my sanctuary. My...home." He lifted his hand, palm up. Wisps of green light swirled around it, growing in brightness and density, until he flicked his wrist.

The green energy burst outward in a wave to encompass the room. But instead of simply casting its eerie glow upon the walls, it *pushed* them.

Kinsley's eyes widened, and her breath hitched as she came to a halt.

Vertigo made her legs unsteady as the walls slid away on all sides and the ceiling rose higher and higher. Nothing touched by that green wave was left unchanged.

The magic faded as quickly as it had spread. Kinsley blinked as though it could set everything right again, as though the room would revert to its prior state, but everything remained...different. She was standing in the center of a huge chamber that could've held the entirety of her favorite bookstore in Portland with room to spare.

Bookshelves twice as tall as Kinsley lined the walls, divided by decorative wood and stone columns. Several sections jutted out from the walls, not quite as tall but just as densely packed with books and scrolls, carving the chamber up into spaces that didn't feel quite so large and daunting. A big table stood just in front of her, laden with writing tools, books, scrolls, and parchments, just like Vex's desk in his bedroom.

Beyond the table, a wide set of stairs led up to a mezzanine level that wrapped around the chamber above the tall bookcases. It too was stuffed with shelves upon shelves of books.

She tipped her head back, looking higher still. Spiral staircases and walkways with elegant railings connected the first mezzanine floor to two more, stretching high enough that she was briefly stricken with another bout of vertigo. And far, far overhead was the arched ceiling, spanned by ribbed vaulting adorned with intricate patterns and carvings.

Curved panes of glass on the ceiling allowed moonlight to stream into the chamber, filling it with welcoming, silvery light. That light caught upon the spherical stones held on sconces between the bookcases, which glowed milky white and blue.

Moonstones. They were bigger and more beautiful than any she'd ever seen, but she was sure they were moonstones.

Kinsley touched the teardrop moonstone piercing at her navel.

It's not a sign, Kinsley. Just a coincidence.

"My library of old," Vex said, calling Kinsley's attention to him.

He stood at the top of the stairs on the first mezzanine level with arms spread, though he'd not been there a moment ago. Shade hovered over his shoulder.

"This..." Kinsley settled her fingers on the table. It was solid wood. "How?"

"Magic"—he closed one fist—"and memory." He closed the other. "Your imagination does the rest."

Kinsley walked around the table, trailing her fingertips over the items upon it. "But it all feels so real."

Vex lowered his arms to his sides and descended the steps with Shade in tow. "Hands touch. Fingers feel. But it is the mind that perceives all sensation." He stopped in front of Kinsley, dropped his gaze to the table, and brushed his hand along its edge. "This table was real. I spent many nights sitting at it beneath the light of moon and stars, studying, searching… But it has long since crumbled to dust."

With those words, the table disintegrated beneath their fingertips. Kinsley snatched her hand back as what remained of the table—the dust he'd mentioned—drifted away on an unfelt breeze and faded to nothingness.

"What happened to this place?" she asked.

He fixed his eyes upon her. His voice was low as he spoke, laced with bitterness and anger that intensified with every word. "My tower was razed. Torn down around me, stone by stone. Everything I had built, everything I had sought to protect…destroyed."

The library exploded around Kinsley. Books flew from the shelves, stone columns crumbled, glass shattered, and bricks rained from the collapsing walls, all in deafening silence. She jumped with a gasp, squeezing her eyes shut and covering the back of her head as she collided with Vex.

He wrapped his arms around her and drew her into the hard, warm shelter of his body, and she buried her face against his chest.

But nothing struck her.

Vex rested his cheek atop her hair. When he spoke, it was in a raw whisper. "This illusion, this memory, shan't harm you, Kinsley. It is but a phantom from my past."

Kinsley hesitantly lowered her hands to his chest and opened her eyes. They were back in the cottage library, with its soft lighting and lush vines, looking exactly as it had moments before.

"What tomes I could salvage formed the core of this collection," Vex continued, "and the stones formed the foundation of this cottage. It is no glorious rebirth from the ashes of ruin, but...it is mine."

He grew quiet. Kinsley sensed that there was so much more behind his words, a whole story filled with pain and loss. Her eyes moved over the room, which was far simpler but no less magical than what he'd shown her. This room was the more welcoming of the two by far.

And as grand and wondrous as his old library had been, she doubted she could think of it without recalling the horror of it falling apart around her.

There'd been fury in his voice when he'd spoken of the tower's destruction. Fury that had been simmering for a long, long time. Maybe it had been some sort of natural disaster, but the emotions he'd let through, though muted, suggested something far more deliberate had occurred.

Kinsley drew back from him. "Who destroyed your home?"

Vex released her, but not before Kinsley felt the reluctant tension in his arms. His expression was grim, those dark eyebrows low over his smoldering red eyes, the corners of his mouth downturned, his jaw clenched.

Shade floated behind him, flames dimming as they turned their little head to look from Vex to Kinsley and back again.

"It is in the past," Vex replied tightly. "You need not concern yourself with her."

Kinsley's brow furrowed. "Her?"

His lips peeled back, giving her a glimpse of his fangs before he turned from her. "My home of old was destroyed. I've no desire to speak of it further."

She ran her gaze over Vex's back as he stepped away. Tension radiated from him, and the air around him dimmed and warped. She knew him just well enough to understand that this wasn't the time to press him for more answers.

"We're allowed our secrets," she said gently.

Especially when it's a matter of life and death...

"Indeed," he said, glancing at her over his shoulder. "And secrets hold value, human. They should never be given away."

"Would you say the same for names?"

Vex turned toward her, narrowing his eyes. "I would." He stalked across the distance separating them, his eyes pinning her in place. "Not that you *gave* your true name away."

Kinsley tilted her head. "How did I not?"

"You believe you've received naught in return?"

"Maybe I misunderstood our deal, but I don't recall my true name being part of the price. You demanded it of me anyway."

"It was necessary to seal our pact, Kinsley."

"In the human world, the contract would need the names of both parties to be valid."

Shade flitted beside Vex, flashing at him in warning and speaking rapidly.

"This is *not* the mortal world," Vex growled, waving the wisp away, "and your oath remains binding."

Kinsley glared at him and clenched her hands at her sides. "Right. I have to give you a baby. Thank you so much for that reminder."

She spun toward the door, needing to get away from him. Her anger was made all the more frustrating by the tears stinging her eyes. For a fleeting moment, she'd actually sympathized with him. She'd seen his anguish. When he showed those little signs of compassion and kindness, when he offered those tiny glimpses of humanity, it was easy to forget why she was here in the first place.

But he always made sure to remind her in the end, didn't he?

"Stop," Vex commanded.

She ignored him.

His hand closed around her wrist, bringing her to an abrupt halt.

Kinsley turned her glare back on him and gave her hand a tug. "Let me go."

"I sought you out to…to apologize to you, Kinsley."

"Well, you're terrible at it. Let go."

Instead of releasing her, he drew her closer with a smoothness and ease that made it seem as though she'd made no effort to resist. She planted her free hand on his chest, stiffening her arm to keep at least that much distance between them, and focused her eyes there, refusing to meet his gaze.

"Look at me," he beckoned.

When she didn't obey, he caught her chin and forced her face up toward his. Finally, she looked at him. The anger that had so tightly gripped his features was gone. Only sorrow and regret, deeper and older than she could fathom, remained in his eyes. Some of her own anger deflated, and her arm relaxed.

"Hear my words, Kinsley," he said, stroking her chin with his thumb, "for they are not spoken lightly. My behavior has been... unacceptable. I said you need not suffer here, and yet my every word, my every act, has done naught but inflict further suffering upon you. For that I am sorry."

"That apology was better," she said, if a little begrudgingly.

The ghost of a smile passed across his face, curling his lips up ever so slightly and sparking a charming light in his eyes. But his tone was serious when he continued. "I know the pain of having everything you know torn away. Of...of losing your world. No one soothed that pain for me, but I shall soothe yours if you would but allow me to learn how."

Vex eased closer, his fingertips leaving thrilling tingles in their wake as they trailed along her jaw and to her neck. Her lips parted.

"Though we remain bound, I'll not force myself upon you, Kinsley."

His hand moved lower still to her collarbone, where his thumb brushed the hollow of her throat. Her pulse quickened. All she could do was stand there, barely breathing, her gaze locked with his.

"I shall take no more from you than what you offer by your own will." His clever, maddening touch traced her collarbone, then dipped to graze the swell of her breasts. The tips of his claws sent whispers of pleasure straight to her core. "I shall not so much as touch you"—he withdrew his hands suddenly and took a step back, breaking all contact with her—"unless you ask it of me."

A shuddering breath escaped Kinsley. Her hand hovered in the air where it had been resting against his chest. She slowly lowered it. Though he was no longer touching her, Kinsley's skin burned as though she'd been branded. His caresses, his words, his nearness, his darkly sensual scent, and that smoldering intensity in his eyes had ignited something fierce and forbidden within her.

Despite everything, she was tempted to ask him to touch her again, to run his hands over her body, to tease her with those claws. She longed to feel the press of his body against hers, to feel his heat...

Their eyes remained locked for several heartbeats. To Kinsley, it was an eternity. Unspoken words crackled through the air between them, charged and electrifying, only adding to her growing desire.

How long had it been since she'd last been intimately touched, since she'd last felt a physical connection with someone? Any connection at all?

All you have to do is ask, Kinsley. Just...ask for more.

As though he'd heard her thoughts, Vex reached for her. Kinsley's heart fluttered.

Two blurs of bluish light darted up from behind Vex—Echo and Flare, both burning bright and whispering frantically.

Vex's hand halted in midair, curling into a fist, and his jaw muscles ticked. He kept his crimson gaze locked with hers. "This is not—"

The wisps cut him off with more whispers, their voices like the wind blowing carpets of autumn leaves across the forest floor.

He snapped his face toward Flare. "You're certain?"

Flare and Echo nodded vehemently.

A shadow fell across his face, leaving his eyes to glow only brighter. "I must take my leave, Kinsley."

She looked back and forth between Vex and the wisps. Her heartbeat hadn't slowed, though that now had little to do with what had passed between them. "What's wrong? They sound worried."

Vex returned his attention to her. Some of the tension had faded from his expression, but he seemed almost too controlled now, too aloof. "There is an urgent matter to which I must attend. Save for the lab, you're free to move about the cottage. But you must remain indoors until my return."

He moved to walk past her, only to pause at her side, his shoulder brushing hers. Voice lowering, he said, "It would please me, Kinsley, if you came to consider yourself my guest rather than my prisoner."

And then he, Flare, and Echo were gone, leaving her staring at the empty open doorway.

CHAPTER FIFTEEN

Echo and Flare darted through the forest, tendrils of ghostfire trailing behind them. Vex followed, moving from shadow to shadow to avoid the sunlight breaking through the canopy, incessantly scanning his surroundings. Even in the shade, the daylight was bright enough to force him to narrow his eyes.

His woods were quiet. Unnaturally so.

And Kinsley was back at the cottage. Shade could watch over her but couldn't protect her. If she were harmed, if she were killed, Vex would...

He clenched his jaw. For untold years, he'd carried only anger and grief. These new emotions Kinsley was awakening in him—

Distractions. At that moment, they were naught but distractions from the task at hand. The cottage was warded. So long as Kinsley obeyed him and remained inside, she would be safe.

"Here, magus," said Echo as the wisps arrived at the wreckage of Kinsley's car, which was already covered in fresh moss and vines.

"You spied the beast here?" Vex moved into the shade of the tree the car had stricken. There was a faint scent on the air—an earthy musk, a lightning-like tang of magic, and a hint of sickly-sweet decay.

"Signs only," replied Flare, floating to the rear of the vehicle. Their glow fell upon a portion of the silver metal that had been crumpled and gouged as if by claws.

Echo sank toward a small depression on the ground, gesturing down.

With a wave of his hand, Vex cleared away the detritus beneath the wisp, revealing a print in the soft dirt. He crouched to study it. Larger than his hand, it possessed a too-familiar form. Three thick, taloned digits to one side and two more, like a pair of thumbs, to the other.

It was confirmation of what the wisps had suspected.

"Barghest," Vex growled. "A large one at that. Likely female."

"Two breaches in a matter of days," whispered Echo. "It is unprecedented."

Frowning, Vex glanced at the damage on the rear of the car. "The first was…"

Fate.

"It was happenstance," Vex continued, and the lie was like ash upon his tongue. "A fae-touched mortal finding herself on the precipice of death at the border of my realm…a once in an eternity occurrence that shredded the veil between worlds."

Flare flew closer, joining Echo. "And the barghest?"

"The beasts are drawn to magic and death. Both were present here that night."

"Her blood must be potent to have lured such a creature," said Flare.

"It is," Vex said. "She is the descendant of a seelie realmswalker. With the veil weakened by her crossing, it is no surprise a barghest would be lured by her power."

After bringing her belongings to the bedroom last night, he'd gone directly to his laboratory. He'd needed to know. Had needed to unravel the mysteries of her power.

He'd needed to know if her blood would enable him to cross the veil.

His questions had been answered. And those answers had come with despair, with dashed hopes, and with newfound resolve. There truly was but one way to escape the curse.

Vex rose, looking in the direction the barghest had traveled. The trail was apparent now—broken branches, disturbed undergrowth, patches of moss scraped off bark and stone, and scattered tracks in what scant bare dirt was visible.

"None of these signs were evident last night," he said.

Flare's ghostfire brightened. "They lead toward the nearest ley line, magus."

Vex clenched his fists, barely feeling the sting of his claws against his palms. "I'll not suffer an infestation."

The wisps hurried to follow as Vex stalked along the barghest's trail. A molten mass roiled within his chest, radiating heat and tension.

His realm would survive an invasion by barghests. His home would survive. But his Kinsley…

For all their ethereal beauty, most seelie fae were hardy beings. Few things could cause them illness. Barghests were amongst those things—their venom was severe enough that it had been known to kill lesser fae, and their claws carried similar poison, oft inflicting foul, festering wounds that healed with torturous slowness.

Even many unseelie were laid low by such injuries, though they were far less likely to perish due to the venom.

He drew in a deep breath through his nose. The beast's smell was strengthening with his every step.

Kinsley was fae-touched. Seelie blood flowed in her veins. The lifeforce with which he'd infused his mate would sustain her through wounds that would've been deadly to her before, but he had no way of knowing whether it would protect her from a barghest's venom.

Vex's uncertainty, paired with her vulnerability, nearly drove him back to the cottage right then.

But she was safe. His magic would serve as her shroud, her shield, and protect her from harm.

Just like it protected all the others? Like it protected my people?

He growled and pressed onward, following the tracks and the guiding heat of his fury.

Soon enough, a thin fog encroached upon the trail. It made Vex's skin tingle with magical energy wholly unlike that of the mist encircling his realm. Where it had touched the sunlight, the fog had dissipated, leaving erratic empty patches. Vex slowed his pace, avoiding those spots.

Magic pulsed ahead. Most of it belonged to the ley line, but he focused upon the smaller, more insidious force. The primal mana of a beast born from the ether and shaped by brutal instinct.

A low ridge lay ahead. He knew that a shallow gill awaited beyond, where the sunken ground followed the ley line. A perfect nesting ground for a creature whose eggs drew magic directly from such sources to grow at alarming rates.

Vex wove a cloak of illusion around himself and the wisps, masking them from sight, as he crept to the ridge. Despite the magic, he took cover behind a large tree, braced one hand on the trunk, and peered into the gill.

Fog had pooled in the depression, shrouding the ground and making the rocks that jutted up from it seem like mountain peaks in a sea of clouds. Yet several of the things rising from the mist weren't rocks. They were purple-gray and oblong, with leathery textures, and their exteriors pulsed as though with malignant heartbeats.

Eggs.

The beast has made haste since her arrival.

And having been lain atop so potent a ley line, those eggs were likely to hatch within a matter of days—not into helpless pups but full-grown barghests just as vicious and capable as their mother.

And they would consume every scrap of meat in this world before invading another to multiply and devour anew.

A snapping branch shattered the forest's silence. Vex's eyes darted toward the sound, and his fingers curled, digging his claws into the tree.

Farther along the gill, a large, dark shape stirred, making tufts of fog swirl around it. A pair of reflective silver eyes, devoid of any emotion but hunger, turned toward Vex before shifting away.

The barghest's form grew more distinct as it lumbered closer. A female indeed, and certainly a large one. Even on all fours, it was nearly as tall as Vex at its shoulder. Its long limbs disturbed the fog with each of its slow, heavy steps. It had an elongated, vaguely wolflike head, and its body was reminiscent of a bear's—albeit a furless, emaciated bear. Any details on its dark hide were too obscured by the fog for Vex to discern.

As the barghest reached the center of the gill, a mere ten paces away from Vex, it halted. The beast rose onto its hind legs as it sniffed the air with loud huffs. While standing, it looked much more like a gangly, oddly proportioned human than a bear.

And it would've towered over Vex were he not on higher ground.

The barghest's head turned toward Vex, making its eyes gleam, and it leaned toward him, still sniffing.

Vex glanced down. A thick broken branch jutted from the tree trunk at the level of his midsection.

Images flashed through his mind unbidden. Pale flesh, shattered glass, blood glistening in the light of ghostfire. Blue-violet eyes so afraid, so pleading. His throat constricted, and sudden heat scorched his lungs. It was wholly unlike the heat of his anger. This was agonizing, debilitating.

Forcing the memories back, Vex returned his attention to the barghest, which had shifted closer to him.

Whether Vex maintained his illusory shroud or not, he would be discovered by the beast ere long. He knew he could not overcome it in direct combat. It was larger, stronger, and very likely faster than him. More, his wings would avail him not—the trees here were too low for him to maneuver beneath them, and if he flew above the canopy, he'd be exposed to the sun. That would kill him faster than any beast ever could have.

But that did not leave him without advantages.

He drew upon the magic at his core and shaped it without the need for thought.

The magic wove first into a voice—his own voice—that called from the opposite side of the gill.

"This is my realm!"

Straightening, the barghest snapped its attention toward Vex's disembodied voice. The creature took a step in that direction, head shifting as it searched the trees. Its lips peeled back, revealing long, sharp teeth with protruding fangs. Though its mouth did not move, its words formed in Vex's mind in a low, rumbling whisper. *"Death has summoned me to hunt."*

Vex unfurled his wings and stretched them wide as magic thrummed through his body.

An illusionary double coalesced around him. Despite the situation, part of Vex thrilled in the making of such magic, just as it always had—and always would.

Especially when his illusions instilled wonder in those who witnessed them, as they had with Kinsley earlier.

His form split with that of his double, and the thrumming ceased. The illusionary Vex moved into place in front of the broken branch. Wasting no time staring at his own back, Vex crept away, seeking a new vantage.

"*Show yourself,*" said the barghest in its disembodied voice.

Vex released the double from its magical concealment and spoke, his words coming from the illusion's lips. "Here, I am the hunter."

The barghest's eyes darted to the illusion. It loosed a call that was part wolf's howl, part lion's roar, and part the wailing of the damned before dropping onto all fours and charging at the double. Its footfalls were as loud and powerful as the hoofbeats of a galloping stallion.

Vex glided down into the gill, landing atop one of the large rocks that stood over the fog.

With sheer strength, the barghest bounded up the embankment and launched itself into the air. Maw gaping and claws poised, the beast struck the illusionary double, which vanished.

The barghest crashed into the tree, shaking the boughs, rustling the leaves overhead, and snapping the branch. It snarled in pain. Sinking its claws into the tree, it shoved itself away. Part of the broken branch protruded from its chest, and black ichor oozed from the wound.

"*Tricks,*" it growled in his mind, nostrils flaring as it scented the air.

Vex bent his magic into another illusion. A dozen seelie warriors in resplendent armor rose from the mist. They readied their weapons—spears and swords forged of gleaming gold.

Snarling, the barghest held its ground, its reflective eyes sweeping over the illusionary warriors, its nostrils opening wider still. "*More tricks.*"

The warriors charged, carried up the embankment by their multihued, diaphanous wings. They rained blows upon the barghest, their illusory weapons barely able to damage its tough hide despite the magic with which they were infused. The beast snarled, batting at the fae, but its claws and gnashing teeth struck only empty air.

"*No more, goblin,*" the creature rasped.

The beast's jaws opened wide, and thick, billowing fog spewed out, building so quickly that the creature was soon shrouded from view entirely. The mist spread in a wave that engulfed the gill and Vex along with it. So dense was the fog that he could scarce see Echo and Flare, though the wisps remained over his shoulders.

"Go," he whispered, "lest the beast devour your essences."

"*The wisps would make a fine snack, yes,*" the barghest purred in his mind, "*but your flesh is rife with magic, goblin. It will feed my clutch well.*"

Vex let the illusionary warriors fade, recalling the mana into himself.

Leaves crunched somewhere to his right; debris rolled down the embankment to his left. And the sound of the barghest scenting the air seemed to come from all around. Yet still the wisps lingered.

Something tugged at Vex's heart. He did not deserve such devotion—not from them, not from anyone.

Vex dropped a hand to his belt, curling his fingers around one of the two daggers sheathed there. Even through the leather and cloth wrapping the grip, he felt the heat of the golden tang building on his palm. "I'll not repeat myself."

With mournful sighs, the wisps darted upward, their blue glows vanishing in the fog.

"*I will feast upon the mortal myself,*" the barghest continued. "*Its scent stirs my hunger. Long has it been since last I tasted such succulent manflesh.*"

"Never again will you taste anything," Vex snarled, drawing the golden dagger and sending out a burst of magic with a pump of his wings. The magic blasted away the fog around him, sending swirling tufts of it up into the boughs overhead.

A huge black shape darted out of the dissipating fog, flying straight toward Vex.

He leapt aside with another pump of his wings. The barghest's claws sliced deep across his right thigh, and its body twisted, colliding with his legs and throwing him into a spin. He crashed onto the ground on his side, a rock digging into his ribs and forcing the breath from his lungs. The barghest landed heavily behind him.

"*Your tricks cannot mask your scent, goblin.*" The beast lashed out with a long arm, burying its claws in the same leg it had cut.

Vex growled in pain. His concealing shroud fell as the beast dragged him closer, its ravenous silver eyes fixed upon him. He grabbed at the ground but found no purchase. The beast rose over him, plunging him into the darkness of its shadow.

I shall not die like this.

With its fanged, slavering maw yawning, the barghest lunged. Vex thrust out his magic, creating a pair of sorcerous hands that caught the beast's jaws and stopped them mere inches from his face.

The beast snarled, shifting its other arm as though to grab at him. Vex jabbed the dagger into the underside of its jaw.

Flesh sizzled and blood boiled as unseelie flesh reacted to the gold. The barghest wrenched its head back, pulling free of the blade and spraying its thick blood onto Vex. He pushed with his magic appendages, forcing the creature back farther still. When the claws tore out of his leg, deepening the gouges, he cried out. His own hot blood ran over his flesh.

The barghest toppled onto its back and thrashed, kicking up leaves and detritus.

Somehow, Vex managed to regain his feet. Though his right leg wailed in protest and fresh blood ran down his shin, he retreated several steps. His pain was only a distant thing, a concept his mind could not fully grasp. How could he perceive the fullness of that pain when his rage left no room for it?

"I am master here," he grated.

Shaking its head fiercely, the barghest planted its oddly split, clawed hands and feet on the ground and pushed itself onto all fours. It sides heaved with ragged breaths as it swung its gaze toward Vex. Faint smoke wafted from the wound on its jaw. "*You are food.*"

Vex spread his arms and wings. Illusionary doubles split off him, fanning out to either side, each holding its own phantom dagger but for one, which clutched the real weapon in hand.

Growling, the beast reared back on its hind legs, towering over

Vex despite its hunched posture. *"The bite of your little blade matters not, goblin, and your blood scent betrays you. I will guzzle the mana from your bones."*

Vex pointed his illusory dagger at the beast. His doubles rushed toward the barghest, attacking. The creature did not react to their insubstantial blows. It stared at him unwaveringly as it stepped forward.

"You came at death's beckoning," Vex said through his teeth.

The illusion bearing the true dagger sliced the weapon across the back of the barghest's leg. The beast snarled in surprise and pain, twisting to rake its claws at the double, but Vex's magic had already passed the blade to another illusory hand. The weapon leapt from double to double, always faster than the beast could follow. It opened a gash along the beast's ribs, and another across its gut, then more on its arms, its back, its legs, striking in rapid succession, each time from a different angle, a different image.

Every wound sizzled and smoked, and globs of dark blood splattered the forest floor.

Vex raised a hand as he shaped his magic into a new form—another sorcerous hand, which grew and grew as he poured mana into it. Arcane energy crackled through his limbs, suffusing him with heat that would soon grow unbearable.

The beast roared as it flailed in defense, but there was nothing solid for it to strike, no enemy for it to wound. It finally stumbled and crashed onto the ground. Clawing at the dirt, it dragged itself toward Vex as the dancing dagger shredded its flesh.

The massive arcane hand caught the barghest in a crushing grip, flipped the beast onto its back, and held it in place. The double of Vex clutching the real dagger poised the weapon over the creature's exposed chest. Black blood burned on the blade, bubbling and hissing.

"In this place, I am death," Vex declared, "and you will *not* take her from me."

The barghest thrashed and roared in pain and hatred. The dagger sped down, plunging deep into the creature's chest.

That roar ended with a choked grunt. The barghest's final exhalation released a faint cloud of fog into the air. The beast sagged, limbs falling limp, and darkness overcame its reflective eyes until they were blacker than its skin.

"Are you harmed, magus?" Echo asked, racing down to Vex on a blazing trail of ghostfire.

"You should not have endangered yourself so!" Flared declared, arriving just behind their counterpart.

"Necessity dictated otherwise," Vex replied.

The illusions dissipated, leaving behind an arcane hand around the grip of the dagger, which tugged the weapon free. The larger hand faded to nothingness.

Tendrils of smoke wafted from the barghest's many wounds, which emanated orange, emberlike glows. Nowhere was that glow more intense than the wound on its chest. The corpse was burning from within.

Such was the fate of any unseelie creature pierced through the heart by pure gold.

If only death had been so quick for all those who'd perished because of Vex's failures.

He drew in a deep breath through his nose. If the queen's curse served as his shackles, the past had been his chains, binding him to this place in misery, sorrow, and regret. He could allow those chains to weigh him down no longer.

There was someone here to protect, the most important someone to have ever entered his life. His mate. And he'd eliminated a threat to her today. He'd succeeded despite his past failures, despite his curse. If he continued to succeed in safeguarding her…

With Kinsley, he would shed those chains, would cast off those shackles. He would be freed from this prison.

When he called his weapon back to him, the barghest's blood had already burned off the golden blade. Vex's leg and ribs throbbed with pain as he guided the dagger into its sheath, feeling the heat radiating from the metal even after it was secured.

Tearing off a wide strip of his sash, he wrapped it around his wounded thigh and tied it firmly in place. The ache only deepened. He willed his wings away, clutched an arm to his tender side, and limped along the gill without a backward glance at the corpse, which was already crumbling to ash.

The wisps lingered behind him; he felt their gazes on his back.

"Come," he said. "Our hunt is not yet concluded. We've eggs to dispatch."

VEX PAUSED at the bedchamber door. The quiet inside the cottage allowed the night songs to flow in—insects chirping, the sorrowful calls of nocturnal birds, and the continued sigh of wind through the boughs. The great tree behind him, which had sheltered his home from the harsh light of the sun for untold years, creaked and groaned softly.

It was in stark contrast to the utter silence that had reigned in the forest when he'd left hours ago, while the sun had still been high. Now the moon and stars ruled the sky but Vex was in no state to enjoy their soothing glow.

The battle against the barghest would've been meaningless had he not thoroughly searched the area for her eggs afterward, a task that had escalated his pain and weariness into agony and exhaustion.

I am home now.

And his home, for once, was not empty. For all the time he'd spent locked away in his tower, secluded from the very people he'd sought to help so he could think and study without interruption, it was pleasant to have someone here waiting for him.

He would be sure to build upon the progress he'd made with Kinsley earlier.

Carefully, he opened the door and stepped into the bedchamber. The room was dark but for the soft glow of the crystals. Kinsley lay upon his bed, wrapped tight in the blankets, her breathing steady and slow, her eyes closed. Shade hovered over her, backed by the round window with its carved tree.

As Vex limped toward her, his battered body pulsed with a myriad of aches, and pain shot up and down his leg, suffused with a building warmth that was anything but pleasant.

Shade drifted toward him, their ghostfire sputtering with alarm. "Magus, you—"

Vex lifted a finger to his lips, silencing the wisp. He stopped beside the bed and fixed his gaze upon Kinsley.

Her beauty was only enhanced in her repose, and under Shade's blue light, Vex could almost see a hint of her fae blood. There was a delicacy to her features that whispered of inhuman ancestry, but when combined with the rest of her...

She is unlike anyone I've ever beheld.

Something stirred low in his belly, spreading a different heat through his veins. For the first time since departing for the hunt, he allowed himself to reflect upon the short time he'd shared with Kinsley in the library.

The light of curiosity in her eyes, the sparkling wonder, had roused an indefinable joy in his soul, and the way she'd jumped to him, seeking security in her fear, had made his chest swell with satisfaction and possessiveness. Her skin had been so warm and soft against his hand, and her alluring scent had enveloped him, taunting and teasing. She'd fit against him so perfectly.

And all of that paled in comparison to the light that had been in her eyes after he'd withdrawn, to the desire that had radiated from her. Had they not been interrupted...

The fae queen had coveted Vex. She'd sought to possess him, to make him part of her collection, another toy to play with as she fancied. But Kinsley...Kinsley *wanted* him.

And he wanted her. He craved her.

Needed her.

"You are mine, Kinsley Wynter Delaney," he rasped, reaching for her.

He needed to claim her, to feel the bond he'd forged with her in all its fullness, to strengthen it. To solidify it. To ensure there was no question—she was his, his mate, *his*. There was no going back. There was no breaking their bond.

They were linked in a way few mortals ever experienced, a way few mortals could ever have imagined. Their very souls were already intertwined; why should they wait to connect their bodies, as well?

Vex halted his hand an instant before his fingers would've touched her. He was covered in dirt and gore, and his leg was far worse than it had been even an hour ago. His fingers curled, but he could not bring himself to withdraw his hand, could not bring himself to look away from her.

Waves of honey brown hair were spread on the pillow around her, beckoning him to comb his fingers through them. Her full lips begged for a kiss, promising to yield to him, to caress him like nothing else could.

In that moment, he wanted nothing more than to climb onto the bed, wrap his arms around her, and draw her body against his. He wanted nothing more than the feel of her skin and her heat. The feel of her.

He wanted nothing more than to feel the sort of connection he'd never experienced with anyone in all his years.

He leaned a hair's breadth closer.

Fresh agony rippled through his leg, making his knee buckle. Shade hurried closer as though to catch him, but Vex snatched his hand back to avoid hitting Kinsley and braced it on the nightstand. The items atop it rattled. He pressed his other hand over his wound. Vex barely kept himself upright, breathing harshly through clenched teeth to ride out the agony.

Kinsley started, sucked in a sharp breath, and opened her eyes.

"Sleep," Vex commanded, infusing the word with magic.

"Vex…" Kinsley whispered as her eyes drifted shut once more.

Had it only been his imagination, his own foolish hope, that had filled her voice with such longing and concern as she'd said his name?

Her body relaxed, and the pain in his leg diminished to a raging firestorm made tolerable only because it had been preceded by so much worse. The beast had inflicted a tainted wound upon him, and even the diluted poison from its claws was proving too much to bear. He could afford little further delay in attending to it.

He tore his gaze away from Kinsley, forcing it down. The shadows cast by Shade's glow danced upon the floor, flickering with the wisp's concern and uncertainty. Keeping his hand tight over his wounded thigh, Vex forced his legs into motion, hobbling toward the bathing chamber.

Once he'd removed his tattered, soiled clothing and washed himself, he could treat his injury properly.

But still, he found himself pausing at the hearth, where he sparked a mana-fueled fire. Once the flames were emitting suitable heat, he entered the bathing chamber with Shade just ahead of him.

He glanced back from the doorway. The firelight blanketed the bed in long shadows, but he could see Kinsley's face as clearly as ever. Something tugged in his chest, urging him back toward her. All he needed was a single touch. The lightest stroke of her cheek, or the tracing of her rounded ear with his fingertip. Perhaps the brush of his thumb across her plump lower lip…

Jaw clenched, he exhaled heavily and closed the chamber door.

It was all he could do not to admit the truth…

One touch would *never* be enough.

CHAPTER SIXTEEN

BOOMING thunder vibrated the floor beneath Kinsley's feet. She sliced through the halved melon on the counter and glanced out the kitchen window. The storm had left the world outside a bleak, gloomy gray, and both the building and the tree through its center were groaning ominously in the raging wind.

Most of her time here had been spent in the shade of that mighty tree, but the weather had been calm and often sunny. The storm had transformed these woods from an enchanted wonderland into a dark, forbidding forest.

"Does the weather here always match the weather on the other side?" she asked, glancing at Echo.

The wisp hovered beside Kinsley, their glow providing a little extra light. They shook their head.

"So this place really is in its own world, isn't it?"

Echo nodded.

"Does it ever snow here?"

With their blue fire fluttering, Echo whispered a response to her. Though Kinsley still didn't understand, she sensed there was a story in those words. The wisp punctuated their reply with another shake of their head.

Kinsley sighed and picked up the melon slices, dropping them into a small bowl. Since Vex had left her in the library five days ago, she'd neither seen nor heard him, not even once. The wisps had assured her he was alive when she'd asked, but they hadn't elaborated—not that she would've understood anyway.

Before he'd left, Vex had told her, quite solemnly, to remain inside until he returned. Despite her rebellious streak urging her to sneak out, she had obeyed.

And her obedience had been rewarded with unfathomable boredom.

She'd tried working on her scrapbook, but she'd found little inspiration. She'd spent hours looking through tomes in the library, but she couldn't read any of them. In five days, she'd explored every accessible inch of the cottage, and the most amazing discovery had been the pantry and root cellar connected to the kitchen, which were stocked with dry ingredients, cheese, butter, meat, and preserves. And as much as she enjoyed the company of the wisps, one of whom was always with her, the conversations were rather one-sided.

Kinsley was…lonely.

She found herself longing for Vex's company. She wanted to learn more about his world, more about him. He'd always been so guarded, but he'd opened up to her in the library, if only a little. He'd even given her glimpses of his softer side. And she'd been so close to asking him to…

To what? To touch her? To kiss her?

To…have sex with her?

Even knowing what he wanted from her, she'd been tempted, if only to have a taste of intimacy again. If only to feel wanted.

She was also worried. There'd been neither sign of nor word from him in all this time.

Where is he?

An acrid, bitter smell filled her nose. Her eyes widened.

"The scones!"

She spun toward the fireplace. Grabbing a cloth, Kinsley wrapped it around the handle, lifted the large iron pot from where it hung over the fire, and lowered it onto the hearthstone. Kneeling, she removed the lid. Black smoke billowed out. She scrunched her nose and waved the smoke away. Echo floated over, shining their light into the pot as they peered in alongside Kinsley.

Black charred lumps sat at the bottom.

"Ugh." Kinsley set the lid down next to the pot. "It'd be so much easier if I could just poof food into existence."

Echo extended an arm and patted Kinsley's hand with a ghost-like touch.

"Why does Vex even have a kitchen when he can just use magic?" she asked.

Kinsley was no stranger to cooking outdoors. She'd often made food on portable grills, small wood stoves, or over open fires. Why was she struggling now?

Because you're preoccupied with thoughts of having sex with a goblin. Nope, not going there. Moving on.

She stared at the blackened lumps longingly before pushing herself to her feet. "Well, no scones for breakfast today."

Kinsley sat at the table, listening to the storm and the cottage's creaking as she ate her meal of fruit and cheese. Her attention fell on Echo, and she tilted her head as she regarded the wisp, who mimicked her movement.

"Are there more of your kind?" she asked.

Echo nodded.

"But not here. It's just you, Flare, and Shade, isn't it?"

Another nod before Echo tilted their head to the opposite side.

"Are you trapped here too?"

When Echo nodded again, Kinsley's brow furrowed. "But I saw one of you that night on the road. You were outside the fog, beyond the barrier. How?"

Echo floated over to the empty plate Kinsley had set out for Vex just in case he decided to join her. They pointed toward the edge of the plate and spun slowly. Then, with equal slowness, they drifted toward the edge. Once the wisp crossed over, their light began to fade, becoming dimmer and dimmer until she worried that they'd truly be snuffed out. Before that could happen, Echo retreated. They brightened as they moved back to the center of the plate.

"You can go outside it, but not for long or far."

They nodded.

"Could that...kill you?"

Their light faded again, and they hung their little head. It was answer enough for Kinsley.

"I wish you could tell me more. I wish I could understand you."

Echo glided over to Kinsley and nuzzled her shoulder, whispering softly. Kinsley cupped her hand around them, smiling at the warm, gentle tingle they caused on her skin.

After she finished eating, she cleaned up the kitchen, wiping away the specks of flour on the counter that had escaped her notice earlier, and disposed of the charcoal lumps in the pot.

Still, Vex did not appear.

On her way back to the bedroom, she stopped in front of his lab. There was no flickering light beneath the door to indicate he was inside. Just darkness and silence.

Every time she'd passed this door, she'd wondered what was inside, wondered what secrets he kept within, what sort of potions he brewed. Did he have a big black cauldron like a fairytale witch? The mystery ate at her constantly.

It was the one place in the cottage she hadn't seen, the one place she'd been forbidden to go. That was like telling someone not to press the big red button.

Being told *no* only ever made you want to do it more.

"Well, he's not here to say no, so…"

Grinning, Kinsley picked up the skirt of her dress and hurried to the bedroom. Echo flitted beside her, speaking rapidly and flashing to get her attention. She ignored the wisp and crossed to the desk, where she dug through her purse until she found her makeup pouch. Inside, at the very bottom, were her bobby pins.

With her tools in hand, she returned to Vex's laboratory door and knelt before it, bending the bobby pins into the shape she needed. Echo floated in front of her face, waving their little arms and shaking their head.

Thunder rolled outside, making the floorboards tremble.

Nope. I refuse to take that as an ominous sign.

Kinsley gently shooed Echo away. "If Vex doesn't want me going inside, then he should be here to stop me." She leaned toward the lock and inserted the bobby pins. "I've never done this before, but it's not like I have anything better to do."

Echo dropped toward her hands briefly, their fire wavering, before darting straight at the door. The wisp passed through the solid wood, leaving nothing behind but a single lick of blue fire that vanished in an instant.

"What do they think I'm going to do, blow the whole place up?" Kinsley squinted and caught her bottom lip between her teeth as she carefully worked the pins.

Echo returned with Flare, startling Kinsley. She drew back and looked at them as they spoke in insistent whispers.

"I won't touch anything. I promise," Kinsley said, returning her attention to the lock. "I just want to see what's inside."

Flare lived up to their namesake, burning bright and gesturing vehemently.

Kinsley stilled when something clicked. She glanced up at the wisps, and they stared back at her, seemingly sharing in her disbelief that she'd actually made progress. Then the wisps zipped back through the door.

Making sure to maintain tension, Kinsley turned one of the bobby pins like it was a key. There was a louder click as a bolt snapped into place.

Kinsley blinked, gaping at the door. "I did it?" She grinned wide and withdrew the pins. "Oh my gosh, I did it! It actually worked!"

Standing, Kinsley flattened her hand against the door. She hesitated. There was a voice in the back of her mind telling her that she shouldn't go inside, that Vex had told her not to, that she was about to trespass. And yet...

Another voice, belonging to the childish curiosity she'd possessed all her life, urged her onward.

Kinsley pushed against the door.

It opened slowly, and the widening gap revealed the soft glow of crystals from beyond. She glimpsed a stone wall, and steps leading down.

The door halted abruptly. Long, black fingers tipped with wicked claws curled around it from the other side, and a dark figure shifted into the opening, blotting out the crystals' light. Vex's red eyes blazed at her from his shadowed features.

Kinsley gasped, her heart feeling as though it had leapt into her throat. The pins fell from her slackened fingers.

"Apologies for my absence, Kinsley." Vex's voice was low with a harsh, ragged edge to it. "But was I not clear in that you are not to enter this chamber?"

Her wide eyes flicked from him to the door and back again.

"Oh, this room? *This* is your lab?" She released a nervous laugh. "My mistake."

His eyes narrowed. "Indeed."

Echo and Flare hovered behind him, their fires uncharacteristically dim.

Feeling like a child about to be scolded, Kinsley dropped her gaze and wrung her hands in front of her. "Really! I was just…um…I…haven't seen you and…"

The door creaked as he opened it further, calling her eyes back up to him. The darkness around him dissipated to allow her an unhindered view of him.

Her breath caught.

His lean torso was bare. The muscles of his chest led down to a toned abdomen, and his prominent Adonis belt pointed down further to pants slung low at his hips. The black skin of his hands continued up his arms, fading into green at his broad shoulders, around which his long dark hair hung loose.

Her fingers twitched to touch him. How had she never realized green skin could be so sexy?

Swallowing thickly, she dragged her gaze back up to his face.

Despite the darkness that had clung to him having faded, she could tell something was off. His features looked a bit sharper, his skin was paler, and there were shadows beneath his eyes.

"Are you okay, Vex?" she asked softly.

"I am…well."

"Oh. That's good to hear."

Not that she really believed him.

In the silence that followed, his gaze raked over her, and something dark and hungry gleamed within it. Her belly fluttered.

He leaned toward her, his chest and shoulders flexing, and a long lock of his hair fell, enticingly brushing over his skin. Desire bloomed in Kinsley's core. She wanted to reach out and grasp that hair, to playfully tug him closer, to run her hands over him, to feel his lips—

"Is there aught you require?" he asked.

Just you.

Shush!

Kinsley quickly shook her head. "No."

The faintest crease appeared between his brows, and his jaw ticked. "Then I trust you'll not repeat this mistake."

She smiled up at him, letting her hands drop to her sides. "I'd tell you I won't, but I know how binding promises are here."

A glint of mirth danced in his eyes. "I shall seek you out later, Kinsley."

"Okay."

Keeping his eyes upon her, Vex eased back and slowly closed the door. The lock clicked into place.

Kinsley stood there, staring at the door. Her heart was thumping, pouring heat through her veins.

It's because I got caught in the act.

Sure, Kinsley. Keep telling yourself that.

She barely noticed when the floor rumbled with more thunder.

Echo's head popped out of the door's wooden face, casting their blue glow across it. Tentatively, the wisp emerged fully, floating in the air before Kinsley with head bowed.

"Why didn't you tell me he was in there?" Kinsley asked, her voice barely a whisper.

Though Echo didn't have eyes, she swore the wisp gave her a look that said, *Are you for real right now?*

CHAPTER SEVENTEEN

Kinsley sat up, smoothed her hands over her wet hair to rinse out the last of the soap, and opened her eyes. The bathroom was dark but for the glow of the rose quartz tub and the crystals on the walls, which were brighter than normal due to the lack of moonlight outside. Between that dimness and the sounds of water trickling on the wall and lapping against the sides of the tub, Kinsley could almost imagine she was in a cave instead of a cottage.

She slid back, lying down with her head resting on the tub's rim. Lavender, rosemary, and peppermint filled her nose, and steam swirled up from the bubbly water, making the air ripple with warmth. Closing her eyes, Kinsley skimmed her palm over the water's surface and took in a deep breath, letting those scents soothe her.

Baths were a luxury she'd never really been able to enjoy. The tub in the house she'd shared with Liam had been small and narrow, and the apartment she'd rented after their separation hadn't had a bathtub at all. And when she was out on the road or camping, well… Hot springs had been few and far between during her travels, and a dip in a cold stream wasn't the same as soaking in a huge, deep, magical hot tub.

But since coming here, she'd often taken the time to just relax in the tub. It wasn't like she had much else to do. And this…this was nice.

She let her hand sink back into the water as a small smile spread across her lips.

"Never have I seen a more lovely sight."

Kinsley shrieked as her eyes snapped open and she quickly scrambled to sit up, covering her chest with her arms. Water sloshed over the sides of the tub to spill onto the mossy floor.

Vex stood at the foot of the tub, tall and dark, dressed in his usual formal black tunic with a silver sash. The soft lighting cast deep shadows upon his features, but those glowing red eyes were vibrant.

And they were fixated upon her.

Squeezing her thighs together and drawing up her knees, Kinsley glared at him. "What are you doing in here?"

"I said I would seek you out, Kinsley."

"And you couldn't wait until I was out of the bath?"

He smirked and sat on the edge of the tub as though it were the most natural thing to do in that moment. "I could not."

"Hey!" She sank a little deeper into the water to hide herself. "Don't just...just make yourself comfortable! You're not supposed to be in here."

Tilting his head, Vex lowered a hand, trailing his fingers through the water. "So you alone have leave to trespass?"

"I told you that was a mistake."

"Ah. Well then, I must apologize." His long, dexterous fingers glided in slow circles, making the water ripple in hypnotic waves. "I thought this was the library. It appears I was mistaken."

"You know damn well this isn't your library."

"And you knew that was my laboratory."

Kinsley let out a frustrated growl. "Okay fine! I knew it and I was trying to sneak in."

"Even though I told you it was the one place you could not go."

"Probably *because* you told me it was the one place I couldn't go."

Vex's smirk softened, and something shifted in his eyes. Kinsley had the sense that he was looking *into* her and seeing something that shouldn't have been discernable at a glance. That should've made her more uncomfortable, should've made her feel even more naked, but the way he looked at her felt...right.

"I shall endeavor to remain mindful of your rebelliousness," Vex said gently. "But surely you did not act merely to spurn my command."

"No. I was just curious. And bored. I can't read any of the books in the library, can't understand the wisps, and you…" She looked down at the water, at his hand and the bubbles clinging to his fingers. "You just left me here alone for five days."

His hand stilled, tension drawing out the tendons on its back. "You missed me?"

"I…" Brow creasing, Kinsley swept a hand toward him. "You just left! I didn't know what happened, didn't know if you were hurt, or…" She hugged herself a little tighter, and her voice softened. "I just didn't know."

Vex was keeping her here against her will, and yet… There was something inside her that had worried about him during his absence. She should've hated him, should've been railing at him, fighting him, demanding that he let her go.

But part of her wanted to stay.

"I've never meant to cause you distress, Kinsley," he said, coaxing her gaze back up to him. "An unwelcome beast crossed into my realm. I had to eliminate it with all possible haste."

Alarm flared within her chest. "Were you hurt?"

"You needn't concern yourself with my wellbeing, Kinsley."

Kinsley frowned. Something had happened. Why else would he have looked so haggard, so…diminished?

"How did the beast get in?" she asked. "I thought nothing could get through the mist."

Now Vex looked down, watching his hand as he traced patterns on the water and the bubbles spread outward in its wake. "This is a place caught between worlds. It is not your realm, but neither is it a fae realm. It is…layered amongst them. There exist means of traveling between worlds. An unfortunate number of monstrous creatures possess that ability, though some few fae also hold the knowledge and power to traverse the planes at will."

Vex lifted his eyes to meet hers again. "And fewer still are the fae-touched mortals who may cross between worlds."

Kinsley eyed him skeptically. "Why are you looking at me like that?"

He raised his hand from the water, shaking droplets off his

fingers. "You've fae blood, Kinsley. Greatly diluted, but it is undeniable."

"Wait, wait, wait. Are you saying that somewhere down the line, one of my ancestors was *fae*?"

"Yes."

"How do you know?"

"You saw the wisps. In your world."

Kinsley shook her head. "It was dark, and they're made of fire. Anyone would've seen them."

"Ghostfire. More akin to magic than flame. But Echo, Flare, and Shade are tied to this realm. Even when they venture beyond the mist, their essences are far too diminished for most mortals to perceive them."

"People have seen wisps and ghosts and...and creatures for as long as there have been people. I can't be the only one. That doesn't automatically make me fae, right?"

Vex stood up and walked around to the side of the tub, his eyes upon her all the while. "Your conveyance carried you to the edge of this realm in your world. But it was you who tore through the barriers between worlds. As your mortal life faded, the fae blood in your veins unleashed its magic."

He sat down on the bath's edge. "When I retrieved your belongings, Kinsley, I also collected some of your blood. Every test I've performed upon it has confirmed my suspicions. One of your distant ancestors was seelie. A realmswalker. And diluted though it may be, their magic flows through you. *You* breached this realm, Kinsley. You opened the way. Else we never would have met."

Hope roused within her, and she sat up a little straighter. If that power really was inside her and she'd already used it once... "Does that mean I could open the way again and go home?"

The ghost of a frown curved his lips downward. "Even were you on the precipice of death again... No, Kinsley. Mayhap you could open the way, but you cannot leave this realm."

"Because you won't let me go."

"Because you are bound to me," he said, voice falling low and raw, "and I am bound to this place."

"What? You..." She leaned closer to him. "What does that mean, Vex?"

"This realm is my prison, Kinsley. I cannot cross its borders." He exhaled heavily. "You recall the day you attempted escape, do you not? When you fled through the woods?"

Kinsley's fingers bit into her arms as she recalled the pain she'd felt upon entering the fog. "Yes."

"You thought you journeyed straight and true." He dipped a finger into the water, tracing a straight line, but then bent that line into a wide curve. "Yet your path was of my choosing, warped by illusion. I sought to keep you from the mist, to protect you from it. Still, it grew apparent that you'd not relent until you *knew* there was no way out."

Vex's eyes fell to her wrist. Kinsley glanced down to see the strange ivy and thorns marking glowing a faint green around it.

"The pain you endured, the disorientation, the confusion and fury... They are shadows of my own." He lifted his finger and swirled it. The steam thickened and gathered on the water's surface, creating a cloudlike ring around a ghostly miniature forest. At the center of the forest, tiny but unmistakable, stood the eight rune stones that lay beneath the cottage.

"I've tried to cross the mist countless times, Kinsley, knowing full well the inevitable outcome," he continued. A miniscule figure strode into the mist and vanished, only to reappear in the center of the ring—the stone circle. "And every time, I suffered a hundredfold what you did in your attempt. I say it not to diminish your pain, but to praise your tenacity, for I would not wish a fraction of that agony upon any but the one who sealed me here with a curse."

He waved his hand, and the steam dissipated.

Kinsley met his gaze. "The one who destroyed your tower trapped you here, didn't she?"

Vex nodded.

"And the wisps?"

"I bound them to myself to spare them from her wrath, lest they perish with all the rest. Had I known they would become prisoners because of it, I..."

Her chest constricted. The pain and guilt he must've carried all this time... "You would have done the same to save them."

A small crease formed between his eyebrows as he regarded her. "You speak with such certainty, Kinsley."

Kinsley shrugged. "I might not understand what they say, but they are loyal to you. They care for you. So you can't be all that evil."

"Have you not considered that their loyalty may be a result of the binding?"

She arched a brow. "I don't recall being compelled to obey despite being bound to you. I've done quite the opposite, in fact."

The corner of his mouth quirked. "You have indeed. Yet our connection is different."

"How so?"

"You shall discover that in time, Kinsley."

The gleam in his eyes was full of wicked promise, and it stirred something deep within her.

"As for now"—he turned to face her fully, curling a leg atop the tub's rim—"I should like to discover more of you."

Kinsley narrowed her eyes at him. "I hope you don't mean that the way it came out. What about your no touching promise?"

"More *about* you," he replied flatly.

She knew he was avoiding more of her questions, knew he'd left so much unsaid, but she could be patient.

Kinsley cocked her head and tapped a finger on her arm. "So you want to know more about a lowly mortal?"

"My only other sources of conversation are the wisps, and we've naught new to discuss but you. So yes, human. I wish to know more about you."

"Annnnnd this couldn't have waited until *after* my bath?"

Bracing a hand on the edge of the tub, he leaned closer, dancing the fingers of his other hand toward her across the surface of the water. "Are you not warm? Comfortable? Suitably relaxed?"

"Warm, yes. And absolutely vulnerable, while you're"—she waved a hand toward him without uncovering herself—"fully dressed and in power."

"I shall remove my clothing and join you, if you'd prefer."

"No! No, that's okay. You just…sit right there."

Vex grinned, showing his fangs. "As you'd like."

Kinsley stared at his mouth. Why were those fangs so captivating? She should've feared them, should've been alarmed by the thought of them sinking into her flesh…

But the only mental image she could conjure was of those fangs grazing her skin, setting her every nerve alight with a dark thrill, and awakening a forbidden desire that she'd be helpless to resist.

"So…what do you want to know?" she asked, squeezing her thighs together against the sudden, aching heat pooling between them.

"Everything."

She chuckled. "Maybe you can narrow that down a little? At least while I'm naked in the tub."

"Are you of noble blood?"

"What kind of first question is that?"

He held his palm up. "Your conveyance—your *car*—is wrought of metal, and I am told it needed neither wind nor beast to carry it. That suggests you are a human of some means."

Kinsley snickered and shook her head. "Most people drive cars. I mean, some cars are worth more and are only owned by wealthy people, but cars are common. I'm not from a rich family, and I don't have noble blood. Just some seelie blood, apparently."

"You've a trade then?"

"I was a receptionist in a dental office before I became a fulltime vlogger."

His thick, dark brows angled downward, and she grinned. Kinsley could almost see her words flying over his head.

"A receptionist is someone who sits at a desk all day and greets people, takes calls, and schedules appointments. I mean, there's more to it than that, but does that give you an idea?" When he nodded, she continued. "A dentist is a doctor for your teeth."

"You've doctors dedicated solely to teeth?"

"Aren't there fae dedicated solely to teeth? Like…the tooth fairy?" Kinsley's eyes widened. "Is there really a tooth fairy?"

"Unseelie who obsess over teeth are not the sort you should want to encounter. They are unsettling creatures." He waved a hand dismissively. "But no more talk of such things. What is a *vlogger*?"

"That…might be a little harder to explain. We record videos, which, um…" She pursed her lips and glanced around the room before the idea struck her. "Oh! Do you know how you create illusions? How you showed me your old library, and what happened to it?"

Vex nodded.

"Well, humans use electronic devices to capture images from life and replay them on screens. Like...moving pictures? Moving paintings?"

"So your machinery is able to replicate magic?"

"Well, no. We're a long way away from being able to do anything like what you can do. We can fabricate a lot of visuals, but that fully immersive thing of yours can't be matched." Just thinking of the illusion he'd shaped around her—the memory he'd shared with her—was enough to awe Kinsley anew. It had felt so real, like she'd been in that long-gone library, like she'd been in his tower.

And if she was correct, the only limit on Vex's illusions was his imagination. What wonders could he conjure if he allowed himself the freedom to do so?

"Anyway," she continued, "a vlogger records parts of their lives and shares those recordings with other people. Sometimes I made videos about scrapbooking, but I mostly covered camping and hiking in the woods. It let me share my experiences and love of nature with people, helped encourage them to get out there themselves, and gave those who couldn't do it a glimpse of something they wouldn't otherwise see."

A thoughtful hum vibrated in his chest. "I should like to see these videos. Summon one, that I may better understand."

Kinsley gave him a droll look. "I'm not a wizard. If I could summon things at will, don't you think I'd at the very least be a little less naked right now?"

His lips stretched into a sinful grin as his eyes dipped. "I quite like you as you are."

A blush spread over her skin. While she could hide her body from him, she couldn't hide from the way his gaze and his words made her feel.

"That shade of pink better suits you than any clothing ever could, Kinsley," he said, looking back up at her face.

This is really not fair.

"Anyway," she said firmly, "that's not how videos work."

"You likened them to my illusions, Kinsley."

"Yes, with the caveat that we're a long way away from being able to match your magic. Everything I do is recorded with a phone. A...

little device that allows us to communicate with other people all over the world."

Vex's brows rose. "You've a device that enables you to speak with anyone, anywhere in the world?"

"Well, theoretically, yes. But they'd need to have a phone, too."

"To think mortals have obtained such power..." He shook his head. "And yet it is used so people may watch you wandering the woods?"

"It's used for a lot more than that. Many people use it for entertainment, but it's also a way to connect with others. The world is so big, and even when you're surrounded by people, it can feel so... lonely. Sometimes it's nice to know that there are others out there who relate to you, even if you've never met, and you can make friendships you never would've had otherwise."

Kinsley looked down at the water, her damp hair sliding over her shoulder. "There was a time when I felt alone, and those connections helped me through it."

Was *a time, Kinsley? Who are you trying to fool?*

The hesitancy in his voice was contrasted by a harsh edge in it when he asked, "Did you not have a mate in your world?"

CHAPTER EIGHTEEN

Kinsley stilled. The silence that followed Vex's question pressed in on her, making it hard to breathe.

Why? Why had he asked *that*?

She drew her legs closer and dug her fingers into her arms. Her eyes stung with the threat of tears. She'd already felt so vulnerable sitting naked before him, but somehow that question made her feel impossibly more so.

"Kinsley…"

"I had a husband," she whispered.

His voice hardened. "You were wed?"

Kinsley bit down on her bottom lip and drew in a deep breath as she attempted to keep the tears at bay. She couldn't cry, wouldn't cry. She'd shed enough tears over Liam to last her a lifetime. "I was, but not anymore."

Slowly, Kinsley lifted her head and looked at Vex. Her heart leapt at the sight of him. One of his hands was clenched in a fist, while the other gripped the edge of the tub so tightly that his knuckles had paled and his claws had scratched the quartz. His thick, dark, shapely brows were angled harshly down toward the bridge of his nose, his lips were peeled back to display his fangs, and fire blazed in his crimson eyes.

"Are you…angry with me?" Kinsley asked hesitantly.

"No."

"You look angry."

He dipped his chin ever so slightly. "Not with you."

Kinsley searched his face. Was he angry on her behalf, or was he...jealous? And why did the thought of his jealousy make her belly flutter?

She released a fortifying breath and looked back down at the water, allowing the tension to bleed from her muscles. "I was born in the United Kingdom, just outside London, but my family moved to the United States when I was eight. That's a place across the ocean to the west of here, thousands of miles away. Liam was my first friend there. He and I were always close, and as we grew older, we only became closer. We were...inseparable. When I turned sixteen, he asked me to be his girlfriend. It always felt like I was meant to be with him, like he was the one, and I dreamed that we'd be together forever. Sounds like a little girl's silly fantasy, but... I was in love.

"And it felt that way when we got married. We were twenty, we were happy, and we had our whole lives ahead of us. But then our lives seemed to become separate. We both had full-time jobs, and Liam was in school, so we didn't see each other often. We spent what time we could together, but there was just so little of it."

Kinsley closed her eyes, fighting back those burning tears. "Our real troubles began a couple years later."

She curled her lips inward. There was so much she wanted to say, so much she wanted to let out, but she couldn't. Not with Vex. She couldn't tell him of the pain she'd gone through, the loss. She couldn't tell him that the one thing he'd demanded from her in exchange for her life was beyond his reach.

Cloth rustled, and Kinsley opened her eyes to find that Vex had shifted to face her more directly.

He leaned toward her with his head lowered and his gaze fixed upon her. "This pain you carry, Kinsley, this anguish... It is due to him?"

Without intending to, she eased closer to him, loosening her grip on her arms. Something deep within Kinsley urged her toward him to seek solace, to find comfort.

"He was part it," she said. "That distance between us grew, and we both became unhappy. In the end, he found someone who...

who could give him everything he wanted. Even as he told me he still loved me, he chose someone else."

Kinsley's gaze locked with Vex's as her bottom lip trembled. "Why wasn't I enough?"

Vex extended his arm and cupped her cheek with his hand, stroking his thumb across her skin. The fire in his eyes burned in solidarity with her pain; it called out to the anger she'd harbored in her heart, the anger she'd barely let herself feel. The anger she'd buried under her anguish.

Despite the storm in his eyes, Vex's touch was firm but gentle, warm, and soothing. "He did not deserve you, Kinsley."

Kinsley's breath caught, and her eyes flared. Her whole universe narrowed down to the feeling of his touch. Where was the cold, domineering goblin she'd first met? This…this was not the man who'd considered her beneath him, who'd treated her like a foul, intolerable creature, like a tool useful only until she'd served her purpose.

A maelstrom of emotions swirled within her—anger, pain, confusion, all around a core of desire. Her skin sparked to life where Vex touched her, and heat that had nothing to do with the bathwater spread through her body.

The way he was looking at her…

It was as though he'd tear apart the whole world to spare her from pain, as though he'd move the heavens and earth for her.

Had anyone ever looked at Kinsley that way? Had Liam, even for a single moment, ever looked upon her like she was *everything*?

And she reveled in it. She craved more of it.

Vex wanted her, and she knew, somehow, that it wasn't because of their pact. The yearning in his eyes was not for the child she'd promised him, but for Kinsley herself.

She'd been floating in darkness for so long, alone and adrift. Her family had helped, but they could never have filled in the hole left in her heart.

Vex's hand, his touch, his voice…

What if he was all she'd needed? He wasn't a light in the darkness, wasn't a guiding beacon. No, he *was* the darkness. And now that she was getting to know him, she could see that the shadows weren't bad, that they weren't something to fear. They were shelter, a shield from all the harshness and cruelty in the world that masqueraded as everything bright and good. They were a comfort.

He was her comfort.

Why not embrace the feeling of being wanted? Why not indulge in it, why not relish it, at least for a little while?

Without looking away from Vex, Kinsley lifted an arm from her chest, knowing she was exposing her breast to his gaze, and covered his hand with her own. "Did you mean what you said about not touching me?"

His pupils contracted into slits. He sucked in a harsh breath through his teeth, muscles tensing, claws lightly pricking her flesh. She felt the resistance in his arm before he withdrew his hand. Saw the reluctance written plainly in his strained expression.

"Forgive me," he rasped, clenching his fist as it fell to his side.

The roughness of his voice sent a thrill through Kinsley.

Vex wanted her, but his vow kept him from having her. That knowledge granted her a sense of power, confidence, and control that she hadn't felt in far too long.

But it also awoke something sensual in her. Something...mischievous.

Kinsley smiled as she lay back against the tub, fully baring herself. "You can't touch, but...you're welcome to watch."

She skimmed her fingers along her collarbone before moving them to her breast, where she circled her nipple with her fingertips. It hardened in the cooler air.

Vex's attention followed her movements, and his jaw ticked. "What are you doing, Kinsley?"

"I'm relaxing in the bath, Vex." She slid her other hand down between her breasts and into the bubbly water. "You're welcome to leave if you'd like."

A growl rumbled in his chest. "I shall remain."

Kinsley's heart quickened as her hand smoothed down her belly. She'd never done anything like this before, had never played the part of a seductress, not even with Liam, but with Vex... God, she wanted to see him unravel.

Spreading her thighs, she slipped her fingers between them to find her clit. The flicker of pleasure caused by that first brush over the sensitive nub made her lips part with a soft gasp.

Vex's nostrils flared, and his pupils expanded and contracted. He did not tear his gaze away from where her hand had disappeared.

Kinsley cupped her breast as she leisurely circled her clit. Heat gathered in her core, and with every stroke, her pleasure built, flowing through her body and filling her with restless energy. Her lashes lowered, but she didn't dare close her eyes.

She dipped her finger lower, sliding it into her cunt, and pumped. Despite the water, she could feel her slickness.

What would it feel like to have his long fingers inside her, thrusting deep? What would it feel like to have his cock, with all its ridges, stretching her, filling her?

Her inner walls tightened around her finger as she withdrew it and returned it to her clit. She moaned softly.

A shudder coursed through Vex, and dark, leathery wings sprouted from his back as it arched. They snapped out, spanning at least twice the length of the tub from tip to tip. Snarling something that must've been a curse, he shoved himself to his feet and turned away.

"Don't go," she breathed.

Tension rippled through him, making those wings tremble. He stalked behind Kinsley, planted his clawed hands on the rim of the tub to either side of her head, and leaned over her. His hair fell around them, and in the shadows it created, his glowing crimson eyes enthralled her.

Through his teeth, he growled, "Not leaving."

Desire burned at her center as she stared up at him. His spicy, woodsy scent strengthened, and Kinsley greedily breathed it in. She kneaded her breast, pinching and twisting her hardened nipple and sending a bolt of pleasure right to her clit, which she continued to stroke. Her skin tingled as those sensations grew, winding tighter and tighter, and the empty pressure within her core expanded. She pressed her toes against the tub and moaned.

Vex's claws scraped the quartz. His crimson eyes blazed, hot and feral, into hers.

Kinsley quickened her strokes. Her pelvis rocked, making the water lap against the sides of the tub. Her breath came in shallow pants. As she edged closer and closer to that peak, her body quivered, her skin tingled, and her brow creased.

"Vex," she rasped as the pleasure coiling within her burst. Her body went taut, and she cried out, squeezing her thighs together and locking her hand in place as her sex contracted. Waves of sensation crashed through Kinsley, but she kept stroking.

Baring his teeth, Vex captured her jaw in hand and lowered his face to hers. "I did not vow it by my true name."

He crushed his mouth against Kinsley's. He swallowed her cries, stole her breath, and she closed her eyes and succumbed to him. His kiss was ravenous, demanding, feral, delivering pleasure that was only sharpened by its lasciviousness. His fangs scraped against her lips; his claws pricked her cheeks.

Vex consumed her.

And then he ripped away from her.

Kinsley bolted up with a gasp and spun around, sloshing water onto the floor. There was no sign of him. Only his lingering scent and the pulsing memory of his mouth on hers proved he'd been there at all.

She pressed her trembling fingers to her bruised lips.

He'd touched her. He'd...*kissed* her.

I did not vow it by my true name.

No, he hadn't sworn not to touch her by his true name, had he?

"You're playing a very dangerous game, Kinsley..."

And the stakes were much higher than she'd thought. She feared it wasn't just her life on the line...her heart was too.

CHAPTER NINETEEN

Vex slammed the door shut, flattened his hands upon it, and leaned forward with head bowed. His wings flexed and stretched involuntarily.

He curled his fingers, sinking his claws into the wood. "You accursed fool."

The ache in his groin had grown so immense that it threatened to swallow him. With each heartbeat, his cock throbbed, fighting the confines of his trousers. With each heartbeat, his need hurt a little more.

He shoved away from the door and hastened down the steps into the laboratory, clenching his fists at his sides. He paced along the walls, passing shelves filled with potions and reagents, baubles and trinkets, pots, jars, and bottles.

His rapid steps sought to match the rhythm of his racing heart. Each footfall echoed through the chamber, swelling into a boom that was like the pounding of a battering ram against the gates of his self-control.

Vex's defenses were in shambles. He could not ward off another attack.

Once, fornication had been naught more than a distraction to him. A source of fleeting pleasure, of temporary satisfaction. A brief diversion from his work. He'd never pursued such desires because no one had ever awoken them in him. And after the queen had taken him...

He'd not been aroused since he was cursed. He hadn't craved sex, hadn't wanted it, had done his best not to think about it. He'd given himself no such pleasure, no release. The queen's attentions had soured his appetite for eternity.

At least, that was what he'd believed.

Kinsley was proving that his desires hadn't died. They'd just hidden away, building over countless years—waiting for her. Now they were too vast, too potent, for him to resist.

Growling, he tightened his fists. His claws dug into his palms deep enough to draw blood.

Pain is a distraction.

And that was exactly what he needed—a distraction from all his thoughts, his feelings, his desires.

The flickering blue flames of a wisp flitted into the edge of his vision and hovered there, keeping pace with him.

"Magus?" Echo asked, their voice soft, uncertain, and concerned.

"Go," Vex commanded. "I require solitude."

Echo hesitated, ghostfire swirling.

"I said go!"

Shrinking back, Echo made a soft, sad sound and darted away.

A pang of guilt pierced Vex's heart like a knife, its blade coated in remorse.

But neither the wisp's intrusion nor the pain Vex had inflicted upon himself were enough to divert his thoughts. The air around him wavered, and shadows gathered in the corners of the chamber, gradually flooding it with darkness. Only a single source of light broke through—a glowing mass of rose quartz shaped into a large basin. Bubbles, shimmering with tiny rainbows, rose above the rim.

Gritting his teeth, Vex stepped toward the tub.

As though touched by a gentle breeze, the bubbles parted. Kinsley emerged from the steaming water, arms crossed over her chest, her pale skin glistening with moisture in the rose quartz's luminescence.

Vex halted beside the tub. Peering up at him, Kinsley moved her arms, revealing her full breasts. She took one of her pink nipples between her fingers and—

"No more!" Vex slashed his arm through the air.

Bubbles, quartz, and steam wavered and faded to nothingness, taking the phantom image of Kinsley along with them.

He was standing before the alcove where he'd kept his bed since bringing Kinsley to the cottage. There was no naked female awaiting him, only crumpled blankets piled on a sleeping mat like the nest of some sad, lonely creature.

But by silver and starlight, were Kinsley here now, he'd never want to leave this pallet. His whole world could've been reduced to this spot and he wouldn't have cared.

Hissing, he clamped a hand over his erection and squeezed against the maddening ache. Molten heat flowed in his veins. Something tugged on him, urging him back toward the door, back to his bedchamber.

Back to his mate.

"I'll not surrender my will," he growled. Releasing his cock, he turned away from the pallet and resumed his pacing. His wings brushed the shelves and tables, their tips scraping the floor stones, but he barely noticed any of those sensations.

Images of Kinsley danced through his mind's eye. Memories of the lust that had been in her eyes, the desire. Of the playfulness, the teasing, which had sparked such uncontrollable, frightening heat within him.

He quickened his stride, but he could not outrun those images. She was in his mind, his heart, his soul, and she would not be dislodged. He was powerless to exorcise her from himself.

He saw again and again the way she'd touched herself, the way she'd reacted to his touch, to his kiss.

He saw again and again the way she'd stared into his eyes as she'd climaxed. And he heard his name, breathy and broken, from her lips.

Vex halted and slapped a hand atop the worktable to steady himself as the pressure in his groin increased tenfold. His other hand again grasped his throbbing cock, bunching the fabric of his trousers. Need crackled through him, carried on a firestorm of yearning so hot and bright that it blinded him to all else.

His harsh breaths filled the laboratory's quiet.
She is a means to an end.
The key to the shackles that have bound me here.
And I...
"I am a master of illusion," he grated, "and none fall prey to my craft so thoroughly as I."

She was his mate. It mattered not that he'd forced that bond, that it had been made under dire circumstances. How it had been formed was inconsequential because now it *was*.

And to pretend he wanted her for naught but the child she'd promised was the height of foolishness.

His fingers flexed, and his claws scraped the tabletop. Though he'd not sworn on his true name, he had given Kinsley his word that he would not touch her, and he'd broken his word it tonight.

But her lips, her warmth, her *passion*...

His cock twitched, and his breathing stuttered.

Vex hurriedly untied his sash, tore off his tunic, and ripped open the lacings of his pants. His cock sprang into the cool air, throbbing with desire. He closed his fist around its base and squeezed. "Ah..."

He closed his eyes as his wings spread reflexively.

The ghost of Kinsley's honey-touched, orange blossom scent teased his nose. Vex drank it in and opened his eyes.

The illusory tub had returned, replacing his lonely pallet with its warmth and radiance, and Kinsley was there inside of it. He watched her caress her breasts, watched her nipples swell to pink buds, their flesh yielding to her fingers. He watched her cheeks redden and her eyelids grow heavy with pleasure.

Vex pumped his hand along his shaft. Sensation shuddered through him with each brush of his palm against his ridges, the movements slickened by the blood from his self-inflicted cuts.

Kinsley's hand dipped into the water, hidden by the bubbles. He knew what those fingers were doing. Even through the strong fragrance of the bath oils, he'd smelled a hint of it—of her arousal, her essence—and its memory teased him now. He longed to bury his tongue between her thighs, to coat it in her essence, to drink from her depths. He longed to know her true, intimate taste. A taste for him and him alone.

His breaths grew ragged as his hand quickened. Pleasure made the muscles in his belly flutter and tense, made his legs unsteady. He clutched the table and stroked his cock faster. Sensation coiled in his core.

He looked down at her, thrilling in her stunning face and captivating eyes, which were made brighter and more violet by ecstasy. Her abundant breasts shook with the tremors coursing through her. He could just make out the silhouette of her lush body beneath the water. Those shapely legs, those wide hips, that hand, so delicate but sure.

Vex's hips twitched, and his breathing faltered. The pressure in him was unbearable; it would be his undoing.

Her lips parted, her brow creased, and a small whimper escaped from the back of her throat. She said his name as she climaxed, wrapping it in reverence, wonder, sensuality, and need.

He kissed her, closing his eyes.

Echoes of the heat he'd felt when their lips met sizzled across his face and raced straight to his cock. He could almost feel her face in his hand, could almost taste her skin and her sweet breath. Could almost feel her.

"Kinsley," he growled. All at once, the pressure released. His pelvis jerked, and seed burst from his cock, spattering the floor and mixing with the blood on his hand. His wings spread, and he pumped faster and faster, forcing out every drop, until the sensation became too much.

Vex blinked his eyes open. For an instant, he was confused to find himself in front of his temporary bed rather than the tub. A bed devoid of his passionate, tantalizing human. The illusion had been so close to real…

"But it is not enough," he rasped. "It could never be enough."

He glanced down at the seed pooled on the floor, then at his cock, still pulsing in his fist. He'd not experienced a release in so, so long. But it wasn't total. It wasn't satisfying. There was still something there—a lingering pressure, a need, a deep, deep ache. And he knew he could never relieve it himself.

His tongue slipped out and ran across his lips unbidden. He groaned; there was still the faintest trace of her taste there, just enough to make him shudder anew, to coax another drop of seed from his cock.

He shut his eyes again. It was her face he saw behind his eyelids, her desirous eyes, her full, pink lips.

"When next I spill my seed, it will be inside you, my Kinsley," he vowed. "My mate."

CHAPTER TWENTY

Kinsley closed the bedroom door as she stepped into the central chamber. She glanced at Flare, who flitted about nearby, whispering excitedly and waving her along.

"Yes, yes. The human needs to eat. I know."

Flare flew closer and tugged on the skirt of Kinsley's light green dress, pointing toward the kitchen.

"Okay!" Kinsley chuckled, following them. "I'm not all that thrilled about burnt scones for breakfast again, but lead the way."

The slits in her long skirt parted with Kinsley's every step, and cool air flowed over her bared skin, making it prickle with goosebumps. She'd never been much of a dress wearer, but her entire wardrobe here consisted of dresses—beautiful, revealing dresses. This one had a low, square cut bodice, shoulder straps that looked like ivy, and a diaphanous skirt adorned with leaf patterns. The matching shoes were delicate, with soft soles and ribbons that tied around her ankles.

There'd never been an occasion to warrant wearing anything like this at home, and it certainly wasn't practical for hikes through the woods, but... The dresses made her feel pretty. Made her feel desirable.

Still, she would've killed for some modern loungewear.

Flare paused in front of the kitchen doorway and looked back at her before zipping inside.

Kinsley shook her head, lifted her skirt, and walked down the steps. "I really don't know what the hurry—"

She froze, eyes widening, when she glanced up to see Vex before her. He stood tall, his long black hair hanging loose around his shoulders. Gone was the pallor from yesterday, the sunken cheeks, the dark flesh around his eyes. He looked healthier today. Stronger.

And the heat in his crimson gaze was fiercer than ever.

Kinsley's heart quickened as her attention settled upon his mouth. The memory of his kiss, of its ferocity and voraciousness, made her lips tingle and her sex clench. If that had only been a taste of the passion he kept locked away, what would it be like when he broke his restraints?

"Good morrow, Kinsley," he said, mouth slanting into a smirk. "Has the dawn found you well?"

She couldn't help but grin as she forced her gaze up to his. "It has. A hot, *relaxing* bath was exactly what I needed for a good night's sleep. How was your night?"

His eyes boldly raked over her body. "Not quite so relaxing as yours, I imagine."

Kinsley's nipples hardened, and it felt like a thousand butterflies had taken flight in her belly as he perused her. The thought of him locked away in his lab, yearning for her and bristling with unfulfilled desire, stirred the eroticism she'd first felt in the bath last night.

She stepped closer to him. "I see you're not hiding from me this morning." Tipping her head back, Kinsley traced the silver ivy embroidery on his tunic with a finger. "Were you eager to see me, Vex?"

He covered her hand with his, pressing it flat against his chest. She could feel the beating of his heart beneath her palm. His long fingers were warm, strong, and rough, but his hold was gentle.

He lowered his face toward hers, coming near enough that she could feel his breath tease her skin. "Yes."

"Oh."

Was that her heart pounding a million times a second?

Why yes. Yes, it was.

Releasing her hand, he stepped back. "I've a gift for you."

Kinsley almost followed him. Blushing, she lowered her arms to her sides and released a soft, shuddering breath. "A gift?"

Vex gestured to the dining room. "Come sit, Kinsley."

She turned her head toward the table, where all three of the wisps hovered above an array of food. There were bowls of mushrooms, beans, porridge, fruit, clotted cream, and jams, as well as plates piled with thick cut bacon, eggs, and the scones she'd been craving so much. The best part? There wasn't a burnt spot to be seen on the pastries.

Chuckling, Kinsley stepped to one of the chairs. "Is it okay to say how much I missed magic food? Because I really did."

As she sat down, Vex strode up behind her chair and grasped its back. "I was told you've encountered some difficulty."

Kinsley glanced up to see him smiling down at her. "It was just the one time."

"Ah." He slid her chair in as easily as though it were unoccupied before seating himself next to her.

"Why do you even have a kitchen and a stocked pantry when you can just create magic food?"

"Because contrary to appearances, I typically prepare my meals without the aid of magic."

Kinsley ran a skeptical eye over him. "You cook?"

Vex leaned back in his chair and tilted his head. "You've difficulty believing that?"

"Well, yes." She waved at him. "Look at you. You're like…a goblin king in all your finery. I just can't picture you with your sleeves rolled up, covered in flour."

The quiet, tinkling sound of laughter drifted over from the wisps.

"Come now, Kinsley. I know you've more imagination than that. But if it would help…" With slow, deliberate movements, he folded his sleeve up, revealing his dark, toned forearm. He repeated the process with the other, and she watched the play of muscle and tendons beneath his skin, her fingers bunching the fabric of her dress in her lap.

How could arms and hands be so sexy?

Why were hands with *claws* so sexy?

"Mind you"—he leaned forward, resting his arms on the edge of the table—"I'll not be covering myself in flour. You shall have to conjure that image on your own."

She laughed. "I don't know, I'm still having trouble seeing it."

Vex's expression sobered as he stared at her.

Kinsley's smile fell. "What?"

His lips parted, but he hesitated before saying, "It is the first time I've heard you truly laugh. I find myself rather fond of the sound."

She clenched her skirt a little tighter as warmth flooded her. "I...guess you don't have other people around for there to be much laughter here."

Vex frowned, a small crease forming between his eyebrows. "I am fond of *your* laughter, Kinsley."

The heat beneath her skin increased, and Kinsley dropped her gaze. She was sure her cheeks were bright red. "Oh."

Where was the bold temptress who'd bared herself to his hungry gaze just for the thrill of teasing him? Why was she being so bashful now when she'd literally masturbated in front of this man last night?

Because this is beyond lust, Kinsley. You know it. You feel *it.*

This was something much, much deeper, and no matter how much she wanted it...

It was harder to take the plunge when she had no idea what lurked under the surface.

When she'd already had her heart broken.

Releasing her grip on her skirt, she smoothed the delicate fabric and composed herself before smiling at him. "You...mentioned a gift?"

"I did." He lowered a hand beneath the table, reaching for something at his waist. When he lifted it again, he held a small glass vial between the claws of forefinger and thumb. He offered it to her.

The wisps spoke to each other animatedly. Even Shade was a little brighter than normal.

Carefully taking the vial, Kinsley studied it. The liquid inside was dark purple, but as she rotated the vial, she could make out swirls of shimmering green within it. "What is it?"

"My way of granting one of your wishes."

She tilted her head as she looked at Vex. "What wish?"

He nonchalantly waved toward the wisps. "To understand our companions."

Shade, Flare, and Echo gathered around Kinsley.

Her eyes widened, and she held the vial closer as she glanced between the wisps. "Really?"

"Yes," Vex said. "It bears what is commonly known as the blessing of tongues. Once you've partaken of it, no spoken language will escape your understanding."

"Oh, wow. Okay. That's…a lot." Kinsley lifted the vial again and took hold of the little cork stopper, wriggling it loose. She peeked up at Vex. "You're sure you're not poisoning me?"

His features darkened, and he narrowed his eyes. "Never."

There was venom in his voice, a grave promise, and it vanquished any doubts she might've held about him. Vex would not harm her. And Kinsley…trusted him. Crazy as it might've been, she did.

Smiling, she looked at the wisps. "Okay, here we go."

She brought the vial to her lips, tipped her head back, and drank quickly. The liquid was sweet and cool upon her tongue, going down with surprising ease, and it warmed pleasantly in her belly.

Kinsley set the vial down and licked her lips. "Am I supposed to—oh!" She braced her elbows on the table, covered her face, and closed her eyes as a wave of vertigo struck her.

Countless voices whispered in her mind simultaneously, each speaking a different language, creating an indecipherable cacophony. It was like everyone in the world was talking to her all at once, their whispers weaving into a roar.

"Vex?" she said with a tremor of uncertainty. "I don't like this." She felt like her head was going to explode.

Somehow, Vex's voice cut through all the noise in her mind. "It will pass, Kinsley."

"It's too much. It hurts." Kinsley gripped her hair. "And I don't… don't understand what they're saying."

Vex's fingers smoothed over her cheeks to cradle her face. "Look at me."

His touch was a balm, dulling the noise and pain. Kinsley loosened her grip and opened her eyes to meet his gaze.

"You do understand," he said firmly. His eyes were unwavering, captivating, commanding. "And it is nearly through. Just breathe."

Keeping her eyes locked with his, she did as he'd instructed, taking in a deep breath and slowly releasing it.

He brushed his thumbs over her cheeks. "Good. Just like that."

Little by little, the voices grew clearer. And with that clarity came meaning—first a word here and there, then phrases and sentences. As that knowledge expanded, the voices faded until, finally, her mind was again quiet.

Vex continued stroking her cheeks. "I should have better anticipated the stress it would place upon you, Kinsley. Should have warned you. But it is through now."

"Is she well, magus?" someone asked in a soft, airy voice.

"Has the enchantment taken effect?" asked someone else with a slightly raspier voice.

"I...I can understand them." Kinsley's lips stretched into a smile. "I can understand them!"

Releasing her, Vex sat back in his chair. Though his smile was subtle, the warmth it sparked in his eyes was anything but. He almost looked like a different person. Were it not for her wonder at the potion's effects, Kinsley would've had a much harder time prying her gaze from him.

She looked at the wisps, and her grin somehow widened. "I can understand you!"

"Would that the magus had not waited so long to offer this gift," said Flare, a tiny lick of their ghostfire lashing at Vex.

"It would certainly have eased these ones' vigil," said Echo.

"And Kinsley's boredom," added Flare.

Shade turned their head toward Vex. "Her worry, as well."

Kinsley reached a finger out to Shade. "That would've been nice."

The wisp brushed their ghostly arm along her finger. "This one agrees."

Vex huffed, folding his arms across his chest. "I expect you'll wish to undo this enchantment ere long, Kinsley. They are like to prattle until your ears bleed."

She chuckled. "I don't think I will. I've enjoyed their company."

He arched a brow. "Mayhap because you've not been able to comprehend their speech."

"Mayhap the magus is jealous," Flare said, swelling a little larger, a little brighter, "because these ones will offer more entertaining conversation than he."

"I am not jealous."

"This one thinks the magus is," Echo said.

Vex planted his hands atop the table and rose from his seat. "I am not."

Though it was so quietly that Kinsley could barely hear it, the wisps laughed.

Frowning, Vex began serving food onto Kinsley's plate. "It seems your presence has emboldened them. But loath as I am to admit it, I've undoubtedly made for poor company during much of our time here. We've you to thank for the change."

"Gradual though it may be," Echo whispered.

Kinsley's smile was soft, touched with a hint sadness at knowing their circumstances. "But at least you weren't alone."

"Indeed," Vex replied.

The pile of food on her plate grew, soon surpassing what Kinsley would've been able to eat. Not that she was particularly hungry this morning—she'd awoken bloated and a little crampy.

"Vex?"

"Hmm?"

Kinsley eased a little closer to him. "I think that's more than enough."

He paused, and for the first time since he'd begun serving food, glanced down at her plate. The wisps laughed again, a little louder this time. Vex's nostrils flared with a heavy exhalation. He retook his seat and leaned back, propping an elbow on the arm of his chair.

She tried to hold back a grin but failed. He just looked so…flustered, and she found it adorable. Vex must've been out of his element, having been without company besides the wisps for a very, very long time.

Unless…it had something to do with what had happened last night.

Blushing at the memory, she picked up a scone and split it in half. "Thank you."

Vex nodded. His blazing eyes were fixed upon Kinsley as she spread cream and jam on the scone, unwavering in their intensity.

"Are you going to eat?" She took a bite, nearly groaning at how good it tasted.

"For now, I am content to watch."

"You know it's rude to stare."

His brows rose slightly. "Is it not also rude to speak with one's mouth full?"

Kinsley chuckled, covering her mouth with a hand. "You sound like my mum."

"Doubtful."

"You do." She swallowed before speaking again. "It's a bad habit of mine. Always has been since I was a kid. And she always calls me out on it, even as an adult." Frowning, she stared at the scone in her hand. Talking about her mother only reminded Kinsley what her family must've been going through.

Shade glided closer, the ghostfire around their darker core dwindling. "You miss your kin?"

"I do, and I know they're worried about me. I spoke to my mum before the accident, and I was supposed to call her back when I reached the cottage I was renting, except... Well, here I am." She looked up and forced her smile back into place. "At least I'm alive, right?"

Something softened in Vex's gaze. "You are."

"I just wish there was a way to let them know that."

"Your kin...they dwell across the ocean, as you did?"

Kinsley nodded, taking another bite of the scone. "My parents and older sister still live in the United States. I moved back to England a few months ago and lived with my aunt for a little while to get my bearings before setting out on my own. I just...needed to get away."

"To escape your pain." Vex scowled and clamped a hand on the arm of his chair, digging his claws into the wood. "Because of Liam."

Kinsley paused her chewing to stare at the grooves his claws were making. She recalled his words from the night before.

He did not deserve you, Kinsley.

Vex *was* jealous.

But he was also right. Escaping was exactly what she'd been doing. She could dress it up as much as she wanted, make all the excuses in the world, but that didn't change the truth.

"I was looking for a fresh start," she said, setting the remainder of the scone down on the edge of her plate. There were smears of cream and jam upon her finger and thumb when she released it. "At least, that's what I've been telling myself."

She chuckled. "Funny thing is, I was heading to a cottage in the middle of nowhere…and that's exactly where I ended up. I mean, it's not the cottage I intended, and this is a lot more middle of nowhere than I thought was possible, but…pretty much the same in the end, right?"

"No. It is not," Vex replied.

"How so?" Kinsley lifted her hand toward her mouth, intending to lick the cream and jam off her fingers.

Vex sat forward and caught her wrist before she could do so, his eyes holding hers. "Because here, you are not alone."

As if his sudden movement or the smoldering passion in his voice hadn't been enough to catch her off guard, he drew her hand toward him, parted his lips, and slipped her finger into his mouth.

Kinsley sucked in a sharp breath, and her eyes rounded. His gaze didn't waver as his lips closed and he gently swirled his tongue around her finger. And what she felt, it…it couldn't be right.

It felt like his tongue was somehow caressing her finger from two sides.

He slowly withdrew her finger, letting his lips glide along its length, then turned her hand slightly before trailing his purple-tinted tongue—his *split* tongue—up her thumb to lick the jam and cream from it.

Heat pooled in her core, and her pussy clenched with the surge of desire sweeping through her. In her imagination, that split tongue wasn't on her thumb, but between her thighs, caressing her clit.

"Ohhhh God," she breathed.

"There are no gods here," he said with a dark, sultry chuckle as he released her hand and sat back. "Only me."

That heat encompassed her, flooding her cheeks, and she dropped her hand into her lap. "This is payback, isn't it?"

Resting an elbow on the armrest, he propped his chin on his fist. The light in his eyes might've been mirth, or lust, or some maddening combination of them. "I fear I do not follow, Kinsley."

Oh, you naughty goblin, you know exactly what I'm talking about.

"Payback?" Echo inquired. "What debt must the magus repay?"

Kinsley flicked a glance at the wisps. If it were just her and Vex, she might've been more direct, but with an audience?

Time to play.

With the hand Vex had licked, she fanned herself. "Is it hot in here?"

Vex narrowed his eyes. "No warmer than a moment ago."

"I'm just feeling so flustered all of the sudden." Reaching down, she parted the slit in her skirt and tugged it higher up her thighs, uncovering her legs.

His eyes followed her hands, and he drew in a sharp breath through his nostrils. A barely audible growl rumbled from him.

Shade eased closer to Vex. "Magus?"

"Are you unwell, Kinsley?" Flare asked in a worried tone.

Kinsley rucked her skirt as high as it would go to reveal curve of her ass. "No, just hot." Hooking a finger on the center of the dress's neckline, she gave it a tug, baring more of her breasts as she resumed fanning herself. She was sure one of her nipples was threatening to give him a show.

The muscles of Vex's forearms flexed, and his jaw bulged. He shifted uncomfortably in his chair.

"Kinsley..." he grated through clenched teeth.

Smiling coyly, she leaned toward him, allowing her hair to fall over her shoulder—and affording him a better view of her cleavage. "Are you hot too, Vex?"

His eyebrows slanted down as he stared at her breasts.

But a hint of a smirk returned to his lips when he dragged his gaze back up. "Now that I think upon it..." He moved his hands to the front of his tunic, and those long, deft fingers unfastened the clasps one by one to expose his chest a little at a time. "I am."

Okay, not what I expected him to do. Abort!

Snatching up a strip of bacon, Kinsley tossed it at him with a laugh. "Eat breakfast with me."

Vex's hand darted out, plucking the strip out of the air. His eyes blazed at her as he opened his mouth, clamped his fangs on the meat, and tore off a chunk.

Oh, he looks like he wants to eat something all right. Just not breakfast.

"This one understands not what just transpired, magus," said Echo.

"Mayhap it has to do with their flesh," suggested Flare. "Flesh brings strange sensations, it seems."

Strange cravings, too.

"It is not for these ones to know," Shade said. "It is between Kinsley and the magus."

"Why do you call him magus instead of Vex?" Kinsley asked before eating a spoonful of porridge.

"Magus is his title," replied Flare.

"And we would honor him through its use," added Echo.

"The magus has watched over these ones for many centuries," Shade said, ghostfire swirling. "He has guarded these ones' true names and essences for all that time."

"Essences?" Kinsley arched a brow. "Do you mean like your souls, or…"

"These ones' very beings. The magic with which these ones are formed."

"Wisps are birthed from the ether," said Vex, drawing Kinsley's attention back to him. His expression had softened, and the light in his eyes was no longer fiery and passionate, but warm, affectionate, and just a little sorrowful. "They are beings of pure mana, with no distinction between body and soul. Some say they are amalgamations of lost souls, or echoes of ghosts long since passed on. Others claim they are the will of the primal forces of magic themselves, granted form and consciousness. I know only that these three have been my steadfast companions for almost as long as I can recall."

The wisps brightened. Echo floated down from the table until they hovered a couple feet above the floor. "These ones have been with the magus since he was small."

"Long before he grew into his ears," said Flare.

"Since before he grew into his ears?" Kinsley looked at Vex and laughed at the mental image of him as a child with overly large ears. "He must've been adorable."

Vex's cheeks darkened. He inhaled deeply, regaining his composure, before leaning toward her with his elbows on the table. "And what of me now, Kinsley?"

Kinsley ran her eyes over him, stopping them at the V of his open tunic. "*Adorable* is not the word I would use."

Dark. Beautiful. Otherworldly. Sexy. Any of those would do.

Vex chuckled. "A response that avoids answering all together."

"The magus was rather solemn as a child," said Flare, "and has little changed in that regard."

"This one would say the change is more than a little," Shade said, turning their head toward Kinsley. "At least as of late."

The implication of Shade's words was not lost on Kinsley, and that blush returned to her cheeks. "So, Shade, Echo, and Flare are not your true names?"

Diversion! Nailed it.

"They are not," Echo replied, returning to Kinsley's eye level. "True names are to be held close. They hold power."

When she frowned, Shade drifted closer and said softly, "It is not the same for mortals. The power is diminished."

She looked at Vex, her frown deepening. "But you said I have fae blood, right? So what does that mean for me? What power does my true name really hold?"

"If you seek the truth"—Vex turned his palms up—"I cannot offer it. I know not, Kinsley. Diluted as your fae blood is, your true name should have no power to compel you, but I cannot declare that with any certainty."

"So my oath that night?"

"It was binding because you swore it upon your true name. As it would have been for anyone, whether mortal, fae, or otherwise."

Kinsley lowered her spoon into the half-eaten bowl of porridge and picked up a piece of fruit. "And what about you? Vex isn't your true name."

"It is not." His features darkened; it was like watching storm clouds block out the sun and cast deep shadows across the land. "It is a name I adopted long ago. Not my true name, but one with meaning nonetheless."

Kinsley searched his eyes. As much as she wanted to ask more questions, to dive further into his past, she knew he wasn't ready to tell her. Why would he share such closely guarded secrets with her anyway? Why would he reveal his pain, his vulnerability, when Kinsley was just...

Just a means to an end.

She returned the uneaten fruit to her plate and glanced toward the window. "The storm finally passed. Would it be okay to go outside today?"

Vex arched a brow. "You've hardly eaten."

"I'm not very hungry this morning."

He frowned, releasing a thoughtful grunt. "I see."

Kinsley looked down at her plate, plucked up another scone, and smiled. "I'll take this with me in case I get hungry."

"If such is your wish," he said with a hint of hesitancy. "I must ask that you not venture too far from the cottage. As you are aware, this forest is not without its dangers."

"You're not coming?" She couldn't fully disguise the disappointment in her voice.

"Though I'd enjoy little more than accompanying you, I've research to attend here." Grasping the arms of his chair, he slid it back and stood up in one smooth motion. He held out his hand to her, palm up, as he glanced at the window. "And goblins do not find sunlight particularly...agreeable."

Kinsley placed her hand within his, allowing him to help her stand. Her skirt fell back into place around her legs. "What do you mean?"

He curled his fingers around her hand and brushed his thumb across her knuckles. "It is rather uncomfortable. But I shan't stop you from enjoying the sunshine, Kinsley. The wisps will escort you. I'll not have you out there unguarded."

Releasing her hand, he gestured at the table. The food that had been atop it vanished so quickly that afterimages of it lingered in Kinsley's vision when she blinked.

She chuckled. "No wonder it stays so clean here. You even poof away messes."

"Cleaning grows tedious after decades with little else to do," he said, smiling softly. "Though not cleaning becomes equally boring in its own time. Should you require aught else, Kinsley, do not hesitate to seek me. I shall be in my laboratory."

"I thought I'm not allowed in there."

"You're not. Surely you're familiar with the practice of knocking?"

"Ah. So picking the lock is out of the question, huh?" Smirking, she snapped her fingers. "Dang. Just when I was getting good at it."

Vex's gaze ran over Kinsley from head to toe and back again. Lips curling wickedly, he leaned toward her, captured her chin, and stroked her bottom lip with his thumb, tugging it down. Kinsley's breath caught, and her heart stuttered.

"I'm certain we'll discover all manner of unknown talents in the days to come, Kinsley," he said, his low voice filled with promise.

"Oh…" Kinsley stared at his mouth as her thoughts returned to their kiss. Her lips tingled with the memory, and she longed to feel it again, to be consumed by his fire and passion, to be devoured by his desire.

He drew closer, his lips a breath away from hers. Her lashes fluttered closed.

"Enjoy the sunlight, Kinsley," Vex whispered. "I look forward to tasting it upon your skin."

Then his touch was gone.

Kinsley opened her eyes, brow furrowing as she glanced around the room.

Vex was gone.

"Damn it!" She groaned, letting her head drop back as she willed her body to calm. "Why does he keep doing that?"

"He is solemn," said Shade quietly, "and often overly dramatic."

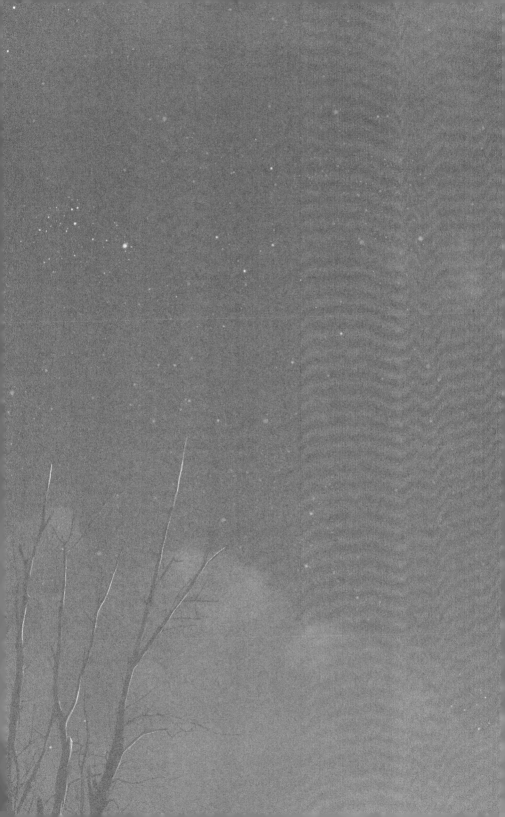

CHAPTER TWENTY-ONE

THOUGH MUCH OF the forest remained damp after the storm, it was vibrant and full of life. Warm, bright rays of sunshine streamed through breaks in the canopy, creating scattered pillars of golden light. Dew drops glistened upon thick ferns, tree branches creaked and leaves rustled in the gentle breeze, and birds sang their songs to the late morning. Kinsley had even seen a few rabbits peeking out from the nearby undergrowth.

She sat cross legged upon a blanket she'd spread on the forest floor, admiring her surroundings and breathing deep the woodland air. It was sweet with the scents of earth, vegetation, and rain.

The serene landscape was more than worth the dull ache in her back and the mild cramping in her pelvis.

Turning to the craft tote beside her, she lifted the lid and removed her journal, laying the book on the mossy log in front of her.

"I missed this," she said as she opened the journal.

Echo fluttered closer to the log. "Missed what, Kinsley?"

She motioned to the woods. "All of this. Before I came here, I was living in London with Aunt Cece. London is a huge city with buildings taller than the trees of this forest, and streets filled with cars and people. But while it has some of the loveliest parks I've ever seen, it's just not the same. It's not...*this*."

Kinsley smiled at the wisps, who hovered before her. Though

they'd positioned themselves out of the direct sun, their glows were diminished by the daylight, making them appear more ghostly than ever. But none of them seemed bothered by it.

"Back home," she continued, "I explored so many forests and national parks. I love being outdoors, in nature, breathing the fresh air. I love just being away from it all." She turned her face toward the trees. "And now I am. It's strange, but as much as I miss my family, I...feel at home here."

But it isn't just this place, is it Kinsley? It's Vex.

She wanted to deny those thoughts, but she couldn't. It wasn't the trees or the land. It was him. She was drawn to Vex. Since the night of the crash, she'd sensed him, she'd felt him. His voice, his touch, had dragged her out of the eternal darkness that'd been swallowing her.

And she knew, despite the scars on her heart, despite the pain she still carried, that her feelings for him were more than lust. Though he'd initially been cold and abrasive, he'd come to show warmth and compassion, thoughtfulness, and surprising patience. He'd even offered glimpses of playfulness—something she doubted he'd ever shown to anyone, given the way the wisps had described him.

Yet what would come of it? What future could they share? Why would an immortal being, who commanded such power, care to spend any more of his time than was absolutely necessary with someone like Kinsley?

Necessary... That's the key, isn't it? He's spending this time with me because it's necessary for him to achieve his goals.

Still, she couldn't entirely believe that. If he truly only saw her as a tool, a means of getting the child he wanted, why would he have shown her vulnerability? Why let her see his real, raw emotions, why offer a look into his painful past? Why accept her teasing, and why tease back?

One thing about their relationship was clear, even if nothing else was—Vex could have taken what he wanted at any moment.

But he hadn't.

If only she and Vex had met under better circumstances. If only they'd been drawn together not by death, not by their bargain, not by the...the thing he wanted.

Flare brushed her arm, their touch bearing a hint of warmth. "These ones are glad to share a home with you."

"Glad too that you have made it your home," said Echo.

Home.

Was this her home now?

Her chest constricted with yearning for this place to truly be her home. Yearning for true, unconditional love.

For...Vex.

"Thank you for sharing it with me," Kinsley said.

Taking hold of the journal's leather cover, she thumbed through the pages to the place where she'd left off. She skimmed her fingers along the edge of the journal as she stared at the blank white paper. Kinsley had spent so many hours pouring her emotions into this book, had cried so many tears. There were pages of pain, loss, and heartbreak, pages of despair.

Pages of hope.

And now, Kinsley wanted to fill the remaining pages with wonder.

Shifting aside the items in her tote, she picked up a stack of colored paper from the bottom. She flipped through it until she found a couple sheets of black, which she glued into the journal as a base. Next, she tore a leaf-printed paper into strips, distressed the edges of the strips with brown ink, and added them onto the black.

Soothed by the sounds of nature, she lost herself in the art. She added little stickers of mushrooms and ivy, and even glued a bit of moss from the log onto the page.

And then came the wisps. With great care and attention to detail, she sketched her little friends, depicting their forms as though they were flying around the pages. Then she painted them; blue paint and white highlights, with a hint of gray mixed in to make Shade a little darker than the other two. After a moment's consideration, she added a sprinkle of blue holographic glitter to each wisp, granting the images a bit of sparkle.

But there was something missing. The black remained a little too expansive, a little too empty. Her hand was already reaching for her red paint when she realized what belonged there. Leaning over the journal, she added Vex's crimson eyes at the center of the spread, one on each page, glowing in the darkness.

Normally, red eyes glowing in the dark would've been a terrifying sight. Yet this was comforting. It made her feel safe, made her feel...seen.

With a silver marker, she wrote in flowing script—*There is always magic to be found in the darkness.*

The wisps drifted closer, studying the journal. Kinsley blinked and lifted her head. She'd been so focused on her work that she'd forgotten she wasn't alone.

"What do you think?" she asked.

Shade stroked an arm of over the dimmest wisp of the three. "You painted this one."

Kinsley smiled. "I painted all three of you."

"These ones are honored." Shade bowed their head, the gesture mimicked by the other wisps.

"These ones offer thanks," Flare said.

"This one is lovely," said Echo, twirling in the air over their painting.

Kinsley chuckled. "I'm so happy you all love it."

She extended her hand into the sunlight shining on the blanket next to her. Warmth bathed her skin. Frowning, she glanced skyward.

The sun had already crept past its midday zenith, leaving the wisps even more faded than before, and a thin fog had begun gathering in the shady parts of the forest despite the sunshine.

"I'm sorry," she said. "I didn't realize how long I was working on it."

"You need not apologize," Shade said gently. "These ones were enrapt watching you create."

"You don't think Vex will mind that we've been out this long?"

Flare's ghostfire swelled. "If the magus desired a swift return, he should have escorted you himself."

"He might also have stated such beforehand," said Echo.

"Either way, we should probably get back." Kinsley smiled down at the journal. "Should I show him this?"

Echo shrank slightly. "The magus may be envious."

"Why would he be envious?"

"You have depicted these ones with such beauty. He will be unable to deny that it surpasses his own."

"It is not for these ones to guess how the magus will react," said Shade, "but this one believes he will appreciate your work."

Kinsley lightly touched one of the painted wisps to make sure it was dry before closing the journal. "Let's go show him then. He's likely still cooped up in his stuffy lab."

Returning the journal to the case, she closed the lid, latched it, and stood, shaking her skirt back into place. She bent and picked up the tote.

"Kinsley, you are wounded!" Flare said with alarm, flashing bright.

Shade and Echo made soft, concerned sounds, and all three wisps flitted before her, their ghostfire flickering.

She furrowed her brow. "What?"

"Your lifesblood." Flare gestured frantically toward the blanket beneath her.

"And on the back of your dress," added Shade.

Kinsley looked down. There, bright red against the blue fabric, was a patch of blood. Setting down the tote, Kinsley grasped her skirt and twisted to look behind her. More blood stained her dress.

"Oh no," she groaned. She lifted her skirt and bent over. Sure enough, crimson was smeared on her inner thighs. "Damn it, I should've known."

The bloating, the cramps, the lower back pain—all the signs had been there, but she'd dismissed them.

Thank God I have some tampons in my purse.

But those wouldn't last long. Kinsley smirked as she lowered her skirt. How would Vex react if she were to ask him to conjure up some menstrual products?

Flare darted back and forth through the air, ghostfire bristling. "We must hurry to the magus before she loses more blood."

"It's okay, Flare," Kinsley said.

Echo's little body trembled. "Flesh bleeds when wounded. Wounds are bad."

Though embarrassment colored her cheeks, Kinsley laughed. The sound was a little louder than she'd anticipated; only then did she realize that the birds had fallen silent. She shook off the unease that slithered into her.

"It's not a wound…" She scanned their surroundings. It must've been a trick of the shifting sunlight, but everything seemed dimmer. She looked back to the wisps. "This is perfectly natural, I promise. It's often an...inconvenience, like now, but it's normal."

The wisps exchanged looks that were decidedly skeptical despite their lack of facial features.

"It is normal for humans to bleed without a wound?" asked Flare.

"Yes. It's, uh..." *Deep breath, Kinsley.* "It's part of the reproductive cycle. It happens every month when...when there's been no conception."

"It is no wonder your kind is so short lived," said Shade.

Kinsley smiled despite the reminder of what she could never have. "We don't normally lose so much that we bleed to death."

Something moved amongst the trees at the edge of her vision.

Heart quickening, she turned her attention in that direction, seeking the source of the movement. The fog had unquestionably thickened, having pooled in every hollow and depression. A chill raced along her spine.

Nothing animals were in sight.

It was probably just a deer or a rabbit.

Please, just be a rabbit.

Why was she suddenly so paranoid? Why was she filled with a sense of dread? She'd spent so much time alone in forests familiar and unfamiliar, and never once had she experienced this inexplicable fear.

"This one does not understand," Echo said. "Why must humans bleed if—"

"Hush," Shade rasped.

A breeze swept through the woods, rustling the leaves and carrying a scent to Kinsley, faint but disturbing—the scent of rot. Of death.

"This mist..." Flare said.

A large, dark shape stirred in the fog ahead. The creature slowly grew clearer as it prowled between the gnarled trunks. An elongated head, a long, lean body and limbs, hunched shoulders.

Not a deer or a rabbit, but a dog. A very big, very disconcerting dog.

"Echo, inform the magus at once," said Shade hurriedly. "You must away to the cottage, Kinsley."

But she couldn't look away from the approaching beast. It turned its head toward her, and a pair of silvery, reflective eyes locked with hers.

The chill inside Kinsley deepened and spread, freezing her limbs and wrapping around her heart. The tiny hairs on her body rose in unease.

Tufts of fog swirled around the creature as it walked, its pace unhurried, unconcerned, confident.

That was no normal dog. It was off, wrong, impossible, and her brain only registered it as a dog because she could not comprehend what it really was.

The wisps were rapidly speaking to her, their voices overlapping into an indecipherable mess.

But those ravenous eyes held Kinsley captive. The creature rose onto its hind legs.

No, *rose* was not the right word. It unfolded, like a wolf shedding the sheepskin with which it had disguised itself. The creature stood taller than Vex, with spindly limbs, long claws, and a jarringly humanoid form.

Though it had drawn alarmingly closer, she could make out no notable features but for those eerie eyes and jaws lined with frightening, pointed teeth. The beast was darkness manifested in physical form, but it wasn't the comfortable, soothing darkness Vex represented. This was the darkness of the void, of emptiness and eternal hunger.

And it moved closer still.

Only then did Kinsley find the willpower to retreat a single step.

A gravelly, inhuman voice clawed into her mind. *"Your fear smells delicious, human."*

Flare darted in front of her face, ghostfire surging blindingly bright. "Kinsley, flee!"

Whatever horrifying, supernatural hold the monster had taken on Kinsley shattered. The thunderous beating of her own heart rushed in, nearly drowning out the malicious chuckle that sounded in her head.

Again, the beast spoke in her mind. *"The meat of rabbits and birds will not compare to the sweetness of your flesh."*

No. Not here, not like this.

Kinsley stumbled backward a few steps before turning around, avoiding a fall only by bracing a hand on a tree. Shade fell into place to her left, Flare to her right, their glows offering her the only shreds of stability and normalcy she could possibly have found in that moment.

She felt the beast's eyes upon her back, sensed its advance.

Without a backward glance, Kinsley ran.

The monster's laughter kept perfect pace with her, echoing in her skull.

CHAPTER TWENTY-TWO

THE FOREST WAS a blur around Kinsley. Only the way forward remained in focus, a corridor through knotted trees and tangled undergrowth leading back to the cottage, back to safety.

Back to Vex.

Though her lungs burned, and her muscles ached, though her feet throbbed from the prodding of countless roots and stones through her delicate footwear, she kept her legs moving.

She had to be close. She hadn't gone that far, had she?

Fiery tingles crackled across her back. She sensed the monster behind her on a primal, instinctual level. She didn't know how far back it was, but she knew it was there, and she knew it was drawing closer with each beat of her heart.

Don't look back. Keep running.

Flare flew just ahead, ghostfire trailing as they led the way. Shade remained beside Kinsley, flickering in her peripheral vision.

And behind her, foliage thrashed, and branches snapped. Tendrils of mist snaked into the edges of her view to either side. It flowed around her bare legs, raising goosebumps with its frigid touch, and spread out ahead of her.

Kinsley's heart stuttered. She stumbled and cried out, but she somehow managed to remain upright and wrest more momentum from the near fall.

The monster chuckled. *"Your fear will saturate your flesh and sink into your marrow, making you all the sweeter."*

That hot, alarming sensation shifted from her back to the right side of her body.

No. No, no, no, please no.

The monster's dark figure entered her peripheral vision. It loped on two legs, hunched at the shoulders, its unnaturally long arms grasping tree trunks to help propel its grotesque form.

Silver eyes flashed as the beast turned its head toward Kinsley.

She veered to the left without conscious thought, driven only by the instinct to escape.

"Kinsley!" one of the wisps rasped.

Her eyes widened. The altered course had brought her to an embankment that descended sharply into what must've been a dried stream bed.

She didn't even have time to think of a suitable curse before her foot went over the edge. It fell much farther than she'd anticipated, the impact jolting into her heel and up her leg, rattling her bones. Her other foot landed an instant later with just as much force, but the earth beneath it was much less forgiving, and crumbled away.

Kinsley fell. Her ass took the brunt of it, sending another jolt from her tailbone up her spine. She reflexively dropped her hands, scraping her palms as she tried to catch herself. But the decline, paired with her momentum, made it impossible to stop herself.

She slid until the uneven ground pitched her to one side. Hair flying into her face, she tumbled to the bottom, where soft moss, grass, and vegetation cushioned her.

"Kinsley, have you come to harm?" Shade whispered, their voice unsteady.

Pushing herself onto hands and knees, she flipped her hair out of her face. New aches radiated through her from head to toe, and she felt spent and sluggish, but none of that had surpassed her fear. That had to count for something, right?

She groaned and lifted her head. "I'm okay."

The stream bed was wide and deep, creating a gap in the boughs overhead that allowed sunlight to stream through unhindered. Lush plants and wildflowers carpeted the ground, basking in the golden radiance. The rest of the forest was dark and foreboding when viewed from this spot.

"*A fitting place to feast,*" the monster said in Kinsley's head. "*Here upon the very ley line that spawned me.*"

Kinsley's eyes darted up to the top of the embankment.

Fog swirled along the ridge, flowing down from it in waves. The beast stood at the center, a black, towering shape, its silvery eyes boring into her.

"You must rise, Kinsley," Shade urged, their ghostly touch running over her shoulder with muted insistence.

The unnatural fog filled the stream bed slowly, but wherever it met the sunlight directly, it dissipated or receded. And still, the monster lingered at the top, staring at her.

Vex had said goblins were uncomfortable in the sun. Was that true for this creature, as well? Would she be safe in the light?

Gritting her teeth, Kinsley climbed onto her feet. A dull ache radiated from her tailbone, but her legs were steady, despite everything.

"Flee," Flare said.

But she knew she couldn't. She couldn't outrun this thing, and she'd only made it this far because it had been toying with her. Curling her hands into fists, she met the monster's malevolent gaze.

From somewhere deep within, Kinsley found her voice. "You are not welcome here."

The monster tilted its head and slowly bent down—*folded* down—to plant its clawed hands on the ground. It sniffed the air.

Please, Vex...hurry.

"Leave," Kinsley said louder. Were her heart beating any faster, it would've burst right out of her chest.

Flare and Shade moved in front of her, their ghostfire burning more intensely than she'd ever seen.

"You *must* go, Kinsley," Flare said.

The monster huffed. "*The scent of death lingers upon you, mortal. Death has touched you, and it calls. You are mine to devour.*"

Around the sunny clearing, the mist had grown so thick that it seemed solid, but still none of it had crossed into the direct light. It made the monster's form more indistinct, more terrifying.

Kinsley swallowed. She didn't know what this creature was,

what it could do, or how to overcome it. But she knew her next words would either call the monster's bluff or seal her doom. And she knew she was almost out of time either way.

"You...you hold no power in the light."

A low, reverberating growl emanated from the monster, making the mist around it ripple and billow. Those long legs bunched, and the beast sprang forward, landing only feet away from Kinsley with the front half of its body in the sunlight. Its skin was darkest black, its lupine face almost skeletal.

"Oh, shit," she breathed, stumbling back.

The wisps darted at the beast's head, a pair of tiny blue firestorms. The creature gnashed its teeth at them.

Kinsley's heart leapt, and she reached for her friends. "No!"

Those toothy jaws nearly snapped shut on Shade, prompting the wisps to hastily withdraw. They positioned themselves between Kinsley and the creature, which advanced, drawing more of itself into the light. Muscles flexed beneath its dark hide.

"Shade, Flare, go." Kinsley continued her retreat until her heel bumped into something large, hard, and unyielding. She glanced over her shoulder to see a huge boulder at her back.

The wisps shrank back, hovering over her shoulders.

"These ones will not leave you," they said in unison.

The monster's voice was like the scraping of claws inside her skull. *"Now you understand, human..."*

She flattened herself against the boulder.

For the second time in less than two weeks, Kinsley was staring death in the face. She still didn't want to die, but this was different. So much different. For the first time in so long, she felt like she had more to lose than her own life.

The monster drew close enough for Kinsley to feel its breath, hot and rancid, upon her face. Bile crept up her throat. The thing stared at her with eyes that would've devoured the heavens themselves, were it possible.

"The sun cannot shield you."

"Nor can it shield you!" someone roared, the deep, furious voice echoing along the stream bed.

The monster's head jerked to the side just before something big slammed into it from the same direction. Kinsley glimpsed green skin, leathery wings, and long black hair, which shimmered like silk in the sunshine.

Vex!

Whether she'd spoken it aloud or had only thought it, his name swept through her soul, suffusing her with warmth, with relief, with hope.

Vex and the monster crashed to the ground in a tumble of flailing limbs and slashing claws. Dirt, leaves, and tattered flower petals flew into the air around them.

The two separated suddenly, both regaining their feet in a flash.

"Come, Kinsley," Echo said, tugging her hand. "You must return to the cottage."

But her eyes were fixed upon Vex. His tunic was torn, and blood had further darkened its black fabric. The green membranes of his wings were blistered and blackened.

The sun.

It was much more than a discomfort to him. It was burning him alive!

Her chest constricted, and air refused to pass through her tightened throat.

Before she could say anything, before she could so much as complete another thought, Vex bared his fangs and lunged at the monster. The air around him fractured and shattered like breaking glass. From each shard, Vex emerged—a dozen of him, indistinguishable from each other, each holding a gleaming golden dagger. The clones converged on the monster, lashing out with wild, relentless attacks. The ground beneath the beast shifted and buckled as though it were being torn asunder by a devastating earthquake.

Somehow, the earth under Kinsley's feet remained unmoving, though the world still spun around her.

The monster scrambled to defend itself from the assault, retreating out of the sunlight.

Steeling herself, Kinsley pushed away from the boulder. The wisps were speaking frantically, begging her, pleading for her to go.

She shook her head. "I can't. I can't abandon Vex."

Not when he was risking himself for her. Not when he was fighting for her.

And something inside Kinsley, something powerful, something buried at the core of her soul, refused to let her turn her back on him.

The fog churned as dark, indistinct forms battled within it. Snarls, grunts, and roars echoed from the mist, all savage and bestial, but not all belonging to the creature.

The figures receded further, until she could no longer make them out.

All at once, everything went quiet, and the fog settled. The wisps also fell silent, drawing around Kinsley with their ghostfire dim.

Kinsley's pounding heart marked the passing seconds as she scanned the mist, seeking any sign of movement, any sign of Vex.

A shadow appeared in the fog, soon taking a humanoid shape as it moved toward her with an uneven gait.

Kinsley crouched, pried a fist-sized rock from the ground, and rose, clutching the improvised weapon. If it was the monster, the rock wouldn't help. But damn it, she wouldn't leave him behind. And she wouldn't die without a fight.

Holding the rock high, she called, "Vex?"

The figure swung its arm as though swatting a buzzing insect. The fog parted, rolling to the edges of the stream bed and over the embankment. Kinsley let out a shaky, grateful breath.

It was Vex.

He had one arm clamped across his stomach. His hair was disheveled, his stride was clipped, and his wings were gone, but it was Vex all the same.

The rock fell from her suddenly limp fingers. She rushed toward him, the wisps racing along to either side of her.

"Are you okay?" Kinsley stopped before him, taking in the darkened, wet fabric of his clothing. "Oh my God, you're—"

Vex caught her jaw with his free hand, turning her head from side to side as he rapidly examined her. "Did the barghest harm you? Even the slightest scratch or bite?"

Her brow furrowed. "No."

"I smell it, Kinsley. Your blood." He dropped his hand, grasping her wrist to lift her arm and display her scraped palm. His eyes, wide and frantic, met hers. "More than this. Where are you hurt?"

"Vex, I'm okay," she said calmly. "But you... Please, we need to get you help."

"You arrived in time, magus," said Shade. "The beast did not touch her."

But Vex only took hold of her shoulder, forcing her to turn around. His grip tightened as he sucked in a breath. "There is bl—"

"I'm fine!" Kinsley tore out of his grip and spun to face him. "But you aren't."

"I will survive," he said through his teeth.

Kinsley shook her head, looking him over again. His clothing was torn and bloodied in several places, and some of the flesh on his face was blackened and raw, having burned in the sun. And the way he kept that arm clamped across his belly suggested a more significant wound than he was letting on.

"We need to go back to the cottage to get you cleaned up," she said firmly.

Echo brushed a tendril of ghostfire against Vex's arm. "Come, magus."

"No." Vex staggered back a step. "I missed one. There may yet be more of the beasts out here. I cannot rest until we know."

Frowning, Kinsley closed the small distance he'd opened between them. "You're in no state to take on another of those things."

His features darkened, brows angling down sharply.

"You would be naught but food for another barghest," Flare said, pointing forcefully at Vex.

Before the growl building in Vex's chest could fully emerge, Kinsley silenced it by placing her hand over his heart, calling his attention to her.

"Please, Vex," Kinsley begged.

"The cottage is warded," Shade said. "All will be safe until you have healed."

Vex released a heavy exhalation. "If there is another barghest, it will wreak havoc on these woods. Destroy what little remains to us."

Flare bowed their head. "These three will scout while you recover, magus."

"These ones will keep vigil that you might rest," added Echo with a bow of their own.

Vex's gaze shifted between the wisps as his jaw muscles ticked. "Take great care, my friends. At the slightest sign of trouble, return to me. Do not risk yourselves. And Shade... I ask that you remain with us for the time being."

Shade nodded, lingering close to Kinsley and Vex as the other wisps sped away, moving in opposite directions.

Seeing the beads of sweat on Vex's skin, which was noticeably pale where it hadn't been burned by the sun, deepened Kinsley's worry. Though he was hiding it well, she knew he was in a great deal of pain.

She reached out and wrapped her fingers around his. "Let's go."

Despite Vex's longer stride, it was Kinsley who had to slow down to keep pace with him. His limp became more pronounced as they continued onward, and his breathing grew only more ragged. Seeing this man—who'd been so strong, confident, and seemingly invincible—weak and suffering like this was heart wrenching.

When he stumbled, she moved against him and slipped an arm around his waist for support.

"You need not treat me like a weakling," Vex grumbled as he glowered at her.

"I'm not," Kinsley replied, glancing up at him, "but if you fall and can't get up, don't expect me to carry you."

"So you'd abandon me after I saved you?"

Kinsley rolled her eyes. "Of course not. You may not be a weakling, but I am. I literally would not be able to carry you. You're heavier than you look."

Vex snickered, settling his arm around her shoulders and leaning against her lightly. "And you are stronger than you look, Kinsley. Never forget that."

By the time they reached the cottage, Vex's pallor had worsened, and he was leaning upon her much more heavily than he likely realized. She knew he was trying to keep as much weight off her as he could, but he was flagging. His feet dragged with every step.

"Take me to the laboratory," Vex rasped as they climbed the stone stairs out of the foyer.

Kinsley frowned. Sweat trickled between her breasts and down her back, which ached only more fiercely after this trek. "I thought I wasn't supposed to go in there?"

"Gloat, human. I've not the energy to argue."

But Kinsley couldn't summon any excitement at the prospect of seeing the room he'd forbidden her from entering. Her only concern was for Vex. Tightening her hold on him, she braced a hand on the cold stone wall and helped him up the last step.

The central room with its rune-inscribed tree and glowing crystals didn't seem nearly as magical as Kinsley and Vex staggered to the laboratory door. They paused in the alcove, where Vex rested his shoulder against the wall and flicked his wrist. The door swung open silently.

Shade flitted past them, lighting the way.

If Kinsley had expected it to be easier going downstairs, she'd been wrong. Though it was only a short flight of stairs, she found herself supporting Vex more and more despite his efforts to use the wall for additional support during their descent.

Her relief upon reaching the bottom was short-lived. Vex's legs buckled, and he began to fall. Kinsley shifted, straining to keep him upright, but managed only to drag him in the direction she'd moved.

Her back hit the wall hard, knocking the breath from her, and Vex fell against her. His claws scraped the wall as he caught himself, his face stopping against her neck, his breath hot and heavy on her skin.

"Forgive me," he rasped. "This…is not how I envisioned such intimacy between us."

"Really?" Kinsley asked, unable to stop her cheeks from warming. "You're joking about that now?"

He brushed the tip of his nose along her neck and up to her ear, making her shiver. "I'm quite serious, Kinsley." With a pained grunt, he straightened his arm, easing the pressure of his body against hers. "Just a few more steps."

She kept her arms around him until he was steady on his feet. Without relinquishing her hold on him, she moved deeper into the room, examining her new surroundings.

The place was part alchemist's lab, part dungeon, and part wizard's sanctum. Soft light came from at least a dozen different sources—crystals of various colors, yes, but also some of the jars and several of the more enigmatic items on display. There were shelves stocked with jars, pots, and bottles, many of them labeled in cryptic writing. Thankfully, there were no body parts floating in glass jars.

At least not that she could see, anyway.

Various vials, stands, and tools stood atop a large worktable, along with numerous loose parchments bearing scrawled notes and more leather-bound books. And everywhere she looked there sat another bauble or trinket, many of which emanated strange, subtle energy. She had no way of knowing if those objects were magical…

But she *did* know. Some part of her, buried deep within, recognized the feel of magic, even if she didn't know what it meant.

To one side was a large metal door adorned with symmetrical, esoteric patterns and tiny runes.

But Vex called her attention away from it, pointing to the opposite side of the chamber. "Take me there."

Kinsley followed his gesture with her eyes and frowned. He'd indicated an alcove on the far wall where several blankets had been piled atop a big cushion. Amidst the wonder and mystery of this chamber, that spot was so…mundane. So lonely.

She frowned as they neared it. "You've been sleeping here?"

"Yes."

"While I sleep in your grand bed?"

Bracing a hand on the wall to steady himself, Vex stepped away from her. "Yes."

With his back toward her, he finally relaxed the arm across his midsection. It trembled as he pulled it away. Movements stiff, he untied his sash and let it drop before undoing the fasteners of his tunic. He peeled the garment down, revealing several inflamed cuts and scratches on his arms and back, only to groan when the fabric over his belly, sticky with blood, clung to his skin.

Drawing in a hissing breath, he tore the tunic free and tossed it to the floor. He turned back toward her.

Kinsley gasped. "Oh God…"

The wounds on his stomach were deep, leaking fresh blood that trickled down his abdomen. But even more frightening were the black lines branching out from the wounds in weblike patterns.

"What is that?" she asked.

"The barghest's claws. Poison the blood." Claws scraping the stone wall, he slowly lowered himself onto the pallet. His movements coaxed out more crimson from his stomach. Expression contorting with pain, he lay on his back.

Kinsley stepped closer to him, reaching out to touch him. Her own fingers trembled. She pulled her hand back. "You need stitches."

"I will heal. But the wounds..." He squeezed his eyes shut as a shiver wracked his body. "Already ill. Already tainted."

"What can I do to help?"

Vex's eyes opened. He lifted an unsteady hand, waving vaguely toward the rest of the room, as his eyelids fluttered shut again. "Tincture. Will ease..."

Panic rose within her, constricting her heart. "That's not helpful, Vex! I don't know what any of this is. What do you need?"

Shade brushed Kinsley's shoulder, drawing her attention. "This one will show you."

The wisp led her to a nearby shelf and indicated one of the bottles. Kinsley hurriedly plucked it from its place. White liquid swirled inside, shimmering in the soft light.

"A few drops upon his tongue," said Shade.

Kinsley returned to Vex and knelt on the cushion beside him. "Vex, I have the tincture."

If he'd heard her, he made no indication of it. Perspiration coated his face, and though his eyes were closed, there was no peace to be found in his strained features. He'd moved his hands to his belly to clutch the bloody wounds, but his curled fingers and claws only worsened the bleeding.

"Stop!" She took hold of his hands and drew them away. "Please, Vex, you're hurting yourself."

Shifting closer to his head, Kinsley brushed aside the damp strands of hair clinging to his forehead. His flesh was burning. He turned his face toward her as though seeking more of her touch.

"Shade said you needed to drink some of this." She wiggled the cork stopper free before gently grasping his cheeks and forcing open his mouth. Tipping the bottle, she allowed one drop, followed soon by a second, to spill onto his tongue.

"Are you sure that's enough, Shade?" Kinsley asked as she released Vex and recorked the bottle.

"For now," the wisp replied, hovering over Vex. Their ghostfire was dimmer than ever around their dark core. "He will need more in time."

"So there's nothing else I can do to help him?"

"You are here. That is far more than he had before."

Kinsley's brow furrowed. "Before? This is what happened the other day, isn't it? When he left me in the library?"

"Yes."

"He was gone for five days..." She recalled his appearance when he'd caught her trying to enter this very room. Haggard, pale, tired. There'd been a hint of it even when he'd visited during her bath. "He was recovering that whole time?"

"He was. Fae suffer not the illnesses of mortals, but wounds inflicted by a barghest can make even the strongest unseelie fae sick." Shade's ghostfire dwindled. "This one searched with Echo, Flare, and the magus for eggs after the mother-beast was felled. These ones failed."

"Why do you think you failed?"

"The barghest that attacked you was fresh hatched, infused with magic from the ley line. Magic siphoned while within its egg." Shade brushed her with their ghostfire. "The magus bade these ones to keep vigil. To keep you safe. For seelie, a barghest's bite is death."

And since Kinsley was seelie...

That was why Vex had been so distraught over whether the barghest had injured her. Despite his own wounds, despite knowing what would befall him, all his fear and concern had been for her wellbeing.

Kinsley stared down at him. His chest rose and fell with quick, shallow breaths, his face was taut, and his fingers clawed at the bedding as his head lolled.

Leaning closer, she smoothed her hand over his brow and stroked the scars at the corner of his eye with her thumb.

"Rest, Vex," she said softly. She turned and started to withdraw her hand, meaning to go get some supplies to clean him up, but was stopped short when he caught her wrist. When Kinsley looked back down, she was surprised to find his eyes upon her.

"Stay," he rasped.

Her heart quickened even as something tightened in her chest. The masks he'd worn during their short time together had fallen away, leaving a direct view into his soul. A direct view into his pain, his loneliness, his fear, his need.

His need…for her.

Despite the dirt and blood, she could not leave him. Not yet.

Kinsley shifted her body to lie on her side next to him and slid her hand to his cheek. "I will."

His eyes fell shut, and some of the tension in his body eased. Though he did not stir again, he also did not relinquish her wrist. His hold was gentle yet possessive, pleading yet considerate, endearing and heartbreaking. When the pad of his thumb brushed over her pulse at her inner wrist, warmth blossomed within Kinsley.

CHAPTER TWENTY-THREE

Vex spun about, seeking sign of anyone, anything, but there was naught to be seen. Darkness stretched in every direction, endless and all-consuming.

No, not darkness. Nothingness.

Had he... Had he been here before, in this place that was not a place? Why was it so familiar?

Neither warm nor cold, neither welcoming nor foreboding, it was nothing...and yet did not his presence make it *something*? Some*where*?

His head throbbed, and whispers of pain coursed through him. But the pain was distant, detached, and his body... Somehow, it was distant and detached too.

Mayhap he wasn't in this nowhere at all?

Voices jarred his thoughts. They echoed gently through the void, emanating from somewhere far off, from an unclear direction —from everywhere and nowhere. They were familiar, just like this place. Familiar but impossible to identify.

Vex poured all his focus into listening, determined to put names to those voices, to trace their sources.

He walked forward, or at least he seemed to. The blackness around him remained unchanging, unwavering, affording no indication that he'd moved at all. Pain and sound washed over his being in waves, but only the former was sharpening.

One of the voices was so warm and soothing. It beckoned him, and he longed to hear more of it. Though it was not his own, he had the sense that it belonged to him all the same.

But it was a different voice that reached him with sudden clarity. It was a soft autumn breeze sweeping through the darkness; beautiful, sorrowful, ephemeral.

"You've visitors without, magus."

Vex had heard those words before, long ago.

Shade. That had been the wisp speaking.

A response came in low, rumbling thunder, powerful, commanding, and aloof. "Turn them away."

Vex's voice, Vex's words. But he had not spoken them. Not here, not now.

"Would the magus not so much as gaze upon these travelers before casting them out?" Shade asked with far more patience and gentleness than Vex had deserved.

Something rose from the nothingness around Vex. Gray mist swirled and coalesced, solidifying into a floor, walls, and a high ceiling. A huge window with intricate metalwork inlaid in the glass took shape before him—a window high in his tower.

A lone figure stood before the window, staring out with hands clasped behind his back. The long black hair and pointed ears, the broad shoulders and lean waist, the stance and posture; all of it belonged to Vex. He was looking upon himself, but the goblin before him was not Vex.

This was the magus. This was who he'd been long before he'd taken Vex as his name.

Beyond the glass lay the magus's realm, whole and hale. Silvery moonlight shimmered on the loch's dark waters and illuminated the glen's hills and ridges. The reflections of innumerable stars danced on the water's surface. The trees swayed in the breeze as though to unheard music, already wearing their autumnal reds, oranges, and yellows.

Something was amiss below. The woods in the tower's shadow were always dark and quiet. Serene. Uninhabited. Yet orange light now glowed beneath the canopy, and tufts of pale, diffused smoke escaped through the leaves.

Campfires.

"Visitors?" the magus growled. "This is an invasion."

The air around him rippled and warped with the release of raw, unbridled magic. Vex felt none of it—not the slightest stirring in his blood, not the faintest tingling on his skin. There was only the dread pooling in his gut, cold and heavy, sending out icy tendrils to creep through his bones.

The travelers in the woods needed to be turned away. They were not safe here.

Shade flitted into the space between the magus's face and the window. "They are of your kind, magus. They are goblinfolk."

The magus tensed. Vex screamed, bending his will toward this ghost from his past, imploring the magus to make the right choice, the only choice that could've protected everyone.

Cast them out! Banish them from this realm, deliver them from their doom!

Vex felt his body moving someplace else, somewhere removed. He felt the ache in his muscles, felt the heat coursing through him with every thump of his heart. Discomfort crawled beneath his skin. But all those sensations were muted, separated from his mind by unseen, incomprehensible barriers.

Until a hand—warm and soft—brushed his cheek.

He stilled, mind and body.

That hand, Kinsley's hand, stroked from his cheekbone to his jaw and back again, instilling him with calm. She spoke to him, but he was too far away to understand what she said.

Still, her tone was not lost on him. Compassion, caring, concern.

Darkness swallowed the tower around Vex and closed in on him, robbing him of her voice, her touch. But he would not let it take her. He would not let it take his mate from him.

There was oblivion in the dark. There was pain. There was heat enough to make Vex feel as though he were melting, and cold enough to convince him that his very heart had turned to ice. Time passed, but it held no meaning to him.

Something was roaring nearby, making a steady, hungry sound, and phantom heat stung his skin. Only then did he realize the darkness had taken on a red-orange tint.

A child's cough echoed in the void, which was slowly filling with hellish light. Not Vex's cough, but it had been once.

When the child spoke, his voice was innocent and frightened. "Mother? Sire?"

Not Vex's voice, but it had also belonged to him. Before he'd been Vex, before he'd been the magus. When he'd been called Reed by his clan.

Vex turned his gaze to the drainage ditch in which the child had hidden. With the telltale shimmer of powerful but unrefined magic, Reed flickered into view as though from nothingness, peeking over the edge of the ditch.

The child hadn't been conscious of the illusion that had rendered him invisible. How could he—so young, so naïve—have understood that his magic was the only thing that had saved him?

He will learn soon enough. Will learn that had he only possessed some control, some discipline, he might've saved others.

Might've saved them all...

The goblin child's eyes rounded as he surveyed the devastation. The village he'd called home was ablaze. Flames raged within the stone buildings, turning them into huge furnaces. Ash and ruin covered the ground, and the charred corpses of his kin lay scattered like driftwood washed onto an uncaring strand. Flakes of ash drifted away from the bodies on the wind, breaking them apart bit by bit, erasing them. Golden blades protruded from many of the fallen goblins, the weapons nearly as expendable to those who'd wielded them as the lives they had taken.

Black smoke billowed into the sky, blotting out moon and stars and leaving the fires to stain the world crimson.

The echoes of those fires blazed in Vex's core.

Arcane residue clung to some of the corpses and detritus, adding splashes of vibrant color to the nightmare. What little magic the clan had been able to muster had not availed them.

Tears welled in the child's eyes as he called out again. They were tears of loss, disbelief, and terror, tears from a youth who did not yet fully comprehend what had occurred. And their spilling would soon enough make way for fury.

Reed's eyes snapped toward movement in the distance. Radiant, gold-clad fae astride fierce-eyed steeds galloped around the edge of the village, barely discernable through the haze. Fear radiated from the child, who ducked into the ditch again, struggling to steady his breathing as his little heart did its best to beat right through his chest.

Vex's heart sped to match the pace of Reed's, and his breaths grew short. Both sensations remained distant, but they built a pressure in his chest that was more difficult to ignore with each labored inhalation.

Thoughts fluttered through Vex's head—his own and Reed's, blended; two voices made one.

Gone. All gone.
They can't be gone.
Why did this befall us?
Why has this happened?

The roar of the flames became deafening. Reed huddled in the ditch, embers and ash falling upon his soot-stained skin and dirty clothing. Names and faces tumbled through his mind, all of them lost to the world, lost to time, lost to everyone and everything but Vex.

The child's wail of grief and pain emerged from Vex's throat, rattling him to his core.

"Shh," someone soothed, their voice gentle in his ear. The light from the accursed fires faded.

Fingertips trailed across his face, cool against his heated skin, and smoothed damp hair from his forehead.

Kinsley.

Vex tried with all his strength to speak, to say her name; no sound emerged. But he could feel his body, could feel something beneath him, something atop him.

His pallet. His blankets. And that touch on his face, that voice—his Kinsley. His mate.

He strained for her, but he could not move, could not reach her.

"Easy," she said as she stroked his cheek. "You're all right. You're not there, not anymore. We're here, Vex."

She sounded weary, even...afraid, her voice just a little raspier, a little thinner. A little unsteady. What was wrong? What had happened?

Vex's heart quickened further. The barghest. He'd fought

another barghest, one he'd missed. Were there more? Had Kinsley been hurt? Had she...had...

The flames lost their battle with the darkness.

In his mind, Vex clawed for purchase, fighting to remain there with Kinsley, but his awareness of her was already vanishing. No more touch, no more heat, no more sweet, soothing voice. Only nothingness.

Nothingness and agony.

Vex drifted on a churning, violent sea, at the mercy of swells of pain. The distance between his mind and body padded his suffering less and less as moments, or hours, or days went by. Memories swirled through his head and all around him, indistinguishable from what must've been feverish imaginings. Voices called to him from within and without, their ghostly words swirling around the maelstrom that held him prisoner.

Shade, Echo, and Flare. His people—both his clan and those who came later. The mortals and immortals with whom he'd dealt. Kinsley.

More than anyone, he heard Kinsley, and it was her voice that became the strongest, the clearest. She was his only tether to reality. But he had not the strength to draw himself closer to her, had not even the strength to part his lips and utter the slightest sound.

Nothingness swallowed him again, holding him prisoner, until finally the darkness receded. He watched the magus, clad in hooded cowl, heavy robes, and an illusory shroud, walk the camp that had been pitched in his tower's shadow.

His anger stirred anew as he gazed upon the bedraggled goblins in the camp. He noted their tattered clothing, their weariness, their wariness. Their burns and scars, far more than any of them could ever have deserved.

And his anger collided with self-loathing as he witnessed the gleams of hope, threadbare but undeniable, in their eyes.

Return to your tower, he urged the magus. *Deny them sanctuary. Let them not falsely hope for what you cannot provide!*

But the magus strode on, entering the elder's tent.

The goblin elder sat bare-chested in the dirt, pungent herbs burning in a bowl before him. His body was smeared with paint—

black for the new moon, for the dark that had devoured his kin. Black for mourning.

The elder's gray eyes were piercing as he looked at the magus.

"You trespass in my realm," the magus said flatly.

"We seek sanctuary," the elder replied evenly. "Tales of a dark wizard led us to this glen."

"What need have you of a dark wizard?"

"To shield us from the light."

Something pierced Vex's heart, echoing what the magus felt in that moment.

"I've no alms to offer," said the magus.

The elder turned his palms up and bowed his head. "We need but land upon which to make a new home. We ask for naught more."

"What you have asked is much and more already."

Sighing, the elder closed his eyes and lowered his hands to his knees. "Many creatures whisper in these lands. They whisper of a dark wizard, aye, and whisper of his blood. Some claim he is our kin. Goblin. Much and more I ask of you, magus, indeed. Much and more... But goblin or not, you know what I truly ask."

No. Hearken not to his words, you damned fool. He knows not what he asks!

The elder opened his eyes, locking his gaze with the magus's. "I beg your leave, magus, that my people might live. No more, no less. I think you know, do you not? Know what it is to have no place, no peace? Know what it is to be hunted for what you are and naught else."

The magus tilted his head. "You assume much, elder."

"Mayhap," the elder replied with a nod. "Yet I can but speak my heart. My truth."

Within the illusionary shadows masking the magus's face, his lips were curled in a small, wistful smile. He had already decided.

And that the decision could never be unmade.

Nothingness reclaimed Vex. He floated through it, distraught, exhausted but unable to sleep, parched but unable to drink, hungry but unable to eat. Only Kinsley's little touches broke his suffering. Only her softly spoken words eased his torment. Those words, those touches, all just for him, came from a world he could not reach, could not navigate, could not see.

From a world he would fight to return to until he ceased to exist.

He felt soothing warmth on his brow, and a hint of moisture. Kinsley was speaking to him again, dabbing a warm, wet cloth on his face. Caring for him.

What have I done to deserve this? To deserve her?

It mattered not. He would do everything in his power to keep her.

Her voice and touch soon escaped his awareness again. Still, he could not cling to her, could not grasp her presence and draw himself back to her. For all the power he wielded, he was utterly helpless. Utterly useless.

Just as when the seelie swept through my home. When they slaughtered my kith and kin.

Vex squeezed his eyes shut. Or mayhap they'd been shut all along? He could not tell. The darkness behind his eyelids was the same as that surrounding him—boundless, inescapable, familiar.

But it wasn't empty. It had never been empty, not truly. Kinsley was still there. She wasn't touching him, but she was close, and her presence was unmistakable. His soul recognized it, reached for it, called to it, yearned for it. For her.

Still, she remained out of his grasp. Though he felt her presence, she was not in this darkness with him, and that was for the best. She deserved so much better than *this*.

Sound tickled at his ear. It was faint, as though carried on the wind over a great distance—like so many of the sounds in this void. But as he focused, it took shape. Not just one sound but several layered together to form a greater whole.

Music played on drums, pipes, and lyres. He'd not heard its like in...in centuries.

Vex opened his eyes to find himself looking through the same tower window as before. The reflections of moon and stars shimmered upon the loch as though restless to escape the temporary bounds in which they'd been caught. The forest and hills were lush with summer growth, the wildflowers pale beneath the night sky.

But instead of campfires and tents, buildings of stone and wood were nestled amongst the trees and along the shore, with large awnings of hide and canvas sheltering much of the space between. Cookfires glowed here and there, but their light could not compare to the multihued glows of the many candles and faery lights the goblins had hung in their settlement, which were complimented by dozens of wisps flitting about between the structures.

A great many goblinfolk had gathered in the center of the new village, where they danced to music that Vex could only just hear from his tower.

He'd long appreciated the songs of his forest—melodies of wood and root, of wind through leaves and water lapping the land, of birds and beasts, of life. This music was different. It hailed from a past nearly forgotten, from ancient days when a child called Reed had run and played with his clanmates, exploring rugged highland glens, climbing the tallest hills, and wandering the darkest woods they'd dared to enter.

It hailed from a past that had been burned away by fire and gold.

In the vague reflections on the window, Vex did not see himself. There was only the robed magus, his red eyes aglow, and the indistinct blue flames of three wisps hovering around him.

"They are a distraction. Naught more," the magus said in a low voice.

Vex's chest ached. He did not know if it was an imagined pain or one from his body, wherever it lay in that moment.

A distraction, yes. But so much more. A reminder.

A failure in waiting.

"This one would join the festivities," Flare said from behind Vex.

"As would this one," added Echo.

The magus waved dismissively. "I'll not deny you your revelry. But I've other matters to attend this night."

With delighted little trills, the two wisps darted away.

"You need not tarry," the magus said.

"This one simply wishes to admire the view a moment longer," Shade replied.

The magus huffed, stepping closer to the window. "It is…" *Doomed.* "Heartening."

"Could it be that the magus is happy?" asked Shade.

"They are happy. That...is enough."

Fire and ice—rage and grief, pain and sorrow—pulsed through Vex's being.

It isn't enough. Wasn't enough.

All that power, all that knowledge, and you couldn't comprehend that simple truth.

He awaited the darkness, the nothingness, and the release it would offer, but it did not come. He didn't know how long he stood at the window, watching the memory. Didn't know how long the musicians played, how long the goblins danced, or how long the children roamed in packs, playing tricks on each other and their elders. He didn't know how long the moonlight shone upon the village below his tower.

At some point, he became aware of a new sensation, cool and wet, upon his lips, tongue, and in his throat. Water. Drops at a time, slaking some of the thirst he'd been unable to quench. It wasn't the first time, he knew, but he'd not yet felt it so clearly.

"We're still here," Kinsley said. "You're still here."

A few more drops of water slid down his throat.

If only he could move his lips. If only he could force a sound out of his mouth to tell her he was there, that he could hear her, feel her. If only his body would respond to his commands. If only he could escape the nothingness and return to her.

Warmth flowed into his hand, accompanied by gentle pressure; it was Kinsley's hand upon his. That warmth spread up his arm and through his body slowly, soothing away the lingering aches and pains. He was aware of naught in that moment but her.

The memory had long since faded, cocooning him in restful darkness that thrummed with her heat, with her voice, with a whisper of her scent.

"Kinsley?" Echo asked.

"He's starting to look better, isn't he?" Kinsley's tone held a heart-wrenching blend of hope and desperation.

"He is," said Shade.

"Tend to yourself a while, Kinsley," said Echo. "These ones will hold vigil."

"I can't leave him," she replied, tightening her hold on Vex's hand.

His chest swelled, and his heart beat faster.

My mate. My Kinsley.

Shade spoke with the gentleness and patience with which they'd conducted themselves for as long as Vex had known them. "If you do not tend to your own needs, Kinsley, you will be unable to care for the magus."

"I'm fine, really."

"It would ease this one's mind," said Echo.

"I... I don't... He hasn't woken yet, and I..."

Vex ached for her. The rawness in her voice, the concern...it was more than he ever would've expected.

"He is deep in a healing slumber," Shade said. "You've time enough for a hot bath, a warm meal, and a bit of restful sleep. Should the magus's eyelids so much as twitch, this one will hasten to your side bearing word."

In the silence that followed, Vex could almost sense her indecision, could almost feel her mind battling itself—a battle echoing within him. He did not want her to go, yet he could not stand the thought of her suffering, least of all on his behalf.

"All right," she finally said. "I'll get something to eat and take a quick bath."

Vex was vaguely aware of something shifting near him, and then Kinsley's other hand stroked his face.

"I'll be back soon, okay?" Kinsley withdrew from him. "I promise."

Biting cold swept in to replace her warmth. Vex reached for her, cried out for her, but his body didn't move, and his voice didn't work. There was only blackness again, and now it was jarringly empty.

The wisps spoke to each other, but it was too late. He was already too lost to understand them, spiraling deeper and deeper.

Somewhere in that vast nothingness, he spied something. It was distant, tiny, indistinct, but he sensed it drawing steadily closer.

A pinprick of light.

Fear slithered through his consciousness and wormed into his being. He didn't want to go to that light, didn't want anything to do with it, wanted only to be as far from it as possible. Yet all his struggling could not alter his course.

The light expanded and intensified. It was the sun, blinding in its radiance.

Not the sun, not the sun, that is not *the sun.*

Vex closed his eyes, but the light remained visible. It would not be denied. He clawed at the darkness, desperate to remain in its embrace. It offered no salvation, no escape. He was falling. Tumbling toward that terrible, malevolent light.

Then all motion halted. Vex opened his eyes, and his heart stuttered.

He knew this place. He knew the marble floors and columns with their golden veins, delicate filigree, and inlaid gems. He knew the intricate stained-glass windows depicting a resplendent female fae. He knew the alabaster carvings, the detailed silk tapestries, and the flowers crafted from gems, which sparkled in every conceivable hue.

He knew the light. Not just that cast by the crystal chandeliers dangling from the high, vaulted ceiling, but *her* light.

No. He'd never wanted to return to this place, not even in memory. He'd never wanted to so much as think of it again.

A dais stood on the far end of the chamber, backed by the central stained-glass window, which was the tallest. Atop the dais was a throne made of gold-veined marble with saffron velvet cushions. And upon the throne sat the fae queen, emitting light to rival the sun—so much light that her features were indiscernible but for her cold, entrancing eyes.

The robed figure of the magus approached the throne, his face shrouded in illusory shadow. Behind that illusion, his eyes were slitted against the luminescence.

The queen spoke. Her voice was high, melodious, and beautiful, and it chilled Vex wholly. "It is customary to kneel before your queen."

This place...he shouldn't have been here, should never have come. Not now, not then, not ever.

"Thus, I remain standing," the magus replied.

Slowly, the queen rose. Her light refracted off the crystal chandeliers, making flecks of color dance around the chamber as she stepped forward. The illumination diminished, revealing her features, as she descended the steps.

Vex fought to turn his head, to retreat to the darkness, but he could not look away. And no matter how hard he wished otherwise, the magus stood his ground.

Tall and elegant, the fae queen was a creature of unparalleled beauty. Her face was perfection—a delicate, slightly upturned nose; full, bowed lips; large, luminous, opalescent eyes; high cheekbones and thin, expressive eyebrows. Dark lashes contrasted her golden hair, which was in turn complemented by the golden torc around her neck.

She wore a white dress made of diaphanous material with the faintest shimmer of blue and gold as it moved, hinting at the lithe, seductive body beneath.

But her perfection was cold. Her light shed no warmth, offered no comfort. Long had the magus—had Vex—dwelled in dark places, amongst unseelie, encountering creatures great and terrible. None had instilled fear in him like the queen.

But the magus had believed himself her match...because submission had never been an option.

The queen paused mere paces away from the magus, tilting her head as she regarded him. Her opalescent eyes were a pair of compassionless abysses, eager to devour anything they beheld.

No! You should never have come, should never have stayed. Should never have uttered a single word to her.

But Vex's shouts could do naught but reverberate through his mind; no one could hear them, least of all his past self.

The queen flicked her wrist.

The illusions shrouding the magus fell away, revealing him as he was—a green-skinned goblin with long black hair and red eyes. Silver earrings adorned his long, pointed ears. He wore a short tunic cinched by a wide belt, also decorated with silver, and black trousers with tall boots. The midnight blue cloak over his shoulders was fastened with a silver brooch in the shape of the crescent moon.

"So, the rumors prove true. A goblin." One corner of the queen's perfect lips ticked up. She closed the distance between herself and the magus. Her long, graceful fingers, tipped with sharpened nails, lightly touched the underside of his jaw, tilting his face up. "I'd no idea your ilk could be so fetching. Those eyes, those brows, those lips... You put some of my courtiers to shame."

Vex longed to slap that hand away, but the magus made no such move.

"I have accepted your invitation in good faith," the magus said, subtly leaning back to escape those fingers. "State your business with me, that I may take my leave with all possible haste."

She chuckled, the sound light but pointed, and stepped around him, circling like a predator sizing up its prey. "Curious that one such as you should possess so much power, is it not? It is quite rare for goblins to wield high sorceries."

"I've not come to be gawked at as a curiosity," the magus replied.

Standing behind him, the queen lifted several strands of the magus's long hair, brushing it between her fingers. "You've come because I summoned you. Your purpose here is dictated by my decree. By my whim."

Vex felt his chest, felt his lungs struggling to fill with air. He felt the breath caught in his throat. But he could not draw in more, could not satiate that need.

The magus stepped forward, again escaping the queen's hold, and turned to face her. "You mistake me for one of your subjects. I am master of my realm, bound to neither king nor queen."

Again, the queen closed the distance, her lips parting in a grin to reveal perfect white teeth. "Such a quaint understanding of authority. How does one manage to be so grave and yet so naïve?"

"How does one manage to be so sophisticated and yet so presumptuous?"

"A sharp tongue. We shall put that to good use."

"We shall do no such thing, as I am taking my leave."

The queen halted the magus with a hand on his shoulder. Keeping that hand there, she strutted around to his back, letting her eyes, half-lidded, dip in her perusal of him. "As ever, my instincts prove correct. You, *magus*, shall serve as the most interesting diversion."

Flee, damn you! Escape! Do not allow her to sink in her claws.

But Vex's pleas couldn't alter anything. The world around him warped and changed, wrenching him through time and space.

The queen's bedchamber, unlike the throne room, was dimly lit. The marble posts of her huge bed stood from floor to ceiling, and over it was a glass dome through which the moon and stars twinkled in a clear night sky. The pure silver of the moonlight was tainted by the soft yellow and orange glows of the gems embedded in the columns.

Atop the bed, amidst silk and velvet pillows, cushions, and blankets, reclined the queen. She was bare, her ivory skin on full display—pert breasts, a narrow waist, flaring hips, and long, lean legs. The magus stood at the foot of the bed, clad in a loin cloth. The torc around his neck was engraved with flowing, golden seelie script, its metal deceptively delicate.

Vex raged, but his wrath had no outlet, no release. It could but serve as shield between his consciousness and the pain at his core.

The queen lifted a hand and crooked her finger, beckoning the magus. When he didn't move, her brows angled downward. That subtle change made her face all the more threatening. "I tire of this."

The magus stared at her, his crimson eyes smoldering with contempt. "I might have sympathized, had you not brought it upon yourself."

"Were that tongue not so clever in other ways, I would have removed it long ago."

"Should you wish to be free of your current frustrations, you need but release me." The magus's expression remained hard, unchanging, and defiant despite the situation, but Vex knew what it hid—the fear, the uncertainty. The racing thoughts and lurking fears.

The queen closed her fist. Molten metal materialized in it, forming a thin chain, link by link, that stretched out to hook on the magus's collar. The metal cooled into polished, gleaming gold. She tugged on the chain, and the magus stumbled toward her, barely catching himself on the bed.

She leaned toward him, her face a hair's breadth from his. "You shall grant me what I desire, pet."

And Vex could only watch, helpless to avert his own damnation and prevent the suffering and death that would be wrought because of it. Helpless to right any of the wrongs of the past.

Baring his teeth, the magus growled, "I care not for your desires."

"Nor for your life," the queen hissed, coiling the golden chain tighter around her fist. The fury writ upon her face—which typically displayed only indifference or cruel mirth—was a rare sight. "And what of the lives of the misbegotten denizens of your paltry realm?"

A crack formed in the magus's mask, and a pang of pain and guilt sharper than any blade pierced Vex's chest.

The queen's red-painted lips split into a sultry, menacing grin. "Ah. So, you haven't a care for your own life, but theirs..." With her free hand, she caressed the magus's face, grazing his skin with her long nails. "You are just beautiful enough a creature for me to offer mercy, my pet. A deal."

The magus stilled as she shifted her head, nearly pressing her lips to his ear. "Sire my child, and I shall release you. Your realm, and all who dwell within it, shall be left in peace."

Tension gripped the magus's muscles, and his claws tore into the bedding as he clutched it in his fists. Vex felt that tension in himself; it was a pressure so great that his heart ceased beating, that his lungs threatened to burst, that his whole being was about to collapse into itself.

No. He wanted so desperately for the answer to be no, for the magus to reject the offer, to reject the queen. Wanted so desperately to stave off what would be—what was—the greatest folly of his life. And yet he knew at heart it would've changed nothing.

But he knew, too, the thoughts swirling in the magus's mind. He knew the torment of that decision. Knew the magus was weighing the scales, plotting, planning, hoping. Hoping there yet remained a way out, that he was clever enough to escape.

What pained Vex the most was that the magus had been right—he'd found a way to escape the prison in which she'd trapped him. But he'd never had a chance of escaping the queen.

After a long silence, the magus nodded.

The queen's grin widened. "Swear it upon your true name. Give me your oath."

Lips barely moving around his fangs, the magus whispered his oath to the queen, granting her his true name.

Cold dread coiled around Vex, crushing him slowly, heart and soul. A true name once given could never be rescinded. And an oath broken...

The queen laughed. Her skin brightened until golden light flowed from her—the light of day, the light of the sun, blinding, withering, scorching.

In truth, the queen hadn't consumed him with light, but she'd consumed him all the same.

That light engulfed him, forming a blazing golden void around Vex. All he'd worked toward, all he'd fought for, all he'd come to cherish...all of it had been annihilated by that light. And now, finally, it would annihilate him too. It would give him the release he'd been denied for so, so long...

No. It is not over. I am not done.

He'd long believed that everything had been taken from him save his life, but that had never been true. He had the woods, cursed yet his own. He had the wisps, faithful, unwavering companions whose care had sustained him. And now he had Kinsley.

His mate.

He felt Kinsley then. Felt her presence, felt her hand on his, her thumb brushing his knuckles. Felt her smoothing back his hair and tracing the scars by his eyes.

She had returned. Returned to him.

"You're not there, Vex," Kinsley said. "You're here with us. With...with *me*."

The queen's aura had been malevolent, diminishing, oppressive. It instilled awe and fear and drove people to their knees. Kinsley, in contrast, exuded serenity. There was fire in her, undoubtedly, but it was the fire of passion, warm and gentle. Not the cold, harsh flame that burned in the queen's heart.

If the queen had been sunlight, destroying all in its path, Kinsley was moonlight—soft, caressing, ethereal.

It seemed as though an eternity had passed since last he'd looked upon his mate's face, since last he'd touched her. All that time lost. When he dragged himself back to reality, back to Kinsley, he'd have much to make up for.

Gradually, the sheer white void gave way to the embrace of blackness. Vex sank into it willingly.

With Kinsley there again, it wasn't nothingness. A new light, small but unmistakable, shone in the darkness. A soft, silvery light.

My Kinsley. My mate.
My moonlight.

CHAPTER TWENTY-FOUR

A sense of heaviness settled over Vex, and with it came awareness. Awareness of his body and its weight. Awareness of his leaden limbs and the dull aches with which they throbbed. Awareness of the taut skin on his belly, of the bedding beneath him, of the blanket draped over him. Of his thirst and his hollow, gnawing hunger.

Awareness of...warmth.

His eyelids fluttered as he struggled to open them, but they were as heavy as the rest of his body, if not more so.

He inhaled. The air was like a scorching desert wind to his raw, dry throat. He released the breath with a weak, broken sound that was halfway between a sigh and a wheeze.

Vex's awareness expanded. He was lying on his back, propped up on pillows to allow a bit of space for the arms of his wings. One of those wings was folded against the wall of the alcove, while the other was stretched out, dangling off the pallet.

Someone was tucked against his side, their head resting upon his arm, their soft hair spread over his bare skin, positioned so their weight wasn't atop his wing. That body was the source of the delightful warmth.

Vex had no desire to move. This was exactly where he was meant to be. Why spoil it, why throw it away?

This was *right*.

This was a memory worth lingering in.

When he took another breath, it was tinged with a sweet, alluring smell—orange blossoms, so exotic; sweet honey; a fresh spring rain.

Brow furrowing, he forced his eyes open. His vision blurred and wavered in the bright light, and his heart quickened, thumping against his ribs. Sunlight, overwhelming, scalding—

No. Not sunlight. He recognized the soft, multihued glows cast upon the ceiling. This was his place. His lab, his home.

Vex sighed, willing himself to ease. Everything he'd seen, everything he'd relived, had existed only in his memory. In the distant past.

Barely holding in a groan as his stiff muscles protested the movement, he turned his head.

It was Kinsley who lay with him, her cheek on his arm. Kinsley whose honey brown hair was draped over his skin, whose soft body was against him, whose warmth radiated into him.

Heat flared in his chest and spiraled outward through his veins, tingling to the tips of his fingers and toes. Kinsley was lying with him, sleeping with him, and he'd not known until now. How hadn't he been aware?

The barghest.

His eyes fell shut and his throat constricted as the memories rushed to the forefront.

Limiting himself to teasing Kinsley had proven exceedingly difficult, but somehow, he'd restrained himself and allowed her to go outside. He'd allowed her to find joy in something from which he could never take any—the sunlight.

And he'd felt so...light. Aroused, but so light, so free. So hopeful and hungry. Because when she returned, he would've pressed that passion, that desire. Would've done more than merely tease.

But then Echo had come. Echo, frantic, speaking almost too quickly for Vex to understand.

Barghest. Hunting Kinsley.

Dread had nearly frozen Vex in that moment. It mattered not that she carried some of his immortal lifeforce. Kinsley could not stand against a barghest. Naught in his possession—not his magic, his knowledge, his herbs and potions, his willpower, his rage—could have saved her had she been bitten.

He recalled the trees passing in a rush. Recalled the sting of sunlight upon his skin, and the scrape of branches as he crashed through the canopy.

Clearest of all, he recalled the moment his eyes fell upon Kinsley, his mate, with the barghest grinning its sharp-toothed, hungry-eyed grin only a few paces away from her. A predator just as cold, ravenous, and calculating as the queen.

His heart had ceased beating.

Vex remembered the fog, the struggle, the pain. His abdomen pulsed with the memory of claws shredding his flesh, and he shifted his free arm to run his hand over his stomach. His fingertips brushed across unmarred skin.

But after the brief, brutal battle, after the barghest lay unmoving in a pool of its own black, wretched blood and Kinsley had helped him back home, he remembered…

Darkness. A universe of darkness.

No, that wasn't right. There'd been memories in the darkness. Nightmares. Yet through it all, there'd been one constant, one shred of hope, one thing to latch onto as he rode the waves of oblivion.

There'd been Kinsley.

Her presence, her touch, her voice. Her compassion, attention, and will. There'd been her. His moonlight.

Vex opened his eyes.

Her features were relaxed in sleep, but even slumber's serenity couldn't mask the dark circles under her eyes or the weary paleness of her skin.

You're here with us. With…with me.

Swallowing thickly, Vex shifted, lifting his head and propping himself on his elbow. She wore a simple white nightgown, and her hair was damp and loose.

"Magus," Echo whispered, their ghostfire shining at the edge of his vision.

Vex lifted his finger to his lips and shook his head. The wisp shrank back but did not dim.

Gently, Vex reached down, hooked a strand of Kinsley's hair, and brushed it out of her face, tucking it behind her ear. She didn't stir.

Throughout his ordeal, his suffering, his…delirium, this human had stayed with him. Had tended to him.

She deserved better than sleeping on a pallet in this dark room, where the air was fouled with the odors of countless herbs and the tangs of ancient magics. She deserved better than he'd given her.

She deserved everything.

And he… He would not sleep alone again.

Moving with exaggerated care to counteract the stiffness and weariness permeating his body, he dismissed his wings, withdrew his arm from beneath her head, and sat up. When he slipped off the pallet and got to his feet, his legs trembled, uncertain of whether they intended to support him. He stood on his toes and lifted his arms over his head, stretching his back with a soft groan.

Echo danced excitedly nearby, casting shadows that mimicked the wisp's movements. They whispered, "This one will tell the others."

Vex nodded, offering them a wave, and turned to face Kinsley as the wisp flitted away. Kneeling, he slipped his arms under her and lifted her from the pallet.

She moaned and turned toward him, her fingers curling against his chest as though to grasp him.

"Sleep," he said gently, infusing the word with what little magic he could muster.

Kinsley settled, nestling against him.

Holding her just a little tighter, he carried her to the stairs. It was impossible to ignore his weakened state, but each step roused a little of his vigor, undoubtedly aided by having Kinsley in his arms.

All three wisps awaited him at the entrance to the bedchamber. They brimmed with excitement, bouncing in the air, their ghostfire swirling, but remained silent as Vex brought Kinsley inside.

He strode to his bed, willed aside the blanket with a flick of a finger, and carefully—reluctantly—laid Kinsley down. After arranging the pillow beneath her head, he combed his fingers through her loose, damp locks and drew the blanket over her. Thankfully, the enchantment kept her slumber unbroken.

Vex cupped her cheek in his hand, stroking her soft, smooth skin with his thumb. "Ah, Kinsley…"

He'd not been sure how to feel when he'd first brought her here, when he'd first laid her in his bed. Having a stranger, a human, in his bedchamber had been…unsettling. But the implication of her presence had been too important to deny. His solitude was a small sacrifice to make in his quest for freedom.

Now he could not imagine his bed any other way. He could not imagine his home any other way. She had already become such an integral part of his life that even he, an immortal who'd watched centuries pass like leaves falling in the autumn wind, could not fathom existence without her.

Leaning over her, Vex pressed his lips to her forehead. He let the tender kiss linger. It afforded him the merest hint of her taste and allowed him a few more moments to drink in her fragrance, to relish her feel.

When he finally withdrew his lips, he whispered, "Rest easy, my mate. I shall return to you anon."

Vex forced himself away from the bed and gathered a fresh tunic, trousers, and a pair of boots. He dressed quickly and exited the chamber. Once the door was closed, the wisps, who'd waited patiently for his emergence, all spoke simultaneously, their excited voices blending into unintelligible chatter.

Though their words were jumbled, their worry, gratitude, and relief were clear.

He chuckled, quieting them with a gentle gesture. "Be at ease, my friends. Though I am not fully recovered, I am hale enough to warrant no further worry. I must ask you to quiet yourselves. I would not have Kinsley awoken before she's had adequate rest."

"She remained at your side throughout, magus," said Flare.

"How long has it been?"

"Eight days," Shade replied.

Eight days? Had Vex truly lost that much time to the illness inflicted upon him by the barghest's claws? Rage coiled in his belly, hot and sharp, but he tamped it down.

"She scarce tended to her own needs," added Echo.

"I know." Vex's chest tightened with a strange mix of sorrow, pride, happiness, and guilt. "Thus, we must allow her to sleep. What of our unwanted guests?"

Flare dimmed. "No sign, magus."

Shade drifted a little closer, their core darker than usual. "These ones scouted ceaselessly during your recovery, magus. If aught else is to be found, it is beyond this one's perception."

"But these ones apologize," Echo said, their ghostfire also dwindling. "Had these ones been vigilant enough, naught would have been missed. You would have been spared your wounds, your suffering."

Vex frowned, studying the wisps. "None of this is any fault of yours. Indeed, your actions have spared me considerable suffering. Kinsley is safe. Naught else matters. You've done more than I could have asked of you, and yet...I must ask more still."

"Anything, magus," said Echo. "These ones are simply glad you have awoken."

Vex smiled, but the expression quickly faded. "One of you remain with Kinsley. Watch over her in my absence. Should she rise before my return, inform me immediately. The others, with me."

Shade tilted their fiery head. "Where are you going?"

"Firstly, to the kitchen. Then into the woods to ensure we've no other unexpected visitors."

Echo's ghostfire flared. "In your state, magus, is that—"

"It can be delayed no longer," Vex said firmly. "I assure you that all due caution shall be exercised, but I must know that we are safe."

That she *is safe.*

"Yes, magus," said Echo.

Shade floated to Echo, touching their companion with a tendril of ghostfire. "Come, Echo. These two shall accompany the magus."

Flare sketched a small salute. "This one shall watch."

"Thank you." Vex bowed his head before walking to the kitchen, where he drank deeply of cool, fresh water and ate the first food he could find—a few pieces of fruit and a chunk of bread that was only just beginning to harden.

When he stepped outside, the forest was peaceful beneath the shroud of night. He wrapped himself and the wisps in an invisibility illusion and took wing. Air rushed by as he swept along the ley lines, seeking any signs of more barghests. When he was satisfied that there were none, he laid rudimentary wards along the ley lines that would alert him should they be crossed.

The sky was cloudy, but the moon occasionally broke through, casting silver beams down to the earth. It felt good on his wings, which all too well recalled the sting of the sun. Yet the moon's caress, however comforting, was not what he craved. He wanted *his* moonlight.

He wanted his mate.

Vex landed when something out of place caught his attention. A blanket, crumpled on the forest floor, and a clear box filled with colorful supplies nearby. This was where Kinsley had been that day. Where the barghest had attacked her.

He clenched a fist, pressing his claws into his palms, as he crouched. He spread the blanket out, and his expression twisted into a scowl. The blanket was damp and muddy, but the dark stain upon it was unmistakable. He would've known it by the smell even if it had been further diluted by the elements.

Human blood. Kinsley's blood.

Images threatened to assault his mind—the metal carriage, broken glass, crimson glistening upon Kinsley's too-pale skin.

"She was harmed," Vex growled, clutching the blanket tightly enough to tear the fabric with his claws.

"She was not," Echo replied hastily.

Vex glared at the wisp and held the bloody blanket up to their light.

"It is natural for humans," said Shade. "Kinsley said it is part of the *reproductive cycle*."

"The reproductive cycle…" Vex blinked and stared at the stained cloth. Was this a sign, then? A sign that she was ready to receive his seed?

That she was ready to receive him?

Flames stirred in his blood again, and he clamped his jaw against the surge of desire that welled up from his core. He lowered the blanket, drew in a steadying breath, and picked up her box.

The material—plastic, she'd called it—was spattered with mud and detritus after a week in the woods. He huffed through his nostrils as his desire shifted toward anger. If her belongings had been ruined, he would…

I'll what? Find a means to restore the barghest's life that I may kill it again?

He unclasped the latches and opened the lid. Fortunately, it had been sealed tightly enough that no moisture had crept inside.

Echo bobbed in the air in front of Vex. "The magus must see!"

"Must see what?"

"What Kinsley created." The wisp gestured toward the book inside the box.

Delicately, Vex lifted the book from its place. He opened the cover and perused the pages, experiencing anew the waves of emotion that many of them induced. Then he reached something new, and he stopped, staring down at it.

A pair of black pages. Paintings that were not necessarily lifelike and yet brimmed with life stood out against the black—the wisps, each depicted with loving detail to capture their colorations and brightness. The painted wisps glittered with tiny metallic flecks.

Echo beamed in delight, spinning and swirling, and even Shade brightened a little.

Vex smiled. That she had brought his longtime companions such joy warmed his heart, but something else on the page escalated that warmth into heat.

A pair of crimson eyes stared out of the darkness. Eyes brimming with menace, wonder, intensity and depth, mystery and longing, passion. They were Vex's eyes. And if this was how Kinsley saw them, how she saw him…

Moonlight broke through the clouds, falling directly upon Vex. He glanced up to glimpse the moon and a small patch of starry night sky. When he looked back at the book, the words Kinsley had written in silver ink shone.

There is always magic to be found in the darkness.

Vex brushed the tip of a claw across the flowing letters. His heart thumped, spreading molten heat through him. He rasped, "All the magic at my command will be yours."

Echo's voice, uncertain and soft, broke Vex's thoughts. "Magus?"

"It is time we returned," Vex said, closing the book and putting it back in the container.

"Is all well?" Shade asked.

"Better than I could've hoped." Vex closed and latched the case, tucking it under his arm. "But I am long since due for a bath and a real meal, loath as I am to be away from Kinsley any longer."

The wisps fell into place at his sides as he walked, their ghostfire flickering at the edges of his vision, but all his attention was directed forward, toward his home.

Toward Kinsley.

Immortal or not, Vex understood better than most that time was finite. He would not waste another moment with her. He would not spend another night alone, and he would not go another day with their mating bond unsealed.

He would share his bed with her, and he would do so as her mate—in every way.

Tonight, he would make Kinsley his.

CHAPTER TWENTY-FIVE

THE SOFTEST OF caresses on Kinsley's face lured her out of her dreams. Fingers traced her brow, her lashes, her cheek, nose, and lips, leaving whispers of pleasure in their wake. She breathed in deep, released a contented sigh, and smiled, turning her face toward that touch. It was warm and gentle, but firm.

She knew it, had felt it before.

"Awaken, my moonlight."

She knew that deep, velvety voice too. It had been her protector in the darkness. It had shielded her from death's clutches, had coaxed her back to life.

Vex.

Kinsley opened her eyes.

Vex was leaning over her. He lay on his side next to her, propped up on an elbow, crimson eyes bright amidst the shadows cast upon his face by the firelight. His black hair was swept back over his shoulder, revealing a long, curved ear adorned with a gleaming silver cuff. The scarred symbol beside his eye was stark against his green skin in the warm orange glow.

Her gaze trailed down the column of his throat to his bare chest. Shadows played upon the lean muscles there, contouring them into sculpted perfection.

The heat that sparked within Kinsley had nothing to do with the crackling fire.

She placed a hand on his chest, over his heart, which pounded beneath her palm. His skin was hot and smooth.

"I'm still dreaming," she said. Why else would Vex be here in bed with her, half naked, caressing her face with such gentleness?

Vex cradled her cheek in his big palm, drawing her eyes back up to his, and flashed those white fangs in a smile. "If this is a dream, Kinsley, surely it is my own."

Kinsley brow furrowed. "It's not a dream?"

"It is not."

She glanced at her hand on his chest. "I'm awake?"

Vex smoothed his hand along her arm until it settled upon hers, holding it securely in place. "It would seem so."

"I'm awake... I'm..." Her eyes widened. "You're awake!"

She touched the back of her other hand to his forehead. He was no longer burning up with fever, and though it was hard to tell in the firelight, it seemed his sickly pallor had vanished.

"How do you feel?" she asked.

The corner of his mouth quirked up. "Better than I have in a long while. And you, Kinsley? I'm told you've taken little rest this past week."

Warmth flooded her cheeks as she lowered her hand to her belly. He refused to let go of the other, curling his fingers tighter around it.

"I'm fine. I..." Kinsley dragged her eyes away from Vex, only then noticing her surroundings. "I'm back in your room. In...your bed."

"You needed rest," he replied, combing his fingers into her hair, "so I brought you here. It's far more comfortable than the laboratory, is it not?"

His mention of the laboratory only reminded her of everything she'd seen during his slow recovery. Many times, his magic had transformed the chamber into bygone places, and those illusions had been so vivid, so real. So heartbreaking.

She'd watched Vex as a child, terrified and alone, gaze upon the fiery ruins of everything he'd ever known. His people, his family, his home, all gone, consumed by flames so intense that Kinsley had almost felt their heat.

His healing slumber had been anything but serene. During

every illusory scene, she'd seen the pain etched upon his face, had felt the strain in his writhing, feverish body. And he'd only calmed when she'd laid her hands upon him and spoken to him.

Kinsley might've thought them nightmares projected from his subconscious mind, but the wisps had told her the illusions hadn't been dreams at all—they'd been memories. His memories.

She'd seen the loneliness in his eyes as he stood in his tower, looking down upon the goblin village. The lively music from below had been made sorrowful and haunting by the distance that separated it from Vex. But she'd seen something more behind his mask.

Longing. Longing and a glimmer of hope.

Vex had lost so much at so young an age, and he must've felt alone for so long...

Even through those seemingly harmless moments, Vex—her Vex, in the present—had been restless in his slumber. He'd writhed and muttered, his body as tense as it had been during the more horrifying scenes.

She'd wondered why those memories had troubled him so, until she recalled what he'd said in the library.

My tower was razed. Torn down around me, stone by stone. Everything I had built, everything I had sought to protect...destroyed.

His restlessness had been rooted in guilt, in grief and pain over what had been lost.

Over not only what had been taken, but *who*.

Tears of anguish and rage stung Kinsley's eyes. Everything Vex had suffered, everything he'd endured, had paled in comparison to what the fae queen had done.

She'd made Vex her slave and threatened to kill everyone in his realm to keep him. A threat Kinsley knew had been carried out.

Kinsley curled her fingers against his chest. "Vex, the things I saw while you slept..."

He clenched his jaw, and his hands flexed, pricking her scalp with his claws. "What did you see?"

"I saw you. Your past, the other goblins at your tower...the queen."

Though his skin paled, Vex's expression darkened. His body did not ease. "Ah. That is...regrettable."

A tear spilled from the corner of her eye, trickling into her hair beneath his palm. "I'm so sorry for everything you went through. For all you lost."

A crease formed between his eyebrows, and his lips parted with a silent sigh. "You need not be sorry, Kinsley. All you witnessed occurred long ago. It is in the past, where it shall remain."

"The past stays with us, Vex. I know that too well. The pain I saw in you...that wasn't pain you buried in the past, it's pain you're still carrying with you. It's still present."

He hummed thoughtfully. Gentling his touch, he took a thick strand of her hair between finger and thumb and stroked it idly. "After all these years, I ought to have learned the wisdom you've just shared. At heart, I know that no matter how much I wish it were otherwise, the queen is with me still. Thanks to her curse."

His crimson eyes met hers, gleaming with something raw, something vulnerable. "You could have let me die, Kinsley. You could have been free, released from our pact. Why did you aid me?"

Kinsley scowled. "You seriously think I'm that kind of person?" She tugged her hand out of his grasp. "That I'd just let you—"

Vex buried his fingers in her hair, angled her face toward him, and slanted his mouth over hers.

Kinsley's eyes widened, and she thrust her hands out, meaning to stop him. But she found herself unable to resist. His lips crushed hers, hungry and fierce, demanding, yearning. Just like when he'd first kissed her, Kinsley closed her eyes and gave in to him.

But this time, she returned the kiss with equal fervor.

Their lips molded to each other, hot, firm, and passionate. Every breath was shared between them.

Vex's arm slipped beneath her, cinching her against him, and her hardened nipples brushed his chest through her nightgown. The sensation sent a jolt straight to her clit that made her whimper. A growl rumbled from him in response.

Flames curled low in her belly, licking at her core, and their heat spread through her body. Every thought vanished. Only Kinsley and Vex existed, here, in this moment. She could focus on nothing else but him—the solidness of his body atop hers, his spicy scent enveloping her, his heat radiating into her, and his taste... Oh God, his taste. She needed more.

The heavy ache in her core expanded, and her cunt pulsed with need.

Kinsley slid her hands up Vex's chest to capture his face between them. When she parted her lips, his tongue swept over them and delved into her mouth, where its tip split to caress hers.

The feeling, both foreign and erotic, startled Kinsley. With a gasp, she tore her mouth from his and shoved against his chest. Surprise flashed across his features as he fell back onto the bed, allowing Kinsley enough time to scramble away.

Nearly tripping on the hem of her nightgown, she climbed off the bed and turned toward him. Her chest rose and fell with her rapid breaths, her body trembled with unfulfilled arousal, and her inner thighs were slick with her desire.

Kinsley wanted Vex, craved him, and yet...

She clutched fistfuls of the nightgown at her sides, squeezing.

He wanted something from her, something she could not give him. And that secret was a chasm, wide and deep, stretching between them.

They shared more than a magical pact. So much more. She felt it, deep in her heart, deep in her soul. Being with him was right. It was...fated.

Yet how could she give in to her lust while keeping that secret?

Tell him. Just tell him, Kinsley.

I...can't.

What would he do to her when she found out? What would he do when he discovered she'd mislead him, lied to him?

Vex rolled onto his hands and knees and fixed his glowing red eyes upon her. Kinsley could only watch as he stalked toward her like a prowling cat, his movements powerful, graceful, sensual. Her heart beat faster with every inch of distance he closed.

But rather than pounce, Vex swung his legs over the edge of the bed and sat before her, settling his long, claw-tipped fingers on his thighs. Strands of hair hung in his face and over his chest and shoulders, making it only harder to look away from him.

"You flee as though I've burned you, Kinsley," he said, his voice low and husky. "But it is I who burns."

Something fluttered in her belly.

I burn too.

Kinsley's lips parted, and her brow furrowed. "We shouldn't do this."

"I see the same yearning in your eyes. Why should we not take what we both want?"

Her chest constricted. "The pact. That's…that's all this is about."

"My desire for you has naught to do with our pact, Kinsley. I want you. I've wanted you since the moment I set my gaze upon you."

"But that's only because of what you want from me."

"No," Vex growled through his bared fangs. "It is because you are *mine*. Pact or no, I want you. You were always destined to be mine."

Kinsley's heart quickened.

Pact or no, I want you.

She swayed, taking a small step toward him before hesitating.

"What do you want, Kinsley?" he asked. "For what does the fire in your eyes burn?"

"You," she whispered. That single, simple word resonated through her very soul.

His chin tilted down, and he crooked a clawed finger. "Then come to me, my moonlight."

CHAPTER TWENTY-SIX

S̲p̲e̲l̲l̲b̲o̲u̲n̲d̲ ̲b̲y̲ ̲t̲h̲o̲s̲e̲ ̲c̲r̲i̲m̲s̲o̲n̲ ̲e̲y̲e̲s̲, Kinsley stepped toward Vex. He held out his hand, palm up. It was an offering, an invitation, a temptation. All she had to do was take it.

You want this, Kinsley. You want him.

She did. She'd been cast aside, made to feel unwanted, unworthy, unloved for so long. She craved the connection and intimacy promised in Vex's smoldering gaze.

Dismissing her hesitation, Kinsley placed her hand within his.

A slow grin spread across his lips as he curled his fingers around her hand. He drew her closer until she stood between his thighs. Though his hold was gentle, she couldn't have resisted even if she'd wanted to.

"Were I given the choice"—he hooked the low neckline of her nightgown with a claw—"there is but one memory by which I'd be tormented."

Wisps of green magic flickered beneath his claw. His hand dipped, and that claw sliced through the fabric without resistance. Kinsley's eyes widened as she looked down.

"Your body"—he moved his hand lower still, and the magic spread like green flames from the edges of the tear, the fabric vanishing in its wake—"bared to me, yet out of reach."

Tingles arced across Kinsley's skin, making her shiver, as the nightgown dissipated thread by thread, leaving her naked. Exposed to both the air and Vex, her nipples grew taut.

Vex captured her chin, drawing her gaze back to his. "Never again shall you be beyond my reach."

Kinsley lifted a hand and lightly traced the scars near his eye. "I'm here, Vex. And I am yours."

An appreciative growl rumbled from him. One of his hands glided up her arm, while the other slid down her neck. The darkness in his eyes expanded even as their heat intensified; they would swallow Kinsley up, and she welcomed it.

His thumb caressed her throat before his hands reached her shoulders. He followed her collarbone with his fingertips, his claws teasing her and stoking the fire at her core. Then he moved his hands down. The backs of his fingers swept over the swell of her breasts and, with maddening, deliberate delicacy, brushed her hardened nipples.

Sensation jolted through Kinsley, and her breath caught in her throat as her hands flew to his shoulders.

"This is perfection," he said, voice low, thick, sultry. "*You* are perfection."

Had those words come from anyone else, Kinsley would've refuted them. But from Vex...she believed them. *Felt* them.

He cupped her breasts, squeezing and kneading them, as his long, clever fingers stroked and pinched her nipples. Her clit twitched with his every caress. Brow furrowed, Kinsley clung to his shoulders and caught her bottom lip with her teeth. Heat pooled in her core as her pussy swelled with need.

Faint tremors coursed through his hands, and he released a shaky breath.

Then it occurred to her—Vex had been trapped in this place for centuries. Alone.

Kinsley brushed a strand of hair back from his face, hooking it behind his long, pointed ear. "You don't have to hold back, Vex."

"Ah, Kinsley," he purred. "My restraint is not for your sake, but my own. I mean to savor every moment."

Vex leaned forward. His tongue slipped out, and he licked a path up between her breasts, making her heart quicken. "I've awaited this for so long. Awaited you."

Turning his face, he captured her nipple in his mouth and sucked.

Kinsley gasped at the thrilling sensation.

He dropped his other hand to her ass, curling his fingers in a tight, possessive grip as he tugged her closer. A whimper escaped Kinsley, and her eyelids fell shut. She thrust her fingers into his hair, needing something to hold onto, something to ground her.

And then she felt his tongue. It swirled around her nipple and split, its twin pointed tips lavishing her flesh. Her knees nearly buckled. It was heaven, it was bliss, sending tingling currents through her and making her sex clench. She never wanted it to stop.

Liquid heat seeped from her, dampening her inner thighs, which she squeezed together. It did nothing to alleviate the heavy, hollow ache growing in her core. She needed more.

"Vex," Kinsley breathed.

He released her nipple, though not before grazing it with a fang. "You need not beg, Kinsley…but I shan't forbid you."

"Please." She clutched his hair and arched toward him. "Please don't stop."

He chuckled as he ran his nose up between her breasts, his breath hot against her skin. "Mayhap I *should* make you beg. I do love the sound of it."

Kinsley opened her eyes and met his gaze. There was a teasing light within its depths that matched the curve of his upturned lips. This was a side of Vex she'd never seen, a side she might never have imagined he possessed.

And somehow, she knew he'd never shown it to anyone else. This was just for her.

"Touch me, Vex." She released his hair to cup his jaw. "Kiss me."

Vex's otherworldly gaze softened, and he reached up to wrap his hand around the back of her neck. He pulled her down until their lips were but a breath apart. Kinsley stared into those eyes, which glimmered in the firelight.

"My moonlight, I shall give my all to fulfill your every desire."

He pressed his burning lips to hers. Kinsley's lashes fluttered closed again as she fell into the kiss. Their mouths caressed and nipped, their tongues flicked and coaxed, and Vex held her captive as he deepened the kiss.

His claws bit into the skin of her ass, but the sensation only heightened the pleasure unfurling within her. She returned her hands to his shoulders as she leaned further into the kiss, into him, breathing in his heady oakmoss and amber scent.

The kiss was carnal and tender, ravenous and generous, utterly intoxicating. His split tongue twined around hers, its every stroke making her core pulse. Her slick ran down her inner thighs, and it felt as though she were on the verge of coming from his kiss alone.

Too soon, he pulled his mouth away. Kinsley swayed toward him, desperate for more, but his strong hand stopped her by angling her head to the side. The brush of his lips and the scrape of his fangs blazed a trail along her jaw, dipping lower and lower.

"I will taste every bit of you, Kinsley," he rasped against her neck.

His tongue swept along her collarbone before his kisses continued down between her breasts, which ached with need and thrummed with the memory of his attentions. But he only continued downward, his hand sliding along her spine to follow his progress.

When he reached her belly, he pulled his head back. Releasing her ass, he hooked the tip of a claw behind her navel piercing, lifting it gently. The teardrop moonstone glittered as the light hit it from a new angle.

"This pleases me." He brushed his thumb across the stone. "But it is too plain."

Soft green light, like dim, ghostly fire, enveloped his hand, but it produced no heat. That light—that magic—snaked out to either side of her piercing, solidifying into the tiny, delicate links of a chain. Kinsley's skin tingled as the cool metal settled against it.

Tiny moonstones dangled from the chain, each shimmering with its own rainbow in the firelight. When the magic faded, the chain had encircled her midsection.

Awed, Kinsley ran her fingers over the chains. Their solid metal warmed against her skin.

"Much better." Vex's hand followed the chain's path to her hip, where it stopped.

"It's beautiful," Kinsley said.

He lifted his gaze to hers. "Your beauty is far more brilliant, my moonlight. You outshine even the brightest of stars in the night sky."

Warmth filled Kinsley's cheeks, and she smiled as she caressed his jaw. Turning his face into her touch, he kissed her palm, making her heart flutter.

"If I'm your moonlight, what are you to me?" she asked.

"I am your darkness. Your cloak, your protection. The shadow that shields you from the ravages of the day, the shroud that lulls you to sleep so you may wander in the bliss of your dreams."

Tears prickled her eyes, and her chest constricted with swelling emotions. "Will you be waiting for me in my dreams?"

Eyes never leaving hers, Vex curled his fingers around the belly chain and drew her closer, brushing his lips just above her piercing. He settled his hands on her hips. "Awake or asleep, Kinsley, I am with you always."

He'd offered those words with such vehemence, such solemnity, that they sounded like a vow, an oath, a binding promise. How could his words have been so meaningful after so short a while? She and Liam had been best friends for years before they'd married, and his vows... Well, they'd meant nothing in the end.

This should've been the same. Kinsley and Vex hardly knew one another, and the circumstances that had brought them together, that kept them together, were dire. He'd made his goal clear to her from the beginning.

But she believed him. Despite everything, she believed him with all her heart.

"Vex," she said softly. It was the only thing she could say in that moment, even though there was so much she wanted to tell him.

He inhaled deeply and shuddered, his slitted pupils expanding as his hold on her hips tightened. Shadows coalesced behind him, solidifying into his batlike wings. "Ah, Kinsley... I can smell your desire."

Before she could even consider a response, he grasped her ass and lifted her astride his stomach as he lay back on the bed, spreading his large wings to either side. Kinsley yelped, her eyes rounding and hair falling forward. She flattened her hands on his chest to catch herself.

"I must taste you in full," he said. "Must drink of your essence."

Kinsley gaped at him. "You...you what?"

He grinned, revealing those wicked, wicked fangs as his eyes dropped to her exposed sex. "If I must speak more plainly, I shall." He dragged her farther up his chest, covering his skin in her slick. "I want my tongue in your cunt."

Kinsley's eyes widened.

Oh God.

"Wait, wait, wait!" She braced her hands on his shoulders, stopping his progress. "I... You... You want me to sit..." Cheeks blazing, she lifted her hands and covered her face. "I've never done that, Vex."

Though she'd always carried some extra weight, it had never stopped her from doing the things she enjoyed. She loved her curves. But like any human being, she had moments of self-consciousness, of vulnerability, and this...this was one of those moments.

Vex took hold of her wrists and guided her arms down, pressing a kiss to each of her palms. "You've naught to fear from this. From me."

Kinsley looked down at him. There was pure adoration in his eyes—adoration and yearning.

"I'm not scared of you," she said. "I'm just...shy."

He chuckled, the sound vibrating against her sex. "Cast out your hesitation, Kinsley. I offer only pleasure." He slipped one of her fingers into his mouth and sucked, the tips of his tongue twirling around it as he slowly withdrew it. "I hunger for you. *Thirst* for you."

Another aching pulse swept through Kinsley, followed closely by anticipation. Her heart was beating so fast that she wondered if it would sprout wings and fly away.

She nodded. "Okay."

Vex growled, palmed her ass with both hands, and tugged her forward until her knees were on either side of his head. A shiver coursed through her when she felt his warm breath upon her slick, intimate flesh.

"Light consume me, you are so wet." Flicking his crimson eyes up to hers, Vex said, "And you are mine."

His mouth met her sex, and Kinsley gasped.

Curling hands around her thighs, he ran the flat of his tongue along her pussy from bottom to top, where its tips brushed around her clit.

"Vex!" she rasped as her pelvis twitched with a spike of pleasure. "Oh fuck."

"Exquisite." He clenched her thighs, pressing his claws into her skin, and held her firmly in place. His eyes locked with hers as he swept his tongue through her folds. He licked, sucked, and nipped, leaving no part of her untouched, teasing her clit but never giving it his full attention.

She leaned back and braced her arms behind her, gripping his sides. Her breath came in soft pants. With each flick of his hot, delectable tongue, he edged Kinsley closer to her peak. She could feel her pleasure coiling tighter, could feel the pressure building in her core. Her skin tingled with awareness, set alight by the overwhelming sensations.

But Vex pushed her no further. His unwavering, possessive gaze pierced her, holding her in place as securely as his hands.

"Please," Kinsley whispered, undulating her pelvis. "Please Vex. If you want me to beg, I'm begging you now. Make me come."

He skimmed her clit with the tip of his nose, and Kinsley nearly bore down upon it, eager for more. He once more breathed in her scent and hummed.

"Not yet." Again, the glow of magic enveloped his hands, but this time it broke away from them—assuming their shape as floating, ethereal copies. "I crave more of you."

Those arcane hands whispered over her skin, brushing across Kinsley's belly until they reached her breasts and closed over them. However ghostly their appearance, their touch was real, tangible, thrilling, and they massaged and caressed with all the familiarity of Vex's touch.

Kinsley arched her back with a moan as those fingers pinched and twisted her nipples.

"I want you writhing." Vex nipped her inner thigh with his teeth, forcing another gasp from her, then soothed the sting with his tongue. "I shall have you breathless, mindless in your need."

He swirled his tongue around her clit, and she nearly sobbed with the pleasure it wrought before he abruptly pulled away.

"I want you lost to ecstasy, awash on a sea of pleasure. No room for thought, only sensation. Only me."

Those apparitions flowed over her body, touching, soothing, stroking, stimulating every part of her as Vex grazed her thighs with his claws.

"Vex..." Kinsley breathed.

He growled and lapped at her clit, coaxing more liquid heat from her. "And when I'm through, I shall bury my cock inside this delicious cunt and fill you with my seed."

"Yes! Yes, just *please*. I need you now."

"I will claim you soon, my mate."

Mate?

He thrust his tongue deep into her.

"Oh God," she moaned, her sex clenching around it.

Vex's tongue pumped ruthlessly, delving ever deeper, and Kinsley was helpless but to move with it, craving relief from the maelstrom raging inside her. And those ghostly hands continued their tantalizing exploration of her body.

Gripping his hair in one hand, she rocked her pelvis, needing his tongue deeper, needing more, and soon lost herself to sensation.

Were she a spectator, she would not have recognized the creature she'd become in that moment. A woman of lust, a woman of power, a woman taking pleasure from the goblin beneath her, who was so willing to give her everything. Her every inhibition had crumbled.

She bounced upon him, grinding against his mouth, and he growled in encouragement, the sound resonating in her core and fanning the flames burning there.

But it wasn't enough. Her body trembled with need for release.

As though hearing her unspoken plea, Vex withdrew his tongue, clamped his lips around her clit, and sucked it into his mouth.

Rapture struck her like a bolt of lightning. Her nerves buzzed with pure, potent energy, and her muscles seized in white-hot pleasure.

"Vex!" Squeezing her eyes shut, she threw her head back as sharp, breathy cries tore from her throat and heat flooded her core.

His tongue stroked her pulsing clit relentlessly, drawing out her cries and holding her at that peak; he did not allow her to descend, did not allow the sensations to dull even slightly. She fell forward, planting her palms on the bed as she ground her pussy against his mouth, unable to stop, driven purely by instinct.

Vex's hands cupped her ass, holding her in place and guiding her movements until another burst of pleasure swept through her.

She screamed, bunching the blanket in her fists as more heat spilled from her and ran down her inner thighs, and Vex drank from her pussy as though unwilling to waste a drop.

"Please, no more," she pleaded when her sex contracted again. "Enough!"

The ghostly hands vanished. Vex's hold tightened, and Kinsley's world flipped. She landed on her back, cushioned by the soft bedding. Before she understood what had happened, he crawled over her, wedging his hips between her thighs. His wings spread behind him, blocking out the firelight. Only those glowing eyes remained, dangerous, intense, and fixated upon her.

He grasped her chin and growled, "I will *never* have enough of you."

CHAPTER TWENTY-SEVEN

Vex stared down at Kinsley. He reveled in her pink-stained cheeks, her parted lips and panting breaths, her full, lush breasts. Her body quivered in the aftermath of her climax. She was radiant. His moonlight, his goddess, lost to the pleasure he'd provided.

He ran the tips of his tongue across his lips. Her essence lingered there, ambrosial and alluring, ensuring that his hunger would never be sated. He would spend eternity craving more, more, more.

But another need was stronger still. It flowed through his veins like fire, pumped by the blazing heart in his chest. It reverberated through his entire being, body, mind, and soul, devouring him, compelling him.

Claim her.
Make her yours.

And the heated gleam in her half-lidded eyes held the same desire. She wanted him. She wanted to be his.

Kinsley flattened her palms on his chest, and Vex groaned as she smoothed them down his abdomen to the waistband of his pants. But they didn't stop there. Boldly, she cupped his cock. Vex hissed through his teeth and shuddered at the overwhelming pleasure.

With a coy smile, she said, "You know, this might work better with your pants off."

Vex chuckled, and something swelled in his chest—something

warm and rich that had naught to do with the flames of his desire. This was Kinsley. His teasing, playful, brave, stubborn mate. She who had brought light and laughter into his world.

When had he last found reason to laugh, to smile? When had he last known joy or lightheartedness? When had he yearned for aught but revenge and freedom? The wisps had found their bits of contentment in this nether realm, and Vex had convinced himself that was enough.

He had not been deserving of the same.

But now that she was here, he'd take all the joy he could. And when his curse was finally lifted, when they were finally freed from this place, Kinsley would want for naught, and her happiness would be his own.

"You're correct. They'd only make things unnecessarily difficult." Vex willed his trousers away. Arcane energy swept over his skin, dissipating the fabric and leaving him exposed to the cool touch of the air on his backside.

Yet he paid no mind to that chill. With the final barrier eliminated, Kinsley's soft, smooth, warm hand was directly upon his cock. Her touch was like a branding iron, scorching but sweet.

Kinsley's eyes flared in surprise and dipped. "Oh..." She tightened her grip and brushed his ridges with her thumb. "These... these will feel *very* nice."

"Kinsley," he growled. His muscles tensed, and both his wings and his cock twitched. That slight change of pressure, that little stroke, and he was already on the verge of exploding.

Her eyes met his, and she smiled. "And I take it this feel nice?"

She wrapped her fingers fully around his shaft and pumped her hand. Vex gritted his teeth and curled his fingers, puncturing the bedding with his claws. Tingles coursed just beneath his skin, and the ache in his groin deepened. His wings stretched wider as seed seeped from his cock.

Kinsley swiped her thumb over the tip, gathering his seed, and spread it along his shaft with another pump of her hand. She pressed her lips lightly against his shoulder. "Is that a yes?"

Succumbing to such pleasure, such bliss, would have been easy. It would've required no thought. All Vex would've had to do was feel.

But he didn't want this to end. Not now, not like this. He'd made a vow.

When next I spill my seed, it will be inside you, my Kinsley. My mate.

Vex caught her wrist, drawing her hand away from his cock. The last brush of her skin over his nearly undid him; he clenched his jaw and held back the tide, refusing to give in.

He guided her hand over her head, pressed it onto the bed, and laced his fingers with hers. "*Nice* is far too inadequate a word. Yet I desire more."

Vex shifted until the head of his shaft aligned with the enticing heat of her sex. "I desire *all* of you."

Flexing his hips, he slowly pushed into her. She squeezed his hand and clutched his side, breath hitching.

He felt every inch of her slick inner walls as they glided around his shaft. That friction sent waves of pleasure through him, all of which wound tight and low in his belly.

It took all Vex's willpower to stop himself from thrusting into her too quickly. He wanted to savor this—the feeling of her body taking him in ridge by ridge, of her cunt stretching around him, so wet, so tight, and by silver and starlight, so hot. He wanted to relish the look of pleasure upon Kinsley's face, wanted to revel in her every reaction. The tiny twitches of her body, the sensual whimpers from the back of her throat, the fluttering of her lashes, the parting of her lips with her shallow breaths.

She was perfect.

And she was his.

Tension gripped his limbs as his pleasure built to a new, impossible height. His self-control was bound only by a fraying twine, and those sensations sliced through each thread, one by one, until the restraints finally broke.

With a growl, he snapped his hips forward, burying himself in her fully.

Kinsley gasped and arched her back, brushing her hard nipples against his chest.

Vex wrested back his control, if only barely, and paused. Her cunt pulsed around him; he felt every tremor, no matter how small, every quiver, felt even the beating of her heart. She fit around him perfectly. Her body welcomed him, beckoned him, begged him for more and offered everything in return.

Never had he been so connected to anyone. Never had he been so close to anyone.

All the desire roaring in his soul like a ravenous beast, all the need, could not prevent him from appreciating this moment, this intimacy. Could not prevent him from appreciating his Kinsley.

"We are one, my mate," he rasped, dipping his head to brush his lips across her forehead. Even that small movement caused enough friction to shake him to his core and quicken his heart.

Raising her knees, Kinsley tipped her head back and trailed kisses along his jaw toward his ear, where she whispered. "Please don't stop."

Vex drew back his hips and lifted his head. Staring into her eyes, he thrust again. This time, a shudder wracked them both.

"Oh God, I can feel those ridges." Kinsley lifted a hand to his face and stroked his scars before slipping her fingers into his hair.

Despite the overwhelming sensations flooding him, he was stricken with pride. The corner of his mouth quirked as he pushed into her again. "My cock pleases you?"

"Very much," she said with a moan. Her sex clenched around his shaft upon his next withdrawal.

That moan urged him on, and he continued pumping into his mate with slow, measured thrusts, each deeper than the last. She moved with him, flowed with him, in complete unison. Their fingers remained tightly laced, neither of them willing to sever the connection.

An inferno blazed through his veins, severe and agonizing, blissful and thrilling, incomparable. The flames burned hotter with each movement he and Kinsley shared. He welcomed the heat, embraced it, craved it.

That fire glowed in her blue-violet eyes as well, not merely a reflection but an exact match, a kindred flame just as fierce, just as consuming.

How long had he unknowingly awaited her? For how many centuries had he endured an emptiness he'd not recognized because *she* was the one thing missing, the one thing he needed, the one thing for which he'd been destined?

He did not know how his life, so fraught with tragedy and pain, had come to this point, but he knew this moment had always been fated. And he wouldn't have traded it for anything.

This was not merely the coming together of their bodies, driven by loneliness and desperation. He felt her soul, her lifeforce, already tinged with his own, dancing with his, twining together irrevocably. He felt that bond—which transcended any oath they'd made, any pain they carried, any curse that plagued them—sealing into something unbreakable.

"My Kinsley," he rasped, his rhythm growing more urgent. "My mate, my moonlight."

She spread her thighs wider and met him thrust for thrust, welcoming him ever deeper. Her brow furrowed, and her grip on his hand tightened. Her voice was strained, aching, and raw when she said, "Vex, I need you."

"You have me."

He dropped his head and captured her mouth with his as Kinsley tensed around him. She cried out, and he took that cry into himself eagerly. Her nails scraped his scalp, and her sex contracted around his cock, sucking and pulling as heat rushed from her.

Kinsley's pleasure was his undoing.

His muscles seized, making his rhythm falter, and his breath caught in his throat. The pressure at his core swelled, suddenly too great for him to bear, and each tiny movement of Kinsley's body only intensified the sensation.

Vex's thoughts fractured. Everything he'd wanted, everything he'd seen and done, everything he'd experienced and suffered, all of it broke apart into meaningless shards but for one thing—his mate.

A snarl ripped out of his throat and his wings snapped outward as seed erupted from him. His free hand darted to her hip, pinning her in place. He continued pumping his hips forcefully, erratically, resisting the oblivion promised by his climax for as long as possible.

Wrapping her arm around Vex's neck, Kinsley held him tight as her body quivered. She squeezed her eyes shut and pressed her forehead to his. Their breaths came in short pants, mingling with his low groans and her soft moans.

Curving his body over her, sheltering her, protecting her, Vex thrust into Kinsley one final time, burying his cock deep, and held himself there while pleasurable shocks echoed through them.

Basking in the aftermath of their joining, they slowly eased. Vex's wings settled around them like a shroud, blocking out the rest of the world. Only he and Kinsley remained—their soft breaths, their heat, their mating scents. Their hearts beating in tandem.

Vex lifted his head to look down at her. Even with naught but the crimson glow of his eyes to light her face, Kinsley was radiant.

He brushed the backs of his fingers down her cheek, and she looked up at him with a content smile. His heart clenched.

"I was lost in the shadows, alone and bereft, until you brought light into my world, Kinsley."

Her eyes glistened with tears as they searched his face. She withdrew her arm from around his neck to tuck his hair behind his ear, where her fingers lingered. "I won't leave you alone in that darkness again."

Cupping her cheek, he wiped away one of her escaped tears with his thumb. He pressed his lips gently to her forehead, letting his eyelids fall shut, letting himself relish their closeness, their warmth, their bond.

It was more than he'd ever dared hope. She was more than he'd ever dared dream.

When he lifted his head again, he said the only words his ragged voice was able to produce. "Thank you."

Unwilling to withdraw from her and relinquish the rapturous heat of her body, unwilling to sever their connection, Vex slipped his arm behind her shoulders and rolled onto his back, drawing Kinsley atop him. He wrapped his arms and his wings around her, cocooning her in his embrace.

I will never let you go, my moonlight.
I could not bear it.

CHAPTER TWENTY-EIGHT

Kinsley dared not move, dared not even breathe, lest she awaken Vex from his sleep. They lay on their sides with legs intertwined, facing each other. One of his wings was tucked beneath her, while the other, along with his arm, was draped over her in a warm, loose embrace.

Soft daylight shone through the window above them, chasing away the shadows. It fell across Vex's skin without causing him any apparent injuries or discomfort, unlike when he'd crossed into direct sunlight while fighting the barghest.

His quiet repose was so far removed from the fitful sleep she'd witnessed as he healed; she'd never seen him this relaxed and untroubled. She knew he hadn't yet fully recovered. Not even a goblin wizard could battle fever for eight days after being nearly eviscerated and then jump out of bed as though nothing had happened.

But when he'd come to her last night, he'd been so vigorous, passionate, and alive. So present.

Kinsley smiled. Her body still thrummed, and her sex still ached from their lovemaking. But it was such a good ache.

It had been so long since she'd been intimate with anyone, so long since she'd been touched, since she'd felt loved… And her connection with Vex had surpassed anything she'd ever experienced. What they'd shared had been so much more than physical. It was like their souls had come together in a sensual, spellbinding dance, and were now blissfully, eternally joined.

Thoughts like that, feelings like that, only happened in romance novels. They were fantasy.

But look at me. Look at where I am, look at who is sleeping beside me.

Her very own broody, beautiful, sorcerous goblin king.

There was magic in this world.

Unable to resist any longer, Kinsley reached out and lightly traced the swirling scars next to Vex's eye.

A deep hum rumbled from his chest, and he drew her a little closer.

She shivered as her tender nipples brushed his chest and his hard cock pressed against her belly. Kinsley recalled the feel of each and every one of his ridges as they'd stimulated her from within. A bloom of arousal unfurled in her core, strong enough that she nearly groaned. She squeezed her thighs together.

His heat lingered inside her, and she wanted more.

She wanted to feel his weight, his strength, his solidness, wanted to feel the hard grip of his hands, the bite of his claws, the thrusting of his cock.

And I can tell him all that with one simple little gesture.

Kinsley slipped her hand between their bodies, wrapped her fingers around his shaft, and stroked him. Those ridges were prominent against her palm.

He sucked in a breath, opened his eyes, and grasped her hip, the tips of his claws pressing against her skin. A devilish grin stretched across his lips as he met her gaze. "What a delightful way to awaken."

The sound of his deep, rough voice made her toes curl.

Kinsley smiled. "I can make it even better."

Fire sparked in his eyes. "Oh?"

Releasing his cock, she pressed a hand to his chest and gently pushed. "Lie on your back."

"As you command." He withdrew his wing and his arm, leaving cool air to flow over Kinsley's bare skin, and rolled onto his back.

Mindful of the wing beneath her, Kinsley shifted onto her hands and knees and looked upon him. Her breath stuttered. He was beautiful, he was…glorious. His long, thick hair, mussed from sleep, was spread out around him, and those crimson and black eyes captivated her. He was long of limb and leanly muscled, but still exuded a powerful, dominant presence. His leathery wings extended past the edges of the bed, making him appear larger than life.

She trailed her eyes down his body. The skin of his hands, feet, and scrotum was black. That color ran upward and faded to a rich olive green at his shoulders, thighs, and along his shaft, where her gaze settled.

His erection stood straight up, with a bead of iridescent green cum at its tip glittering in the morning light.

Kinsley brows rose in surprise. "It's green?"

Vex chuckled. "I fear I must ask you to clarify the subject of your inquiry, Kinsley."

She hummed. "I guess quite a lot of you is green, but..."

Crawling over one of his legs, she situated herself between his thighs, which he spread wider for her. She ran a finger up from the base of his cock, over every ridge, watching the grin fade from his lips as a shudder coursed through him. When she reached the tip, she gathered the bead of cum.

"I was talking about this." She brought her finger closer to her face for inspection. His seed was a light, translucent green, and as it caught the sunlight, it truly looked like tiny motes of glitter shimmered within.

His legs and abdomen flexed as though he were about to sit up, but Kinsley stopped him by flattening her other hand on his belly.

"Kinsley," he rasped.

She smoothed that hand down until she wrapped her fingers around the base of his cock. He grunted, and his shaft twitched, producing another droplet at its tip.

"What does it taste like, I wonder?" she asked.

Breath ragged, Vex bared his fangs. He stared at Kinsley with a wild glint in his eyes—like a beast about to pounce, pin her down, and rut her. "No need to wonder. Taste me."

Keeping her gaze locked with his, she slipped her finger into her mouth. His flavor struck her immediately. It was sweet and potent with a hint of tartness, reminiscent of berries. It was...so delicious.

Slowly, she pulled her finger free and bent closer to him, bracing that hand on his thigh.

His crimson eyes darkened. "Kinsley..."

She closed her mouth over the head of his cock and sucked.

Vex's pelvis thrust upward, pushing his shaft deeper. "Gods!"

Tightening her hold on him, Kinsley slid her lips back up to the top of his cock, where she flicked her tongue along its slit to gather more of his cum.

A tremor coursed through Vex. He clenched the blanket in his fists and raised his knees on either side of her.

As she worked her mouth up and down his length, he writhed, panted, and shuddered, uttering her name in ragged, desperate pleas. Then one of his hands moved to her head, grasping her hair and guiding her motions with trembling need.

His feral reactions intensified Kinsley's desire. Her breasts hung heavy, her hard nipples ached, and her cunt clenched, hollow and eager to be filled. She was so aroused that her slick trickled down her inner thighs. She craved the feel of his cock inside her, but at the same time, she was unwilling to give this up. Unwilling to stop.

Kinsley dragged her tongue up his shaft, swirled it around the head, and sucked, coaxing more of that sweet berry taste from him. His flavor was a drug that she couldn't resist, an aphrodisiac, and she wanted more.

Vex growled, tightening his fingers in her hair before he forced her mouth down, making her take all of him. Relinquishing her hold on his shaft, she planted her hand on the bed and let him use her.

With every thrust into her mouth, he grunted, growled, and snarled. He was usually so refined and controlled, but this was a different side of him. A thrilling side.

Kinsley reveled in it.

His toes dug into the bedding, the ends of his wings curled upward, and his body grew taut an instant before his cock swelled and his seed burst across her tongue, flooding her mouth. Vex roared.

Kinsley closed her eyes and drank as much of him as she could. What she'd sampled before hadn't prepared her for his true flavor—

saccharine and intoxicating, ambrosial, irresistible. She wanted every drop. With each suck, she coaxed more from him.

He snarled, and his hips bucked with every spurt.

Those bestial sounds combined with his unrestrained release only aroused her further.

Finally, Vex's grip eased, and his body relaxed. He petted her hair with those strong hands. "Ah, Kinsley…"

Kinsley opened her eyes and met his gaze, running her tongue up his shaft one last time.

Vex's chuckle was deep and sultry. He caressed her face and brushed a thumb along her bottom lip, wiping away a drop of his seed from the corner of her mouth. "I trust my taste is to your liking, my moonlight."

"Mmm, it was." With a grin, Kinsley crawled atop Vex to straddle his waist, trapping the length of his cock against her pussy. Pleasure spiraled through her as she ground against him.

He clamped his hands on her ass, firmly pressing her down onto him as he groaned. She could feel his shaft throbbing, could feel him shuddering with need, as though the release she'd just granted him had done nothing to assuage his hunger.

And that wasn't surprising, was it? Her own appetite had only been whetted.

She teasingly licked his lips before rubbing the tip of her nose against his. "But there's something else I crave more."

His grip tightened, and he lifted her hips. His cock sprang up and pressed against her entrance, hard, hot, ravenous. "Your craving is my own."

Vex thrust up into her sex even as he pulled her down onto him. His shaft plunged deep, stealing her breath. Kinsley grasped the bedding and moaned as her pussy contracted around him.

This. This was what she needed.

Biting her lip, she sat back and widened her legs, taking him deeper.

Vex smoothed his hands over her thighs until they reached her pussy, which he parted with his thumbs. His gaze focused on the spot where their bodies were joined. A growl rumbled from him, and he stroked her clit, making her gasp and jerk.

"How perfectly we fit," he said, brushing her clit again to wring a whimper from her before his hands covered her breasts. "How beautiful you are."

Kinsley caught his wrists as he kneaded her flesh. Unable to hold still any longer, she rocked on him, feeling every one of his ridges as they glided back and forth inside her.

"Vex," she whispered.

He bared his teeth, and his wings twitched. His eyelids fluttered, but his eyes remained open and locked with hers. "We were made for each other."

As Vex massaged her breasts, she lifted herself and dropped down upon him, gasping at the pleasure rushing through her. She rode him, and Vex bent his legs behind her, matching her with hard pumps of his own.

But that steady pace could not last for long. With every thrust, the heat in her core expanded, its fire licking through her veins and setting her skin aflame. It coalesced in her belly, swelling like a star on the verge of exploding.

Panting, Kinsley grazed his chest with her nails. Her sex clenched, her thighs trembled, and her motions faltered. The pressure within her was so immense, so potent.

She needed more, but it was too much. Too overwhelming. She was right there, she was so close. But she couldn't push just that little bit further, couldn't make her body take what it so urgently needed, couldn't—

"Vex, fuck me," she begged. "*Please*. Fuck me hard."

Snarling, Vex dropped his hands to her hips. His claws bit into her flesh as he seized control. He bounced her atop him, eyes fixed upon that point of connection. Fixed upon his cock, glistening with her slick, slamming in and out of her. Each thrust was harder than the last, faster. Fiercer.

"Oh God," Kinsley cried, clutching her breasts.

"There is no god here," he growled. "Cry out for *me*."

Sharp, needy moans escaped her, and the firestorm inside her finally burst. Digging her nails into her skin, Kinsley threw her head back and squeezed her eyes shut. His name tore from her throat on a rush of ecstasy.

Her essence surged from her sex, coating her thighs as her cunt clamped and pulsed around his cock.

"*Kinsley,*" Vex groaned, thrusting into her once more and seating himself deep. His cock thickened before flooding her with stream after stream of his heat.

Kinsley hummed. It was like his magic had flowed into her, swirling and thrumming, and she ground her pussy upon him, wanting to prolong those sensations as much as possible.

After everything had finally waned to a lingering sense of euphoria, she released her breasts and dropped her hands to his thighs, panting.

Vex stroked her hips, soothing the small cuts his claws had inflicted. Kinsley didn't even register any pain. His palms moved over her reverently, worshipfully, before settling low on her belly.

"Twice you have taken my seed," he said, his voice uncharacteristically soft. "Soon enough, it shall take root, and you will bear our child. Then we will be free from this realm. Free from this curse."

Everything stopped in that instant. Kinsley's heart, her breathing, her thoughts, the world around her; all frozen in time. When the universe lurched back into motion, she was filled with a sickening dread that chased away all her heat, chilling her to the bone.

Opening her eyes, Kinsley sat straight and looked down at Vex. "What did you say?"

He smiled at her. His eyes brimmed with layered, complex emotion—adoration, lust, joy, and hope, underlaid by an old, faded sorrow. "To break the curse binding me to this place, I must sire a child. Our child." He brushed his thumb over her belly. "Then we shall be free to go as we please, to make a home anywhere we choose."

Kinsley's heart raced as panic and disbelief closed in on her. How was this right? How was this fair? After everything... After *everything.*

This was why Vex wanted a child, why he *needed* a child. Why he wanted her.

No. No, he wants me. He just doesn't know.

And when he finds out? What then, Kinsley? You've been down this road before.

Inadequate, insignificant, unworthy.

Defective.

She shook her head, tears burning her eyes as she struggled to breathe. "No. This... This isn't happening."

Vex planted a hand on the bed and pushed himself up, brow furrowed and mouth downturned. He cupped the back of her head, forcing her to look at him, and searched her gaze. "What ails you, Kinsley? What is wrong?"

But Kinsley couldn't speak, and all she could see was the hope that had been in his eyes. Hope that he would finally be free of the prison he'd been trapped in for so, so long.

A sob burst from her, and she tore herself out of his grasp, away from his body. His seed, the very seed that was meant to create life, ran down her thighs as she climbed off the bed. She grabbed the rumpled blanket and wrapped it around herself, needing that barrier, needing that protection, though it did nothing to diminish her sense of vulnerability.

The bedding rustled behind her as Vex moved, and Kinsley tightened her grip on the blanket, tears spilling from her eyes.

Why? Why does it have to be this way?

"After what we've shared, you withdraw from me as though repulsed?" he asked. "I've not forgotten your objections to our pact, Kinsley, but this... It is the natural outcome of what we've done, of what we've become. And the breaking of the curse will not be the end. There can be no end to us."

Kinsley's chest constricted, and her breaths came in short, shallow bursts. Guilt and pain surged inside her. "I can't."

He took hold of her shoulder and forced her to turn toward him. He'd risen from the bed, wings gone, eyes blazing, features taut. "Can't what, Kinsley?" His gaze softened before he lifted a hand to brush away the tears on her cheek.

But Kinsley stepped away from him, shaking her head. "I can't give you what you need."

Vex moved as though to follow her, only to halt abruptly and lower his arm. His jaw muscles bulged. "I do not understand."

More of Kinsley's tears fell, and her next words felt like glass shredding her throat. "I lied. That night that you saved me."

"What do you mean?"

Her lower lip trembled. "I didn't understand what you were asking. I...I was dying, and desperate, and I just agreed. And I..."

His brows lowered. "You what?"

Kinsley's reply came out in a broken cry. "I can't have children!"

He stared at her, his face an unreadable mask, his eyes devoid of emotion.

"I can't." She took in a deep, shuddering breath. "I tried and tried and tried, and it nearly killed me. So I… I chose to prevent myself from getting pregnant again."

When Vex remained silent, the pain inside Kinsley's heart unfurled, spreading its thorny vines through her chest. Why wasn't he yelling at her? Raging at her? Why wasn't he doing *anything*? Somehow, that would've been easier to face than his silence.

"I didn't know, Vex. I swear, I didn't know this was how you broke the curse. And I-I thought if I told you…"

"That I would kill you." His voice was so low, so flat, that she barely heard it.

"Yes," Kinsley whispered.

Something flickered across his features. A shadow—darkness, pain, betrayal? She couldn't tell, and that only intensified her agony.

He turned away from her and strode toward the door. "Remain here."

Kinsley took a step to follow him. "Vex…"

"I said remain here!" he roared, twisting toward her.

Kinsley flinched. Green magic flared around his hands and blazed up his forearms, and his fingers were curled, claws on full display. A furious light smoldered in his eyes.

They stared at one another. A new crack formed in Kinsley's heart with each passing moment.

Then he tore his gaze away from her and stalked to the door. With licks of magic trailing behind him, he cast the door open, stormed across the threshold, and slammed it shut. The entire cottage shook with the thunderous bang.

Kinsley's legs gave out, and she crumpled to the floor. She trembled in the bedroom's deafening quiet until it was broken by a new sound—the anguished wail that clawed its way up from her chest as her heart shattered.

CHAPTER TWENTY-NINE

Vex's fists trembled at his sides as he stalked away from the bedchamber. A maelstrom swirled in his chest, massive, catastrophic, violent. It churned with raw emotion—bitterness, despair, sorrow, hopelessness. But coiled throughout was fury, its scalding barbs sunken deep, its molten heat fueling the fire in his gut.

Shadows crept in at the edges of his vision, snaking along the walls, floor, and ceiling in his wake.

I am your darkness. Your cloak, your protection.

I can't have children!

The flames inside Vex roared. He gritted his teeth against the pressure. His rage hungered for violence, for destruction.

For catharsis.

And I-I thought if I told you...

That I would kill you.

His heart stuttered, his claws bit into his palms, and his stride faltered.

He could feel her in the bedchamber. Could feel her shattered heart, her grief, her pain. It was inextricable from his own, caught in the same storm. But everything inside Vex had been touched by his indignation, scalded by it, tainted by it, and he could not separate it from the other emotions.

Though his anger was not directed toward Kinsley, he could not trust himself to protect her from it.

Just another failure to add to the tally.

Vex forced himself onward, climbing the stairs and entering the library. Wrath thrummed in his bones, stronger with each thump of his heart, and the creeping shadows thickened along with it. His body could not contain all his magic, not with the torrent of emotions inside him.

Growling, he strode along the shelves, raking his gaze across the books that filled them. This was a fraction of his old collection, but these tomes held thousands of years of knowledge and wisdom.

Heat crackled through his limbs, and the internal pressure swelled.

A ragged roar ripped out of him. Vex's arms lashed out and swept the books off the shelf in front of him. The tomes fell heavily around his feet.

Once the floodgates had been opened, he could not shut them.

Wordless cries of rage and frustration escaped Vex as he cast more books into the growing pile. Pages flapped and fluttered, thick volumes thumped on the floor, and parchment tore.

A forceful wave of his hand blasted magic at the next section of shelves. Books tumbled from their perches to land in a heap. Vex's claws raked paper, leather, vines, and wood—but something inside him yearned to rend flesh, to spill blood.

Why did she not tell me?

Why did she condemn me to...to hope?

"Magus..." Flare intoned from behind Vex.

Shoulders heaving with his ragged breaths, Vex paused. His wings, which had emerged unbidden, sagged and shook with the same tremors that coursed through his arms. The shadows were closer now, thicker, shrouding much of the library in darkness.

"Please," whispered Shade. "This is not you."

Vex's teeth ground together, and he balled his fists again. "But it is. No more fantasy, no more illusion. I see all this"—he waved his hand at the shelves, at the fallen books, at everything—"for what it is. *Nothing.*"

"You do not mean that," said Flare.

Vex snatched one of the few remaining tomes from its place.

Subtle arcane energy coursed beneath his fingers; this was a book of spells, bristling with residual magic. "All this knowledge, all this power, and what has it won me?"

He turned toward the wisps. Flare and Shade were a pair of tiny blue flames against a backdrop of impenetrable blackness, both uncharacteristically dim.

That vinelike rage wound tighter still in Vex's chest, constricting his lungs, his heart, his soul. He brandished the tome, stepping toward the wisps. "Everything for which I toiled, everything I built, dreamed, and desired, it has all amounted to naught."

Flare's ghostfire intensified. "You must not say such things, magus."

Vex clutched the book, claws piercing the cover. "I shall not shy from the truth. What has power and knowledge availed me? None of these books protected this realm and its people from the queen and her golden host. None of these spells stopped the slaughter. No artifact repelled her curse, and no tincture can break it."

He spread his arms. "Gaze upon my power, my kingdom! My ruin."

"Your words are overly harsh, magus," said Shade, moving closer to Vex.

The library shuddered as a wave of magic flowed from Vex. "All I have cherished has met doom and damnation. For a fleeting moment, I dared believe that would change. As ever, my folly sows woe to be reaped by those closest to me."

"You are not yet defeated," Flare insisted. "Hope is not lost."

I am your darkness. Your cloak, your protection.

Rage boiled in Vex's blood, tinged with the sour tang of helplessness. Arcane energy radiated from him, raw and unbridled. The cottage groaned as magic shook its beams and stones. Books and baubles rattled on the shelves, bouncing out of their places to fall like scree in a landslide. The tome in his hand buzzed, generating its own heat.

"My mate cannot bear children," he growled. The illusory shadows closed in around him. Sorrow and pain twisted in his chest, adding their piercing chill to the crushing grip of his fury. "This realm is my tomb, my eternity. Your eternity." His voice broke into a rough rasp. "Kinsley's eternity. The queen damned my mate centuries before she ever existed."

The waves of magic fizzled as the fire and ice inside Vex collided. His throat closed, and his heart quickened. The shadows around him swirled and changed. A clear, star-sprinkled night sky bled across his vision overhead, and Vex's glen sprawled below, bathed in sweet, silvery moonlight. He looked out over his loch, his forest, his hills.

Kinsley would never witness this herself. She would never be able to gaze upon the realm he'd made his home, his sanctuary. Her only glimpse would be through hollow illusions drawn from his memory.

He would never see it again. Not this place, not anywhere. He would never see the world from which his mate had hailed, would never watch the moon rise over the ocean, would never walk lands foreign to both him and his mate.

The landscape receded to darkness, but a figure emerged from it, sculpted from scorching radiance. The queen.

Vex stared into her cold, alluring eyes. In them, he saw his contempt amplified, saw his rage echoed, saw his guilt and grief reflected. He saw all that could've been. All that had been taken.

"It was not enough to take from me and my people," he said, stepping closer to the queen. "Now you've taken from her. From my mate."

The fae queen did not reply. She simply maintained the expression he'd seen her wear all too often—like she was gazing upon a mildly interesting but ultimately intrusive insect.

With a snarl, Vex hurled the book at her. It passed through her face, making her arcane visage waver, before vanishing in the shadows behind her.

Ancient, impotent rage quaked with him. Again, the library shook, and more books, now masked by darkness, hit the floor with heavy thumps.

Claws hooked, he swung his arms outward. The queen's flesh cracked like porcelain and tore open. Light poured from the widening wounds. Breathing raggedly through clenched teeth, Vex watched as she slowly came apart, watched embers spark and devour her skin, burning the pieces to char.

But her expression did not change. Even after all this time, and despite all his fury, he could not imagine fear in her eyes, could not imagine her face contorted in pain. And he'd never have the satisfaction of witnessing either firsthand.

"Damn you," he rasped. "Were you to die a thousand deaths each day until the end of time, it would be a mercy compared to the suffering you deserve. Would that everyone had seen through that stony mask to the venomous monster lurking beneath."

He growled and closed his fists. The queen shattered, and each tiny piece blazed to ash, which faded into nothingness as the glowing embers cooled.

Vex lowered his arms and squeezed his eyes shut. The darkness behind his eyelids was no different from that enveloping the library.

My mate cannot bear my child.

A memory—fresh, vivid, and heart wrenching—banished the darkness. In his mind's eye, Kinsley flinched away from him. Fear and hurt glimmered in her eyes.

She hadn't been reacting to the queen's curse or the revelation that she was trapped here forever. She'd reacted to *him*. To his harsh manner, his foul temper.

She fears me.

Bile and brimstone churned in his gut.

Vex turned and staggered, blindly throwing out an arm to catch hold of an empty shelf and steady himself. His wings drooped to either side of him.

Kinsley's voice echoed in his head.

And I-I thought if I told you...

He clutched the shelf, gouging the wood with his claws. "Sunlight take me, I am a fool. It was not the queen who doomed Kinsley." His throat constricted, but he forced his next words out regardless. "It was *me*."

Vex pressed his free hand over his chest. It did naught to relieve the pressure, the pervasive ache, the crushing weight. His fingers flexed, and his claws pricked his skin. "And if not for this curse, would ever I have found her? If not for me dragging her into my damnation, would ever I have had her?"

A gentle, tingling sensation spread across his back—a hint of warmth, phantasmal and familiar. He opened his eyes to find the shadows gone. The wisps' gentle light danced upon the bookshelves, emphasizing their emptiness.

His wings shuddered; he drew them in tight and clenched his jaw. "I am sorry, my friends. When I brought you here, I never intended for it to be forever. I sought not to entrap but protect."

"Without the magus, these ones would have been extinguished long ago," said Flare. "These ones yet burn only because of you."

"And these ones are content here," added Shade. "In this forest, with the magus and Kinsley, these ones are home."

The two wisps drifted to Vex's front. Compared to the queen's light, theirs was dim, weak, underwhelming. But to Vex, it had always been purer, more beautiful. It had always been warmer and more welcoming. It had always been more real.

"Would that these ones could wander afar, could soar amidst clouds and stars with you," Shade continued, their ghostfire core burning darker. "Yet these ones want for naught."

A tendril of Flare's ghostfire brushed Vex's knuckles. "These ones have a place. A purpose. And friends. These ones are not alone, adrift in the night."

Shade dipped their head toward Vex. "Nor are you, magus."

"I…" A broken chuckle escaped Vex. He stared at the wisps, searching their flames. How could beings so small, seeming so simple, hold such depth and complexity in their hearts? "I fear I've been selfish. I've overlooked much. All these years, I've never asked your thoughts regarding our situation, never addressed your feelings. I simply assumed my anger was yours."

Vex tugged his claws free of the wood and lifted his hands, cupping them beneath the wisps. Their ghostfire settled lightly on his palm.

"All this while, I've isolated myself in my anguish," he said, stroking the edge of Shade's flame with a thumb. "But never have I truly been alone. You three have remained steadfast through my dark moods, my rage, my despair. You have offered guidance and compassion even when I was undeserving of it."

He touched his fingers to Flare, coaxing a brighter light from the little wisp. "And I do not believe I've ever thanked you. Not properly."

"These ones have no need for thanks," Flare replied.

"Mayhap not, but you deserve my eternal gratitude all the same. Without you three, I'd have lost myself to this curse long ago. Thank you. And I will be sure to say the same to Echo when next I see them."

Flare curled their arms around Vex's fingers. "These ones want only for you to know happiness, magus."

Shade nuzzled Vex's thumb. "And Kinsley has awoken within you a joy like these ones have not witnessed. The sight sparks warmth within. That is something the queen cannot steal away."

Tension bled from Vex's muscles, and the storm inside him abated. The answer to his rage, his bitterness, his grief, had been in front of him since the moment he'd first seen Kinsley in her carriage and something inside him had growled, *Mine.*

Kinsley could not make it all go away, could not make him forget, but she made it bearable. She made healing seem possible. She made *living* seem possible.

Vex hummed softly. "Had more folk recognized the wisdom of wisps, the world might well have been very different."

"If the magus's world is different, that is enough for these ones," said Flare with a deep bow.

Smiling, Vex stepped back. His awareness expanded, and with clear eyes, he beheld the chaos he'd wrought. Seeing books scattered across the floor, their pages bent and torn, caused a pang of remorse in his chest, but it was the shelves that caught his attention. It was the shelves that made his heart sink into his stomach.

Without books, the shelves were desolate, robbed of their purpose. Only sorrow and loss lingered in the empty space—a jarring reminder of the richness and wonder they'd previously held.

It was an unsettling sight. It was...wrong.

It was a glimpse of life without Kinsley.

Vex swept his gaze across the chamber. He'd built this place. He'd shaped it with his hands and his magic over years, over decades, had crafted it from rubble and ruin. He'd always thought of it as his home, but only recently had it begun to feel like one.

He combed his fingers through his hair, drawing long, loose

strands back from his face. The grazing of his claws across his scalp grounded him further.

Kinsley was the piece that had always been missing. She was the key—not to unlocking his curse, but his heart. She was the final word of a spell he'd unknowingly been chanting for most of his life.

"I've no need for freedom," he said, "no need for release from this curse." He turned about, and the cottage sprawled in his mind's eye, each part crafted with care and thoughtfulness. But it was the wisps he settled his gaze upon, wishing Echo were present. "Everything I require is here."

And everything he desired was just downstairs, in his bedchamber.

Kinsley was his mate. Her heartbeat was the sensual rhythm of his yearning. Her laughter was the song of his soul. Her passion was the wind that filled his wings, carrying him high into the night sky, where earthly matters held no importance.

This place, which Kinsley looked upon with such wonder, could be *their* home. It was not an eternity of damnation stretching before them, but of life. A shared life.

A *happy* life.

And would not their togetherness, their contentment, be the ultimate refutation of the queen's victory? Despite all the suffering she had inflicted, all the power she'd mercilessly wielded, Vex had found his mate.

Here within a cursed realm, he'd found joy, wholeness, and purpose. What the queen had intended as unending punishment had become something wholly unforeseen, something pure. It had become a paradise for Vex and his mate.

A paradise he'd disrupted in his fury.

Frowning, Vex bent down and picked up a fallen book. Its pages were creased, its threading had loosened, and the cover was marred by gouges from his claws. He turned his head to glance back at the bare shelves.

"Only empty if I make it so," he whispered through the tightness in his chest.

"What do you mean, magus?" Flare inquired.

"Merely thinking aloud." Drawing upon his magic, Vex ran a hand across the book. His palm tingled as the pages straightened and the creases disappeared, as the binding resecured itself, as the marks on the cover healed. When it was done, he gently closed the book, carried it to the shelf, and set it in its place.

He collected another tome and repeated the process, and another after that. One by one, he picked up the books, repaired the damage he'd done, and returned them to the shelves. A bit of the weight lifted off Vex's shoulders with each piece put back in place. A bit of the pressure in his chest eased. Little by little, the library recovered.

Shade and Flare followed him, casting their soft light on everything he touched. Though they could not aid him physically, their presence was enough. Vex could only wish that he had reached that understanding many years before.

When the last book was finally restored and returned, Vex again surveyed the library. Everything looked just as it had before he'd torn it apart, but nothing felt the same. It felt...warmer. Fuller. Somehow, everything fit together better now, as though all the books—the same books that had always been here—held more promise, more wonder.

A snare closed around his heart and cinched tight, pulling on it. His legs itched with the need to move, and the muscles of his back ached with a yearning to fly to the one place he needed to be more than anywhere else at that moment—at his mate's side.

"It is well past time I attend Kinsley," he said, striding toward the door. Each step came quicker than the last, until he was quite nearly sprinting for the exit.

Fire swept through his veins, sweet and sweltering, only hastening him further.

He needed to claim Kinsley so she would know that he was hers, whether free or bound by the curse.

But first...I must right the wrong I have done her.

CHAPTER THIRTY

Kinsley sat in the dining room with her chin propped on her palm as she twirled the bottom of the wine bottle around and around atop the table. Her head was light and fuzzy, her skin warm and tingly, and her sex still pulsed with echoes of pleasure.

But nothing could dull the pain in her chest, in her heart. Nothing could distract her from it.

So, she'd turned to raiding the cellar, where Vex stored his wine. Perhaps the alcohol could spare her by providing the oblivion she so desperately sought.

Kinsley brought the bottle to her lips and tipped it back, taking another long drink of the sweet wine. When she lowered it, she hiccupped.

"I ruined everything, didn't I?"

Echo drifted closer, casting their ethereal blue glow on Kinsley as they brushed a tendril of ghostfire over her arm. "You ruined nothing."

Kinsley sniffled as her vision blurred with tears. Her eyes were puffy and tired from crying, but as much as she'd wanted to just curl up in bed and sleep away her pain, she couldn't. Every time she'd closed her eyes, she'd been haunted by the look that had been on Vex's face, by his anger…

God, his anger.

That had led to her current plan of drinking away her pain.

Except it wasn't working. "He's going to hate me. He's going to cast me aside. What use am I?"

The wisp dimmed, their flame reminiscent of a candle sputtering out. "Do not speak so, Kinsley. The magus does not hate you. He cannot hate you."

"But he will. I'm worthless to him now." Kinsley scrubbed a hand over her cheek to wipe away her fallen tears.

For so long, she'd felt...*defective*. Oh, how she hated that word. But she'd been unable to see herself any other way after Liam had left her.

She'd given everything she could to Liam, but she'd been unable to give him the family he wanted.

He'd made her feel incomplete. Like less than a full person. And though she'd known deep down it wasn't true, that poison had crept in and festered in Kinsley's heart.

How could it not have, when Liam was supposed to have been the love of her life? He'd been her best friend, her childhood sweetheart, her husband, the one person she could trust above all others, who was meant to make her feel cherished, safe, important.

Liam had claimed he loved her even as he'd broken her heart. Claimed he loved her while he watched her crumble to pieces, while he walked away to a new life.

Liam said he loved me, but I just wasn't enough for him.

Why couldn't she have been enough?

And it was happening all over again with Vex. She'd allowed her heart to get involved only for it to break again. But this time, it was much, much worse. His freedom relied upon the thing she couldn't give him. Because of her, Vex and the wisps would remain trapped here. They'd remain cursed.

"I've doomed you all," Kinsley said with a sob.

Echo made a soft, sorrowful sound, and rubbed against Kinsley's arm. "No share of the blame is yours. The queen laid her curse upon the magus long before you first drew breath."

Kinsley hiccupped again and took a few more swallows of wine. As she wiped her mouth with the back of her hand, she set the bottle down harder than she'd intended, nearly knocking it over. She hurriedly righted it, holding it down firmly as though it would topple the moment she released it.

"The queen is a bitch." Kinsley tentatively let go of the bottle and wrinkled her nose. "A mega bitch, and I hope she gets cursed with… I don't know, the worst thing ever. An endlessly itchy butthole or something."

The wisp tilted their little head. "Is that the worst fate a mortal might suffer?"

"Probably not, but it still sucks." Groaning, Kinsley covered her eyes before another hiccup escaped her. "Why does it have to be so bright in here?"

"It is not bright. The tree shades this place from the morning sun."

"I know." She sighed before lowering her hand and looking at Echo. "I am worth it, though. I'm done thinking I'm not. I'm tired of feeling lesser. I… I'm not a baby making machine. I'm not defined by what people want from me. I'm a person with my own feelings, my own wants, my own dreams."

Sitting back in her chair, Kinsley grabbed the wine bottle by the neck and took another draft. "I came here to get away from all that. To put it all behind me, start a new life, and…find myself. And Liam…he's a fucking asshole. I refuse to settle for someone who doesn't want me for *me*. I deserve better. I deserve to be loved."

"You deserve *everything*," Vex said.

Kinsley started, clutching the bottle against her chest, and swung her wide-eyed gaze toward his voice.

Vex stood mere feet away with Shade and Flare floating behind him. He was a vision of dark sensuality—long black hair, glowing red eyes, tempting, sculpted lips, claw-tipped fingers, powerful, batlike wings… He wore only a pair of dark trousers, leaving his lean, toned torso bare. Kinsley found herself fighting a wild, insistent urge to lick him.

But then she remembered everything anew. Remembered the silence that had followed her confession, a silence so thick that it had strangled her.

She remembered how he'd left her.

Kinsley scowled. "I didn't invite you to my pity party."

"I've no need for an invitation. This is my home."

She flattened a hand on the table to help herself stand. "So I'll leave."

With a growl, Vex closed the distance between them until he loomed over her. "You shall do no such thing."

Kinsley plopped back down onto her seat with a pout, still hugging the bottle to her chest.

At a glance from Vex, the wisps reluctantly retreated from the room.

"I bade you remain in the bedchamber, yet you left. Now I ask that you remain here so I may speak with you."

"You didn't *bid* me, you yelled at me." She took another drink and blushed when an involuntary hiccup followed. "And since when do I ever listen to you anyway?"

The corner of Vex's lip quirked. "You do not."

"I don't want to talk to you."

His smile faded. Kinsley hated how much it hurt to see that expression disappear.

"You need but hearken to my words," he said.

"Didn't we just establish that I don't listen?"

He glanced at the wine bottle, brow furrowing. "You're drunk."

"I'm not drunk. I'm just a little tipsy. But I plan to get very, very drunk."

Vex sighed, reached out, and grasped the bottle. At his gentle urging, Kinsley relinquished it. When he set the bottle on the table, Kinsley stared at it, unable to look at him as fresh tears flooded her eyes.

"You hurt me," she said, voice small and broken as she placed her hands in her lap.

"I know." He took hold of her chin and turned her face toward his. Regret tempered the heat in his gaze, deepened the crease between his eyebrows, and drew down on his lips. "And I am sorry."

"Sorry." Kinsley tugged her chin away with a bitter laugh as she lowered her gaze to the floor. "Sorry. That's exactly what my ex-husband said. He was sorry that it didn't work out. Sorry that we got divorced. Sorry that he hurt me." She angrily wiped away her tears as they spilled. "He told me over and over that he was sorry, just as often as he told me that he loved me. And neither of those words meant anything. They lost their meaning, and they just became…empty."

"Kinsley…"

"No. You...you don't owe me anything. It was just sex. There's nothing between us, right? Nothing except the pact we made." She clenched the material of her nightgown in her fists. Every word was more painful to utter than the last, but she kept going. "You've made it clear that I'm the one who owes you, and now you know I can't pay the price. You're stuck here. So you'll...you'll just have to wait for the next woman to crash into your woods and hope she can give you the baby you need."

"*No*," he grated.

Kinsley turned her teary eyes to Vex. "What?"

Holding her gaze, he dropped to his knees and spread his wings, curling them around her. His big hands settled over hers. "I want no other. You are all I desire, Kinsley Wynter Delaney."

Kinsley's heart quickened. "I-I don't understand. You're...you're choosing me?"

He squeezed her hands. "Yes. With all my heart and soul."

"But what about the curse? You and the wisps will be trapped here because I can't—" She pressed her lips together and curled them in, biting down.

Because I can't give you the child you need for your freedom.

Vex lifted a hand to her face, caught her chin, and gently pressed his thumb beneath her mouth until she released her lips. "Better a single day here with you than an eternity out there, free to roam without you."

Kinsley's head swam, and the wine's effects blurred the lines between her conflicted emotions. Her lower lip trembled. "Vex, please don't do this to me. Don't lie to me. Don't say sweet words you don't mean. There's nothing I can give you."

"You can give me everything I desire. *You.*" He soothed her lip with tender strokes of his thumb. "Love me, fear me, command me, obey me. I will be your master and your slave, your worshipper, your equal. I will be your everything, just as you will be mine."

Kinsley wanted to believe his words, wanted them to be true with all of her being. She searched his eyes for deception, for the illusion, but instead found sincerity, yearning, and something much vaster and deeper. Something that made her heart thump ever faster and harder even as it wrapped her in delicious heat.

What would he have to gain by lying?

Nothing.

Vex moved his hand to cradle the back of her neck, his firm but gentle hold keeping her face from turning away. "Something urged me into the woods that night before the wisps ever told me what they'd found. That pull strengthened as I approached the strange carriage, and the moment my gaze fell upon the mortal within, I knew. I knew she was mine. The female who sat there terrified, dying, desperate, whose light would be extinguished before ever I had a chance to know her, belonged to me.

"You agreed to be bound to me. To be my mate. Yet you were my mate before that moment, and you will be forever after." His expression darkened, and shadows coalesced in his eyes. "And I'd have done everything in my power to save you, even had you refused."

Kinsley's eyes flared. "What?"

"You are my mate, Kinsley. My fated one."

She tried to shake her head in denial, tried to pull away, but his hold remained secure. "Y-You're talking about...about soulmates. That isn't—"

Real.

But why wouldn't it be real when there was proof of magic all around her? She was living in another realm, where will-o'-the-wisps, goblins, and fae existed, where illusions bent reality, where magical fog acted as an impassable barrier. If all that was real—if Vex was real—why couldn't soulmates be real too?

Because your heart's been broken once, and you're terrified of it happening again.

Kinsley blinked back more tears. "The way you treated me... You were cruel. You almost raped me, Vex!"

His lips peeled back not in anger but in anguish, and he pressed his forehead against hers, reducing her world to his glowing gaze. "Neither words nor actions will erase the suffering I have inflicted. Of all the regrets I must carry into eternity, it is the heaviest. I was desperate, at war with my instinct to claim you and my yearning for freedom. All the anger I've held for so long, all the pain and grief, it all surged to the surface because you were the key, the thing she never wanted me to obtain.

"Yet none of that justifies my behavior. None of it excuses what

I have done to you. You are my *mate*. You are Kinsley Wynter Delaney, you are my moonlight. Naught else matters. And I will spend our eternity atoning for the wrongs I have done you."

His voice was ragged and raw, so full of emotion. It pierced to Kinsley's soul. She pressed a hand to his chest, over his strong, pounding heart. "I forgive you, Vex."

"I..." Vex searched her gaze. "I remain undeserving of your forgiveness, yet I accept it with more gratitude than I can express. Thank you." He lingered there briefly, as though lost in her eyes, before finally lifting his head. "There is something more you must know. Something I should've told you long ago."

Kinsley's brow furrowed. "What is it?"

"You are not mortal, Kinsley. Not since the night I found you."

Her heart had never thumped as loudly as it did in the quiet that followed his words.

Not mortal? Not...mortal.

Whether addled by the wine or not, her mind simply couldn't process what he'd said. She didn't feel any different...did she?

"I don't understand," she said. "I'm human. How could I not be mortal?"

The muscles of his jaw bulged, and he released a heavy exhalation through his nose. "I had but one means of saving you. But one means of delivering you from the threshold of death." He released his hold on her neck and moved his hand to hers, pressing it more firmly over his chest. "I drew upon my lifeforce, my soul, my immortality, and wove it into yours. We are bound. So long as my heart beats, so shall yours."

Kinsley curled her fingertips against him, uncertain of what to say, to do, to think.

She was immortal. She wouldn't grow old, wouldn't die. She would live on as all the people she loved faded away. Her family, her friends. Everyone she'd ever known.

And she was trapped here. She'd never see her loved ones again, would never get to say goodbye.

She choked on a sob as more tears flooded her eyes.

You would have died anyway, Kinsley. Death was the only alternative.

She knew that. She *knew*. Vex had done what was necessary to save her, and she was grateful for that, so grateful. But that didn't lessen the impact of this revelation.

Vex brushed away her tears as they flowed. "Would that I could take away your pain."

Kinsley sniffled and drew in a shuddering breath. "I...I think I need to feel this. To mourn. I won't be able to see my friends and family again, won't be able to talk to them, and...and I think it's better this way. They probably already believe I'm dead."

She lifted her other hand and swept loose strands of hair from his face, hooking them behind his ear. "I left home to begin a new life. I can do that here. With you." Her brow creased. "But are you sure I'm what you want? I...I can't grant you freedom from this place."

"I choose you, my moonlight. So long as I have you, I shall never need for aught else." He tightened his grip on her hand. "Do you accept me?"

I choose you, my moonlight.

Those words played over and over in her head. The fear, doubt, and rejection she'd felt for so long burned away like fog in the morning sun, and her soul soared.

Kinsley smiled. "I do."

She'd spoken those simple words at her wedding, and they'd been so easy at the time, so natural. It was different now. They were heavier, and more impactful, meaningful, and heartfelt than she ever could've imagined. She understood that those two little words encompassed *everything*. Good and bad, joy and sorrow, life and death.

She hadn't known it back then, but those words had never truly been meant for Liam. They'd always been meant for Vex. And somehow fate had brought her here, to him. This was where she was meant to be, this was what felt right.

This was where she felt at home.

"Ah, Kinsley," Vex growled. "My mate."

He closed the distance between them and captured her mouth with his. She closed her eyes and leaned into the kiss, succumbing to him. There was nothing to hold back. She wanted him, wanted this.

Vex's scent enveloped her with oakmoss and amber, with earth and spice, with everything that was wholly him. His lips were hot, spreading tantalizing heat through her body. His kiss—his passion, his desire, his choice—consumed her, and she welcomed it.

She craved more of it.

But he ended the kiss far too soon.

Vex drew back, cupping Kinsley's jaw to prevent her from following. She opened her eyes. His blazing crimson gaze locked with hers, his desire plainly written within its depths.

"Join with me tonight," he said, voice low and gravelly. "Join with me in the way of my people, beneath the moon and stars. Join with me in the mating hunt."

Kinsley's brows rose. "Mating hunt?"

Vex chuckled and stroked her cheek with his thumb. "It is not the sort of hunt that must've come to mind. It is an ancient rite my people have performed since time immemorial. My clan held their ceremonial hunts during the equinox each spring and autumn. The females would gather, and those ready to seal their mating bonds were adorned with paints of their chosen color.

"When the moon reached its zenith, the females would run into the forest, and the males would give chase. It is a...primal affair. Instincts reign, and passion heats the night. I did not understand when I was young. I knew only disappointment, for I could not join the game. But many years later, I watched from my tower as the clans who sheltered within my realm held their hunts."

His fingers flexed, and his claws grazed her skin, making it tingle. "And I yearned to one day partake with my own mate."

Her heart ached for him. She'd witnessed how he'd held himself apart from everything. She'd seen his loneliness, his isolation, his longing. And she understood now. After what had happened to his clan, he'd secluded himself for protection. He hadn't allowed anyone close besides the wisps because his fear of loss was too great.

"Should a male and female return before the morning light with her paint smeared upon their bodies, all the clan knew they were mated and bonded forever," he continued. "And I would perform this rite with you. Tonight."

"But it's not the equinox."

"I care not. This is our realm. We dictate its customs."

Something wicked coiled low in her belly at the thought of participating in this tradition with him, and she thrilled at the idea of being hunted down by him.

Yet there was much more to what she felt. It was in the way he'd said *our realm*. He'd infused that phrase with such devotion, such dedication, such adoration. This would be more than sex. It would be the coming together of two lonely, wounded souls, in the way he'd always longed for. With his mate.

With her.

But there was one lingering worry, one thing she could not forget.

"What about the barghest?" she asked. "Are there more of them out there?"

"No. I scoured the forest to be certain." The glow of his eyes intensified into a dangerous, fiery light. "And should any more unwelcome beasts enter our realm, they shall *never* touch you. I vow it."

Kinsley smiled and brushed the tip of her nose against his as she turned her hand to lace their fingers together. "Then let's get freaky in the forest."

Vex laughed and shook his head. "Though that is a curious way to describe what we intend, I will embrace it. But first…" His wings withdrew, tucking neatly against his back, and he turned his head to look at the table. Releasing her, he pushed the wine bottle farther away. "You require *real* sustenance. You'll need all your strength for what is to come. After we eat, I shall prepare you."

"Prepare me?"

He leaned back and raked his gaze down her body with a hunger that made her nipples ache. "We've no clan to aid you, so I shall paint that delicious body of yours."

He gripped her hips and slid her closer until her knees were on either side of him. Kinsley's eyes widened, and she placed her hands on his shoulders.

Vex's lips curled into a sinful grin. "Let every stroke, no matter how tiny, remind you, Kinsley… You are mine for the taking."

CHAPTER THIRTY-ONE

Vex couldn't stop himself from glancing at the bathing chamber door. Kinsley was on the other side of it, bathing and preparing for the hunt. Preparing for him. She would emerge at any moment and present herself to him.

His limbs itched with restlessness, and his heart pounded. He kept the maddening heat from flooding his veins only through force of will, and that willpower would only last so long. All that passion, anticipation, and desire had to be saved. He could let it build and build, but he could not release it until the hunt.

He couldn't release it until he'd captured his prey. Until he was claiming his mate in full.

He turned his attention to the small table he'd moved to the foot of the bed. It bore deceptively mundane items—a jar of freshly mixed silver paint, a paintbrush, and a cloth. Simple tools with which to enact the most important rite of his life.

But when he lifted his gaze to survey the rest of the bedchamber, he frowned. Conducting this ceremony with Kinsley was right. He harbored no doubts; he'd never been more certain of aught in all his existence. Honoring his people, who he'd lost so long ago, and uniting with his mate...it would be a profound occasion. Yet initiating it here seemed almost too ordinary.

"Does something trouble you, magus?" asked Echo, who hovered nearby along with Flare and Shade.

Vex grunted, still studying the chamber. "It is not right."

"What is not right?"

"This place," Vex muttered. "The...ambience."

"This is the bedchamber you now share with Kinsley," Shade said.

"Yes, and yet it needs..." Vex waved his hand, searching for the proper words but failing to find them.

Kinsley would be ready soon, but he couldn't quite determine what was missing. Something small, something easy...something he was overlooking, overthinking.

"This one does not understand." Flare drifted over the bed and threw their little arms to the sides. "Does not the hunt occur in the woods? Of what matter is the state of this chamber?"

The wisp's light danced across the surface of the bed. Despite its softness and subtlety, it altered the appearance of the bed completely.

"Just so!" Vex declared. "Your brilliance has solved my dilemma."

Flare tilted their head. "This one still does not understand."

Vex willed his magic outward to shape his vision. Shadow enwrapped the glowing crystals, allowing only pinpricks of light to shine through like distant stars in the dark of night. At the same time, an arcane spark ignited in the hearth. With the usual soft blue glow so muted, the flames cast their warm orange radiance across the chamber, deepening the shadows and making them dance and flicker.

Though darkness had never been a hindrance to Vex, he'd always appreciated firelight. It reminded him of his youth, of his clan, of the fires they'd kept in their huts and the way such light could transform a space into something more inviting, more intimate.

Fire could be destructive, ravenous, and deadly, but he refused to see the flames that had erased his clan when he looked upon at the fireplace. If Kinsley, through her struggles and pain, had clung to wonder and positivity, he could remember the good rather than the bad. The comforting rather than the devastating.

This fire was perfect for tonight. A small way to remember his people, to remember the life he'd once had.

But this night was not merely about honoring the past. No, above all, it was about embracing the future.

His eyes fell upon the window over the bed. With the sun having set and the tree's lush boughs blocking out the sky, the world beyond the glass was black as pitch. The carved tree adorning the window was dark too, with only its more prominent ridges highlighted by the fire.

Vex's magic wove across the window. A faint, grayish glow illuminated the panes, growing steadily brighter and purer until it was a beam of silver light spilling through.

Moonlight.

The shaft of illumination stretched across the bed, undiluted by the firelight. The carved tree now stood in clear silhouette—Vex's shelter, his home, strengthened and defined by moonlight.

By his mate.

The wisps made soft, awed sighs like wind blowing through long grass.

"Now this one understands," whispered Flare.

Vex brushed his fingertips over the bedding, watching the moonlight play across his black skin. Here he would mark his mate. Here he would bridge past and present, opening the path to a future he'd never imagined but wanted more than anything.

"Again, I must thank you three for all you've done," he said, dipping his head solemnly, "but what remains of this night is for myself and my mate."

The wisps offered bows, their ghostfire bright.

"Of course, magus," said Echo. "These ones would not dare to intrude."

"May moonlight smile upon you," Shade intoned.

"And fortune bless your hunt," added Flare.

The wisps departed, speaking quietly amongst themselves.

Fire kindled low in Vex's belly once they were gone. The moment was nigh. His union, his binding, his moonlight...

His heart marked the passing time, pounding so rapidly that it stretched each second into an agonizing eternity. To keep his fingers from twitching, he smoothed a crease in the bedding and tugged it tighter over the mattress.

"All must be—"

The bathing chamber door opened; he spun about and looked upon his mate.

Kinsley stood in the doorframe with her honey brown hair cascading over her shoulders, clad in a light green gossamer robe that concealed naught of her lush body.

"—perfect," he rasped.

Holding the robe closed just beneath her breasts, Kinsley smiled and stepped toward him. The fabric parted and flowed around her legs, and the firelight mingled with the moonlight to lend unique vibrancy to her pale skin.

The fire in his belly spread, blazing outward to set his body alight. His cock stirred beneath his trousers, thrumming with the ache she'd awoken in him. It was all he could do not to stalk across the chamber and take her right then.

"This is beautiful," she said as she glanced around the room.

"You outshine it all, my moonlight." Vex beckoned her closer. "Come. I am eager to see the light caress you."

Her eyes returned to Vex and brightened with a mischievous gleam. Stopping in front of him, she lifted her hands and lightly ran her fingertips down his bare chest. "I would rather your hands caress me."

Vex shuddered at the sensation—and at the implication and invitation in her words. His back itched with the urge to release his wings, and he didn't fight it. They formed already spread, their muscles taut, and cast large, shifting shadows across the floor.

Kinsley's hands dipped lower.

He growled and caught her wrists, halting her teasing fingers before they could reach the lacing of his pants. "Not yet, Kinsley. A hunt requires patience. Disrobe."

"Is that an order?"

"*Now.*"

She chuckled and took a step back. He released her wrists, and she moved her hands to the front of her garment. "I love it when you're bossy."

Taking hold of the lapels, Kinsley parted the robe and let it fall from her shoulders. The fabric whispered down her body to pool at her feet. Vex groaned. All was revealed to him—her beautiful,

HIS DARKEST DESIRE

supple skin, her glorious curves, and the subtle silvery marks upon her belly.

Her pink nipples hardened, tempting him to take her breasts into his hands, to caress them, worship them.

Soon. Soon, her body would be his for taking. But not yet.

"Sit," he said, voice low and husky, as he nodded toward the bed.

Keeping her eyes locked with his, Kinsley retreated a couple more steps and sat on the bed. She scooted back just enough for her legs to hang over the edge before reclining, propping herself up with her arms behind her. Smiling, she parted her knees—and her cunt.

The moonlight shone upon the slick coating her inner thighs and glistening upon the small patch of short curls above her sex. He stared at the pink flesh of her cunt, his restricted cock twitching uncomfortably as seed seeped from its tip.

A growl reverberated in Vex's chest as he planted his hands to either side of her thighs and leaned over her. The heady scent of her arousal filled his nose. "By silver and starlight, female, you tempt me."

Kinsley shifted a leg between them, pressed her toes to his belly, and gently urged him back. "Patience Vex, remember?" She twirled a finger around one of her nipples as she ran her gaze down his body, settling it on his groin. "Shouldn't you remove those? It'd only be fair."

He hissed through bared teeth. Unbearable pressure pulsed within him, already threatening to burst. "That would risk ending the hunt before ever it began."

Her toes slid farther down to rub along the length of his shaft. "What better way of practicing restraint?"

A tremor coursed through him, and his cock throbbed. His discomfort had escalated to pain, and there was only one way to relieve it.

It would've been so easy to give in. So easy to succumb to his appetite.

Vex shoved away from the bed, breaking that maddening contact with Kinsley. "My little seductress." He drew in a deep breath, seeking clarity, strength, resolve. But his need only deepened, growing ever vaster as he beheld his mate with her legs spread before him. "When you are pinned beneath me tonight, I shall make you beg for every flicker of pleasure I lavish upon you."

His eyes fell to her sex, and hunger yawned within him, immense and insatiable. But he would not be outplayed by his alluring mate, not tonight. He lifted a hand, and with a casual flick of his wrist, set his magic to work. His pants dissipated thread by thread, the arcane energy casting a faint green glow upon Kinsley.

The touch of cool air against his cock nearly made him shiver, but he held his composure.

Kinsley's eyes dipped. The heat that flared within them lured him, inviting him to bury himself in her hot cunt.

Instead, Vex walked to the desk, grabbed the chair, and carried it back to the bed, positioning it in front of his mate. He sat down and settled his palms upon her thighs.

"I gaze upon you now and hesitate." He smoothed his hands down, hooking them behind her knees. He guided her legs to lie across his with her knees at his sides. "What could my markings do but mar your perfection?"

She looked away from him, but not before he caught the uncertainty in her eyes. "I'm not perfect, Vex."

He hooked a finger beneath her chin, coaxing her gaze back to him. "You say that only because you cannot see yourself through my eyes, my moonlight. You are perfect to me. For me. Naught else matters."

With tears glistening in her eyes, Kinsley smiled. "I see it. When you look at me, I see it."

"Good." He brushed his thumb beneath her lip. "Never forget it." He released her chin, turned to the small table, and removed the lid from the paint jar. "Now, we've a matter to attend, and I'll accept no further delay."

Kinsley chuckled as she glanced down at his erection, which stood tall between them. "Are you sure you have the patience?"

Vex gave her a droll look. "I've endured an eternity awaiting this moment. A few more heartbeats shall not be my undoing."

Or perhaps they shall.

He could feel her gaze like a physical thing, weighty and fiery. It was the promise of a touch, of the glide of flesh against flesh, of pleasure unimaginable. He could still recall the feeling of her tongue, the warmth of her mouth. By the look in her eyes, she was just as hungry for him. His cock twitched as more seed beaded on its tip.

Kinsley caught her lip between her teeth and smirked.

"Hence mates were separated for this part of the rite," Vex growled, snatching up the brush. He dipped it in the paint. "The hunt would never have occurred otherwise."

He leaned forward, only to start and curse inwardly when the head of his cock brushed his stomach. Kinsley laughed. Vex glared at her, but the expression quickly gave way to a smirk of his own.

Sliding his free hand to her back, he drew her slightly more upright and set the paintbrush to the skin of her breast. His smirk widened when her breath caught, and she shivered. With light, confident strokes, he painted his marks on her—swirling ivy, vines, and thorns. Her body provided all the inspiration he needed, and instinct guided his hand.

The flowing patterns mimicked her collarbone, dipping down at the center into the valley between her breasts. He trailed the paintbrush around her breasts, drawing close to her nipples but never touching them. The whisper-light touch roused her nipples to bud. He was not sure how he resisted the urge to take them between his fingers, to nip them with his teeth, to taste them with his tongue, but somehow, he restrained himself and continued.

Vex painted intricate designs on her belly, which quivered with his touch. As the brush trailed steadily lower, caressing her, he glanced up at her face. Her eyes were half-lidded and molten with lust, and her lips were parted with her soft, heavy breaths. Heat radiated from her core, and his cock pulsed in response.

He shifted his hand to her hip and slid his chair back to bend down as he painted lower still. The sweet scent of her arousal filled his senses when he reached her supple thighs. Her cunt was right before him, already dripping, desperate to have him.

Clenching his jaw, he added to the patterns, drawing them toward her inner thigh—toward the source of all that heat, of that tantalizing fragrance. Toward that heady beacon of desire. Kinsley's body trembled, and his hand flexed on her hip, pressing his claws into her skin.

Need roared in his mind, in his soul, and instinct raged within him. He needed to claim her, dominate her. Conquer her. Have her in all ways, *now*.

He inhaled deeply, meaning to steady himself, but all he could smell was her. All he could feel, all he could see, all he could want was her.

Vex lifted the paintbrush from her skin and planted his hands to either side of Kinsley, curling his claws into the bedding to keep himself from grabbing her. He bowed his head and gritted his teeth. His hair fell, cascading over her legs.

"You must go," he growled.

She lightly touched his hair. "Vex?"

"Go. Run. Hide." He lifted his face and met her gaze. "I will find you, my moonlight. I will catch you. And when I do, I will fuck you with a savagery that will unmake you. You will beg me to put you back together. To give you more."

With wide eyes, Kinsley withdrew her legs and climbed off the bed. Vex remained in place, listening to her quiet footfalls as she hurried away. Her scent lingered. He drew it in, his breath growing more ragged and his heart beating faster and faster as instinct roared within him.

Chase her.

Catch her.

Claim her.

The illusory moonlight flickered, and the glow of the crystals intensified as his control over his magic faltered. He squeezed the bedding in his fists. Every muscle was tense, stiff, burning, and everything in him was being pulled toward Kinsley.

Find her.

Rut her.

The artificial moonlight vanished, leaving only darkness outside the window.

No more waiting.

Vex thrust himself up, nearly tearing the blanket off the bed, and darted for the door.

She is mine tonight and every night hereafter.

Mine for eternity.

CHAPTER THIRTY-TWO

Kinsley's heart raced, urging her feet to match its pace as she ran through the woods. She'd hiked many trails in her life, had explored many forests and camped in the wilderness more times than she could count, but she'd never once exposed herself to the elements like this.

And it was thrilling.

Though night had long since fallen, the woods weren't dark and foreboding. The light of moon and stars streamed through the canopy, and crystals she'd never noticed during the day glowed everywhere, morphing the land into the enchanted forest it had felt like from the beginning.

Kinsley slowed to a stop. Her chest rose and fell with her ragged breaths as she studied her surroundings. She didn't know where she was, hadn't even bothered to pay attention. There'd been no need. No matter where she was, Vex would find her. And when he did...

She squeezed her thighs together as her core pulsed in arousal. Her pussy was already swollen and slick with need, and her nipples ached. It'd been torture sitting there as he'd painted her. The titillating strokes of the brush, the firm grip of his fingers, his teasing breath, his body heat, the tickle of his hair; it'd been maddening. All while he was positioned between her legs, his cock so hard it wept cum.

Her only comfort had come from the knowledge that he was just as tortured as her, and that the wait would be worth it in the end. More than worth it.

Combing her fingers through her hair, Kinsley tilted her head and listened for the sound of his approach.

She was greeted by the forest's night song—the gentle chirruping of insects, the soft rustling of the wind through the foliage, the erratic pattering of twigs and leaves falling to the ground. But there was something else there, something felt rather than heard. A hum, faint and indistinct but no less real. A sense of...magic. Magic all around, in everything, everywhere. Magic to which she was connected. To which she'd always been connected, just like she'd imagined as a child.

Then a new sound joined the chorus, muted and yet impossible to ignore. The heavy flap of wings in the night sky.

Kinsley snapped her face in that direction. The small hairs on her arms and neck stood on end, and a shiver coursed up her spine.

She darted forward, her feet falling upon patches of fallen leaves, soft moss, and smooth stones. Anticipation thrummed through her. There was a hint of fear mixed with her lust, the fear of prey being hunted. It was primal, instinctual, and it only heightened her excitement.

Another beat of wings from somewhere above, just before a shadow crossed through the beams of moonlight ahead.

Kinsley's eyes widened, and she sprinted to the right, slipping between the trees. But when that shadow crossed her path again, she skidded to a halt. Something crashed through the canopy a few dozen feet in front of her.

A dark form landed on the forest floor.

Breath catching in her throat and heart nearly pounding out of her chest, Kinsley sank low and retraced her steps as quickly and quietly as she could.

"You cannot hide," Vex called from behind her, his voice echoing through the forest.

She ducked behind a boulder, willing her breathing to ease and her heart to slow so she could listen. Heavy footsteps drew near to her, disturbing the vegetation, and she knew she was caught, knew it was over.

But those footfalls darted past on the other side of the boulder, moving rapidly away from her.

When they'd fallen silent, she lifted her head, raking her gaze across the area. She spied no movement but that of the gently swaying boughs overhead. There was no sign of Vex. Releasing a slow, measured exhalation, she crept forward.

Vex's voice came now from the direction in which he'd run. "You are mine, Kinsley. I feel you here. *Smell* you."

Bracing a hand against a trunk, she peered around it. The ancient trees and mossy rocks were motionless in the ethereal night glow. She could make out every detail, tinted blue by the preternatural light, but she could not discern Vex's shape amidst all of it.

Yet he'd gone in that direction. Where was he?

Pushing herself away from the tree, she turned. Her gaze met a pair of glowing crimson eyes.

Kinsley's breath hitched, and her sex clenched.

Vex stood before her, bathed in silvery moonlight that made his ear cuffs glint and his hair shimmer.

Barely suppressing a grin, she tensed, meaning to run.

His wings swept downward, propelling him with an impossible burst of speed. Before she could move an inch, he'd caught her wrists, raised them over her head, and pressed her against the tree. The bark was surprisingly smooth and warm on her back, contrasting his rough, fiery hold.

"*Mine*," he growled, leaning over her. Strands of his long hair fell to tickle her shoulders and chest.

She stared up at his face, transfixed, paralyzed, aroused.

Vex dipped his head and kissed her neck. Eyes closing, Kinsley tilted her head to grant him more access, gasping when he nipped her with his fangs. Desire shot through her, flooding her core with heat.

His lips were hungry, hot, desperate, and his hold on her wrists tightened. Though he did not press his body to hers, the head of his cock brushed her belly.

She arched against him. Her body trembled with need, ached to be touched. She craved his hands on her, his mouth, craved his cock. She craved all of him. She was so aroused that her slick was dripping down her inner thighs.

His mouth vibrated against her skin as he groaned. "Mmm, your scent."

Kinsley turned her face toward him and licked his ear. "Vex, I need you."

He glided his palms down her arms and sides, sending tingles across her skin, while his lips trailed lower, following her collarbone down to her breasts. He captured one of her nipples between his lips and sucked.

She moaned and dropped her hands to his head, slipping her fingers into his hair. "Vex..."

Every flick of that split tongue, every pull of his mouth, sent a jolt of pure pleasure straight to her clit. She clenched his hair and whimpered, forcing her eyes open to look down at him. He stared up at her with a predatory, possessive gleam in his eyes that only aroused her further.

He released her nipple and brushed his mouth over her breast. Silver paint dusted his lips as he moved them to her other breast, giving that nipple the same attention as the first. Kinsley squirmed, but he held her securely against the tree, exactly where he wanted her.

Kinsley's lips parted with her panting breaths. Her clit twitched, eager, and her skin hummed, hyperaware of every sensation. She'd never orgasmed just from someone sucking on her nipples before, but she was so, so close.

With a final hard pull and the tantalizing scrape of a fang, he released her nipple. She leaned forward and pulled him close again, but Vex only continued the downward trail of kisses. His mouth smeared the paint on her belly, each brush of it making her quiver with need.

A breathless plea escaped her. She didn't know what it was —*please* or *more*—but it didn't matter. He continued his deliberate descent with his blazing eyes fixed upon her. His hands slid down to her hips, and finally his lips whispered across her pubic hair.

Vex drew in a deep breath. He let it out in a growl that teased her sex and made her shudder. Grasping her leg, he threw it over his shoulder and closed his mouth over her pussy.

Kinsley tightened her grip on his hair. "Oh fuck!"

A single rolling caress of his tongue over her clit was all it took for Kinsley to combust. Pleasure rushed through her, so intense it bordered on agony. It stole her voice, stole her breath, stole her every thought. Her sex contracted, and Kinsley dug her toes into Vex's back beside the arm of his wing.

That sensation was prolonged when he sucked her clit into his mouth and stroked it with the tips of his tongue.

Squeezing her eyes shut, Kinsley threw her head back, pressing it against the tree, and released a strangled cry.

Wet heat spilled down her leg. With a snarl, Vex released her clit, strengthened his grasp on her, and pulled her closer to his mouth to greedily drink from her cunt. He coaxed everything from her.

Kinsley bit down on her lip to stifle her moans. She savored every swipe of his tongue, every prick of his claws, every rumbling growl as her orgasm shook her. Gradually, the intensity dwindled, and her muscles eased.

Softly panting, Kinsley opened her eyes and looked down at Vex. The black slits of his pupils had expanded, nearly erasing his red irises. The way he stared at her as he continued to leisurely lick her pussy was so primal and erotic.

Vex withdrew his head and ran his tongue across his lips. "I shall forever thirst for your divine nectar."

Blushing, Kinsley smiled and caressed his ear. "You make it sound like I'm some goddess."

"Ah, my moonlight, you are." He lowered his face toward her pussy once more, his eyes not leaving hers. "Eternity is not time enough to worship you." He kissed her clit, sending a jolt of pleasure through Kinsley before he lowered her leg from his shoulder and rose.

He caught her chin and tipped her face up toward his. "Now, on your hands and knees."

That sudden shift from worshipful to dominant was more arousing than Kinsley could ever have dreamed.

Thighs trembling and sex throbbing, Kinsley stepped away from the tree and lowered herself to the ground. The moss, leaves, and grass carpeting the forest floor were soft beneath her. The caress of cool air on her heated skin made her shiver; she felt it strongest of all against her inner thighs and wet, exposed sex.

Swiping her hair to one side, she twisted to look at Vex over her shoulder.

He moved to stand behind her, wings partially spread. Holding her gaze, he ran his hands down his chest and abdomen, smearing silver paint across his green skin. Marking himself. That paint glittered in the forest's ambient glow. More silver shone on his face, contrasting the shadows around his eyes and his blazing red irises.

He was a god in his own right—a dark, wicked, sensual deity, the lord of a realm full of shadow, mystery, and wonder.

Though Vex sank onto his knees, he still towered over her, powerful and commanding. "I claim you, Kinsley." He clamped a hand on her hip and gathered her hair around his other fist just tightly enough to produce an enticing sting on her scalp. The head of his cock pressed against her dripping sex, hot as molten steel.

Tremors of anticipation raced through Kinsley's limbs, and she released a shaky breath.

"Beneath the light of moon and stars," he said, "I claim you. You are *mine*."

He growled that last word, punctuating it with a snap of his hips. His shaft plunged into her hard and deep, instantly filling her, stretching her, assailing her with a wave of withering pleasure and overwhelming pressure. Her arms and legs nearly gave out, and her head would have bowed were it not for his firm hold on her hair.

The sensations he'd produced with his clever tongue and ravenous mouth rekindled rapidly, building to new heights, to new intensity.

It was so much; it was everything. There was room for nothing inside her but Vex. It was delirious pleasure, it was burning, titillating pain. Her body clenched around his cock, her inner walls fluttering, even as he stretched her further. Once again, she couldn't breathe, couldn't speak, couldn't think. Every ridge, every vein, every bit of his cock was known to her, embraced by her, craved by her.

"Now and forever," he said, releasing her hair. With both hands on her hips, he drew his pelvis back, the slide of his shaft leaving delightful fire in its wake even as it offered respite from that pressure.

She whimpered as fresh slick trickled down her thighs.

But Vex cut that respite short. His fingers and claws dug into her hip, and he tugged her back hard as he thrust forward again. Kinsley's breath caught in her throat, her eyes closed, and stars danced behind her eyelids.

He drove into her again and again, allowing her no time to recover, no time to react, dictating every move with strength and confidence. The rhythms of their flesh meeting, of their ragged breaths sawing in and out of their lungs, of her moans and his growls, added to the night's song, reverting the woods to the primordial wildland it must once have been.

She forced her eyes open and looked back at him to see the bestial light in his eyes, to see his bared fangs and the sweat glistening on his dark skin. To silently beg him for *more*.

Vex snarled and banded an arm around Kinsley's waist, clutching her belly as he bent over her. He braced his other hand on the ground. The muscles of his abdomen were flush against her backside, and his dangling hair brushed her back and shoulders. Each tiny point of contact, each little sensation, added to the pleasure.

His wings curved, forming translucent walls around him and Kinsley that were backlit by the moonlight. Vex pressed his cheek to her hair. His breath, hot and heavy, teased her ear.

"My mate," he rasped, pounding into her harder, faster. "My moonlight. Mine."

Kinsley's toes and fingers curled, digging into the soft moss and leaves.

Vex's growl vibrated through her very soul. "To whom do you belong?"

"You," she breathed.

He slammed into her even harder, and her elbows buckled with a blast of ecstasy. But Vex held her up, his hold unwavering, firm, and possessive.

"Sing it to the night," he demanded, shifting his hand up to her breast to pinch her nipple.

"You!" she cried out as pleasure pierced to her core. "I belong to you!"

Rapture overcame her, devoured her, and those inner flames engulfed her. She clutched at his arm and filled the night with breathy moans as her pussy contracted around his cock.

Vex snarled. "And I you."

He thrust deep into her once more and remained there while his shaft thickened, and his claws pricked her skin. She felt his body, already hard as a rock, tense further, and then his seed erupted within her. His heat sharpened the pleasure, and his gravelly, rumbling roar resonated through her, layering a new sensation atop her ecstasy. She bowed her head and gave over to the spasms wracking her body, gave over to him, as she would again and again.

Her mate.

Mine.

Vex ground his cock inside her, seemingly unable to get deep enough as he held her tight. She felt him shudder, felt more of his heat flood her, felt his breath against her back as he hissed. Kinsley smiled through her own pleasure, content with the knowledge that she could undo him this way—the same way he undid her.

They remained like that, consumed by the flames of their passion, consumed by one another, until those fires dwindled to embers.

Embers that could never be extinguished.

"You are my heart, Kinsley," he said, nuzzling her hair. "My soul."

His wings bent toward her protectively, and he shifted his hand to rest his palm over her heart, which beat in time with his steady pulse. "I'd have endured centuries of loneliness just for this single night with you, my moonlight."

Kinsley covered his hand with her own and closed her eyes. Her heart swelled with overwhelming emotion. "You'll never be alone again."

CHAPTER THIRTY-THREE

Vex brushed his nose over Kinsley's wet hair and hummed appreciatively. Despite the strong fragrance of the bath oils, he could smell her unique scent—along with that of their coupling. Those scents stirred his desire, even though he'd taken his mate over and over until they'd both lain exhausted on the soft forest floor beneath the moon's silvery light.

Their current position certainly didn't curb his arousal. They sat in the bath together, Kinsley tucked between Vex's legs with her back against his chest. He was supposed to be tending to his mate, cleaning her and soothing her worn body, yet all he could think about as he ran the washcloth over her breasts was sinking his cock back into her heat.

His erection twitched against her.

Fuck, he'd never have enough of her.

Vex smirked. *Fuck.* He'd learned the word from Kinsley, who had cried it out many times as he'd claimed her. What a versatile, impactful, arousing word.

Kinsley chuckled and turned her face to look up at him. "I can't believe you're still hard after all that."

"My sweet, beautiful mate is bathing with me, her delectable body against mine, skin to skin. I feel her every intake of breath, her every word, her every quiver." He moved the washcloth up along her collarbone, following it to her shoulder. Trails of glittering silver paint ran down her skin to swirl atop the rose-tinted water before slowly dissipating. "You should praise my restraint, Kinsley."

Her smile stretched into a grin. "Aww, you've done such a good job, haven't you?"

Vex arched a brow. "Disregarding the mockery in your tone, yes. I have. Yet I wonder..." He slid the washcloth down, brushing it over her reddened nipple, which stiffened at his touch.

Her breath hitched as she faced forward to watch his progress.

He moved the cloth lower, dipping it under the water and over her belly, toward her sex. He felt her thighs quiver against his, heard the provocative whimper from the back of her throat. "Shall I continue my good behavior?"

Kinsley caught his wrist. Voice thick and airy, she said, "Yes. At least until morning. I don't think my poor body can take any more."

Vex took gentle hold of her chin with his free hand and turned her face back toward his. "I am sorry, my moonlight. I should have been more controlled. Should have been gentler."

Kinsley narrowed her eyes. "Don't you dare vow to be gentler. Tonight was perfect. *You* were perfect."

His fingers flexed, and his chest constricted. "It was perfect because of you. You are beyond anything I could ever have dreamed. Thank you, Kinsley. For being mine...and for accepting me as yours."

Her features softened, and her eyes, looking more violet than blue in this lighting, glimmered with tears. "I should be thanking you for that. For accepting me as I am. Even if it means..."

"Ah, Kinsley..." Vex dipped his head, brushing his lips over hers in a soft kiss. "Now that our secrets have been laid bare, tell me. Tell me what he did to you." He trailed the backs of his fingers down her cheek and along her neck. "Allow me to carry some of your pain."

Her brow creased. "Are you sure you want to hear me talk about my relationship with Liam?"

In truth, Vex had no desire to hear about the human who'd treated Kinsley so foully, who'd hurt her, discarded her. The human who'd wed her. He wanted only one thing regarding Liam—to saturate the earth with the man's blood.

But he sensed that speaking of Liam was important to Kinsley. Sharing her story, her pain, would help her heal, and so Vex would suppress his contempt for her sake.

"If you wish to speak, my moonlight, I shall listen," he said.

"Okay." Kinsley drew in a shuddering breath. "I told you how Liam and I met, and how we wound up together. I said we just… grew apart, but it was more than that. A lot more. We thought we knew each other. How could you not when you've known someone for more than half your life? At the time, I couldn't have imagined anything in the world that would ever tear us apart. I couldn't have imagined a life without him."

Vex's hold on her tightened, and an unbidden growl rumbled in his chest. "You were not meant for him."

Well, he'd tried to hold back that contempt. It'd been foolish to believe he could ever have done so entirely.

Kinsley smiled at Vex and smoothed her hand along his arm beneath the water. "I know that now. I didn't then."

Pressing his cheek to her hair, Vex strengthened his hold on her before releasing a huff and willing his muscles to relax. "I know, my moonlight. But it does naught to ease my loathing of a mortal I've never met. You are mine now."

"I am."

"Please, continue."

She settled her hand atop his, and when Vex released the washcloth, she laced their fingers together. "Liam wanted a family of our own. So did I. And we were so excited when I got pregnant. But… we lost the baby. I was only nine weeks along when I miscarried. We were told that miscarriages happen often in the first trimester, that it was common, but that didn't lessen the loss we felt. It didn't stop me from feeling like it was my fault, like I should've been more careful, like I must've pushed myself too far, too hard.

"We tried again a few months later." She shook her head. "We lost that one at eight weeks."

The sorrow and pain in her voice was raw, as though undiluted by time, and it pierced Vex's chest like a shard of ice. He hated the thought of her carrying another male's child. It slithered through him, cold and fiery, constricting, choking, crushing. But it was nothing compared to her grief. Her guilt.

The past was done, but her pain wasn't, and Vex's heart ached for her. He couldn't claim to know what she'd been through, couldn't claim to understand, but he'd suffered loss of his own. He knew how it felt to have something right before him, so close he could almost touch it, knew how it felt to be awash with hope and excitement only for everything to be snatched away in an instant.

Vex gave her fingers a squeeze and rubbed his cheek against her hair. "My moonlight..."

Kinsley rested her head against him. "I fell into a depression after that, and Liam was just...absent. He was working full-time as a mechanic and studying part-time to get into law school. I was working as a receptionist then, so I was occupied during the day, but at night and on the weekends, I was alone. So, I worked on my scrapbooking and vlogging channel. I couldn't share my hikes with Liam because he was too busy, so I shared them with the world instead.

"And some of those days were hard. I never talked about personal things on social media, so I was always having to put on a smile, but it was hard to pretend that nothing was wrong when all I wanted to do was cry. But I think that was what saved me. It didn't make everything better, but I started to learn that things could get better in time. They *would* get better."

Taking up the washcloth in his free hand, Vex smoothed it over her shoulder and down her arm, wiping away lingering smudges of paint with slow, gentle motions. Though he didn't understand everything of which she'd just spoken, he understood the feelings behind her words. She'd been wounded and had sought fleeting moments of escape that she might heal.

In spirit, it was little different than a young goblin with heavy scars upon his heart and soul constructing a tower in which to seclude himself.

"There was strain in our marriage," she continued, "and a lot of distance. We kept trying to bridge the gap, but it was hard when we rarely saw one another. We waited a year before we tried for a baby again.

"When I found out I was pregnant, I didn't feel joy. I was... anxious. I was scared. I didn't want to lose that one. *Nothing* could happen. So, I was careful with everything I did, with everything I ate, and I followed every instruction the doctor gave me to the letter. I stopped going on hikes. Stopped going anywhere, really. I just...stayed home. And Liam just... He just wasn't involved. It was like he was afraid to hope, afraid to get attached. So I felt even more alone and unsupported.

"It wasn't until I'd entered my second trimester that I was able to breathe a little easier. The fear was still there, and I was still being careful, but I was relieved the baby had made it past fourteen weeks.

"And then I felt a flutter." Something had changed in her voice. There was awe in it, a smile that Vex could not see. "It was the tiniest, strangest, most wonderful thing. I didn't know what it was at first, but when I realized it was the baby moving... I think that was the first time I felt true excitement. It was the moment that I realized it was happening. That a little baby was alive and growing inside me. That it...that it would survive."

Vex's heart squeezed at the sudden catch in her voice.

Kinsley's body shuddered, and a quiet sob escaped her. "But it didn't."

Vex banded his arm around her, capturing her face and cradling it as he held her. "What happened?"

"I don't know. Everything was perfect, but suddenly I felt this horrible cramp, and then there was blood. And I knew. I *knew* I was losing it. I went to the hospital, and I begged them to save it. I couldn't...I couldn't lose another. But there was so much blood... I went into hemorrhagic shock and nearly died."

A void opened within Vex, a vast abyss of silence and stillness. It allowed only one thing to exist—grief.

He could have lost his mate before ever knowing her. Before ever knowing she existed.

He could have lost her, and he would never have known it. He would never have been able to empathize with her, laugh with her, walk with her, would never have shared words or meals with her, and there always would've been an emptiness inside him that he would never have known how to fill.

In all his years, he'd never encountered a sorrow like that in her voice now. He'd never encountered *love* like was in her voice now. Mayhap fae were blessed with eternal life, but humans packed their short lifespans with emotions beyond the comprehension of most fae. Fourteen weeks was nothing to a being like Vex.

But to Kinsley, fourteen weeks had been everything.

Filling his lungs with her fragrance, he tightened his embrace and closed his eyes. He was neither foolish nor arrogant enough to believe anything he could've said would heal her pain. All he could do was exist in that moment, exist for her, and let her take anything she needed from him.

"The doctors told me that any further pregnancies would be a risk to my life," she said quietly. "But I didn't want to try again. I couldn't take the grief and guilt anymore. I ended up getting a tubal ligation to make sure I couldn't get pregnant again. Liam agreed and supported my decision, but he was...unhappy. He wanted kids, and he didn't want to adopt. He wanted his own children."

Kinsley laughed bitterly. "He didn't mean to, but he made me feel so much worse. He made me feel so broken. Our marriage fell apart after that. We didn't feel like husband and wife anymore. Sometimes, it didn't even feel like we were friends. We were like strangers to each other.

"We lived like that for a couple years before Liam asked for a divorce. And even with the way things had been, it hurt so much. I knew it was because he wanted a baby, and I felt like it was selfish of me to deny him the life he'd dreamed of—the family he'd dreamed of. So we went through the divorce proceedings.

"But Liam didn't want to lose me entirely. He wanted to remain in contact, to remain close. I...I thought at the time that I didn't want to lose him either. I thought that despite everything, it was sweet that he still wanted to be there for me, to support me. He'd been my best friend for so long... I didn't know what else to do or say. So we kept in touch. I understand now that he didn't want to keep in touch to help me through it. He wanted to make himself feel better. To alleviate his own guilt.

"He ended up remarrying within a year, and when I saw pictures of him with his new wife and how happy they were, all I could think was why wasn't I enough? Why couldn't he have been happy with me? Why didn't he simply love me for me? And when he announced that they were expecting their first baby...it killed me inside."

Kinsley stroked her thumb against Vex's hand. "And still, I couldn't bring myself to break ties with him. But I knew I needed to get away, to work on myself, to just…be free and start anew. To find my worth. So, I saved as much money as I could and came here. Well, not *here*, but London, where I stayed with my aunt until I could find a place of my own. I finally found a cottage to let in the Scottish Highlands…"

"And here you are," Vex said softly.

Kinsley shifted, releasing his hand and turning in his embrace to face him. Water lapped at the sides of the tub. Her violet-blue eyes were made brighter by the tears she had shed.

"Here I am," she echoed softly. "But I didn't need to move across the world to find my worth. I am worthy, and I always have been. Liam was going through his own struggles, but that doesn't excuse anything. I deserved so much more than him, more than what he made me feel. I'm not broken. I never was. And I'll never let anyone or anything make me think otherwise again."

Vex took her face between his hands and brushed away the tears from her cheeks. "Would that I could take back my words, my actions… I am sorry, Kinsley. Sorry to have made you feel that way. Sorry you've endured so much. But you need never again bear such burdens alone."

She lifted her hand from the water and placed it over his heart. "It hurt when you left after I told you the truth, but I understand. I couldn't imagine being trapped for so long in one place, unable to leave, never seeing another person…" Kinsley searched his eyes. "I still can't believe you're choosing me over your freedom. And really, I wouldn't blame you if you chose otherwise. I don't want you to be trapped here."

"Ah, my moonlight." Vex smoothed her hair back and leaned down, pressing a gentle kiss to her forehead. "My imprisonment has naught to do with you." He kissed her eyelids, her nose, her cheeks, tasting the saltiness of her tears. "And truth be told, I don't feel quite so trapped anymore. Without you, I'd be a husk, a vessel overflowing with bitterness and fury. A beast raging at the bars of its cage."

He tilted her face more toward his and pressed his lips over hers, instilling the kiss with all the warmth and tenderness brimming in his chest. "With you, I am home. I am free in a way I never imagined."

"Vex..." She'd spoken his name in a whisper, in a gentle, pleading cry before she rose and kissed him again. Kinsley slipped her arms around his neck, pressing her soft breasts to his chest.

Vex wrapped his arms around her, pulling her close. Their lips were caressing, tender, and fervent, conveying through touch all the unexpressed emotions and unspoken words roiling inside him and Kinsley. Arousal flared within him, but he ignored it. This kiss was not about lust. It was about comfort. It was about two souls seeking solace in one another. It was about two hearts beating as one.

When Kinsley broke the kiss, she did not pull away; she lay atop him, twirling her fingers in his hair, which hung down past the water line. "Can I ask you a question? And I understand if you don't want to answer."

He trailed his hand slowly up and down her back, grazing her skin with his claws. "There shall be no more secrets between us. Ask, and I will answer."

Her eyes met his. "Why did the fae queen want you to father her child?"

To his surprise, her question did not stir the dread it might have only days before. All he'd suffered remained with him—the pain and anger had not simply vanished—but it was muted now. It was controllable. Manageable.

"I cannot claim to know what thoughts dwelt behind those cold eyes," he said, unable to keep his mouth from sinking into a frown. "Nor would I want to. But she was known to take lovers at a whim. Beauty and power attracted her equally, and she coveted both. She collected consorts the way other monarchs might collect pieces of jewelry. And from such unions, she birthed numerous offspring, unique in beauty and power. Yet they were naught more than experiments to her. Pets. Things to be used, whether for entertainment or war.

"When she learned of me, she was intrigued by my magic. My resistance to her interest only strengthened her curiosity. For one such as her, being denied can sometimes be a novelty. And she was relentless in her pursuit of me. Foolishly, I eventually accepted her invitation to her court, hoping my appearance would appease her curiosity that I might go about my life in peace."

Vex's fingers flexed, briefly disrupting the steady up and down rhythm of his hand along Kinsley's back. "I went as the mysterious, magic-shrouded master of an independent realm. But she saw through my illusions. She saw the lowly goblin who'd defied her, who wielded power beyond his due. She saw an unseelie who stirred deep, burning desire within her. An unseelie she longed to possess.

"She held me in her palace against my will. Used me. And I continued to defy her as best I could. She treated it as a game, delighted to have a toy that would not break like the rest. But her amusement—and her patience—had its limits. The visage of authority and control she displayed to others began to crack around me. She called me a vexation. Irritating but ultimately unimportant."

Kinsley's brow furrowed. "Vex. You told me it was what I did to you, and what I should call you."

Despite everything, he chuckled. "Yes, and you did vex me, little human, by defying me at every turn. And in so doing, you held up a mirror by which I glimpsed what I had become. What I was doing."

"Why would you call yourself that?"

"To spite her. To ensure she would be reminded every time she heard it, every time she spoke it, that regardless of the words she chose, I was the thorn in her side. The one thing she could never master, could never truly own. The one thing she would never fully have."

He ran his claws through Kinsley's hair and traced the line of her spine, delighting in the little shiver he elicited from her. "But you are no vexation, Kinsley. You are my everything."

She smiled, but that smile slipped as sadness filled her eyes. "Why would you continue to use a name you took because of the queen?"

"At first, it was to continue my defiance, despite the curse. It was…hope, in its own twisted way. But over time, it became who I am. Vex is not my rage or bitterness, is not my regret or guilt. Vex is simply…me. The name does not belong to her. It never did. It has always been mine, though I was slow enough to claim it as such."

"But she has your true name," Kinsley said quietly. "While you were healing, I...saw her force you into that deal. I couldn't hear you, but I know you said it."

"Yes," Vex said, voice gravelly. "She took my freedom, my name, my seed. She wanted a child with my looks, my magic, and her blood combined."

He closed his eyes and simply breathed Kinsley in, letting her scent soothe him. "She was not subtle in her cruelty by that point, not with me. She made it clear that the child I sired would be a pet. A thing for her to shape, to control, to display."

Kinsley touched her forehead to his, her grip on his hair tightening, but not pulling. "Vex, I am so sorry."

"I could not allow an innocent babe, *my* child, to be born into slavery, into cruelty. To be birthed by her. I used a tincture to ensure my seed had no potency, a mixture so simple that the lofty fae of her court were unfamiliar with it. That was my only means of defying her until I was able to make my escape."

"But she found you," Kinsley said softly.

"I'd always known she would give chase. But I thought I would've had more time, that I'd exercised appropriate care. I knew she'd turn her fury toward those under my protection. Not for a moment had I believed her threat to be mere bluster. I was weaving a spell to transport my realm and its people out of your world, to shelter them in a plane beyond her reach, when she arrived."

Vex gritted his teeth against the pain, rage, and guilt rising inside him. A growl sounded in his chest, and he clutched Kinsley closer. Her breath hitched, and her body jerked when his claws prickled her skin a little too deeply. He hissed, opened his eyes, and immediately loosened his hold, soothing the hurt he'd caused with gentle strokes of his fingertips.

Kinsley drew back and cupped his jaw. Her eyes, so full of compassion, met his. "It wasn't your fault. *None* of it was your fault. You did everything you could to protect them."

"Everything but fulfil my pact with the queen," he said, the jagged words scraping his throat as they came out.

"A pact you were forced to make. And what would that have accomplished? Had you given in to her, had you allowed her to have your child, they would've been a slave. No, you couldn't have done that. You would have regretted it for the rest of your life. You were a slave to her yourself, and the position she placed you in was vile." Kinsley brushed her thumb over his cheek. "All the blame is hers, Vex, not yours."

"I chose to escape, Kinsley. Knowing full well the consequences, I fled from her, I led her back to my tower. Back to my people."

"But you went back and tried to save them. To bring them all somewhere safe. Because even if you had stayed with her, how long would it have been before she went after those people anyway? How long before she would've started to...to bring them in, to march them in front of you and harm them to get what she wanted out of you?"

He lowered his gaze, as though he could find the answer elsewhere, but Kinsley coaxed his eyes back up by guiding his chin toward her.

"Listen to me, Vex. Hear my words. Their deaths were not your fault."

Their deaths were not your fault.

For hundreds of years, rage and guilt had defined Vex, had consumed him. He'd been left with naught else. And hadn't that been the queen's goal? She could easily have slain him or locked him away in her dungeon for eternity, but she'd chosen this. She'd chosen to keep him alive and alone in this place—his home warped into a prison cell—where the weight of what he'd lost, the weight of his failures, would slowly crush him until the end of time.

Yet the greatest magic of all was before him. Kinsley's words could not erase the past, but they were a balm to his soul. They soothed those old wounds, eased his burden. They uplifted him.

Vex had made mistakes in his dealings with the queen, but her maliciousness, her tyranny, had existed long before she'd ever sought him out. Even had he played every round of her game to perfection, she would've stopped at naught to secure her victory. She would always have won in the end

He lifted a hand and slipped it into Kinsley's hair, cradling her head. "Would that neither of us had been forced to walk roads paved with such hardships to find each other."

She smiled and leaned into his palm. "If we hadn't walked them, we might never have found each other."

"I would again endure all I've suffered and more to ensure you were mine, Kinsley."

"You don't have to endure anything else, Vex. Let go of the past." She smoothed a hand over his shoulder, creating a delightful thrill in the wake of her touch. "We both need to let it go and live for the future. One that we can have together."

Vex grinned and slid his hands to her ass, gripping both cheeks and holding her snugly against him. "Oh, I've fully embraced the future. And I'm never letting you go."

Kinsley laughed and wriggled against his cock, making him groan as pleasure shot through his core.

"Hold on to me for as long as you'd like." She raised her hand, showing him her palm. "But I think we should get out of the tub. We're turning into prunes."

He leaned forward and pressed his lips to her palm. "Few prunes retain their beauty as you have."

Kinsley smirked. "I never would've guessed you were such a romantic when we first met."

"I wasn't."

"Liar," She replied, smirk stretching into a grin as she pushed herself up onto her knees. "Come on. Let's get out of here."

Vex trailed his eyes over her body. Her skin glittered with lingering flecks of paint, and water streamed in rivulets down her chest, dripping from her rosy nipples, tempting him. And Vex gave in to that temptation. With a growl, he sat up, wrapped his arms around her, and captured one of her nipples with his mouth.

Kinsley squeaked, but a moan swiftly followed as he lavished that bud with his tongue. She settled her hands on his head, slipping her fingers into his hair, and in a breathy voice said, "Vex…"

She is tender from mating, you arse.

With great reluctance, he released her nipple, placed a soft kiss upon it, and looked up at her.

Kinsley chuckled as she grasped the edges of the bath and rose to her feet. "You are insatiable."

"And you are irresistible."

Vex stood up quickly. Water sluiced down his body and splashed over the sides of the tub, but he barely noticed as he hooked his hands behind Kinsley's thighs and lifted her, drawing her against him with her legs to either side of his waist. She let out a gasp and threw her arms around him, locking her calves around his hips.

He stepped out of the tub and onto the moss-carpeted floor. As he strode toward the door, magic swirled around their bodies, teasing their skin with cool air that carried away the moisture. Kinsley's shiver nearly undid him, but he somehow maintained his resolve.

Vex carried his mate into the bedchamber, lit the fire with another spark of magic, and walked to the bed. With barely a conscious thought, he willed the blankets to draw back. He laid his mate down and climbed on beside her. Slipping his arms around her, he tucked Kinsley against his side with her head resting on his arm and settled the covers over their bodies with a final flicker of magic.

He pressed a kiss to her brow. "Sleep, so morning will come swiftly and I may have you again."

Kinsley laughed and pushed up onto her elbow to look down at him. Her soft hair fell to brush his shoulder. "I suppose you have centuries of abstinence to make up for."

Vex caught a lock of her hair and curled it around his finger. "I knew not the slightest yearning for carnal pleasures. Not until you."

Smiling, she hummed and lightly traced his brow with her fingertips before stopping them at his scars. "Do these have meaning?"

"We goblins are fae creatures, but few of us possess true magic. Those who do are believed to be destined for greatness. In my clan, children who demonstrated magical ability beyond the usual were marked with such scars. I was told my talent with illusions was apparent even before I could walk. I was expected to one day bring prestige and power to our clan, and these marks were meant to signify the blessing I had received, and the blessings I would one day bring."

"Did anyone else have those marks?"

"A few in my clan, though they were my elders. Most goblin clans I encountered boasted at least one such individual. Sorcerers, shamans, mages...though their titles varied, they all commanded similar respect and recognition."

She traced one of the swirling scars. "It must've been painful, especially for a child."

"I imagine it was," he replied with a soft smile, gently tugging her hair until she brought her face closer, "but I remember it not."

Vex lifted his chin and kissed her lips. She leaned into it, opening to him, and he groaned at her taste. Slipping his fingers into her hair, he pulled Kinsley deeper into the kiss. Their lips caressed and nipped, and their tongues flicked and danced. He relished the feel of her soft breasts against his skin, the teasing press of her hardened nipples, the brush of her leg as she raised it over his, the heat of her sex against his thigh.

He craved more of her. He longed to sink his cock between her thighs, to feel her cunt around him, to thrill in the flames of her desire and passion.

But for now, he would content himself with naught more than this kiss. For her.

Kinsley broke the kiss, but she didn't pull away as she stared down at him, silent, searching his eyes.

"You said no more secrets between us," she finally said.

"And I meant it."

"I have one I want to confess to you."

His brow furrowed. "What is it, my moonlight?"

She spoke after a brief hesitation, and there was a rawness in her voice, a vulnerability. "When you found me, my heart was broken, and I was barely holding the pieces together. You saved my life. That was your part of our pact, that was all you had to do. But…you've done so much more for me. You've been mending my heart, Vex. The cracks are healing because of you, and for the first time, all the pieces are right where they should be. And I don't understand how they're staying together, because I just feel so, so…full.

"So, I'm giving my heart to you for safekeeping. I know you'll protect it as fiercely as you've protected me." She brushed her lips over his and whispered, "I love you, Vex."

Those words flowed into Vex, and everything within him stilled—his heart, his lungs, his thoughts. Warmth blossomed in his chest, spreading a little further with each thump once his heart resumed beating. And with that warmth came a growing sense of fullness. Of…completion.

Love.

Was that the word to describe all his elation, his fear, his yearning, all the jumbled emotions lodged within him? Was that the word that encompassed his adoration and devotion to this female, his need for her? Did it explain why the thought of losing her made his chest ache and his heart race?

Yes. Yes, it was all that and more, and he'd never understood it until that moment. Never could he have imagined so small a word meant so, so much.

And when he stared into her eyes, he saw it shining in them, just for him.

Vex kissed her, slowly and tenderly, savoring her taste and feel. Something new was building in his chest. The last secret he'd kept, the last part of himself he'd hidden. But he knew it was time. "My moonlight… What the queen forced from me through coercion, I give to you freely."

He turned his face so his mouth was beside Kinsley's ear and whispered the name he'd only ever spoken aloud once in his life. The name nestled at the center of his soul, the name that comprised his being, that tethered him to the very universe.

Kinsley looked down at him with wide eyes. Breathlessly, she said, "Is that…"

"My true name," he replied softly. He could feel the name inside her, becoming part of her, becoming one with her. "It is yours to hold, Kinsley. But I would yet have you call me Vex, for it is Vex who found you, who saved you, who was saved by you. And it is Vex who has fallen in love with you."

Tears gathered in those beautiful periwinkle eyes, and his heart clenched.

"Kinsley…"

She closed her eyes and pressed her mouth to his, kissing him firmly, desperately, and he returned the kiss just as fervently, clasping a hand around the back of her neck. Despite his restraint, his desire for her hadn't waned, and it resurged now with overwhelming force. His already erect cock hardened further.

Lifting her head, Kinsley shifted to straddle his waist, planting her hands to either side of his head. She locked her lustful gaze with his as she lowered herself until the head of his cock pushed into the wet, blissful heat of her cunt.

Vex bared his teeth and swiftly grasped her hips with both hands, stilling her. "I've no desire to hurt you, Kinsley."

"You won't. I want this, Vex. I need you."

"Ah, my moonlight. I can deny you no more than I can deny myself." Tightening his grip on her, he drew her down slowly, thrilling in the feeling of her tight sex closing over his ridges one by one, delighting in her whimper and the way her body tensed. He shuddered in utter pleasure when she was finally seated upon him fully.

"My love," Vex groaned as he lifted his hips, pressing into her deeper still, "you are all I desire."

CHAPTER THIRTY-FOUR

Kinsley ran her fingertip over the spines of the books standing on one of the library's high shelves. She felt the indents in the bindings where cryptic runes and arcane symbols were embossed, the meaning of which continued to elude her. Though she could understand any language she heard, the writing in these books remained as unreadable as ever.

So, Vex had assumed the role of narrator. Whether snuggled up together in bed, reclining in the shade of a tree outside, or sitting in front of a cozy fire, he'd read to her many times over the last month, bringing the words to life with a mix of his smooth voice and masterful illusions. He'd made subjects that could've been bland magical and memorable.

Her favorite book thus far had been about astronomy. The star charts within were interesting even without any understanding of the words accompanying them, but Kinsley's imagination hadn't done them justice. Vex had transformed the entire bedroom that night. The walls and ceiling had faded away, leaving only the unbroken dome of the night sky stretching around them.

As he'd named the constellations, they'd brightened in the sky, twinkling with brilliance and splendor that had stolen Kinsley's breath. They hadn't been the stars of Earth, but of a far-off fae world, alien, wondrous, and brimming with magic. He'd sat with her head in his lap, pointing out each formation, explaining its significance, and sometimes dazzling her with almost-real images of the fantastical creatures with which those constellations had been associated.

Even after they'd set the book aside, she and Vex had remained like that, gazing at the stars of another world as he tenderly combed his fingers through her hair.

Kinsley's lips curled into a smile at the memory as she pulled down a brown book with gold etching and turned it toward Flare, who floated beside her. "What's this one about?"

The wisp tilted their head. "Techniques for tanning hides."

Kinsley wrinkled her nose and promptly replaced the book. "I don't think I need visuals for that."

She knew enough about tanning hides to know the process wasn't pleasant.

"How did you come to be with Vex?" Kinsley asked as she gave the tall ladder she stood upon a push. It glided smoothly along its rails to the next bookcase. "You said you met him when he was little. Was that after he lost his clan?"

"It was," Flare said as they followed Kinsley. "These ones found him slumbering in a cave at the heart of a wood where few dared venture, sheltering from a storm. He was not the magus then. A child, lost and alone. Broken. These ones were drawn to him and watched over his sleep. When he awoke, sorrow gleamed in his eyes and quivered in his voice, but he spoke to these ones as equals, with kindness."

Kinsley's heart squeezed. She recalled Vex's memory—a little boy hiding, huddled away from the terrifying flames blazing all around him. She couldn't imagine how scared and alone he must've felt.

She reached out to Flare. "I'm glad you were there for him."

The wisp brushed her fingers with a tendril of ghostfire. "This one is glad you are here for him now."

Kinsley smiled softly. "Me too."

She withdrew her hand and resumed skimming the books. It'd been a little over month since Vex claimed her, since they'd professed their love to one another. That time had been the happiest of her life. She'd seen the change in Vex too. His mood was lighter, his eyes were brighter, and his smile came easier. And when he laughed? God, Kinsley loved the deep, rolling sound of his laugh.

In some ways, she couldn't believe those weeks had already passed. She and Vex had done so much together that part of her insisted they couldn't possibly have experienced all of it in so short a time.

Vex had brought her into his lab and demonstrated a bottomless well of patience in answering Kinsley's endless questions as she'd examined everything. She'd been down there while he'd recovered from his wounds, but she hadn't explored any of it. Her focus had always been on him. Nothing else had mattered.

But being down there again, without a life-threatening emergency to command her attention, was a whole new experience. There was magic in every corner—even in the many mundane ingredients he'd stockpiled down there. It was nothing like the mad scientist's laboratory she'd initially envisioned. It was a wizard's workshop, where potions were brewed, magic was crafted, and ancient artifacts were stored, the most powerful of which lay behind an enchanted vault door.

In response to her interest and enthusiasm, Vex had begun teaching her some of his craft. She'd mixed a few bath oils, helped make a few bars of soap, and even brewed her first potion, which Vex said would help with upset stomachs. Then he'd shown her some real magic. Drawing from sources both physical and arcane, they'd created what he called an everglow.

They'd used a simple glass jar, covered by a waxed cloth seal marked in magical symbols. And inside the jar, they'd created a tiny, constantly shifting aurora. The shimmering colors within changed from green to blue, blue to purple, then to red and yellow before circling back again. It was like having the northern lights bottled up.

But they hadn't spent all their time in the lab, not by any means. He'd been a teacher in the kitchen, too, helping her adapt to the old-fashioned equipment on hand. With his guidance, she hadn't burned a single scone in weeks, and she'd practically become an expert at baking several varieties of bread.

Her sister Maddy would've been proud.

Conjured food was a wonderful luxury, but it couldn't match

the satisfaction of prepping and cooking with one's own hands. Especially when the cooking was done with a partner.

With a *mate*.

Their cooking time had of course led to a few cooking-adjacent activities... More than once, she'd found herself locked in flour fights with Vex that had turned the kitchen and themselves into a powdery mess. Those battles often resulted in spontaneous bouts of lovemaking with the food all but forgotten.

The aftermath always necessitated shared baths.

And shared baths always led to more sex.

Not that Kinsley would complain. Not one bit.

Gardening and foraging in the forest had often brought the same results. Whether tending to his neat patch of vegetables or gathering mushrooms from the surrounding woods, Kinsley and Vex always wound up dirty, heated, and unable to keep their hands off each other. It was like some untamed, carnal creature had been awoken within her, revealing a part of Kinsley she'd never known existed.

And she loved it most when Vex let himself go. When he was unrestrained, wild, bestial. When he held nothing back.

There was no one around to spy on them, no one to judge. This realm was theirs.

Desire unfurled in her core. She squeezed and rubbed her thighs together, but it didn't alleviate the hollow ache blooming inside her.

Books, Kinsley. Think of the books!

"I'll have to get Vex to teach me how to read these." Kinsley pulled out another tome and flipped through the pages. "It'd be nice to know what they're about without having to ask."

"And if such knowledge is forbidden?" Vex asked from behind her.

Kinsley gasped as her heart leapt into her throat. In her startlement, she lost her hold on the book. It snapped shut and fell, and she fumbled to catch it, succeeding only in disrupting her own balance. Her foot slipped on the rung, and her hands were in no position to grab hold of the ladder before she tipped backward.

Rather than the hard, unforgiving floor, her fall was broken by Vex's strong arms, one behind her shoulders and the other under her thighs. They barely gave beneath her weight, moving just enough to gently halt her. She reflexively clutched at him, grasping his bare shoulder.

Of course he was shirtless.

Vex held Kinsley against his chest, his eyes blazing down at her.

"You *really* need to stop doing that," she said breathlessly.

One corner of his mouth quirked. "I can hardly take the blame when you keep throwing yourself into my arms."

Kinsley chuckled. "I'm not throwing myself at you."

"And yet here you are, my moonlight." He spun away from the ladder, twirling across the room, faster and faster, making the blue skirt of her dress flare and flutter.

Laughter spilled from her as he danced and swayed. His crimson eyes were alight, the only constants as the world swirled around her with delightful, dizzying speed. His gaze was her tether, her balance, her anchor. Her solace and her joy.

Finally, he slowed to a stop and leaned over her. His expression sobered as he studied her face. Without a word, he slanted his mouth over hers, claiming her with a kiss deeper and more meaningful than she could ever have expected after that whimsical dance.

Kinsley closed her eyes, settled a hand on his face, and leaned into that kiss. Their lips caressed each other, and their tongues danced in a much different way, fueling the desirous spark in her core.

Breath ragged, Vex pressed his forehead against hers. "You see, Kinsley? There are rewards to reap by throwing yourself at me."

Kinsley grinned as she opened her eyes. "I fell."

"No matter what you call it, Kinsley, the result is unchanged. You are in my arms."

"Did you seek me out just to have your wicked way with me?" She twirled her fingers in his hair. "Because if you did, I'm okay with that."

"Should these ones leave?" Echo asked.

Kinsley turned her head to see the three wisps floating together near the table where she'd stacked the interesting books she'd found today. Next to that stack was a green bottle of wine, a pair of plain bronze goblets, and a plate with sliced fruit and cheese, all of which Vex must've set down while she was distracted.

"That depends entirely upon my mate's current appetites," Vex replied huskily as he nuzzled her neck.

His voice made her belly flutter and her skin tingle. But however much she would've enjoyed sex with him right here, right now, she knew that once they started, they wouldn't stop. Everything else would be forgotten, including the books she'd set aside to have him read and the food he'd just brought.

Would that be such a bad thing?

Was it possible to live solely on sex?

I am immortal now...

God, Kinsley, stop it!

"Nope! You three stay." Kinsley looked at Vex sternly. "It's story time."

He chuckled. "As you command, my love."

Holding her close, he released her legs and let her body slowly slide down his. The action stimulated Kinsley's overly sensitive nipples and sent shivers of pleasure through her. Though it took hardly any time at all, she was already breathless and gripping his forearms when her feet touched the floor.

With a grin, Vex leaned toward her and whispered. "We may yet send them away."

"Tease." Kinsley gave his shoulder a playful nudge. "You know the wisps enjoy story time as much as I do. And we shouldn't let the food go to waste." Keeping her eyes on his, Kinsley lowered her voice and traced his bottom lip with fingertip. "We have all night for…other activities."

Vex hummed thoughtfully, seductively, and caught her hand, holding it in place as he pressed a kiss to her finger. "Nightfall cannot arrive swiftly enough." He released her hand and took a step back. "Show me what has piqued your curiosity today."

Resisting the temptation to drag him back to her, Kinsley walked to the table and waved at the small stack of books she'd collected. "These. But this one"—she picked up the top book—"I really want to know more about."

Vex accepted the book when she held it out, brushing his fingers across the weathered black cover.

"Flare said it was a journal that belonged to a realmswalker?"

"Indeed." He carefully opened the book, smoothing the yellowed parchment within, which was slightly damaged along the edges. "She called herself Alythrii, which means—"

"Carried by wind?"

"Just so," Vex replied with a smile. "It is an ancient unseelie dialect."

Their reading sessions had brought up many such instances— alien words and names that Kinsley understood instinctually thanks to the potion. It had been odd the first few times, but she was growing used to the sensation of...knowing.

"So, she was unseelie. Does that mean she was like you?" Kinsley asked.

Vex closed the book, and with a flick of his wrist, summoned a set of ethereal green hands that collected the food, wine, and goblets. Kinsley followed him to their usual place in the reading nook, where they'd piled pillows and blankets. The wisps and Vex's arcane hands came right behind them.

"I suspect she was not," Vex said as he sat, spreading his thighs to make space for Kinsley. "Alythrii makes no mention of her people in the journal, but she was likely a highborn fae."

Kinsley lifted her skirt, lowered herself onto the cushion between Vex's legs, and lay back against his chest. She smiled and nestled against his warm body as he wrapped an arm around her. "Do the highborn look like..."

"The queen?"

"Yes."

"Some do. They are ethereal, beautiful...cold. At times, it is nigh impossible to tell seelie from unseelie when it comes to the highborn. Regardless of their blood, highborn may travel far more freely than other fae. They are largely feared by lesser beings. Hence my suspicions regarding the writer of this journal."

He held the book out before Kinsley, and she opened it to the first page. The wisps hovered just over them, casting their soft blue glow, which granted the ink on the parchment a faint metallic glint. The magic hands placed the food and drinks on a small shelf built into the nook, easily within arm's reach, before dissipating.

"Herein shall I, who have taken the name Alythrii, record the breadth and scope of my travels," Vex began, his deep voice rumbling into Kinsley. "Of my own accord have I deigned to undertake this journey, that I might better understand what gifts my blood has bequeathed to me. I shall travel as though blind to realms hitherto unknown to me."

Kinsley listened raptly as Vex read, occasionally nibbling on the snacks or sipping wine that had been poured by the magic hands. He did not relinquish his embrace; Kinsley turned the pages when he signaled and fed him bite-sized pieces of food when he leaned his head over her shoulder. No words were necessary for their little exchanges. They were attuned to one another, in sync.

As Vex had implied, Alythrii offered scant information about herself, focusing instead on describing the people, places, and things she encountered in her travels.

Instead of transforming the whole room with magic, Vex created a wide illusory window—though to Kinsley, it was much closer to a movie theater screen. The images within were almost dreamlike, depicting landscapes and creatures too fantastical to be real.

The journal's writing downplayed the wondrous nature of its author's travels across planes of existence. Alythrii offered matter-of-fact observations sprinkled with infrequent opinions and speculations, many of which seemed almost hesitant.

But the places... Vex showed Kinsley alien worlds filled with odd flora and fauna, places with skies of any color, where magic overflowed from every pebble. Alythrii had walked so many worlds, had seen so much.

Kinsley could only wonder who the mysterious author had been. What had she looked like, sounded like? Had she been kind and curious or callous in her desire to see everything? What had driven her to wander for so long, to face such dangers?

And why could Kinsley relate so much to that drive?

The glimpses of those fantastical worlds offered by the journal and Vex's illusions only fanned the flames of adventure and exploration in Kinsley's heart. She'd always loved learning about far-off places, but she loved *experiencing* them even more.

She wanted to see with her own eyes a world where islands floated in the sky. She wanted to walk in a world where flowers were as tall as houses. She wanted to visit a realm where cities drifted across an endless ocean atop the backs of giant sea creatures.

But when the journal described a place called Silverfall, something familiar caught Kinsley's attention. Alythrii spoke of luminous crystals growing from the land in pillars, in cliffs, in entire mountains, defining the landscape as far as could be seen.

Vex's illusion depicted a world shrouded in night—a place with thick, overgrown forests and bogs which stood beneath and around huge formations of raw crystal whose light created as much shadow as it destroyed. Settlements, even whole cities, lay clustered around those formations.

And in some places, the bases of the crystals gave way to veins of silver, though it was unclear whether the crystals had sprouted from the precious metal or it had bled from them.

"Vex, those crystals..." she said, brow furrowing. "They look a lot like the ones here. Just much bigger."

His fingers flexed on her belly, and he tilted his hand, angling the book downward. "Because they are the same. Silverfall is a haven for unseelie. It was my aim with the translocation spell, and here, Silverfall and your world bleed together. Hence the abundant crystal growth."

"Is that where you're originally from?"

"No, my moonlight. My realm of origin was rather more volatile. Alythrii details it in a later entry. She dubbed it Wrathhome. A place of fire and shadow, midday and midnight, chaos and conflict. Where silver and gold clash and blanket the land in death. I know not its state today, but in my youth, it was a realm torn asunder by the unrelenting war between seelie and unseelie."

Kinsley frowned, tucking her head beneath his chin. "I'm sorry. I can't imagine what it must've been like to get caught up in a war spanning multiple worlds."

"I escaped that conflict by coming to your world. Unfortunately, I but delayed the inevitable. My second attempt at escape met with far less success." Keeping his place with a finger, he closed the journal and turned it, examining the worn leather binding. "In truth, much of my knowledge of other realms was garnered from this text and a precious few others.

"Discounting this limbo, I've but once ventured between realms. There existed a portal in the realm of my birth, one I discovered only after years of research, toil, and exploration. Its condition was dire when finally I uncovered it, and I fear my use of it must've depleted it beyond recovery. But it brought me somewhere else... and that was all I'd wanted."

Kinsley felt those words resonate in her soul. She understood all too well that desire to be somewhere else, anywhere other than the place you were. That was what had brought her across a continent and an ocean. And she'd felt that wanderlust, that need to move, the whole time she'd lived with her aunt. The worst part had been the vague but insistent sense that she had...nowhere. Nowhere to go back to. Nowhere she belonged.

But somehow, Vex had silenced her desire to roam. Being with him felt like being at home. Like she was exactly where she was meant to be. Like no matter where life took them, she'd always have her place—she'd always have him—to return to.

"I've felt a lot like Alythrii for as long as I can remember," Kinsley said. "Even as a kid, I rarely stayed indoors, spending most of my time exploring the forest in our back garden. Much to my parents' frustration." She frowned, running her fingers over the book. "If it has to do with my blood, wouldn't one of them also be a realmswalker?"

"At least one of them is undoubtedly fae-touched," Vex replied. "Yet not every descendent will inherit the gifts of their ancestry, especially as the bloodline is further and further removed from the fae progenitor."

"My parents never really understood me. They still don't. My mother is—was—trying to get me to settle down with another career. A stationary career. She always worries about me traveling on my own, especially at night. I, uh, guess her worries were valid considering I got myself impaled by a tree while driving at night."

She shuddered at the memory, which was somehow both vivid and hazy.

Vex's arm curled tighter around her, and he let out a slow, heavy breath. "I shall forever be haunted by that night."

"As shall these ones," Shade said, hovering closer and trailing ghostfire along Kinsley's arm.

Kinsley smiled at the wisp before resting her arm atop Vex's. "I don't blame you. Any of you." She shifted to the side to look up at him. "I don't regret coming here, but *that* was an experience I could've done without."

Brow creasing, Vex leaned down and kissed her temple. "I'd have spared you that suffering, had it been within my power."

"That you were there at all to save me was enough."

"Would that I could take credit for fate's doing." He kissed her temple again, letting his lips linger there, warm and comforting. "Had you reached your cottage, what would you have done? Would it have appeased your desire to wander?"

"No." Kinsley smiled and cupped his jaw, stroking his cheek with her thumb. "I think you were the only cure for that."

Vex's fingers flexed against her, and his crimson eyes glowed brighter as his slitted pupils contracted.

She lowered her hand before the heat in his eyes could further intensify. "The cottage was more just meant as a stop along the way. A staging point. I was planning to vlog my hikes and discoveries here for a time before moving on to my next adventure."

Withdrawing his finger from between the pages, he set the journal aside and combed his claws through her hair. "Mayhap it is time for a new story. Not Alythrii's, but yours. Tell me of the places you've explored. Tell me of your land beyond the sea. Be my eyes, that I may see what you have seen. *Vlog* to me."

"These ones wish to hear also," said Flare, their flames brightening as they floated closer.

Echo bounced excitedly beside Flare. "Please vlog for these ones, Kinsley."

Kinsley laughed. "It's not really vlogging, but I would love to tell you about some of my favorite places." She laid her head against Vex's chest, taking pleasure in the feel of his fingers running through her hair. "When I was twelve, my parents took me and my sister Maddy to the Grand Canyon. Even though Maddy's two years older than me, she was too scared to get close to the railing. She hates heights. But I walked right up and looked out.

"It was breathtaking. So wide, so long, and so, so deep. The sandstone walls were red, orange, and brown, and as silly as it sounds, I remember thinking it looked like a layered cake. And at the very bottom was the Colorado River, bright turquoise and sparkling in the sun. I think standing there, staring out at this immense canyon, was when I first realized how huge the world is. That I was just this tiny little person in a vast place…but that realization never frightened me. It was exciting. Because a world so big meant that much more to explore."

"It sounds unlike anything I've seen," Vex said softly. "And little Kinsley strode, undaunted, to its edge and beheld it with uninhibited wonder."

"I did. And it freaked my mother out when I climbed onto the rail." Kinsley snickered. "She thought I was going to fall in. I mean, if it were my kid doing that, I'd likely freak out too. But I just wanted to get closer, to see farther down. I wanted to hike right down to the bottom and dip my toes in the water. Of course, I probably would've been too tired to get back to the top, and my dad would've had to haul me out… But kids don't usually think that far ahead."

Vex laughed and brushed his knuckles along her arm. "We've no canyons in our little realm, but I'd gladly carry you anywhere you wish to go no matter how far, no matter how deep."

Something warmed within her, but then the potential meaning of his words clicked. She looked up at him. "Carry me? As in…fly?"

"We could soar amongst the stars."

She smiled wide. "Really?"

"Yes." Vex caught her chin and smiled down at her. Desire blazed within his eyes. "You shall be the envy of the heavens, my moonlight." He lowered his voice to barely a whisper. "And I know just how to make you shine all the brighter."

Heart quickening and breath catching, she stared into his eyes. There was something more to his words. A hint of promise, an implication. And whatever wicked thing he intended, Kinsley wanted it.

Her gaze dipped to his mouth, and she parted her lips when he stroked his thumb across the lower one.

"These ones would fly with you," said Echo.

Spell broken, Kinsley blinked, and a blush crept beneath her skin.

"These ones would do best not to claim unoffered invitations," Shade said.

Echo bowed their head. "Apologies, magus."

"No apologies," Vex replied distractedly, his own eyes having fallen to Kinsley's lips. "I shall be selfish and claim Kinsley's first flight for myself. But we will soar with you afterward, my friends."

"These ones cannot wait," Flare said.

"Now"—Vex brushed her cheek—"tell us more about your adventures, Kinsley."

Echo bounced in the air. "Please, share more!"

"These ones would love to hear more," Flare said.

"Uh, right. My adventures." Kinsley cleared her throat, buying herself another moment to regain her composure. The lingering effects of Vex's words proved difficult to shake, especially while she was lying against him, snug in his embrace, with his spicy oakmoss and amber scent enveloping her.

Had he really implied what she thought he had? Sex while flying?

Don't think about it now, Kinsley!

To her credit, she didn't think about it one more time.

She thought about it a couple more times. Well...maybe a *few* more times. Definitely no more than half a dozen.

Somehow, she focused enough to tell Vex and the wisps about some of the other places she'd visited—places that had left lasting impressions upon her. The more she talked, the more her pounding heart, heated skin, and fluttering stomach eased.

She told them about her trip to the Dixie National Forest in Utah, where towering red sandstone formations jutted up from amidst tall pine trees beneath an expansive blue sky. Vex asked several questions about the odd landscape, leading to Kinsley describing the desert comprising the greater southwestern United States and the way it varied from place to place.

Unsurprisingly, he'd never seen a desert. His only knowledge of such environments had come from books.

From Utah, she leapt to the Midwest, detailing the week she'd spent in Shawnee National Forest in Illinois. She couldn't help but smile as she described the varied deciduous trees, the rocky cliffs, the streams and enchanting waterfalls. Though sandstone was also prominent there, it was so different from that at the Grand Canyon and in Utah—gray and relatively smooth, its layers more subtle in some places and jarringly obvious in others.

Her favorite place in that park had been the Garden of the Gods, where those unique rock formations rose above the woodlands, offering stunning views of the surrounding area. Sitting on one of those rocks with the forest stretching out before her and the sky stained red and orange by the setting sun had been an experience beyond her ability to describe.

So many cities had been within a few hundred miles of her that evening—Chicago, Indianapolis, Cincinnati, Louisville, Nashville and Memphis, St. Louis. But on that rock, she'd felt a million miles away from it all. She'd felt wholly surrounded by nature, at one with it.

"Would that we could lie together upon those rocks and bask in the moonlight," he said, skimming his lips along the side of her neck, "while the woods slumber peacefully below us."

A shiver coursed through her as those lips pressed a kiss to the spot just beneath her ear. She caught a strand of his long hair and twirled it around her finger. "We could find a similar rock here."

"Mayhap," he purred. "But you've not yet satisfied my curiosity."

"What curiosity haven't I satisfied?"

He kept his lips beneath her ear, letting his breath tease her skin as he traced little circles upon her lower belly. "Of the places you've journeyed, which is dearest to your heart?"

"Mmm... Here." Kinsley closed her eyes, thrilling in the sensations he produced. And she knew he was fully aware of what he was doing. "Definitely here."

Vex chuckled, creating a rousing vibration, and nipped her ear lobe with a fang, making her breath hitch. "Before you came here."

How could he expect her to think clearly when he was toying with her like this? Her blood was hot, her nipples taut and throbbing, and her clit ached for attention. All she wanted to do in that moment was take his hand and slip it between her thighs so he could feel how wet she was and put her out of this misery.

"Before I came here..." Continuing to twirl his hair around her fingers, Kinsley opened her eyes. Despite the distractions, the answer to his question came quite easily, and the associated memories brought a smile to her face. "A place called Sequoia National Park. It's up in the mountains, and it's pretty popular, but it just... It's special.

"It's named after the trees that grow there, giant sequoias. They're the largest trees in the world. I mean, your tree is bigger, but it's magic and technically isn't in the same world anyway, so it doesn't count. Anyway, the sequoias are so tall that if you stand at the base of one and look up, you might think it's punching right through the sky itself."

She sighed, smile widening. "I went there as an adult, but standing amongst those trees made me feel like a kid looking out at the Grand Canyon for the first time again. They rekindled that sense of the huge, breathtaking world around me. I think I actually got a kink in my neck from staring up at them for so long as I walked the trails."

Her smile faltered, but the frown that replaced it felt more thoughtful than sorrowful. "That was also the first trip I took after Liam left. I was hurting, obviously, but being there... I realized that there were so many things bigger than my pain. Those trees... they're basically adapted to survive wildfires. You can see black spots on some of the trunks where they burned, but they heal over time. They take their wounds, collect their scars, and continue standing tall.

"My scars will never go away. They're part of me. But I grew stronger from them. I stood, no matter how much I wanted to fall sometimes. That park was where some part of me decided that I needed to heal. That I *would* heal. I just needed time."

"Ah, Kinsley," Vex rasped, voice thick, and hugged her tight.

Kinsley turned her face toward him, caught his gaze, and held it. "You will heal too, Vex."

"I am, my moonlight." He kissed her tenderly, and though it lacked the heat of earlier, it made Kinsley melt.

But her thoughts had taken a sorrowful turn. Vex had asked her to tell him about her adventures, to share her experiences and describe the things she'd seen, when he'd been trapped here for centuries while the world outside passed him by. While everything moved on without him.

Kinsley brushed her fingers over his wrist, remembering how Vex had stood atop his tower in his memory, separated from the goblins he'd protected. "Did you ever leave your tower? Before you met with the queen, that is."

"Very little," Echo said.

Vex shifted his head to rest his cheek atop her hair. "Loath as I often was to leave, I *did* venture out from time to time. My aim was knowledge and power. I had seen my clan slaughtered, and I had witnessed countless other atrocities before coming of age. Always it was lesser fae, beings like goblins, who paid the steepest price in the conflicts that ravaged my realm.

"I sought a means of using my magic to protect. My illusions had saved none but myself. All I could do, all my people could do, was hide and hope. Hope that we'd survive another day, another hour, another heartbeat. I wanted more than a means to hide. I longed to fight. To stand against those who treated us as vermin.

"That necessitated travel. I hunted obscure tomes and artifacts, traded for information, scoured ancient places for secrets. I dealt with mortals and fae alike—even seelie, when it served my goals. And I brought it all back to my tower, where I hoarded it." He chuckled without humor, shaking his head gently. "The fool I was, I journeyed about your world with its beauty all around me and still returned to that tower time and again, locking myself away from all of it. Never truly seeing, never truly experiencing. Too focused on my goals to appreciate anything but the pursuit of them."

Flare did a little twirl in front of Vex and Kinsley. "This one told the magus to dance and sing during the celebrations."

This time, Vex's chuckle had warmth to it. "I would only have succeeded in frightening everyone off."

Kinsley grinned, broke Vex's hold on her, and scooted off the cushion. Standing, she shook her dress back into place around her legs, faced him, and held out her hand. "Will you dance with me?"

Fire sparked in his eyes as he glanced from her hand to her face. His lips curled into a sinful smile. "Not here."

Rising, he took Kinsley's hand and drew her against him,

locking her in place with an arm banded across her back. She stared up at him with wide eyes and parted lips.

"Let us take this dance into the sky, my love."

Before Kinsley could respond, Vex lifted her off her feet and whisked her toward the doorway. With a gasp, she wrapped her arms and legs around him, watching the bookshelves streak by in a blur.

"These ones will wait here!" Flare called. The wisps' laughter followed Vex and Kinsley out.

CHAPTER THIRTY-FIVE

THE INSTANT VEX stepped out the front door, his wings burst from his back, and he leapt into the air. Kinsley squeaked and held tight as her stomach lurched and wind rushed around them, but she didn't close her eyes. She watched over his shoulder as powerful pumps of his wings carried them higher and higher, watched as the cottage shrank with distance.

Just like when she'd looked down into the Grand Canyon all those years ago, Kinsley felt wonder instead of fear. She was in the arms of an otherworldly unseelie fae, surrounded by magic and excitement. She was *alive*.

The forest was dark but for the soft glow of crystals and the faint bioluminescence of mushrooms and lichens glimpsed through breaks in the canopy. The light of moon and stars shimmered on the leaves, which rustled in the breeze, making the tops of the trees resemble the surface of a gently rolling ocean.

Her hair whipped wildly around her head. She tugged it back, tucked it behind her ear as best she could, and slipped her arm back around Vex's neck, delving her fingers into his hair.

Vex strengthened his hold on her. "I have you."

Kinsley smiled and grazed his ear with her lips. "I know."

She felt the play of muscles in his back as he carried them higher still. She could see everything now—the patch of forest that had been Vex's world for so long, with a sliver of shoreline on one side, all surrounded by dense gray fog as far as she could see. Surrounded by nothingness.

But the sky above was unrestricted, boundless, infinite. Inky blue and deepest violet stretched endlessly upward, with countless twinkling stars scattered across it. Whole words—entire galaxies—lay out there, looking so tiny. And the more altitude Vex gained, the closer Kinsley was to all of it.

As he crossed the path of the moon, she glimpsed the veins through the membranes of his wings; for all his magic and mystery, he was flesh and blood. And he made her flesh and blood burn, made her crave his heat, his touch, his kisses, his cock.

She lifted her head to look at his face.

Silhouetted by the moon, his features were lost in shadows. They were darker than the night sky, blackness cut out of the fabric of the universe itself, but for the pair of crimson flames that were his eyes. His hungry, adoring eyes.

It was just Kinsley and Vex, flying through a sea of stars. Soaring through the majestic night.

He leaned his head down and kissed her lips, her chin, her cheek, each brush of his mouth as tender as it was ravenous. Tension rippled through his body, rousing the fire within her. "Never have I dared dream I would have anything like this," he rasped against her neck as he slid a hand up her back to cradle her head. "Anything like you."

Vex kissed her neck, nipping her with his fangs, and she quivered, drawing herself impossibly closer to him. His other hand moved down to her ass, pressing her pelvis flush against him, and she felt the hard evidence of his desire. The prick of his claws was a splash of pain followed by a flood of pleasure.

Kinsley closed her eyes. "I am yours."

"You are."

She felt the telltale tingle of magic as her dress disintegrated thread by thread. Felt the rush of cool night air against her bare flesh. Felt the scorching hot brand of his cock press against her belly, no longer restricted by their clothing.

Vex dragged the tips of his split tongue up her throat. "Are you wet for me, Kinsley?"

A slow smile stretched across her lips as she opened her eyes, lifted her head, and met his gaze. "Why don't you find out for yourself?"

He lowered his hand from her head, banding his arm securely across her back. His other hand slid around from her ass until it reached her dripping sex. Slowly, maddeningly, he stroked her cunt.

Kinsley moaned.

"You are dripping." When he raised that hand to his mouth and slipped his fingers in, she nearly came undone. His chest rumbled with a groan as he sucked her essence from his flesh. "Fuck, there is no sweeter taste than yours in this world or any other."

His pale teeth flashed in the moonlight as he bit the claws off two of his fingers. Eyes never leaving hers, he turned his head and spat the claws aside. Kinsley's pussy ached for what was to come. It was all she could do not to grind against him.

"I've yet to have this pleasure," he purred, trailing the tips of his now clawless fingers down from the hollow of her throat. They seared a path between her breasts and over her belly, their slight moisture intensifying the chill of the air against her skin and sending a shiver through her.

Finally, his hand reached her sex. Those long, deft fingers teased her flesh, stroking, exploring, caressing, gathering her slick and spreading it. The heat his little touches sparked inside her immediately chased away the coolness of the night. She clutched at him, desperate and eager for more, but she could only take what he gave.

His fingers delved between her folds, brushing across her clit. Kinsley gasped, digging her nails into his back, and rocked her hips against him, pinning his hand between their bodies.

Vex chuckled, a dark, velvety sound perfectly at home here in the starry night sky. He brushed his lips across her jaw. "So wet for me. So soft." He pushed two fingers deep inside her. "So hot."

"Vex," Kinsley moaned, her pussy clenching around those fingers.

He leisurely thrust them in and out of her, grinding the heel of his palm against her clit. "You feel exquisite."

Kinsley's brow furrowed at the ripples of pleasure spreading through her. Panting, she bit down on her lip and undulated her hips, seeking to take those fingers deeper. He curled them, coaxing more essence from her, and she felt it trickle down her ass.

Vex scattered little kisses on her nose and cheeks until finally capturing her lips. The tips of his tongue flicked against them, seeking entry, and Kinsley granted it. He swept that hot, delectable tongue inside and twined it with hers.

Blazing heat spread over her skin, growing hotter with each pump of his fingers, with every grind on her clit, with every beat of his wings and every thump of her heart, wringing little whimpers from Kinsley's throat as pleasure coiled in her core.

Kinsley dug her heels into his thighs and gripped a fistful of his hair as she rasped Vex's name against his lips.

"No," Vex growled, withdrawing his fingers from her sex and leaving her bereft, hollow, and unfulfilled. He grasped her ass, stilling her hips, as he flew them upright. His fierce eyes held hers, and long strands of his black hair fluttered in the wind.

"When you come"—he lifted her ass and positioned her cunt over the head of his shaft—"it shall be around my cock."

He slammed her down. Kinsley gasped as he filled her, forcing every delicious, ridged inch of himself inside her. Her sex clenched around him greedily, her thighs flush against his hips. She was so close to coming. So close to losing herself to ecstasy. It was euphoric, it was agonizing.

"I love how your body clings to me, how it craves me." Vex shuddered and tightened his grip on Kinsley's ass, the press of his claws only heightening the sensations raging through her. "Shine for me, my moonlight."

The slightest shift of his pelvis rocked her with pleasure; those ridges dragged along her inner walls, stimulating every nerve, triggering waves with every minute movement.

All she needed was a little more. Just a little more of him, from him, and she'd burst.

Another powerful thrust of his wings launched them to the pinnacle of their flight. For an instant, they hung weightless, and she felt like the moon in his night sky, radiant, resplendent. Then he curled his wings in, cocooning her in their warm embrace.

Kinsley's world flipped, and her breath hitched. They were falling.

She clung to him with all her strength—arms, legs, and sex, all clamping in reflexive desperation.

"Trust me," he rasped, cradling the back of her head.

"I do," she breathed.

Vex's wings muted the roaring wind, allowing Kinsley to focus on everything else. The fluttering in her stomach, which had combined with her pulsing, searing pleasure. The rhythm of their racing heartbeats and their harsh breaths. The heat radiating from his skin, now enwrapping her, permeating her. His oakmoss and amber scent overpowering that of the crisp night air.

His hard, throbbing shaft, through which she felt each thump of his heart, each little shudder coursing through him. Through which she felt the vibrating rush of air.

Her cunt clamped tighter still, drawing him in deeper, twitching at the feel of his ridges.

Vex slanted his mouth over hers. His lips were velvet and steel, and he stole her breath as his wings snapped out and caught the air.

The fluttering in her stomach intensified as their course changed, catapulting the sensations to impossible heights. The thrill was too much; it paired with the other sensations perfectly, creating a blend beyond anything she could've dreamed.

She could hear leaves rustling not far below as she and Vex sped over the trees. Vex's hand remained on her ass, holding her in place as he ground his pelvis against her clit, as his thick shaft pulsed inside her, as every flap of his wings vibrated through her.

The pressure inside her swelled. She was there, right on the edge. This excitement, this wonder, this closeness to him, it was everything she craved, everything she needed, everything she wanted for the rest of her life.

He was everything she wanted.

Vex pushed inside her deeper still. His shaft swelled, practically thrumming.

And she surrendered.

White-hot pleasure exploded within Kinsley. It was pure, it was blinding, it was rhapsodic. She raked her nails across his skin, and a soundless cry built in her throat. She was about to shatter, about to be unmade.

Breaking the kiss, she spread her arms to the sides and tilted her head back. Wind swept over her skin and through her hair. She was flying, soaring, free.

Vex roared, and Kinsley's cry escaped, their voices mingling in the night to declare their pleasure to all the world. Heat and ecstasy flooded her. She glimpsed Vex's shadowed face against a backdrop of infinite stars, a dark angel sweeping her away on wings of bliss, before her eyes fell shut and she allowed rapture to consume her.

He buried his face against her neck and dug his fingertips and claws into her flesh. His harsh, hot breath warmed her skin as he ground his cock into her, pushing deeper and deeper, but never seeming to get deep enough. She felt the tension rippling through his hard muscles, felt every twitch of his cock as he filled her with his scorching seed. All the while, they glided through the air, lost in a maelstrom of pleasure. Lost in each other.

She wrapped her arms around Vex and clung to him as she trembled with her release.

When the intensity of their lovemaking ebbed, Vex pressed a kiss over her pounding heart and skimmed his lips up her neck. "My love. My moonlight."

Kinsley angled her head up. Their eyes locked. Vex's crimson gaze brimmed with pure, unmasked love.

Love for her.

Tears stung Kinsley's eyes. She felt that same fierce love burning inside her, a blazing, unquenchable flame that would shine in any darkness.

He touched his forehead to hers. Despite the wind sweeping around them, she heard his words clearly when he said, "I know not how long I've been here, Kinsley, but I've not lived until you."

CHAPTER THIRTY-SIX

"A LOT of people don't like the gloom," Kinsley said as she lifted the skirt of her white dress and stepped onto a large rock, "but it never bothered me. I've always loved overcast, rainy days."

Vex smiled, offering her a hand. "Mayhap you've unseelie in you after all."

Smirking, she placed her hand on his and hopped down. "I do a couple times a day, at least."

When she continued onward, Vex gave her hand a squeeze, drawing her to a halt. "You play a dangerous game tempting me so, my pretty human."

Her mouth stretched into a grin as she looked at him over her shoulder. "Well, I'm not exactly known for my caution." She wiggled her backside.

"This one is confused," said Echo from ahead of Kinsley.

"Then it must be more innuendo," said Flare, who drifted nearby with head tilted.

Cheeks flushing, Kinsley faced forward. "Sometimes I really regret teaching you three that word."

Vex's smile softened as he gently drew Kinsley to his side. For as bold as she often was, the reminder that she sometimes had an audience never failed to make her blush—and he adored it.

"It is good to know," said Shade as they lazily floated by between

Vex and Kinsley's heads. "Now these ones have a word for what is oft heard yet rarely understood."

"Flesh inspires strange hungers," Flare rasped with exaggerated seriousness.

Laughing, Kinsley withdrew her hand from Vex's and slipped her arm around his waist. "Can't argue with you on that."

Vex wrapped his arm around her shoulders and walked at a relaxed pace, wanting to prolong this contact with her as much as possible.

Though it was nearly midday, the overcast sky left the woods heavily shaded, deepening the natural greens and browns. All was lush and alive, suspended in quiet anticipation of the inevitable rain. But even in the gloom, he could not deny how different the forest looked during the day. It was almost like another place.

In the two months since they'd sealed their bond in the mating hunt, Vex felt as though he'd awoken to a new world every day. Kinsley had introduced light, life, and wonder to this realm, changing it more thoroughly than any illusion ever could have.

"I rather enjoy these dreary days as well," he said.

Kinsley chuckled and peeked up at him. "Of course you do. Sunshine doesn't exactly agree with you."

Vex pecked a kiss on her forehead. "That's certainly one reason. I've always viewed such weather practically. As a means to an end, like all else. A cloudy day meant more time to travel and search. More time to chase my goals. Now, I know it for the boon it truly is. It means more time with you, experiencing the world in a way I've so often ignored. Experiencing the light, the color, the vibrancy."

He met her gaze and let himself sink into those shining periwinkle eyes. "It grants me a glimpse of the world as you must see it. And for that, I shall ever be grateful to the clouds."

"Me too," Kinsley said. "Though the nights with you are just as beautiful."

Flare turned toward them. "This one is glad to see the magus outside his laboratory."

"The magus has spent too much time there alone," Shade said.

Vex scoffed. "I've scarce set foot in that chamber without my brilliant assistant at my side."

Kinsley snickered. "More like in your lap or bent over the table."

A low growl rumbled in his chest, and his fingers flexed against her arm. It was too easy to envision his mate as she described, riding his cock with her skirt bunched around her waist, her head tossed back in pleasure, and her fingernails digging into his shoulders. Or bent naked over his worktable with her lips parted and eyes squeezed shut, her hips marked by the grip of his hands and the bite of his claws as he drove into her from behind.

"My point stands regardless," Vex said, trying to ignore the insistent throb in his groin. "I've not secluded myself these past months."

"These ones are happy for it," Echo said.

Kinsley rested her head against him and tipped it back, looking up at the trees. "You know, it was autumn when I came here. The leaves had already changed colors. It's so strange that all this time has passed, but this world hasn't changed at all. The Highlands were so beautiful."

Frowning, Vex swept his gaze across the surrounding woods. He'd not thought about it before, but...how little had this place changed in the countless years he'd spent here? Yes, plants grew, rain came and went, but this realm had been locked in summer for the entirety of its existence. He'd almost forgotten how much everything changed with the autumn, had forgotten what this land looked like in winter's cold, quiet grasp. Had forgotten what spring looked like, when everything was reborn and renewed after seasons of slumber.

For immortals whose lives could stretch from decades into centuries, centuries into millennia, millennia into eternity, changes of season seemed to come with every breath. Yet that made the seasons no less important. That made them no less magnificent in the way they transformed the land, no less profound in the way they altered life itself—plant and animal, mortal and immortal, magical and mundane.

Obeying the unspoken command of his heart, Vex's magic flowed outward in a green wave. Wind raced on its heels, blowing up detritus and shaking foliage, changing all it touched.

The summer greenery gave way to the browns, reds, yellows, and oranges of autumn. Soft golden light streamed through the treetops to bathe the forest floor, which was covered in an expanding carpet of fallen leaves.

More leaves rained from overhead, lazily fluttering to the ground with gentle rustles and patters. No portion of the woods remained unchanged—neither moss nor lichen, tree nor shrub, grass nor fern. Colors that had existed for so long only in Vex's memory now sprawled around him, made vibrant by sunlight he could never have withstood had it been real.

Sunlight he could never have appreciated were it not for his mate.

"Vex…" Kinsley breathed as she drew away from his side to look around. She held up a hand, and one of the illusory leaves settled upon her palm, its crimson stark against her pale skin.

"Autumn will not come to this place, so I've brought it to you," he said. "An illusion, yes…but it is yours, my love."

"I…I don't know what to say." She looked at him with a big, glowing smile. "Thank you. It's beautiful."

The wisps formed a ring with Kinsley at the center. They spun and twirled rapidly, kicking up loose leaves from the forest floor, which flew around Kinsley in a colorful spiral. She laughed and spread her arms, spinning in place as the leaves and wisps fluttered around her.

Warmth spread through Vex's chest as he watched. For all this time, he'd mistaken this realm as his entire world, but the truth was right here. Kinsley and the wisps were his world, his everything. His dearest friends and his beautiful mate. His clan, his family. He needed naught else.

Kinsley met his gaze. So much passed between them in that moment, more than words could ever have conveyed.

Love.

It was there, plain for him to see. To *feel*.

And then she smiled, stepped out of the leaf vortex, and took his hand. "Join us, Vex."

Vex pulled her against him. Kinsley's eyes flared, and her smile widened as she settled a hand on his shoulder. Placing a hand upon her lower back, he twirled her across the forest floor. Wind whipped around them, carrying streams of vibrant leaves in swirling paths that filled the air with color as he danced with his mate through shafts of illusionary sunlight. All the while, he kept his eyes on hers, watching them sparkle with joy. All the while, his heart swelled in his chest.

The wisps flew around them, laughing and fluttering Vex and Kinsley's hair, and she laughed along with them before they flew off into the trees.

Kinsley watched the wisps until they were no longer in sight. "They're happy."

"They are," Vex said.

Kinsley looked up at him. "And so are you."

"I am." He slowed to a stop. Falling leaves pattered on the forest floor around them. "What of you, my moonlight?" Releasing her hand, he ran the backs of his fingers down her soft cheek. "Are you happy?"

She cradled his jaw between her hands, rose on her toes, and pressed a kiss to his lips. "I'm happier than I've ever been in my life." She stroked his cheeks with her thumbs. "I love you."

Leaning his forehead against Kinsley's, Vex closed his eyes and held her. "And I love you."

He knew not how long they stood there, nor did he care. He would've happily remained like that forever without sparing a thought for aught else.

But a distant sound broke through the tranquility of their embrace, an out-of-place sound that had haunted him too many times during his long imprisonment.

The sound of voices from another world.

His ears twitched. Opening his eyes, he raised his head and listened. As always, the voices were muffled, as though heard underwater. They were calling out, their words indecipherable but somehow chillingly familiar.

Kinsley lowered her hands to his shoulders. "What is it?"

The wisps returned, their ghostfire flickering unsteadily, and hovered nearby.

"What's wrong?" Kinsley asked, brow creased.

The voices called again, closer but no clearer.

Her eyes widened as she took a step away from Vex. "Are those...people?"

He nodded. "In your world."

"Shall these ones cross, magus?" Shade asked.

"Yes, but tarry not. I'd not have you drain yourselves unnecessarily."

The wisps bowed their heads. Their forms shimmered, rippled, and finally faded to nothing, leaving only empty air behind. Though they'd safely returned from that crossing many times over the years, Vex could not help his worry—and he could not shake the vague sense of emptiness that emerged in the wisps' absence.

Those voices sounded again, even closer still.

Kinsley's breath caught, and she walked in the direction of the voices. "Vex... That sounds like..."

The wisps reappeared, their ghostfire frantic.

"Three mortals, magus," Flare said hurriedly. "Two females and a male."

"They are calling for Kinsley," said Echo.

"What?" Kinsley spun toward the wisps. "W-What do they look like?"

Vex's brow furrowed. The desperation that had crept onto her face and into her voice was reminiscent of what he'd witnessed during her first days here, but it was layered with something more. Something deep and sorrowful, a wound that time had not yet healed.

Shade floated closer to her, their voice as gentle as wind through long grass. "Fair of skin. The male is dark of hair but light of eye, with a thick beard. The females are golden haired and dark eyed."

"Oh God, it's them," Kinsley rasped before rushing toward the voices.

"Kinsley!" Vex raced after her, but something stopped him from reaching for her, from halting her. He recognized the rawness in her voice. Recognized the loss.

The illusory autumn broke, reverting the forest to its natural, dreary state, and Kinsley didn't miss a step despite the drastic change. Those ghostly calls continued, louder with every step, and though they remained unclear, he knew now why they sounded so familiar.

They were shouting Kinsley's name.

She finally stopped when she reached a mass of vines and moss at the edge of the mist—her car, now entirely shrouded and unrecognizable. Vex stopped behind her.

Those voices were loudest here, as though the humans in the other realm were standing before Kinsley. Their calls echoed eerily off the trees, rippled through the fog, pulsed in the fabric separating their world from this one. And though the words were no more intelligible than before, the distress and anguish they carried were clear.

"It's them, Vex," Kinsley whispered, voice shaky. "They're here."

Vex curled his fingers around her arms. She trembled beneath his touch. Gently, he turned her to face him. Tears streamed down her cheeks, and her eyes glistened as they met his. When those voices called out her name again, she closed her eyes, and her features contorted with pain.

"They're still looking for me," she said brokenly. "They still think I'm alive."

"Kinsley..."

"And I am alive. I'm alive, and I'm *right here*, and I can't even let them know it." A sob escaped her. "I can't comfort them, can't tell them I'm okay. And they'll...they'll just keep looking, wondering what happened to me, never getting any answers. Never getting any closure."

Vex pulled her against him, and she clutched at his tunic as she cried against his chest. His heart ached like a hole had been torn into it. Not since the queen had taken everything from him had he felt so powerless.

Had he not saved her, Kinsley would have died. That would've provided closure to her family. But she would be gone, her spark extinguished, the entire universe left darker in her absence.

She would have been forever lost to Vex.

He would never regret saving her. Would never regret sharing his lifeforce with her, would never regret prying her from the jaws of death. Yet she did not deserve this suffering. She did not deserve to be trapped here, and it was even crueler than his imprisonment because she still had people out there who loved her. She still had people out there to mourn her.

She hadn't forgotten her world, and it had not forgotten her.

Vex slid a hand into her hair and cupped her head, holding her closer. He stared at the mist as the voices continued calling around them, as his mate grieved, as despair flooded his chest.

The wisps hovered near, brushing tendrils of ghostfire over Kinsley, their lights dim.

"Take me home, Vex," Kinsley whispered against his chest. "I...I can't..."

Gently as he could, Vex lifted her into his arms and summoned his wings. She clung to him, face buried against his neck, her tears hot and wet on his skin, and didn't look up even when he leapt into the air. He sent a wave of magic ahead, forcing apart the branches above to clear a path.

Raindrops fell from the overcast sky, breaking cold upon his wings. The slow rainfall mirrored the sorrow of her tears, as though all the realm wept with his Kinsley.

CHAPTER THIRTY-SEVEN

THERE WAS no comfort to be found in the warm red firelight and the dancing shadows it cast. Neither the soft blue glow of the crystals on the walls nor the darkness beyond the circular window could provide solace, and the familiarity of the bed and blankets offered no respite. There was no peacefulness in the steady drumming of the rain on the roof.

Vex would not sleep this night. He'd known it when he'd first lain beside Kinsley hours ago, and it had only become truer with each moment.

He smoothed a strand of hair back from Kinsley's face. His fingers tingled as they brushed her skin, but she didn't stir.

They lay on their sides, facing one another, with her head upon his arm and his wing draped over her. Though she'd succumbed to exhaustion some time ago, the usual nighttime serenity had never settled over her face. The swollen pink flesh around her eyes evidenced the multitude of tears she had shed since hearing the voices of her family that afternoon.

Each sob, each sniffle, had driven another blade through Vex's heart.

He cupped her cheek with his palm, tenderly stroking the skin beneath her eye with his thumb.

By silver and starlight, he knew her pain all too well. He knew her helplessness, her despair. He knew how it felt to have something so tauntingly close and yet entirely out of reach.

His tumultuous thoughts had ensured sleep would keep far, far away from him. He'd tried to silence them, but he would've fared better trying to quiet a raging thunderstorm. He'd tried to direct them, to seize control, to focus, but they'd only spun faster, as difficult to grasp as the leaves that had been swirling through the air as he and Kinsley danced in the forest.

And no matter what path those thoughts followed, they always led to the same conclusion. An understanding that poured dread, cold and thick and heavy, into his gut.

An understanding that constricted his chest and strained his breath, refusing to be ignored. It was impossible to deny.

Vex knew what he had to do.

Whether he *could* do it was a different matter.

Tenderly, reverently, he traced Kinsley's features with his fingertips. The air he inhaled was perfumed by her familiar, enticing scent. By sight, by feel, by sound, smell, and taste, he'd learn every bit of her. He'd commit it all to undying memory.

A shimmer of blue at the edge of his vision coaxed him to lift his head, albeit reluctantly.

Shade had entered the bedchamber. They floated over to Vex, their ghostfire moving with haunting, mournful ripples.

At Vex's questioning glance, the wisp shook their head. Vex's heart sank.

Moving close, Shade whispered into his ear. "Their search took them beyond the boundaries of this realm, magus. These ones were depleted by following. Only one female heard our calls. When the other humans said they had not, she dismissed it as weariness. This one apologizes."

Though it felt like his ribs were collapsing, making every word a struggle, Vex replied in a soft, even tone. "You need not apologize, my friend. I would have you three safe. You have my thanks for trying."

The wisp bowed their head. "For Kinsley and the magus, there is naught these ones would not try."

Vex smiled. The expression bore warmth but no joy. "Rest. I shall call, should we require aught."

After a lingering look at Kinsley, Shade took their leave.

Vex lowered his head, returning his attention to his mate. She'd not stirred during his brief exchange with the wisp, hadn't so much as made a sound.

He wished he could say her slumber was peaceful, but he knew she was troubled in mind and soul.

And still you know what you must do.

Shifting his wing to uncover Kinsley's arm, Vex gently grasped her wrist. Beneath the slow stroke of his thumb, the binding sigil flared to life, a ring of ivy and thorns glowing green on her pale flesh. The shackle binding her to this place.

He absently rubbed the mark, watching its magic wax and wane in response to his touch.

Everything Kinsley hoped to do, see, and experience tumbled through his mind, all the dreams she'd shared in the hours they'd spent talking. He'd lost his past to this curse. She'd lost her future.

Something stung his eyes. It took him a moment to realize it was gathering tears. Drawing in a slow, shaky breath, he willed away the sensation. He would not have this night marred by his tears.

After all these centuries, he'd finally tasted happiness. He'd finally found joy and the courage to throw himself into it with the whole of his heart. He'd found her—and he'd had her all to himself.

There'd be an eternity to rage against all that being torn away from him. He'd have forever to mourn these moments of bliss he'd claimed amidst the millennia of anguish.

For now, for tonight, those moments remained his. *She* remained his. And he would revel in her. He would delight in her. He would ensure they'd be emblazoned upon one another's souls for all time, no matter what happened.

And then he would choose her happiness over his own, just as he always would when given the choice.

Vex slowly slid his hand up her arm, letting his fingertips explore every inch of her silken flesh until they reached her shoulder. Gently, he guided her onto her back.

Kinsley's brow furrowed, but she didn't open her eyes as she flattened her palm on his chest. "Vex?"

He took her hand, brought it to his mouth, and kissed each

knuckle before turning it and pressing his lips to her palm. "I am here, my Kinsley."

She smiled. It was such a soft, subtle expression, but it filled him with warmth.

"So beautiful." After returning Kinsley's hand to his chest, Vex pushed himself up and leaned over her, curling his fingers behind her neck. His lips met hers in a tender caress.

With a quiet inhalation, Kinsley tipped her face up and returned the kiss. Her fingers spread over his skin, and her other hand slipped into his hair just beneath his ear. She came alive at his coaxing, emerging from her slumber into Vex's sweetest dream.

Into their reality.

Heat washed over him, and his cock pulsed, hard and wanting. Her arousal scented the air, stronger and more tantalizing with his every breath. His wings shuddered. The bestial urge to take his mate roared inside him. It gnashed its fangs and swiped its claws, demanding obedience, demanding release, but Vex denied that primal appetite.

He would not rush this.

Breaking the kiss, he whispered, "I've never tasted anything so sweet as you. Your lips…"

He sensually brushed his mouth across hers before moving on to the rest of her face. He kissed her chin, her jaw, her cheeks. Her nose and eyelids, eyebrows and forehead, her temples. He kissed her ears and teased them with the tips of his tongue before moving to her neck.

Her grasp on his hair tightened, and she tilted her head back, baring her throat for him. Planting his hand on the bed, he followed her neck down, relishing the feel of her soft flesh against his lips.

"Your skin," he said against the hollow of her throat.

Vex trailed his kisses lower still; over her heart, which fluttered beneath his lips; over the yielding flesh of her breast. Kinsley's breath stuttered as he reached her nipple. He drew the hardened bud into his mouth and twirled the tips of his tongue around it.

She arched her back and tugged him closer. "Vex…"

He glanced up to find her eyes open, dark and gleaming with lust.

"Your desire," he said as he moved his mouth to her other breast to lavish it with the same attention.

Kinsley bit her bottom lip, but she did not look away from him. She moved beneath him, restlessly rubbing her thighs, petting him with her fingers, and clenching his hair.

Vex drew hard upon her nipple, wringing a gasp from her before soothing it with his tongue. "Your cries."

He settled a hand on her thigh. Her skin was hot, and that heat called directly to the fires raging at his center. At his urging, she spread her legs. He climbed between them, keeping himself raised over her with his arm braced on the bed.

She watched intently as he dipped his head to continue that trail of kisses downward over her soft belly to the patch of hair on her pelvis. Kinsley's breath quickened, and she shivered.

As he slid his body down the bed, he released a shuddering exhalation; the friction of his cock against the bedding sparked a deep, pulsing ache in his groin, prodding the beast he'd kept restrained all this while. He grasped Kinsley's thighs and spread them wider, denying that instinct a little longer.

The petals of her sex glistened with dew, and her aroma filled his nose.

"But sweetest of all," he growled as he lowered his face, "your essence."

Keeping his eyes on her face, he ran the flat of his tongue over her from bottom to top, gathering that dew until the tips of his tongue reached her clit, which he caressed. He groaned at her taste. His wings snapped out before contracting against his back.

"Oh God," Kinsley moaned, closing her eyes as her pelvis twitched upward.

Vex tightened his grip, holding her down. "Cry out to *me*, my moonlight. For me."

He pressed his tongue over her clit, flicking and stroking with its tips. She grasped the bedding in both hands and called out his name in a strained, breathless voice. It washed over him, flowed into him, permeated his heart and soul, and he let his eyelids fall shut as he thrilled in the sound. As he thrilled in her.

"Just so," he purred.

Wrapping his arms around her thighs, he pulled her closer and resumed licking and teasing her intimate flesh. Her essence was the perfect blend of sweet and salty, the pure distillation of her, his mate, his everything. Vex would never forget it. All else would be compared to her for the rest of his eternity, and it would all come up short.

Kinsley writhed in his hold, again grasping his hair with one hand. Her every little movement—the twitches of her cunt, the gyrations of her hips, the scrape of her nails on his scalp—fanned the flames of Vex's need. He relished her soft moans and breathy whimpers. Relished her scent and her warmth, relished the feel of her pounding pulse and her leg muscles quivering beneath his palms.

Everything she did, every part of her, he sealed away at his core. It would be his forever.

She would be his forever.

Squeezing his eyes tighter shut, he threw himself into the joy of her pleasure, into the satisfaction of knowing that all her reactions, her lack of control, were because of him. Her breaths came faster and shallower, and her grip tightened. The tips of his tongue whirled around her clit. She writhed atop the bed, nearly breaking his hold.

Finally, he took that swollen bud into his mouth and sucked.

Kinsley's hips bucked, and her entire body tensed. He opened his eyes to stare up at her as she lifted her shoulders off the bed, mouth open in a soundless scream, only to collapse and arch her back, thrusting her pelvis up at him.

Liquid heat rushed from her cunt. He devoured it hungrily, greedily, delving his tongue into her to coax out more. Kinsley's voice finally emerged in a broken cry of pleasure as her thighs clenched around him, but her hand only pulled him closer still.

"Vex!" she rasped, curling her toes against his back as she met his gaze. "Please, I need you. I want you inside me."

He dragged his tongue over her clit one last time, savoring her taste and the tremors wracking her, before he crawled up over her body. Nestling his hips between her thighs, he braced his elbows to either side of her head. His long hair hung in dark curtains around their heads. He lowered his face to hers as she wrapped her arms around him.

Stroking his hair with her fingers, Kinsley searched his eyes. "I love you."

"And I love you." Vex shifted his hips until the head of his cock was poised against her entrance. Beckoning heat radiated from her, and he didn't resist. He slowly pushed into her hot, wet, welcoming body.

Kinsley's breath hitched. She tipped her head back and widened her thighs, allowing him to settle deeper inside. Her sex closed over him, ridge by ridge. Just as it seemed she could take no more, she banded her legs around Vex, dug her heels into the backs of his thighs, and drew him more snugly against her until she'd taken all of him.

Vex's claws raked the bedding as her cunt clamped around his cock. Just lying there, seated within her, feeling her inner muscles twitch and her pulse race, was nearly enough to make him come.

With his hair blocking out the firelight, there was only Vex and Kinsley. The rest of the world had ceased to be. All that mattered was here, now. All that mattered was her.

"You are my mate," he whispered, brushing his lips over hers as he pulled his hips back. He slowly pumped into her again. "You are my soul."

Kinsley moaned and rocked her pelvis upward, meeting his thrusts as he set a rhythm with slow, steady strokes. She kissed his lips, but he did not yet allow her to claim his mouth fully.

He slid his arm up, combed his fingers into her hair, and kissed one corner of her mouth. "You are the air I breathe." He kissed the other corner. "You are the water that slakes my thirst and the food that nourishes me. You are the trees that bless me with shade and shelter"—he kissed the center of her lips—"and the sky through which I soar."

A crease formed between her eyebrows, but she didn't tear her gaze from his. Panting softly, she cupped his cheek. "Vex... My darkness. My night sky."

Pleasure coiled around him with crushing strength. His muscles tensed, his breathing faltered, and his heart quickened, but Vex maintained his deliberate pace. Their bodies moved as one, giving and taking equally. Their souls sang in harmony.

"You, Kinsley," he rasped, "are *all* to me." He kissed her again, more firmly this time, and felt her tremble beneath him. The press of her lips enhanced every other sensation. "You are the song in my heart. The melody of my soul. I am yours."

She pulled him into another kiss, moaning against his mouth. Their breaths mingled; their tongues danced. Vex closed his eyes. All his other senses heightened, drinking her in. Every shred of his being thrummed with passion, with pleasure, with love. For her, because of her.

Panting, he tipped his forehead against hers, their noses tip to tip. They opened their eyes. Hers were dark, shimmering with reflected light from his.

"You are mine, Kinsley," Vex growled. He caught her bottom lip with his teeth.

She gasped and bucked her hips.

His chest rumbled, and his cock twitched, disrupting his rhythm. Only then did he speed his thrusts, surrendering to their mutual need.

"Naught can change that." He punctuated each word by driving into her harder, deeper. "Neither time nor distance…"

She hooked her arms around him, her clutching fingers and scratching nails urging more haste, more force. Her desire was his, woven with it as surely as their souls were twined.

The pressure in Vex's groin swelled, threatening to overtake him, to sap his strength and wrest control from him.

"Not beast," he grated between ragged breaths, "nor magic, not fate itself."

Her features, stained crimson by the glow of his eyes, went taut. Her cunt clenched, wrenching a fresh growl from his throat. But neither of them relented. They drew strength from one another, carried each other ever higher in their pursuit of ultimate intimacy, of unrivaled bliss.

"Naught…will change it." Vex's pace became frantic, erratic, and his wings snapped out, their tips raking the bedposts. "You. Are. *Mine.*"

Kinsley's voice rang out in time with his declaration, just as bold, just as confident, just as possessive, just as raw. "I am yours!"

Vex's entirety shrank down to a single point—the point of contact between their bodies, their hearts, their souls. It was far too small to contain all that pleasure, all that pressure, all that fire. All that love. Much too small to encompass his whole world.

The universe around him exploded. White hot flames engulfed his senses, his very being, blasting away all thought and sensation and leaving only Kinsley and ecstasy behind.

He roared; she screamed. Vex heard the sounds from afar. The pressure in him burst, stealing his breath on a wave of pleasure so powerful and immense that it would surely drown him. And he welcomed it.

He rode it with her.

Kinsley's every movement, her every sound, and every rush of her hot essence fueled that wave and wrung more seed from him. She and Vex clung to each other. They were one with each other.

Though his eyes were closed, and his mind had succumbed to sweet, sweet oblivion, he saw Kinsley. Felt Kinsley. Around him, beneath him, within him. She was a part of Vex carried outside himself, and he was a part of her. No force could separate them, not in truth. Their souls were bound by threads stronger than any queen, than any monster, stronger than fate, than death.

Gradually, Vex sank into himself. His body, tingling and throbbing in the aftermath of their lovemaking, was warm and heavy. But not as heavy as his heart.

He stroked her hair, and her fingers slid up and down his back soothingly. When he opened his eyes, his chest constricted.

Kinsley was glowing, and it had naught to do with the light of his eyes.

"No eyes, whether human or fae, have ever been so blessed as to gaze upon such beauty," he said, voice low and rough. "It is a sight worth eternity."

Vex kissed her again, slowly, tenderly, worshipfully, willing it to communicate all the things he'd not yet said, all the feelings he'd not yet expressed.

She moved her hand, brushing it across his cheek as she swept his hair behind his ear. "I love you, Vex. With everything I am."

He met her gaze and caressed her cheek with the backs of his fingers. A universe swirled in those periwinkle eyes, an infinite expanse of potential and promise.

Gods, how he longed to cast himself into their depths. To claim all that promise, to hoard all that potential. To have her eternally.

"And I love you, Kinsley." His eyes followed his fingers along her jaw to her chin, then followed his thumb as it stroked her kiss-swollen lower lip. "Never doubt. Never forget."

His heart nearly stopped when she brushed her lips across his and vowed, "Never."

CHAPTER THIRTY-EIGHT

KINSLEY INHALED DEEPLY as she woke. Rolling onto her back, she stretched her arms over her head and arched her feet, pressing her toes into the mattress. She exhaled slowly as she settled and opened her eyes.

Diffused light streamed in through the window over the bed. Rain pattered on the cottage roof, and the tree creaked and groaned softly, its boughs undoubtedly swaying in the wind. The rain must've decided to stick around.

Her thoughts turned back to yesterday, to before the storm began. Back to the moment she'd heard the distorted sounds of her family calling for her from another world. When she'd closed her eyes, their voices had sounded as though they were coming from right beside her, like she could've just reached out and touched her parents. And she'd longed to do so. To comfort them, to tell them that she was alive and well. That she was happy.

But she couldn't. And their grief was hers. She wished there was a way to take that pain away.

Kinsley's chest tightened.

A gentle, familiar caress on her cheek soothed her.

Though Kinsley's heartache would never fully go away, it would lessen over time, and Vex's touch would always soothe that hurt and bring her the comfort she sorely needed.

She looked at Vex, who sat on the edge of the bed gazing down at her, dressed in a tunic, pants, and boots, the dark garments contrasted by a periwinkle sash. He was ever the formal goblin lord.

Her goblin lord.

Kinsley smiled and turned onto her side to face him, tucking an arm beneath her head as she reached out and ran her fingers through his long hair. "Morning. You're up early."

She couldn't recall a morning over the past several weeks when she'd awoken without Vex lying curled up around her.

He covered her cheek with his palm and brushed the skin beneath her ear with his fingers. "I've not slept."

Brow creasing, Kinsley covered his hand with her own. "Are you okay?"

His intense, piercing crimson eyes held hers, amplifying the silence gripping the room. He wasn't merely looking at her, he was looking into her. Those eyes saw Kinsley in her entirety, inside and out. They knew her every hope and dream, her every desire, her every secret. And though she loved being seen by him, there was something different in his gaze now.

A wistfulness. A hint of sorrow. A longing removed from the passion and lust that normally blazed in his eyes, removed from his hunger.

Too soon, he looked away, withdrawing his touch, and shoved himself onto his feet. "I've something to show you," he said as he strode to the wardrobe and opened it. "Don your clothing."

Kinsley propped herself up on an elbow, watching him. There was something off, something she couldn't place. Even the room itself wasn't quite right. The fire that normally burned within the hearth was extinguished, and the crystals were dim.

He was acting strangely. He was acting…distant. This wasn't the passionate lover she'd known. She could still feel echoes of every caress, every kiss, every thrust of his cock from the night before. She could still feel him branded upon her very soul.

Drawing back the covers, she slipped out of bed and rose, walking toward him. The chill of the room made her skin prickle.

"Vex, what is it?" she asked as she stopped next to him.

"You will know soon enough, Kinsley."

She cast him a cheeky smile as she reached into the wardrobe and pulled out a dark blue gown. "A surprise?"

Though his eyes followed her hands, he didn't look at her directly. It added to that niggling feeling of wrongness. He normally gazed upon her naked body at every opportunity, and he always had his hands on her as though he couldn't resist touching her.

When he said nothing more, Kinsley stepped into the gown and drew it up her body, slipping her arms through the short sleeves before tying the belt at her back. "Will the wisps be joining us?"

Vex ran his gaze over her, and something sparked in it, something familiar and heated. But that ember faded too quickly. In a low rasp, he said, "Lovely as ever."

Kinsley stepped closer to Vex and placed her hands upon his chest. "I could…take this off and we could get back into bed?"

He covered her hands with his, squeezing gently as he stared down at them. "Come, Kinsley. It…it shan't take long."

Keeping hold of one of her hands, he led her toward the door. It opened at a flick of his fingers.

A knot of dread formed in Kinsley's belly as she followed him. "Vex, what's wrong?"

The closest thing to a response he offered was the tightening of his grip as they walked around the tree. He brought her down into the foyer, turned, and descended into the chamber she'd only entered once, when she'd attempted to cross the mist.

Vex's ritual chamber.

The crystals on the rough stone walls offered little illumination. As before, most of the light came from the runes carved on the standing stones in the center of the chamber. The tree's thick, gnarled roots surrounded the stone circle, black as pitch in the dim light, and only now did she realize how much it resembled a cage.

"What are we doing down here?" she asked.

Vex led her beneath the roots, between a pair of standing stones, and to the center of the circle. Her skin thrummed, and the small hairs on her arms and neck stood on end. She understood what that feeling was now.

Magic.

Vex turned to face her, though he did not relinquish his hold.

"You feel it. That"—he gestured to the ground with his free hand—"is why I chose this place. It is a font of mana. The ley lines converging beneath our feet carry unfathomable magic."

Kinsley glanced down. The ground, covered with soft moss, looked unremarkable, but the feel of it... She could almost envision the powerful currents running beneath the surface. Could almost envision the magic flowing into everything around her, nourishing, sustaining, enriching.

But she found no comfort in that.

"Here, magics are woven and unraveled." Vex took hold of Kinsley's wrists, calling her attention back up to him.

"Vex..." She searched his gaze, desperate to identify the source of his melancholy, to understand the resigned sorrow in his tone.

He guided her right hand to his chest. Beneath his tunic, his muscles were warm, firm, familiar, and the beat of his heart was strong and steady. "What we share, my moonlight..."

The green glow of the runestones brightened, deepening the shadows on Vex's face. Disturbed by a gentle breeze, Kinsley's skirt brushed her legs, and her hair tickled her face and shoulders.

Vex's hand heated around her wrist. "What we share is beyond magic."

The air changed. It wasn't exactly thicker or heavier, but...fuller. It was charged with the same unseen energy coursing underfoot, and it swirled round and round the circle, bristling with more power after every circuit.

She'd experienced Vex's illusions many times. This magic was wholly different.

He turned her left palm upward and looked down at it as he ran this thumb across it. "What we share, my Kinsley, cannot be unraveled."

She curled her fingers, grasping his tunic. Around them, the circle was tumultuous, fraught with unbridled magic. But as long as she had Vex to steady her, to ground her, she wouldn't be afraid. The universe could fall apart around them, but she'd be fine.

Vex met her gaze. Something in his eyes made time stop, something so grave that nothing could escape its pull.

"Forgive me, my love," he rumbled.

"Vex, I don't—"

Vex's claw slashed her palm. Hissing, she reflexively flinched and tugged her arm, but he held it in place, his lips peeling back to reveal his fangs in an anguished snarl.

Kinsley's hand throbbed around the sting of the cut, from which glistening blood welled. She watched crimson pool on her palm and wondered why that sight—and what Vex had just done—was so much less troubling than the faint tremors she felt in his hands.

Color whirled around Vex and Kinsley, obscuring the rest of the chamber. Green, violet, dazzling white and electric blue, carried on an ever-intensifying wind that pushed and pulled at Kinsley's hair and clothing but exerted no force against her body.

She was in the eye of the storm.

No. I am the eye of the storm...

"Vex, what are you doing?" Kinsley tugged on her wrist again, but he held firm. "I don't understand."

A shiver stole through her when he spoke. It wasn't a reply to her questions, not at all; his words were in a language she'd never heard, a language that crackled with eldritch power.

And she understood every word.

"I call upon the ether that binds this world and all others."

Kinsley's heart thundered. "Stop."

"I seize the veil," he continued, "and will it to part."

"No!" Tears stung Kinsley's eyes as she fought his hold. She shook her head, begging him, barely hearing her own voice, her own words.

Vex raised her upturned hand. "Let this blood be the key and my words the command. Unlock the door."

Kinsley yanked harder, yet his grip only strengthened. "Vex, no! Please, don't do this! You can't do this! Please, please..."

He drew in a deep, shaky breath. Kinsley's eyes widened as the blood from her hand flowed up into the air—first a few drops, then a stream, swirling and weaving in a double column like a model of DNA.

Or like two intertwined souls.

The blood flowed outward to join the chaotic array of magic, adding a splash of crimson to the maelstrom.

Her right wrist heated further. The searing pain should've been debilitating, unbearable, but the ache in her heart was so immense that it swallowed all else.

"Open the way!" Vex called.

Kinsley cried out as she felt reality fracture. A chasm opened within her, around her, between her and Vex. She felt...split. Torn. Two contradictory forces pulled at her—one dragging her toward a far-off place, the other wrenching her from that place back to here, back to Vex.

The floodgates crashed open, and fear and panic washed through her.

With tears streaming down her cheeks, she met Vex's gaze and leaned toward him, chest to chest. Her words were strained and raw, but she forced them out. "Don't send me away. Don't you dare abandon me. Please, Vex. I don't want to go. I love you."

Releasing her raised arm, he caught her chin in his hand. His eyes glistened with unshed tears as he stared down at her. "And I love you, Kinsley."

She gripped his tunic. "Then let me stay. Keep me. Choose me."

"My moonlight," he rasped, brushing his trembling thumb beneath her lip. "I would sooner tear the heart from my chest than hurt you...so that is what I must do. You will understand with time, my love, that I am choosing you."

Kinsley frantically shook her head. "Vex, no. No, no, no."

"For the first time in eternity, I understand. Each moment is precious. A thing to be treasured. All those moments you should've had..." Tears trickled from the corners of his eyes, catching the wild light as they trailed down his cheeks. "Your family seeks you. They need you, just as you need them."

"I need *you*! I want you!"

"Wherever you are, my moonlight, wherever you go, so shall I be there. For you are my heart." Sliding his hand into her hair, he dipped his head and pressed his lips to hers.

Kinsley threw her arm around his neck and embraced him as tightly as she could, refusing to end that kiss, refusing to let him release her. She felt his heat, tasted the saltiness of their mingling tears, smelled his oakmoss and amber scent. She clung to his solidness. She clung to him.

And she tried to tell herself that he wasn't kissing her goodbye. She tried so, so hard to convince herself of it.

Vex's fingers twitched, and his claws pricked her scalp. He let out a shuddering exhalation as he clenched her closer. But his words were clear, steady, and deliberate when he whispered against her lips, "Kinsley Wynter Delaney, I release you from your vow. Our pact is fulfilled."

The stinging pain in her wrist vanished. The swirling colors grew to blinding intensity, so bright that they swallowed up Vex completely. A sound like roaring wind and quaking earth filled her ears. She felt herself pulled in a million directions at once, felt the universe shattering around her, felt reality vanishing from under her feet. Felt herself coming untethered.

But she still felt Vex. He released her wrist and embraced her, and for another instant, she felt him holding her, tighter than ever. For another instant, he was real.

All that sound and light crashed over Kinsley and devoured her. A wave of dizziness swept through her, and she was falling, falling, falling…

And then it was silent. So silent, and so, so still.

Kinsley squeezed her eyes shut and drew in a deep breath as she willed everything to stop spinning. She was bent over, arms on the ground and head bowed. The cold air smelled of moist vegetation and earth, and her dress offered no protection from the chill, especially the skirt, which was wet where she was kneeling upon it.

Eyes snapping open, she shoved herself up on her knees and looked around.

"No," she rasped, her breath coming out in a tiny white cloud. "*No!*"

There was no stone circle, no tangled roots, no rough-hewn stone walls with glowing crystals. There was no cottage.

And there was no Vex.

Gnarled trees stood around her, their bark covered in moss, their branches bare of leaves. All remained still and quiet, as though the land were sleeping.

She looked down to find herself in the middle of a small depression that was ringed by a wide circle of mushrooms, their large, orange-brown caps stark against the dull, dreary surroundings.

A fairy ring. A final bit of magic that felt like a mockery of what had just happened.

"No." Kinsley shook her head. "No, no, no, no. This isn't real. He...he didn't..."

Lifting her hand, she turned her palm up. The wound had already stopped bleeding; only a line of pink, healing skin remained as evidence that she'd been cut at all. Heart pounding and breaths coming quick and shallow, she scratched at her palm. The pain was distant as her nails bit into her flesh until she drew blood.

"Send me back. Send me back!"

She held her hand over the ground and clenched her fist. Time crawled, and her arm quivered with exertion, until finally several drops of blood fell to the earth.

But nothing happened.

Eyes filling with tears, she slammed her hand on the ground. "Send me back! Please!"

A sob wrenched from her throat, followed by another, and another. She crumpled forward, head against her arm, and cried, body shaking as she begged whoever would listen to send her back. She begged her blood to work, her magic to awaken, begged fate to correct itself and return her to her mate.

The world around her remained unchanged; reality didn't so much as ripple.

She thought she heard someone call her name from afar, but she offered them no attention; it hadn't been Vex's voice.

She clutched at the ground. Her heart had been split in two, with half of it trapped in another world, so far out of reach.

Why? Why had he done this?

You were useless to him.

No.

You couldn't free him.

No.

He doesn't want you.

"No! None of that is true."

Vex loved her. She'd seen it in his eyes, had felt it radiating in his every touch. She'd felt it in her soul.

You will understand with time, my love, that I am choosing you.

"But you didn't," she whispered. "You didn't."

Anger ignited inside her. Each ragged breath and thunderous beat of her battered heart fanned the flame until it was a roaring inferno, burning hotter than her agony and heartache.

With a growl, Kinsley shoved herself to her feet. "Damn you!"

Her throat burned as she screamed. The sound echoed through the forest, but she didn't stop, not even when she heard her name called once more.

"Why? Why did you send me away? You had no right! *No right!* It was my choice, Vex. Mine! And you…" A hoarse sob escaped her, and her next words came in a broken whisper. "You took it from me."

She thrust her cold, trembling hands into her hair, gripping the roots until it hurt. It was different from her other pain, but she needed it. She needed something more than the wretched hollowness gnawing at her from within.

"It was my choice," she repeated quietly as tears spilled from her eyes. "I wanted to stay with you. I want *you,* Vex. Why…why couldn't you want me too?"

Vegetation rustled behind her, followed by the snap of a twig.

"Kinsley? Is…is that you?"

Kinsley's breath caught. She lowered her arms and turned. Large, gentle brown eyes, set in a familiar face, met hers.

"Mum?"

"Oh God, Kinsley!" Emily rushed forward and threw her arms around Kinsley, squeezing her tight. "It's you. It's you, oh God, you're alive. Oh, my baby. I love you so, so much."

Kinsley kept still, frozen by the shock of having her mother here. She'd made peace long ago with the knowledge that she'd never see her family again. She had accepted that Vex's realm was her home. Her forever.

But hearing the pain in their voices yesterday had broken her heart anew.

Now her mother was here. Emily Delaney wasn't just a disembodied voice, lost in the mist. She was with Kinsley right now.

You're alive.

But Kinsley didn't feel alive. This…this felt like dying again.

Kinsley wrapped her arms around her mother, clutching at the thick coat she wore. Emily's sweet peppermint scent filled her nose. "Mum?"

"I'm here, love. I'm here." She pulled back and cupped Kinsley's face, wiping away the tears on her cheeks. "You'll be okay now."

Emily turned her head and yelled, "Aiden! Cecelia! I found her!"

Two other figures emerged from the trees, running toward them—Kinsley's father and Aunt Cece.

"Oh, thank God," Cecelia breathed, wrapping her arms around both Kinsley and Emily. She pressed a kiss to Kinsley's temple. "We refused to believe we'd never see you again. Where have you been? Are you hurt?"

"I'm okay," Kinsley said, squeezing her eyes shut and resting her head against her aunt's.

You're a liar.

Their love flowed into her, warm and soothing, but it could only swirl around the gaping hole in her chest. It couldn't fill that void; nothing ever could. Nothing but Vex.

Fabric whispered behind her aunt and mother. They pulled away from Kinsley as her father took off his coat and settled it around her shoulders, blanketing her in heat. She looked up at him. His blue eyes were reddened by his tears, which rolled down his cheeks to disappear in his thick beard.

A soft cry broke past Kinsley's lips. "Daddy."

He drew her into a crushing embrace, cupping the back of her head in his big hand. "I thought we lost you, baby girl."

She wrapped her arms around him. "You didn't."

"You're safe now."

I was already safe. I was exactly where I wanted to be.

I was happy.

CHAPTER THIRTY-NINE

It mattered not how tightly Vex had held on, how fiercely he'd desired or how deeply he'd hoped. Naught could have changed this.

He told himself that over and over as he stared down at his empty arms, still curved as though around her body, as he stared at his open hands, his splayed fingers. As he beheld this... *wrongness*.

Each time he repeated those frantic insistences, those pathetic, fraught self-assurances, he knew they were holding something else back. Something far larger, darker, and hungrier. They were the gates defending against a titanic, rampaging monster.

And the gates were splintering.

"I chose her," he rasped.

His voice echoed off the stone walls, twisting in the chamber's oppressive silence to become a taunting rumble from the dark. His own voice distorted, reflected, stripped and raw, tearing apart his intent, his words, his already tattered heart.

When the echoes died, silence reclaimed mastery of the space. It pressed in around him, squeezing, crushing, demanding he curl his arms inward.

But to do that would...

Would prove his arms were empty, would prove this was no illusion.

It would prove his Kinsley was...gone.

My mate is gone.

Vex's fingers twitched, and his arms trembled. He needed but blink, and all would be right again. Needed but squeeze his arms a little tighter and he would feel her again. He would know she was still right here.

Clenching his jaw, he drew in a deep, shaky breath. It caught in his lungs, laden with the tang of magic and the cloying scents of earth and root. But it yet bore a hint of perfume. A hint of her.

He moved his arms closer to his chest. They encountered no resistance until they touched the breast of his tunic.

Nothingness. He'd been cradling nothingness in his arms, and now it flooded his heart. Now it permeated his being.

Kinsley shouted from another world. Vex held his breath and listened as her voice swept through him, the words lost but the emotions unmistakable. Her anguish and anger, her grief.

Vex balled his fists. He welcomed the bite of his claws against his palms, though it could not shield him, could not distract him.

"What did I expect?" he growled.

He'd known what he was doing, had understood his aim. The spell had worked. Vex had succeeded.

But this success was no more satisfying than his gravest failures.

He forced his hands open and stared at the blood on his palms. Some part of him had hoped her blood would've worked for him, that it would've transported him alongside Kinsley. That selfish, foolish part of Vex had hoped they'd remain together, despite every piece of evidence proving it could never have been so.

Muffled voices sounded around Vex, coming from right beside him, coming from across the universe. Kinsley was no longer alone. These were the voices of other humans—shocked, relieved, brimming with love. Her family.

His legs buckled, and Vex sunk to his knees, falling back to sit on his haunches.

Something hot and wet streamed down his cheeks and along his nose. The tears fell, splashing on his upturned hands, where they mingled with his blood.

Vex didn't fight them. He watched them fall like rain, refracting the light of the runes and crystals. He watched them break upon his hands and the ground, each a tiny reflection of his heart.

Were he to spill enough tears to flood the glen, to flood the world, they'd not be enough to fill the emptiness at his core.

He did not know how long he knelt there—only that his tears persisted after the otherworldly voices faded.

"Magus?"

Soft blue light fell across the ground in front of Vex as the wisps flew to him.

"These ones sensed a surge in the ley lines," said Flare.

"These ones did not think to find you here. What has happened?" Echo asked.

Shade flitted down. Their light dimmed as they studied the ground, Vex's hands, and finally his face. "Magus…" The wisp extended a tendril, lightly touching Vex's thumb. "Where is Kinsley?"

The answer emerged raw and ragged from Vex's throat. "Gone."

"Gone?" Echo joined Shade, looking small and dim.

But when Flare fell into place beside the others, the wisp's ghostfire was bright and bristling. "What have you done?"

"What have I done?" Vex lifted his gaze to the wisps. His heart thumped deafeningly in the gaping void within his chest, and each breath clawed at his lungs and throat. "What was necessary."

"Please, magus. Where is she?" Shade asked, voice gentle but quavering.

"She's returned to her world. Her home."

Flare swelled, ghostfire taking on withering intensity. "*This* is her world. This is her home."

"This was her cage!" Vex dropped his hands and tore up fistfuls of moss and soil. "This is naught but the floor of a cell. This world was her prison, even more so than it is mine."

"Such foolishness is unlike you," said Shade, blazing alongside Flare.

"Is it foolishness to wish her happiness?" Vex threw the clumps down and clutched at his tunic. "Foolishness to pluck out my heart that she might live?"

"She was living," Echo replied. "She was happy."

"She was *trapped*. All her dreams, snatched away. All her loved ones bereft and beyond reach." Shoving himself to his feet, Vex spread his arms and turned in place. "Here, my mate was a caged bird, damned by no folly of her own to wither for eternity. But out there..." His words caught in his throat, a jagged clump echoing the unfathomable ache in his chest.

But he forced them out anyway, embracing the agony they inflicted upon him. "Out there, she is free to soar."

"How can she soar," said Shade, voice low and oddly thick, "when you have broken her heart?"

"You may as well have clipped her wings," added Flare.

Vex stared at the wisps, unblinking, grasped by a terrible stillness. The first movement inside him came in the form of something cold and heavy in his gut, expanding and sinking.

"These ones have not any time to waste," said Echo softly.

"Come," Flare commanded.

The wisps faded from sight. The faint tingling of their magical essences ceased, leaving only the overwhelming thrum of the ley lines amidst the chamber's silence.

There was no question of what the wisps were doing. Yet as much as Vex wanted to know that Kinsley had made it safely, he didn't want the wisps to succeed. What could they accomplish by finding her? What could come of it but for the wounds both she and Vex carried—still raw, still bleeding—being torn even wider?

Lowering his hands to his sides, Vex stood in the silence, in the solitude, forcing himself to feel every moment of it. It could not fill the void either, because it was the void, consuming him from within and devouring him from without.

Only here, now, with the wisps and Kinsley gone, did he truly understand loneliness. Only now did he understand the real depth and weight of isolation.

Anguish, anger, bitterness, grief, and a dozen other emotions raged within him, swirling around and within that chasm, akin to it but always separate, always lesser.

He closed his eyes. Images of Kinsley danced through the darkness behind his eyelids. Her alluring, sensual body. Her full, expressive lips. Her dazzling smile and mesmerizing periwinkle eyes. Her soft, honey brown tresses. Her warm laughter.

The hurt and desperation that had been on her face when she'd realized he was sending her away.

Her pleas echoed in his memory, each word drawing tighter the thorny vines constricting his heart. The way she'd looked at him...

Vex had betrayed her. His mate, his love, his moonlight. His Kinsley. Whatever his intentions, he'd betrayed her. She would carry that pain—the pain he'd caused—forever.

Faint magic rippled through the air. Vex's heart lurched. For an instant, he sensed the veil between worlds, sensed its thinness, its fragility. For an instant, he felt Kinsley's world, which he'd once called home.

And it only made him more aware of her absence.

"These ones could not find her." Echo's soft, whispery voice had a brittleness to it like Vex had never heard.

"She has journeyed too far beyond the borders of this realm," said Shade.

Squeezing his eyes more tightly shut and clenching his fists, Vex asked, "You've searched everywhere within your reach?"

"Tracks lie around the circle on the other side. Human tracks," added Echo.

Flare said, "And human blood lies at its center."

Vex's heart quickened, its beat reminiscent of pounding war drums.

"No more than a few drops," said Shade. "Yet these ones found no other direct signs of Kinsley."

"Just as the magus said," Flare rasped, their tone fiery and harsh. "She is gone."

"Leave me," Vex grated through bared teeth.

"Magus..."

"Now!" Vex's eyes snapped open. His wings burst out, and magic surged inside him, amplified by the ley lines to make the whole chamber quake.

The surrounding light—including that of the wisps—dimmed as shadows coalesced around Vex. Fury thrummed at the heart of his power.

The wisps shrank back, their ghostfire flickering. Their hurt and confusion pierced Vex's heart, yet what could those emotions do but settle atop the heap? When his hurt was already inconceivably wide and deep, how could anything make it feel vaster than infinity?

"Please," he begged, voice broken.

Silently, sorrowfully, and hesitantly, the wisps exited the chamber. Once their light was out of sight, Vex again closed his eyes. He called upon memory, willed images of Kinsley back into his mind's eye. But those images, those memories, refused to come.

Brow furrowing, he strained for cooperation from his mind. It did not comply. Emptiness lingered behind his eyelids. Nothingness reigned. All his mind produced was a voice, cold and humorless. His own voice.

She is gone. Now you gaze upon all that remains for you.

Everything welling inside Vex erupted. Pain and rage, grief and guilt, heartbreak and agony, and there was no one to blame but himself.

The roar began in his belly—in the pit of his soul. It was a banshee's wail of lament, the enraged call of a wounded, starving beast, the cry of an immortal enduring an eternity of self-inflicted suffering.

The sound felt like golden blades slicing his chest and throat, leaving fire in their wake, and its reverberation within the chamber only plunged more blades into him, burying them deep in his heart and soul.

Kinsley was gone. He'd sent her away. He'd forever severed himself from the only light in his life.

Though he did not will it, his roar became a plea—it became her name. And he sounded it until all breath fled his lungs and he collapsed to the ground, where that name echoed cruelly through the ley lines, bounced off the chamber walls, and replaced the sound of his heartbeat.

CHAPTER FORTY

Kinsley was tired. So damned tired. It'd been hours since Vex had cast her out, and she'd felt every second that had passed. She thought she'd felt heartache over Liam? That had been nothing compared to what she felt now.

Half her soul had been ripped away.

Against her protests, Kinsley's family had insisted she see a doctor. During the long car ride to the hospital, her parents and aunt had asked endless questions.

What had happened? Where had she been? What was she wearing? Where was her car?

But Kinsley hadn't answered any of them. She couldn't have. Every time she'd opened her mouth to mutter, *I'm okay*—which would've been a complete lie—she'd started crying again. What else could she have said, anyway? They wouldn't have believed the truth, even if she'd been able to give it.

At the hospital, the long wait in the waiting room had been equally torturous. Yet she had felt little relief when a nurse finally called her back. Kinsley's mother had accompanied her to the exam room, while her father and aunt anxiously remained behind.

She'd felt like an automaton as they'd gone through the usual motions—checking vitals, questions about her medical history, peeing in a cup. After the nurse had left, Kinsley sat, staring at the floor, again waiting.

Waiting for something that would never come.

Waiting for Vex.

She wasn't sure how long it had been before the doctor stepped in. The middle-aged, gray-haired woman with a soothing brogue had introduced herself as Dr. Ames. She'd checked Kinsley over for injuries, but there weren't any to find. Even Kinsley's hand had healed again, without a scar to be seen.

Soon after the doctor had stepped out, promising she'd return once she had some test results to review, Kinsley had received a visit from the police.

The detectives were compassionate but firm. They'd asked many of the same questions as Kinsley's family, along with a great deal more.

What had happened on the night of her disappearance? Had she met someone? Had she been taken, assaulted? Was she avoiding their questions because she was protecting someone, or because she feared for her safety if she shared the truth? How had her car vanished, leaving behind only the path it had cut through the woods and some scattered debris?

Had she been under the influence of alcohol or any controlled substances that night or in the time since?

She understood how it all must've looked. She'd vanished with only the most inconclusive of traces. The local authorities had searched the surrounding area thoroughly, going so far as to have diving teams check the loch, but there'd been nothing to find save a few bits of broken glass, plastic, and metal where her car had crashed.

Then, three months later, she'd suddenly reappeared in the middle of the woods where'd she'd vanished.

No answer she could've provided would have ever satisfied everyone's questions. That she'd been able to muster the occasional shake of her head or an *I don't know* had been a small wonder given how everything felt inside her chest—like there was a huge hole where her heart should've been, swallowing everything up.

But now, thankfully, the police had decided to relent.

Kinsley watched as one of the detectives handed a card to her mother, who was sitting beside her.

"If she remembers anything, ma'am, please let us know."

Emily nodded. "We will."

The detectives stepped out and quietly closed the door.

Emily settled her hand on Kinsley's. "What aren't you telling us, love?"

"Nothing."

"Kinsley, please. You disappeared for months without a word. That isn't like you. Everywhere you've gone, you've always, *always* kept in touch. Always. And then you suddenly appear out of thin air dressed like...like"—Emily waved at Kinsley's body—"that! Like you've stepped out of some fairytale. This isn't nothing."

More tears stung Kinsley's eyes, and her lower lip trembled. "I just want to go home."

Home.

It wasn't the secluded cottage she'd rented, wasn't her room at her aunt's place, wasn't her apartment back in the States or her parents' house. Her home was in another plane, another world.

Her home was Vex.

"We'll take you home soon," Emily said, squeezing Kinsley's hand. "It'll be better once you're back with us. You'll have time to recover, to forget—"

"No."

"What?"

Kinsley pulled her hand from her mother's. "I'm not going back to the States, mum."

Emily drew in a slow, deep breath, and turned her body more toward Kinsley. She spoke her next words calmly. "I understand how much you love traveling and how much your platform means to you. But you've been through something. Something you won't tell us about. And it happened while you were alone and still healing, love. You should take time off to be around your family, so we can support you while you recover from...whatever happened."

Kinsley's heart clenched, and she found herself fighting back the sob catching in her throat. She couldn't speak. She didn't know how to make her mother understand. Going back to Oregon meant being thousands of miles away from Vex, away from the place she truly longed to be. She didn't want to forget him, didn't want to forget what had happened, didn't want to move on. She...couldn't. Not from this.

"We're worried about you," Emily said softly, brushing her fingers down Kinsley's arm.

"Mum, I..."

There was a gentle knock on the door. It opened a moment later, and Dr. Ames stepped inside.

"Results for your urinalysis are in," the doctor said as she rolled a stool closer to Kinsley and sat down on it, settling her computer on her lap. "Perfectly healthy. But there's something I need to discuss with you regarding these results. Are you okay with your mother being here, dear, or would you like me to speak with you alone?"

"She can stay," Kinsley said.

When her mother took her hand, Kinsley didn't pull away.

Dr. Ames nodded, leaned a little closer, and held Kinsley's gaze. "Kinsley, are you aware that you're pregnant?"

Everything froze within Kinsley. Her heart, her lungs, her thoughts—everything but those words echoing in her mind.

Kinsley, are you aware that you're pregnant?

She was...pregnant? That wasn't...

"*What?*" Kinsley rasped, her heartbeat roaring back like thunder in her ears. She must've misheard. There was no way Dr. Ames had said what Kinsley thought she had.

But before the doctor could respond, Emily's fingers squeezed Kinsley's hand. "That must be wrong."

"I take that as a no," the doctor said, frowning. "I could run another test, if it would make you more comfortable."

Kinsley shook her head. "I...I had a tubal ligation. It's not possible."

"A tubal ligation is highly effective in preventing pregnancy, but in very rare instances, pregnancies can still occur. And according to the tests we ran on your urine, this is one of those very rare instances."

Stunned, Kinsley settled a hand on her belly and looked down. She was pregnant. *Pregnant.* She didn't know how it was possible, and she didn't care. After everything she'd seen and experienced these last few months, how could she deny this was real?

Magic existed. *Impossible* didn't hold much meaning anymore, did it?

And if she was pregnant, that meant Vex would be—

"Free," she breathed so quietly that she barely heard her own voice.

Her mother's hand settled on her cheek, guiding Kinsley's face toward Emily's.

With panic gleaming in her eyes, Emily said, "Kinsley, please. Please tell me what happened. If someone raped you—"

Kinsley yanked her face away. "No! He didn't hurt me!"

Emily's eyes widened. "He?" Fury contorted her features as she stood. "So there was someone? What did he do to you?"

"He loved me!" Kinsley cried. "He loved me, mum, and I loved him. But he...he..." God, why had Vex done this? Fresh tears trickled down her cheeks. "He let me go so that I could be free."

"Would you like me to call the constables back in here?" Dr. Ames asked carefully.

Kinsley shook her head. "No. I have nothing to tell them. He didn't hurt me. Nothing happened that I didn't want."

Emily's brow creased in worry. "If you're pregnant, what...what about the risks?"

"I don't care. I'm keeping it."

The danger to her life didn't matter. If there was any chance that this baby could survive, this precious life created by love, she would take it. And if it lived...

Vex would be free.

"Kinsley..."

"Mum, please." Kinsley caught her mother's hands. "I know what you must be thinking, and I...I don't know what I can say to make it better. But I need you, okay? I need your trust, and I need you."

Emily frowned, eyes welling with moisture. "Oh, love..."

She leaned down and hugged Kinsley just as fiercely as she had when they'd first been reunited in the woods. Kinsley closed her eyes, and for that little while, she was able to set aside her conflicted, tumultuous emotions and simply take comfort in her mother's presence, her mother's love.

When Emily finally pulled back, the doctor spoke. "If you're up for it, Kinsley, I'd like to get you in for an ultrasound. That way we can get an idea of how far along you are and discuss appropriate prenatal care."

Lifting a hand to wipe her leaking eyes, Kinsley nodded.

THE RETURN TRIP to the cottage was quiet. She knew her mother still had lots of questions, and her father and aunt even more so, but they respected Kinsley's need to process everything that had happened.

The sun set while they drove, leaving the Highlands dark. But that darkness was not as complete as it had been on the night of the accident. The night when Kinsley's life should have ended...

The night when her life had truly begun.

Her hands cradled her belly. The ultrasound had confirmed that she was, in fact, pregnant—nine weeks along. Which meant Kinsley may well have conceived the first time she and Vex had made love.

Nine weeks. In the past, Kinsley would've been fretting, terrified that something would go wrong. But nothing would happen to this baby. She *had* to believe that. And she would make it so, no matter what it took.

I'm carrying Vex's child.

Kinsley smiled, brushing her thumb across her belly.

The ultrasound had given Kinsley her first glimpse of her baby. Just a little white thing on the black screen, with the teeniest arms and legs. Thankfully, it was too soon to tell whether the baby had wings.

When she'd heard its heartbeat, she'd bawled all over again.

Though the doctor had warned that pregnancies after tubal ligation ran a much greater risk of being ectopic, the ultrasound had shown the baby in Kinsley's uterus, exactly where it was supposed to be.

"Sometimes," Dr. Ames had said, "the human body is far more resilient than we give it credit for. Sometimes we heal even when medicine says it shouldn't be possible."

Kinsley knew it was more than that. When Vex had saved her, when he'd shared his immortal life force with her, she'd been healed. What if it had done more than heal her injuries? What if that binding had restored her, inside and out?

Fate. This had to be fate.

And that sense of being surrounded by destiny's threads, of being guided by them, only strengthened when her father turned the car onto a road she'd only seen once but would never forget. Even though so much had been obscured by the rain that night, she recognized it immediately.

She felt this place.

As they rolled down the dirt road, Kinsley sat up straighter and stared out the window. Her eyes darted back and forth, scanning the trees, seeking even the faintest light in the darkness.

Static crackled across the car stereo. Kinsley's heart raced, and she grasped the door handle, ready to throw it open at the faintest flash of blue.

"Every time we come down this road," her father muttered as he changed the radio station, only to be met with static at a slightly higher pitch.

"Eyes forward, Aiden," Emily scolded.

The radio fell suddenly silent, and Aunt Cece said, "There. Simple as switching it off, isn't it?"

Aiden grunted. "Must be a weird dead zone here or something."

They reached the bend in the road where Kinsley had crashed. She knew the spot, even though it was dark and no evidence remained of her car having gone off road.

Yet no wisps showed themselves. There were no spirits drifting through the night, no eyes watching from the shadows.

Kinsley's heart sank, dragging her down with it. She let her head fall back, and it lolled as the car trundled over the little bumps and irregularities in the road. That alternate world was behind her now. She felt it receding even as its call to her grew stronger.

She returned her hands to her belly and closed her eyes.

Vex loves me. He freed me because he loves me.

But no matter his reasons, it still hurt that he hadn't given her the choice.

I would have chosen you, Vex. I would have stayed.

When the car came to a stop, she didn't open her eyes. Not until her father said, "We're here, Kins. Want me to help you inside?"

Kinsley glanced out the window and beheld the cottage for the first time with her own eyes. It had looked so quaint and enchanting in the pictures. Had looked so magical, so perfect. Something about the listing had been…right.

But it had never been this cottage beckoning her soul. It had been the nearby woods; it had been a nearby world.

"No, it's okay," Kinsley said, reaching for the door handle.

She climbed out of the car and closed the door behind her. As she stood there, clutching the sides of her dad's coat closed around her, she looked toward the forest. Once more she searched for a glimpse of blue between the dark trunks.

There was still nothing.

Tears pricked her eyes.

"Kinsley?" Cecelia inquired.

Kinsley looked at her aunt, who now stood in front of the cottage, holding the door open.

Aiden wrapped an arm around Kinsley's shoulders. "Come on, baby girl. Let's get inside."

Emily followed as they entered the cottage. Cecelia flicked on the light. Just like in the pictures on the listing, the place was fully furnished, old-fashioned and charming. It had seemed perfect those months ago. There was a faint musty, woodsy smell, though it wasn't unpleasant. Once, it might have even been a little comforting.

There were blankets and pillows on the sofa and chair, mugs on the side tables, and suitcases propped against the wall.

"You've been staying here?" Kinsley asked.

"We came here as soon as we found out about the accident," Emily said. "It was close to where you went missing, and the owners have been very kind about all of it. Gordon and Lucy even helped in the search."

Kinsley turned and looked at her family, *really* looked at them. Her heart clenched. Her parents looked more haggard than she'd ever seen then, her mother thinner, paler, her father sporting a few more gray hairs than she'd remembered. There were dark circles beneath their eyes.

"I'm so sorry," Kinsley said.

Cecelia wrapped her arms around Kinsley. "You have nothing to be sorry about. All that matters is that you're safe." She drew away and cupped Kinsley's face, smiling. "We'll go back to London tomorrow, and you can all stay with me while we make travel arrangements."

"I'm not going back to London, Aunt Cece."

Cecelia frowned. "What do you mean?"

"I'm going to stay here."

"Like hell you are," Aiden said with a scowl.

"Aiden..." Emily intoned.

"No, Emily. I'm not going to stay quiet about this." He scrubbed a hand over his face; his eyes were red and glistening when he lowered it again. "This is twice, Kinsley. Twice that...that we've almost lost you. And here, you're so far away from everyone, from everything. What if something goes wrong again? What if..."

He pressed his lips together and spun away, shoulders shaking with a shuddering inhalation.

Kinsley went to her father and slipped her arms around him, pressing her cheek to his back. He placed his hand over her arm.

"I know, and I'm sorry I've caused you all so much pain. But I...I can't leave, dad." Kinsley sniffled and hugged her father tighter. "I can't promise that nothing will go wrong. That's not how life works. But being here...*this* is what's right for me. This is what I want, and what I need."

"How can you know that, love?" Emily asked. "You've been through so much, and you haven't even told us about any of it. About...him."

Aiden turned in her embrace, forcing Kinsley's arms down, and curled his fingers around her shoulders. "Who is he?"

She searched her father's face. She loved her parents, loved them so, so much, but she hadn't lied when she'd told Vex they had never really understood her.

"I..." Her shoulders sagged. "You wouldn't believe me if I told you."

Aiden closed his eyes and let his head drop. With a measured exhalation, he said, "We're listening."

"We're here for you no matter what," said Aunt Cecelia, "but it would be so much easier to help if we know what happened, Kinsley."

Emily touched Aiden's arm, bringing his attention to her. "Let's let Kinsley take a shower and get settled. Give her a moment to breathe." She stepped closer to Kinsley and pressed a kiss to her cheek. "Then you can tell us. Everything and anything you want to share, all right?"

Kinsley nodded. "Okay."

Moving to the one of the suitcases, Emily opened it and shuffled through the contents until she pulled out one of Aiden's shirts and a pair of sweatpants. She handed them to Kinsley. "Sorry, love. I should've thought to stop off while we were in town to pick you up some clothes."

"These are fine. Thanks, mum." Kinsley walked into the bathroom, closed the door, and leaned heavily against it, tilting her head back as she closed her eyes. With every beat of her heart, she felt the chasm that separated her from Vex.

Kinsley placed a hand on her belly. "We'll free you, Vex. I promise." Opening her eyes, she looked down at her stomach and smiled. "And then, little one, I'm going to kick your father's ass."

But her attempt at humor did little to ease her mood. She missed him, so damned much.

And though she truly wanted to tell her family everything, she couldn't do that without remembering every single moment she'd spent with him. Without reopening wounds that hadn't healed— that would probably never heal.

"No," she whispered, shaking her head. "You're not going to hide from it this time, Kinsley. This isn't the end. It's an interlude. And as much as it hurts...there's still hope."

There was still their baby. A part of Vex was growing inside her, and she would carry that life, nurture it, and protect it.

She and Vex *would* be together again.

After Kisley showered, she dressed and rejoined her family in the main room. They were sitting together with plates on their laps bearing unmistakable Aunty Cece sandwiches. Another sandwich waited upon the coffee table for Kinsley.

"Come, love," Emily said, patting the sofa cushion. "Sit, eat, and tell us."

Kinsley picked up her plate, sat beside her mother, and collected her thoughts as she took a bite. In some ways, it felt like only yesterday that she'd been sitting in the back of her car, eating a ham and cheese sandwich Aunt Cece had packed for her. In other ways, it felt like a lifetime had passed.

"I know how all this is going to sound," she said, "but please, just...hear me out, okay?"

"Of course," Emily said.

Aiden reached across Emily's lap and gave Kinsley's knee a reassuring squeeze. "We're here for you, baby girl."

"All right." Kinsley drew in a steadying breath and began her story.

Surprisingly, the beginning was the hardest part to tell. Everything she'd felt that night came rushing back—her fear, her grief, her longing to live, her understanding that she was going to die. The crushing loneliness of being in the middle of nowhere, unable to get help, unable to say goodbye.

With tears in their eyes, her family sat quietly and listened as she described how Vex had come upon her. The deal he'd offered. She'd decided not to leave out any of the magical, supernatural things she'd experienced, no matter how unbelievable. The more she shared, the easier it came.

The only parts she didn't mention were her intimate moments with Vex.

By the time she finished, she was crying again, but the tears felt just a little cathartic. The burden had lightened, if only a bit.

Her mother, father, and aunt sat there in lingering silence, uncertainty upon their faces, eyes downcast. That hurt a little, but it was such a small hurt in the face of everything else.

Aunt Cecelia broke the silence. "I saw a wisp once."

Emily looked at her, brow furrowed. "What?"

"When we were little. Remember when dad hired that caravan, and we went camping in Wales with our cousins? It was dark, and the adults were sitting around the campfire while we played hide-and-seek in the woods."

Emily frowned, but her eyes soon rounded. "I do remember. Tommy was so cross with you because he couldn't find you. You were hiding so long that we thought you got lost, and we were about to tell mum and dad you'd vanished. Then you came back all wide-eyed and smiling."

"I *was* lost. Scared out of my wits. But then I saw this beautiful blue light." Cecelia smiled. "It didn't make a sound, but I swear it called to me. I followed it, and it led me back to everyone."

"You never told me."

"Would you have believed me?"

"I…don't know."

Cecelia chuckled. "No one would have. But I saw it." She looked at Kinsley and smiled with warmth and understanding gleaming in her eyes. "And I believe you, Kinsley."

CHAPTER FORTY-ONE

The forest was at once familiar and alien to Kinsley. There was no mist, no crystals, no lush summer foliage. All around, the boughs were largely bare. Instead of green—or the golds and reds from before her accident—there was only gray, brown, and white.

There'd been a dusting of snow overnight. Just enough to break up the drabness. Just enough to confirm that she'd made it through autumn, that she'd weathered the changes. Just enough to remind her that even in the bleakness of winter, there was beauty to be found for those willing to look.

But regardless of its appearance, and no matter the season, this place felt the same. It resonated in her soul. It…sang to her.

Kinsley could imagine her father pacing in the cottage living room, ready to rush out the front door in pursuit of her. But she could also imagine her mum and aunt, their sisterly bond strong as ever despite how far they lived from one another, blocking that door together. Telling him to have patience. To have faith.

Though he'd been surprisingly accepting of Kinsley's story, he'd become even more protective after listening. Only after some convincing had he begrudgingly agreed to let her step out alone this evening.

As Kinsley walked, snow crunched softly under the boots she'd borrowed from her aunt. These woods were unknown to her, but she had no fear of losing her way. Something within Kinsley guided her. Something within her knew the way.

When that sixth sense compelled her to stop, Kinsley did so.

She glanced down to find herself right where she'd meant to be—the center of the fairy ring. The mushrooms were untouched by the snow, and the ground around each was clear, as though the fungi were too warm for any frost to stick. Yet the snow gathered within the ring was deeper and purer than elsewhere.

She crossed her arms over her chest. Her breath came out in little clouds that lazily floated away before dissipating. She could just imagine herself beneath the tangled roots of Vex's mighty tree, surrounded by glowing standing stones.

"Did you think you could get rid of me that easily, Lord Asshole?" Voice louder and harsher in her anger, she demanded, "Did you?"

In the back of her mind, she could almost see his seductive smirk, could almost hear his dark chuckle and teasing retort. She wouldn't admit to herself that it was just her imagination. Wouldn't acknowledge that, even if he'd heard her, he wouldn't have understood her words.

"You should never have made the choice for me. You should've talked to me, Vex. You should've asked me what I wanted." She reached up and wiped away a tear. "Because I would have chosen you. I would have stayed with you. What good is freedom when half of my heart is still imprisoned?"

Kinsley sniffled, and the cold air burned her nose. "I'm not going anywhere. So your plan to send me off isn't going to work."

She turned in place and surveyed the forest, wishing for a glimpse of glowing red eyes in the shadows. Once, all this forest and much, much more had been his. In the fading daylight, she could see the dark waters of the loch through the trees, reflecting the cloudy sky, and she could just make out the hazy forms of the hills beyond the distant shore.

It wasn't quite the same as gazing upon this land from the top of a wizard's tower—or while soaring through the sky—but it was her first real look at it.

At what he'd lost.

"You didn't lose me. No matter how hard you try, you can't lose me." Kinsley raised her voice to a shout, willing it across the planes. "Do you hear me, Vex? You're stuck with me. I'm going to haunt you for all eternity if that's what it takes."

"Kinsley…"

That low, gentle whisper sent a chill down her spine, but the sensation had nothing to do with fear. She spun toward the voice.

Three wisps, their forms indistinct, hovered at her eye level. Even though they were diminished in this world, she knew each of them at a glance. More tears blurred her vision.

"It's only been a day, but I've missed you three so much," she said through the tightness in her throat.

The wisps flew closer, brushing her cheeks with little tendrils of faded ghostfire, and she lifted her hands to touch them. That familiar tingling sensation wasn't nearly as strong here. Even though they were with her, touching her, it was like their essences remained elsewhere.

"These ones have missed you too," Flare said.

Echo nuzzled her shoulder. "It is so quiet without you."

Shade settled on Kinsley's hand. "Sorrow wanders our halls."

Kinsley blinked, and tears spilled down her cheeks, the winter air making them burn even more. "How do I get back?"

"These ones know not," Shade replied softly. "For wisps, it is natural."

"If I have this magic in my blood, if I'm a realmswalker, shouldn't it be natural for me too? Shouldn't I be able to go back if that's what I want?"

Flare's light dimmed further. "These ones know not the ways of such magic."

"Nor whether you've power enough to cross again," Echo rasped.

Kinsley had hoped it would've been easy to return, that her magic had been unlocked and she'd be able to make use of it consciously. That she would see Vex again and be back in his arms. But that flame of hope sputtered out.

Fortunately, it wasn't the only hope she'd harbored. It wasn't the only way to be reunited with Vex. Just the fastest.

"How…is he?" Kinsley asked.

All three wisps dwindled.

"The magus is but a shadow," said Flare.

"More than a shadow," Shade corrected. "A void, swallowing light and leaving only darkness."

Echo brushed her cheek. "You are his light, Kinsley."

Kinsley closed her eyes against the agony their words roused in her heart. She hated this. She hated that she was helpless to comfort him, to be with him.

I can give him something.

Hope, though, was a dangerous thing. How often had she clung to it only for it to be wrenched away? Hope could make you feel like you were on top of the world and then snatch the world right out from under you.

But hope could also sustain you through the darkness. Even if it was as small as the flickering flame of a candle, it was something. Something that could warm Vex through the long, dark nights to come.

If only Vex had waited, if only he had talked to her...

But she knew why he'd done it. He'd sacrificed his own happiness so Kinsley could have her life and family back. If only he had realized that *he* was the life she would've chosen above all else.

Releasing a shuddering breath, Kinsley opened her eyes and looked at the wisps. "I have something to tell Vex, and since I can't speak to him myself, I need you three to be my messengers."

"What would you have these ones say?" asked Echo.

"First, that he's an asshole. And that I am very, very angry with him."

A soft rustle of laughter came from Flare.

"But tell him that I love him anyway," Kinsley continued. "And that I'm not leaving. I'm staying right here, waiting for him. So his plan to give me freedom was stupid and pointless."

"Waiting for him?" Echo tilted their head. "This one understands not."

"The curse remains," Shade said. "The magus and these ones will not be freed."

"Not yet. I have one more thing for you to tell him." Kinsley smiled at them and placed a hand on her belly. "I'm pregnant."

The wisps brightened and swelled.

Flare's ghostfire danced. "You are with child?"

Kinsley nodded. "I think when Vex saved me, he healed my body completely. If…if there are no complications, our baby will be born in the summer, and you will all be free."

They twirled around her in a rush. Kinsley could feel their joy; it settled warmly within her as they pressed themselves against her chest and she hugged them close.

CHAPTER FORTY-TWO

Vex set a stack of books atop the table with a thump. Their shadow, softened by the glow of the wall-mounted crystals, stretched long over the table's surface.

Something heavy twisted in his gut, coiling through him and sinking into place. It dragged him down, down, down...

Down to the ritual chamber. It insisted he go there. Insisted he belonged there.

Clenching his jaw, he lifted the first book off the stack. Bound in faded red leather, it had been etched with words that had nearly faded over the long years. But he knew it well. He'd read it over and over again, had committed the recipes for potions and tinctures it contained to memory.

He set the book atop another stack upon the table, one filled with tomes regarding brewing and alchemy.

A small, pale-skinned hand settled on the next book from the pile in front of Vex. Beautiful, delicate fingers, capable not only of gentleness but surprising strength and deftness, caressed the cover and brushed along the spine before plucking the book up.

Vex's heart pounded, loud but hollow. He lifted his gaze to see Kinsley, his lovely, radiant mate, examining the tome in her hands.

"What about this one?" she asked, turning those brilliant blue-violet eyes toward him. Her voice was faint, haunting, coming to him from across a rift in time.

Vex opened his mouth. That insidious thing within him squeezed, constricting his chest and choking off whatever response he'd been about to offer.

His reply instead came from behind him. His own voice, echoing across the eternity that had passed since this exchange between himself and Kinsley had occurred.

"Beasts of the Blademarshes," said the Vex of long ago. "A place in the realm of my birth."

Kinsley smiled. "I think I'll enjoy this one."

Molten heat flooded Vex's heart, but it was surrounded by such terrible, impenetrable cold—cold that only strengthened when Kinsley stepped away from the table and vanished like a candle's flame snuffed out by a soft breath.

He felt the invisible tether binding him to his mate pull taut, demanding he follow her. That tether had not once slackened since yesterday morning.

And Vex could not follow her.

Growling, he picked up the bestiary, which had remained at the top of the stack, and strode to the shelves beside the reading nook. Shifting two tomes aside, he slid the bestiary onto the shelf.

"Nature. Fauna," he muttered before turning away.

But he halted when he inhaled. The library had always been dominated by the distinct, comforting scent of books. A different smell lingered in this spot. Orange blossoms, honey, and rain. Each component natural and individually sweet, but in that combination, they became so much more alluring. Became irresistible.

They became Kinsley's.

Her scent lingered on the cushions, pillows, and blankets here, where she and Vex had sat so many times to read together, laugh together, and dream together.

Where they had made love.

Vex clenched his jaw. How long before her scent faded? How long before naught of her remained in this place but his memories?

Kinsley's laughter sounded from the nook, clawing at his heart from the unreachable past.

Vex turned his face away and shut his eyes. He could not bear to glimpse another specter.

"So you really hand wrote this one, too?" she asked. "I don't understand how your hand didn't fall off. The writing is so tiny."

Though his lips moved, his words came from the reading nook rather than his mouth.

"You would doubt me, human? Recall how easily boredom has accosted you in your short time here. Then recall how long I've been here."

She laughed again. "Fair point. But that doesn't excuse your writing being so dry."

Vex opened his eyes and stalked back to the table. The knots inside him drew tighter with each beat of his heart, but he wouldn't let them prevent him from doing his work.

Should have gone down...

"No." He sorted more of the stack, placing books into piles according to their categories.

Should have gone when she called.

"To what end?" Vex slammed down a tome about herbology, fingers twitching on the cover. "Did I not waste all of yesterday in that dank chamber? And to what avail?"

Should have gone...

When Kinsley's voice had rippled through the cottage not long ago, calling from another world, Vex's urge to go down to the ritual chamber had grown stronger than ever. He knew she was in the stone circle on the other side of the veil. Had he but accompanied the wisps down there, he could have…

Could have what?

Been close to her.

Close to her, yet worlds apart.

Could have heard her, yet never understood her.

Could have felt her but not touched her.

Could have been reminded even more thoroughly that he'd chosen this. That he'd sent her away, knowing full well the price he would pay for it.

"Naught would have come of it," he muttered, continuing through the stack. "My time is better spent here. Tending to our—"

His throat constricted, and he gritted his teeth, pressing a hand over his chest as though it could soothe that hollow ache.

"*My* home."

But that correction was a lie, bitter and vile. This place was no longer his. In the short time Kinsley had spent here, it had become *theirs*, and it could never be anything else.

Vex set aside another book, revealing the last in the stack. A tome bound in weathered black leather, its yellowed pages damaged along the edges. He lifted it carefully, hand trembling, and brushed his thumb across the cover.

Kinsley spoke again from the reading nook. "I've felt a lot like Alythrii for as long as I can remember."

He squeezed the tome. That force inside him squeezed his heart. The pressure only intensified when he heard his own words from that same night.

"Of the places you've journeyed, which is dearest to your heart?"

"No," Vex said, shaking his head. "Extraplanar studies. A small section, but—"

"Mmm... Here," Kinsley said.

Eyes downcast, Vex strode to the shelves beside the reading nook. If he were to turn his head aside just a little, he would smell her again, would see her again.

It isn't her.

"Definitely here," she finished.

Vex placed the realmswalker's journal on the shelf. "I've not the time to tarry in memories."

She will never again see her favorite place.

And this place would never again feel like home.

"But there is nowhere else. Not for me. She may yet find somewhere."

She had to find a place, lest all this... No. This could not be for naught. She would heal. She would live.

Kinsley's voice again drifted from memory to haunt him, this time in his head—in his heart.

I'm happier than I've ever been in my life.

Air refused to flow through his throat, and his pulse throbbed at his temples.

"Magus?" Shade called from the library's entrance.

Heat roiled beneath Vex's skin. He'd not sensed the wisps' return.

Had you but followed her call...

"These ones bring tidings, magus," said Echo excitedly.

All three wisps flew toward Vex, their ghostfire bright and spirited.

"She is safe?" Vex asked through the dryness in his throat.

"She is," Shade replied, turning their head as they surveyed the library. "The crossing left her body unharmed."

The implication was clear.

Vex's next words came with abrasive heat and stinging grit. "Then I need hear no more." He moved toward the table, only for the wisps to dart into his path, stopping him.

"Magus..." There was warning in Flare's tone, fiercer than anything they'd displayed in all the time Vex had known them.

"Leave me."

"These ones shall not," Echo declared, swelling to nearly match Flare's intensity.

"I've matters to attend. I shan't repeat myself."

"What matters?" Flare demanded.

Vex threw his arms out. "The reorganization of this library."

"Look upon it, magus," Shade said, mimicking his gesture. "Truly see it."

Scowling, Vex raked his gaze across the library. Whatever retort he'd been about to make faltered before ever gaining voice.

Swaths of shelving stood empty. Piles of books, some stacked almost as tall as Vex, lay not just upon the table but all over the floor. Several looked so precarious that even magical intervention might not have been enough to prevent them from eventually toppling.

The library was a mess. A leather-bound labyrinth.

"Temporary chaos. Necessary to achieve the end goal." Vex waved at the shelves near the nook. "I am arranging them by subject. A far more logical system."

Shade floated to one of those shelves, casting their glow upon the books there. Gently, they said, "These are not arranged by subject."

"Of course they—"

"They are not," said Flare.

Echo joined Shade at the shelf and pointed to the tomes. "You have but gathered the books Kinsley most enjoyed in one place, magus."

Vex's brow furrowed. Scarcely two dozen books were on those shelves; he could've sworn there'd been more. Could've sworn they'd been categorized properly. Yet he recognized every book upon that shelf as one he'd read with Kinsley, especially the last two.

Beasts of the Blademarshes and Alythrii's journal stood at the end, side by side. Hadn't he placed them on separate shelves, in separate sections? Mayhap...mayhap there was an overlap between the two, and he'd simply lost his focus for a moment?

"It has been but one day, magus," Shade whispered.

"One day..." Vex chuckled humorlessly. "Each heartbeat has been an eternity."

Shade and Echo moved to Vex, the former touching his hand. "This will change naught."

"Yet these tidings may ease you," said Flare as they joined the others.

Echo flickered with excitement. "These ones bear a message from Kinsley."

Vex's insides clenched, halting both his breath and his heart. As much as he wanted to hear what she'd said, he wasn't sure if he could bear the pain of it. Wasn't sure if he could bear hearing her words from anywhere but her own lips.

"Speak," he finally choked out.

"You are an asshole," Flare said without hesitation.

The blunt statement struck Vex like a blow; he flinched, pressing his lips firmly together.

"Kinsley's words, magus," said Echo.

Flare gestured to themself. "This one's words as well."

Shade stroked Vex's hand with a tendril. "And she is angry with you."

"Very, *very* angry," Flare amended.

The void at Vex's center grew wider, deeper, colder. That he was wholly deserving of her anger did not diminish the hurt it inflicted. But better her wrath than her hatred.

"Yet she loves you still." Shade rose to hover directly before

Vex's face, flanked by the other wisps. Their ghostfire was strong, steady...hopeful.

"She will remain close," said Echo, "awaiting you."

Jaw muscles ticking, Vex shook his head. "I acted so she may move on. I'll not have her lingering here because of me."

Ghostfire blazed hypnotically around Shade's dark core. "She has good reason, magus."

"There is no good rea—"

"Kinsley is with child," Flare said.

Vex's mouth hung open, remaining that way as his mind struggled to decipher Flare's words. "What did you say?"

"Kinsley carries your child. Your seed has taken root within her womb."

Now it wasn't just pressure from within—Vex was being crushed from all directions at once, the entire universe collapsing upon him.

"That... That cannot be," he finally rasped. "She..."

"Is with child," the wisps intoned together.

Vex knew they were not lying. He also knew Kinsley would not have lied to them, especially not about this. But it shouldn't have been possible. She'd taken measures to ensure she could not conceive, to protect herself from all the heartache and danger she'd faced.

"Gods," Vex breathed, raking his fingers through his hair. "She is with child. *My* child. And I banished her. Sent her away just when she most needed me.

"Fuck!" His claws bit into his scalp as that hole inside him yawned. "I must find a way to reach her."

Breathing raggedly, he hurried to the nearest pile of books, tossing them aside one by one as he sought anything regarding travel between worlds.

Voice quavering, Echo said, "Magus, please."

"She mustn't be alone," Vex growled. He could not stop Kinsley's voice from sounding in his mind, telling him anew of what she'd been through—of what had happened the other times she'd been with child.

He'd sent her away, but he refused to lose her.

He flitted from book to book, muttering the titles upon their spines. There was a solution somewhere. Something he'd misunderstood, something he'd overlooked, something he'd missed. There *had* to be.

"Magus," one of the wisps said with concern.

"Please," another begged as Vex dug into more books.

"Vex."

That name, spoken in Shade's voice, punched through Vex's focus, stilling his hands. His pounding heartbeat pulsed throughout his body, making his soul itself quake.

"You need not a book to tell you, Vex," Shade said, their words like a cool, caressing wind on a hot summer's day. "You know what must be done. Know what you need."

Kinsley.

She was all he needed.

And this news…it meant he might have her again.

No, it meant he *would* have her again.

Vex released the book in his hand and slowly straightened. "Patience and faith. No small things to ask of myself, given the circumstances."

Kinsley carried their child, and he could not reach her, could not help her, could not be beside her were anything to go wrong. He was truly powerless now—and he'd chosen this.

"She shares your lifeforce," said Echo.

"And a strength all her own," added Flare.

Yes, Vex's mate was strong. Strong, brave, selfless, and stubborn. She could see this through. She would. And he'd spend every night in worry, would spend every day cursing not the sun but the barriers separating him from his mate. Helplessness and concern would eat at him.

But he would endure it all. He would endure his guilt, would endure both his mate's anger and the rage he harbored for himself. And he'd voice not a word of complaint, because no price was too great to pay for her.

Already, Kinsley had returned something that he'd thought lost to him forever after yesterday—hope.

"I must beg your aid in sending a message to her on the morrow, should she return," Vex said.

"Aught these ones might do, magus, consider it done," said Shade.

"Thank you. All of you."

The wisps drew in close, and Vex embraced them gently. Their magic hummed against him, relieved and joyous in a way he'd not sensed in many, many years.

When his child was born, he would fly from this place. Naught else would keep him from his moonlight. Naught would keep him from his heart.

He would claim his mate and his child, and no one would ever take his happiness from him again—not even himself.

CHAPTER FORTY-THREE

KINSLEY TURNED toward her family and waved them closer. "I don't know if this will work, but I need you to trust me."

Aiden approached, keeping his gaze angled down toward the circle of mushrooms in which Kinsley stood. "Is that…?"

"A fairy ring."

Emily tucked strands of her short blonde hair behind her ear. The tip of her nose was red from the cold. "I didn't even notice it when we found you."

"Understandable considering the circumstances, I'd think," Cecelia said. Her brow furrowed. "So…this is real?"

Kinsley nodded. "When Vex sent me back, this is where I appeared." She lifted her gaze and swept it around the surrounding woods. The area was so overgrown that it was difficult to picture any building standing on this spot, but she knew this was the place. "His cottage is here. On the other side, I mean.

"I don't know if this will work, but if it does, I'd like you to meet them. Just…don't freak out." Kinsley called out the wisps' names. Her voice carried through the forest to mingle with the creaking of branches and distant bird songs.

She felt a flicker of magic, the faintest tingling along her spine, before the wisps materialized in front of her. She'd come to recognize the sensation over the past few days; every evening, she'd come to the circle and called them. And each time, she'd felt that tingle, had felt the tiniest change in the air, right before they appeared.

Kinsley clung to those little tastes of magic. They were her lifeline to Vex's world. Her proof that even here, magic was real.

Echo and Flare bounced, their bodies animated despite being so dim in this world.

Shade brushed a tendril along Kinsley's arm. "These ones are glad to see you, Kinsley."

"Oh, my God," Cecelia breathed, backpedaling from the circle.

Emily started and reached for her sister. "What's wrong?"

Eyes wide and filled with wonder, Cecelia righted herself and took a step toward the wisps. "They're real."

A crease formed between Aiden's brows as he looked from Cecelia to Kinsley. "What's real?"

"You don't see them?" Cecelia asked.

Emily shook her head. "I don't see anything."

"Most mortals cannot see these ones," said Echo, turning to study Kinsley's family.

Flare moved closer to Cecelia. "Magic has faded in this world, and these ones are bound to another place."

Cecelia's eyes widened. "I can hear them too. Those whispers..." She tentatively raised her hand.

Flare brushed against her fingers. Aunt Cece snatched her hand back with a nervous, delighted laugh.

"So you really can see something?" Emily asked.

Cecelia nodded. "I can. They're real. And they're so...beautiful." She reached out again, and she didn't pull back when Flare touched her. "I saw one of you as a little girl once. It helped me find my way back to my family, and I was just so relieved that I never got to thank them. It was gone when I looked for it, but I knew I hadn't imagined it."

"These ones are drawn to the lost," Shade said as they and Echo joined Flare. "These ones guide them to wherever they must be."

Kinsley's thoughts turned back to that long-ago night when she'd been traveling to a remote cottage in the Highlands. She hadn't been lost in the physical sense, but emotionally, spiritually...

And then she'd seen a blue light in the darkness.

She would've welcomed a less extreme means of following that light, but in the end, she'd been led to the exact place she needed to be.

"I can't understand them," Cecelia said. "Their words are just..."

"Niggling at the back of your mind?" Kinsley suggested with a soft smile.

Her aunt chuckled. "Yes."

Though Kinsley's parents could neither see nor hear the wisps, they remained with Kinsley, asking hesitant questions about what she and Cecelia were witnessing.

Somehow, Kinsley knew their hesitance wasn't due to disbelief but uncertainty. They were unsure of how to engage with a phenomenon that was outside their perception and understanding. But their efforts warmed her heart.

Soon enough, Emily declared it was time to allow Kinsley some privacy. She and Aiden headed back for the car, which they'd parked along the dirt road, very nearly having to drag Aunt Cece along with them.

Kinsley understood her aunt's reluctance to leave. She understood the allure of the fantastic, of the magical, and wondered if Cecelia had been denying that call for most of her life. To finally have her experience validated after so long must've felt amazing.

But Kinsley was glad to have some time alone with the wisps, because she was finally able to blurt out the question that had been burning inside her the entire time.

"How is he?"

"Solemn," Shade replied. "Still pained, but the light has rekindled in his eyes."

Kinsley smiled and slipped her hands into her coat pockets. "When you go back, remind him that we may be apart, but we're not alone. I'm carrying part him with me even now."

The wisps sketched little bows, and Echo said, "These ones shall."

"Is he over there now? In the circle?"

The wisps nodded.

Kinsley drew in a deep breath, filling her lungs with crisp Highland air. "I love you, Vex!"

Her voice echoed faintly between the trees, across the gray winter sky, and over the deep, dark waters of the loch. And in those echoes, she thought she heard Vex's voice calling from beyond this world.

Winter crawled on, strengthening its grasp on the glen day by day, but Kinsley did not break her routine. Rain, snow, sleet, and biting winds would not stop her daily visits to the fairy ring.

Two weeks after she'd returned to this world, Kinsley's father and aunt had to go. Both had been months away from their lives. The tears Aiden Delaney shed while saying goodbye nearly broke Kinsley. He gave her the biggest, tightest hug before he and Aunt Cece climbed into their car and began their long drive down to London.

Kinsley's mother did not accompany them. Magic or not, Emily Delaney was not about to leave her pregnant daughter alone in the middle of nowhere. Fortunately, her company allowed her to resume her graphic design work remotely, even with the time difference between the United Kingdom and the Pacific Northwest.

Every day, the wisps exchanged messages between Vex and Kinsley. They told her of his worry, his excitement, his determination, his love. She spoke to him, wanting him to hear her voice even if he couldn't understand. But she never admitted her own worry. It had dwelt at the back of her mind as nine weeks of pregnancy had turned to ten, then eleven, and now twelve.

She could not cast off that worry, but she wouldn't allow it to take control. One simple, powerful thought—one unshakeable belief—held any doubts at bay.

Our child will live.

Twelve weeks, and many more to go. Twelve weeks, each taken one day at a time; twenty-eight more to take one day at a time.

That was when she received an unexpected call. Her mother saw the caller ID on Kinsley's phone and was about to reject the call before Kinsley stopped her.

Kinsley accepted the call and lifted the phone to her ear.

"Kinsley?"

Hearing Liam's voice for the first time in so long was oddly... anticlimactic. Everything she would've expected to feel was absent. There was just...nothing.

Unprompted, he went on and on about how concerned he'd

been, about how he'd known at heart she would be okay because he just couldn't imagine life without her.

And she was honest with him. She congratulated him on his beautiful family, his adorable child. She told him she was glad that he was happy, and she told him that she hadn't been for so, so long. That he'd hurt her very, very deeply. Had abandoned her. And she pointed out that for someone who claimed he couldn't imagine life without her, he really hadn't seemed to notice how much she'd withdrawn in the past few years.

He was silent for a moment, and when he spoke again, his voice was hoarse and thick. "I'm sorry. I know after everything I put you through, it doesn't mean much, but I am. You never deserved the pain I caused you."

Kinsley had heard so many apologies from him over the years. She'd never found meaning in them before, and that hadn't changed. But she didn't need meaning from Liam's words. Didn't need his sincerity. She didn't need anything from him, didn't want anything from him.

"I know you wanted to keep in touch, but whatever this is between us, it's done."

"Kinsley, please. We can still be friends."

"No, Liam," she replied in a gentle tone that would've made Shade proud. "I lost my friend years ago. Goodbye."

After the call, she felt a little lighter, a little less burdened. She'd moved on from Liam during her time with Vex, and she'd hardly thought about him. But finally saying those things to him, finally speaking up for herself after spending so long trying to keep the peace, felt good. This was…closure.

She quite swiftly—and happily—returned to not thinking of him.

Strange as it was to be living with her mother after years away from home, Kinsley fell into a comfortable routine with Emily. They cooked and ate breakfast together every morning, took walks along the dirt road or the shore of the loch when the weather was fair enough, enjoyed lunches and teatime. They did puzzles together, played a few of the old boardgames that had been stored in one of the cottage's cabinets, and talked more than they had in years.

Kinsley didn't record her hikes and explorations nearly as much as she'd intended, but she still journaled, scrapbooked, and kept in touch with her audience. And she took up another craft, one she used to do as a child, which her followers enjoyed.

She began making little forest displays and fairy houses using items from the surrounding woods—sticks and bark, stones, moss and nuts, as well as leaves and flowers that she and her mother dried and pressed. And Emily joined in occasionally, finding delight in something new to her.

Before bed every night, they called or video chatted with Kinsley's father, and they did the same with her sister and aunt at least a couple times a week. Though Madison remained skeptical and uncertain after being brought up to speed, whether she believed or not made no difference. All Maddy cared about was that her sister and her soon-to-be niece or nephew were safe.

And every evening, before the sun set, Kinsley went to the fairy ring to talk to the wisps and Vex, who she always felt there. His presence was undeniable, more familiar with every visit, but always out of reach. She kept them up to date on the baby, but information was regrettably limited. There were no doctor visits to recount, no test results to share.

That had been the only thing about which she and her mother had fought. Emily had insisted Kinsley go for regular check-ups. Under any other circumstance, Kinsley would've agreed wholeheartedly. Only after a long, emotional, tear-filled conversation had Kinsley finally convinced her mother to see her point of view.

This baby wasn't human. And Kinsley could not risk the truth being found out by anyone outside her family. The potential danger to her child would've been too great. How the hell would they explain it if the ultrasound showed tiny claws on the baby's fingers, or little wings sprouting from their back?

Thankfully, her mother had relented, though on one condition. She made Kinsley promise that if anything went wrong, they would immediately race to the hospital.

With research about pregnancy, childbirth, and home deliveries added onto her daily activities, Kinsley had no shortage of things to do, and she rarely found herself alone. Yet the days weren't easy. Winter's worsening chill had nothing on the cold at the center of her heart. Her trips to the fairy ring sustained her, but each was a single drop of water on her tongue as she faced dehydration in a desert of loss and loneliness.

But the visits weren't the only thing sustaining her. No matter how much Kinsley missed Vex, no matter how much it hurt to be apart from him—and some days hurt more than any pain imaginable—her spirit was always uplifted by the life growing inside her.

Because twelve weeks of pregnancy had turned to thirteen, then fourteen, and she'd spent the next seven days battling rising panic. She'd never carried a child past that point. Had never made it so long, so far, and every bit of her, ever cell in her body, every neuron in her brain, every drop of blood in her veins, willed this child to hold on, to keep going. To live.

Then fourteen weeks became fifteen, sixteen...

At seventeen weeks, she realized she was showing. Just a small bump, nothing that anyone else would've noticed, but she saw it. And the first morning she noticed it, she stood in profile before the bathroom mirror, gently running her hands over that bump and smiling the biggest, warmest smile of her life, barely aware of the moisture gathering in her eyes.

Not long after, she felt the baby's first movements. The very next day, it was all she could do to stop herself from sprinting through the forest to get to the fairy ring and tell the wisps what had happened. While she held her shirt up, they hovered before her belly, their little ghostfire arms tickling her skin. Though the baby didn't move for them, the wisps remained like that for a long while, making soft, awed sounds reminiscent of the wind sweeping over a grassy meadow.

They said they felt the lifeforce inside her, said they sensed the magic, the strength. When they departed, they were brimming with eagerness to share the news with Vex.

Afterward, Kinsley and her mother spent a lot of time sitting in front of a crackling fire with blankets over their laps and their hands on Kinsley's belly, waiting with bated breath to feel even the faintest stirring from her womb.

As the days passed, Kinsley's new crafts blossomed into a modest but fulfilling business. There was demand from her audience for her little displays, so she opened an online store. In addition to building a lovely website for Kinsley, Emily demonstrated an impressive knack for packaging the often-delicate creations, and happily offered to put them in the post during her weekly trips into the nearest town for groceries and supplies.

Even as winter railed against the coming spring, bringing late season snow, Kinsley continued her visits with the wisps. She wouldn't have stopped for anything. But those visits were hard sometimes for reasons that had nothing to do with the weather.

Especially the day when she felt the baby move as she stood inside the circle of mushrooms, talking to the wisps.

In an instant, she went from laughing and smiling to ugly crying.

The wisps' surprise and concern only made her cry harder. They were so sweet, so kind, so thoughtful, but nothing they could've said or done would have stemmed the flow of her tears.

So they waited with her, their dim ghostfire flickering in the gathering dusk. Kinsley's tears sharpened the sting of the cold air against her face, and ice stabbed at her nose and throat with her every trembling inhalation. But finally, she calmed enough to explain her sudden shift in mood.

Vex was so, so close, but he couldn't reach out and settle his hand over her stomach. He couldn't feel what she felt. Couldn't feel the little life they'd created against all odds. Couldn't just...be *with* her.

It was far from her finest moment, especially when she swore at him for taking all that away, for eliminating any chance of them sharing all these experiences, good and bad.

She quickly apologized despite knowing that he wouldn't have understood her words, but it didn't ease her hurt that night.

The next morning came regardless, followed by another, and another, and Kinsley carried on. Winter finally relented to spring. Her little bump grew, and the baby moved more and more. The sun shone warmer, brighter, and longer.

Yet Kinsley found herself yearning for the moon and stars.

She took to filling some of her quiet moments by talking to her baby. She told the little one how much they were loved, told them about the wisps and a tiny, magical world nestled between two others. But more than anything, she told her baby about their father.

The nicer weather meant longer, easier walks, and the glen felt like a whole new place as green again spread over the land. She drank in the fresh air, which was kissed by the scent of the loch and the smell of new life. She delighted in the fragrance of gorse, the prickly bushes with bright yellow flowers that grew in any open space they could find. Before coming to Scotland, she'd been told the blooms smelled like coconut, and she'd not quite believed it. Now she knew firsthand how astoundingly similar the scents were.

But she always found herself wishing for another scent on the breeze—a hint of oakmoss and amber.

The lengthening days only made her feel farther away from Vex. She continued visiting the fairy ring every day without fail, taking advantage of the increased daylight to stay a little longer each evening. Some part of her always wanted to stay until the sun went down, as though somehow the night would enable her to hear Vex, to feel him more clearly, to see him...

Even after the wisps, who could not hold themselves long on this side of the veil, departed, Kinsley would remain at the fairy ring, talking to Vex. She told him about her day, about their child, told him how much she loved and missed him.

And when she closed her eyes, she could picture him in the ritual chamber, sitting with his back against a standing stone or lying at the circle's center with his wings spread across the ground, listening to her talk. Sometimes, she even thought she heard his muffled voice from afar—but it never carried into her world strongly enough to be certain.

In April, Madison visited, having finally staffed her bakery well enough for it to continue operating while she was gone. Kinsley hadn't realized how long it had been since she'd seen her sister until they were hugging each other so, so tightly.

Kinsley couldn't be sure whether she or Madison started crying first. Regardless, both sisters were quickly sobbing as Maddy apologized again and again for not having been there, for not coming sooner, for not having been a better sister when Kinsley had needed her the most.

Kinsley assured her that no apologies were necessary, and that

Maddy and their parents had done so much for her. But in the end, it always would've come down to Kinsley making a choice. She'd had to decide to heal, and though she'd chosen to undertake that journey by herself, she never would've reached that point at all without the love and support of her family.

Though Kinsley had planned to give Maddy a day or two to settle in after crossing thousands of miles and numerous time zones to get there, she couldn't wait. She brought her sister to the fairy ring that evening. And Madison, despite her weariness and continued skepticism, couldn't hide the flicker of curiosity and excitement in her eyes as they stepped into the circle of mushrooms.

Watching her sister, Kinsley called for the wisps.

Madison's eyes swept back and forth as she bounced in place, hands tucked securely in the pockets of her hoody. "So, what am I looking for here, Kinsley? Because I don't see—"

Her words were silenced by a gasp. The wisps had appeared directly in front of her, their ethereal bodies resembling haunting flames.

"Oh," Maddy breathed. "Wow."

A huge grin spread across Kinsley's lips. "You can see them?"

"Yes!"

When the sisters returned to the car a little while later, they told their mother everything. With an exaggerated pout, Emily proclaimed that it wasn't fair. Here not even a single day, and Maddy had already met the will-o'-the-wisps. When would Emily get to see something amazing?

Kinsley sat back and cradled her belly. She could feel what the wisps had sensed—the magic, the power, the wonder of the life taking shape inside her. "Soon, mum. You'll get your chance soon."

The week passed much too fast, bringing another teary-eyed goodbye as Madison headed home. She promised to do all she could to make it back during the summer, after the baby was born.

The highlands felt more and more alive, and the baby grew faster and faster. Only a few weeks after Maddy's visit, Kinsley marked a new milestone—the start of the third trimester.

It came with so many of the things she'd heard mothers complain about. Body aches, swollen ankles and feet, the delightful sensation of being so squished on the inside that drawing a deep breath was a struggle. Her baby bump—which had long since surpassed the word bump—seemed a smidge more ponderous each day. She had to relearn how to move to account for it.

And she welcomed all those things with delight. Every discomfort was worth it, and she'd endure it all a thousandfold for her child. For Vex.

She missed him so, so much. Missed his deep, smooth voice, missed his stories, his dry humor, and his earnest, heartfelt words of love and adoration. She missed the sound of his laughter, his kisses, and his gentle caresses. Missed how perfect she felt while she was in his arms, how perfect *everything* felt while she was in his arms.

Even when they'd spent time in his cottage separately, she'd always been comforted by knowing he was only a short walk away.

The nights were worst of all. They were so lonely without him, and the darkness felt so empty.

She and her mother bonded further over that. Though Emily talked to Aiden every day, it was clear that she felt that sense of loss, felt that distance between herself and her husband. In over thirty years of marriage, Kinsley's parents had never spent more than a couple weeks apart from each other.

Kinsley refused to take anything for granted. She thanked her parents for what they were doing, for all that they'd done. Told them she knew how hard it had been on them.

And they told her they'd always do everything they could for Kinsley and Madison...and for their grandchild.

Though they rarely lasted long, rainstorms often struck the loch. Kinsley got her money's worth out of the rain gear she'd ordered. The sound of raindrops breaking on her raincoat was actually kind of soothing.

When the weather was nice, she'd bring a book along to the fairy ring. The wisps enjoyed listening to her read, but it wasn't just for them; it was for Vex and the baby too.

Spring became summer. The days were pleasantly warm, the glen was breathtaking in its beauty, and the baby was strong. Damn strong, based on how hard some of their little kicks were getting. Kinsley's daily walk from the car to the fairy ring took a little longer each week, and soon enough, her mother insisted on walking alongside her to ensure Kinsley made it down there safely.

Soon.

Kinsley spoke that word more times than she could count during those long summer days. She said it to her mother, her aunt, her father and sister, to the wisps, to Vex, and to the baby. Most of all, she said it to herself.

With every repetition, it became heavier, larger, more solid. With every repetition, it took up more space in her heart. Anticipation, anxiety, impatience, excitement—it was all that and more.

Soon could never be soon enough.

Vex said it right back to her, albeit through the wisps. They said he'd been restless, broody, and irritable, that the fire in his gaze was fiercer than ever. They didn't describe a man fallen into despair and despondency, but a fearsome beast eager to escape his cage so he could rush forth and claim his mate.

Whole lifetimes had passed over the months. Kinsley had watched seasons come and go, had watched the land and her body change. She'd felt the baby change. And as summer approached its pinnacle, the forest increasingly resembled Vex's realm. Her already immense longing for him expanded further.

Every day, she went to the fairy ring. She refused to let anything stop her—not the weather, not her swollen feet, not the belly that forced her to groan each time she got out of a chair. It didn't matter how much she had to waddle to get around, or that she felt like she had to pee every five minutes because she swore the baby slept with a tiny foot directly on Kinsley's bladder. Every day, she showed up to tell Vex and the wisps that she was still there.

She told the wisps *soon* every day, and every day, they repeated that word back to her, carried from Vex's lips to her ears, to her heart. The summer air was abuzz with life, with the future.

When her back ached so intensely that she'd almost been unable to get out of bed, she still made it to the circle. When her eyelids were nearly too heavy to keep open after a long, restless night during which no position known to man or fae had provided even the slightest semblance of comfort, she still made it to the circle.

Until the day she couldn't.

CHAPTER FORTY-FOUR

With one hand under her belly to support it, Kinsley leaned over the arm of the sofa and cried out as she was struck by another contraction. The pain started in her lower back and quickly radiated through her core. She dug her fingers into the upholstery, squeezed her eyes shut, and gritted her teeth.

The contractions were growing in frequency, intensity, and length, and this one was overwhelming enough to steal her breath.

Emily rubbed Kinsley's back. "Breathe, love. Just keep breathing. You're doing so well."

Kinsley forced her lungs to work, drawing in deep, measured breaths. They helped a little. Though she'd watched a dozen videos on breathing techniques and had practiced them so many times, though she'd consumed all the information she could find about childbirth and home deliveries, she didn't feel like she was prepared at all for the reality of labor.

And with each contraction, the anxiety and fear she'd fought so hard to hold back surged in a tidal wave, crashing over her.

Her baby was coming. What if something happened?

Even if I don't survive this, as long as the baby lives, as long as Vex is freed...

The contraction eased, allowing Kinsley a moment's respite. She knew the next would come all too soon.

"Okay," she said, slowly straightening.

Emily handed her a water bottle. "Drink."

Kinsley drank several gulps before passing the bottle back to her mother. With Emily's hand on her lower back for support, Kinsley continued walking laps around the living room. All the furniture had been pushed aside to make space for this. As much as Kinsley wanted to sit down, to rest, to sleep, walking helped.

Despite all their preparations, despite knowing this day was imminent, both Kinsley and Emily had barely been able to quell their panic when Kinsley's water had broken the prior evening. They'd been just about to head to the car for her daily visit with the wisps when it had happened.

Her mother had become a tornado, rushing to prepare the bed, move the furniture, and gather everything they'd need for the delivery as Kinsley changed into a button-down nightgown. Somehow, between all that, Emily had also informed their family that the time had come.

That had been hours and hours ago. Each minute had trickled by slower than the last.

Kinsley walked until the contractions came too fast for her to recover from them. The light of dawn was streaming through the windows by then. Exhausted, she lay in bed, drifting into brief bouts of sleep before being awoken by another agonizing tightening in her core. Every time she woke, her mother was there with words of encouragement, with water for her to sip, with a cloth to gently mop the sweat from Kinsley's face.

But as much as she loved her mother, and as thankful as Kinsley was to have her there, there was one person she longed to have by her side more than anyone.

Vex.

Soon. He'll be here soon.

The hours wore on, and Kinsley bounced between fitful slumber and painful consciousness, finding solace only in the fleeting moments between the two.

It wasn't until night fell, leaving the cabin dark but for the golden glow of the lamps, that Kinsley was stricken by the irresistible urge to push.

Kinsley gripped the bedding and let out a scream.

CHAPTER FORTY-FIVE

Vex paced around the edge of the ritual chamber, eyes downcast and unfocused, as a maelstrom raged inside him.

Every evening since he'd sent her away, Kinsley had visited the fairy ring to talk to the wisps. Every evening apart from the first, Vex had come to this chamber, where he'd listened intently to her voice as she spoke in another world.

Those visits had been his life. His nourishment. His reason. Hearing her voice, even if he could not understand, had been a balm for his tortured soul. He'd spent his days eagerly awaiting her visits, and he'd descended to this chamber earlier and earlier as the weeks passed, unwilling to be anywhere else when her call first sounded through the veil.

Even then, he'd barely endured these long months. Were the time to stretch to years, decades, centuries without her, he would come undone. Never had he been more foolish than when he'd convinced himself he could withstand eternity without Kinsley.

Only the weakest of threads held him together now.

Kinsley had never called for them yesterday evening. The wisps had crossed over to search, but they'd found no sign of her. Worry had gnawed at Vex through the night and the entirety of this day. The wisps had entered her world again and again, and the result had always been the same.

When she'd missed today's visit, a mountain of dread had plunged into Vex's gut.

Heat crawled beneath his skin, and his fingers itched with restlessness. He kept his hands behind his back, clamped strongly enough that they tingled with the threat of numbness. Tremors coursed through his wings. Instinct demanded he spread them and take flight, demanded he soar to his mate.

But neither his wings nor his magic could carry him to her.

"She is fine," he said.

The only response came in his own echo, which followed quickly on the heels of his words and obscured them with rumbling mockery.

If she was fine, she would have come. If she was fine, she would not have deviated from the routine she'd kept for all this time, would not have...vanished.

I would know if she has come to harm. I would feel it.

I would know if she was...

His stride faltered, and his every muscle tensed at once. He clutched at his chest against a rush of pain. Shallow, ragged breaths tore in and out of his throat, burning his lungs.

"She is not gone," he growled.

Again, his echo layered over his words, twisting them, tainting them.

Kinsley carried his lifeforce. They were bound. No distance could break that bond, no magic could sever it. He would have known.

But he could draw no comfort from that. The storm inside Vex was one not of wind and rain, nor of thunder and lightning, but fear and anxiety, helplessness and guilt. She was alive, but was she safe? Was their child safe?

Vex thrust his hands into his hair, tugged it back roughly, and rasped, "Where is she?"

The unknown had burrowed deep into his heart, and he could not cast it out. He could not stop it from touching his every thought, from corrupting his every emotion, could not stop it from growing larger and larger with his every step.

Those emotions were too big and potent for him. They were too much for his mind, for his body, for his soul. They were a beast outgrowing its tiny cage, pushing against the bars with increasing force.

And those bars were already bending. They were dangerously close to breaking.

The fabric of Vex's reality rippled. For a fleeting, torturous moment, he felt Kinsley's world. He did not feel her.

He knew what the wisps would report even before Shade said, "No sign, magus."

"These ones' calls go unanswered," Echo added.

"And night has fallen," Flare said.

The pressure within Vex swelled. The seams of his very being were tearing. His mate, his child, out of reach, out of sight and hearing, lost.

No. They are not lost. Cannot be.

Vex turned his head toward the wisps. All three were dim, their ghostfire diminished. Depleted.

They'd crossed over countless times since the prior evening, and he had no doubt that they'd repeatedly journeyed as far as they could from the heart of this realm in their searches. He'd never seen them so small and weak.

Yet to his shame, that desperate part of Vex demanded he send them back. Nothing was more important than Kinsley and his child. He could not look for her, but the wisps could, so they needed to go back and resume their search. He needed to command them to do so, needed to beg them to do so.

"Rest, magus," Echo said softly as the wisps floated closer to Vex. "These ones will hold vigil here should she call."

As the wisps hovered before Vex and he beheld them, as he felt their dwindled essences, his shame grew into a lumbering monster. That he'd even entertained the thought of putting them at risk was unforgivable.

No one else would pay for his choices. No one else would suffer for his foolishness. He would never again endanger those he loved.

"No. It is well past time you three rest." Vex brushed a finger against each wisp, frowning at the faintness of the tingling against his skin. Somehow, his voice remained steady and calm, though his heart was thumping and there was not a shred of steadiness or calmness within him. "I would not have you burn out your fires, my friends."

"Magus?" Shade tilted their head.

Vex gently brushed the wisps aside and stepped past them, ducking beneath an archway formed by a pair of large roots to enter the circle of standing stones. The ley lines' power hummed beneath his feet, mirroring the restlessness inside him.

"Magus, what are you doing?" asked Echo.

In the center of the circle, Vex stopped. He lifted his hands and reached out to the stones, willing his magic to mingle with theirs, to blend with it. The runes flared, their green light casting the rest of the chamber in shadow.

Overwhelming energy flowed into Vex. It buzzed in his bones, crackled through his veins, roiled under his skin.

"Magus, please," Echo pleaded. "You know it will not work."

"It must," Vex replied through clenched teeth as he struggled to focus that magic. It was a flood, a surging tide, and he had naught save his will to shape it, but there was no other choice.

It mattered not that he'd tried this dozens of times over the months, nor that he'd never once succeeded.

He had to find his mate. He had to be with her.

"You cannot cross," Shade called, but their voice sounded far off now, drowned out by the roaring song of the magic.

The stones were already attuned to Kinsley's world. Vex felt it, a connection so real and solid it almost seemed as though he could reach through and pluck something from the other side. But he didn't need to bring anything here. He needed to send himself there.

His arms trembled with strain as he brought his hands together, focusing on that attunement, on the arcane path the stones had forged between worlds when Vex had unlocked the power of Kinsley's blood. He bent all his willpower toward it.

"The door is unlocked," he rasped. "Open the way."

The air shuddered around him. Fire sparked in his veins, accompanying the arcing magic, searing him from within.

"Open to me!"

The power swelled and swept forward, but it halted before ever leaving his body. Something caught it—a net woven of magic so ancient that it had existed before time, that it had been spun from the very fabric of creation itself.

Vex's soul trembled. He knew that arcane net; it was as familiar to him as his own hands. The queen's curse. It stretched against the magic's force, but only slightly.

"Open," Vex repeated, voice raw. "Open to me!"

The curse solidified. Vex leaned into it, driving more and more magic at the arcane barrier, pouring all the strength of his mind, body, and spirit into it, but the net began to contract all the same. It drew in on him, reversing the flow of magic.

Pain wracked his body as his muscles locked. *"Open..."*

No, no, no! Not now, not again! No!

Green energies burst from the standing stones, and a wave of power crashed over Vex. It blinded him, deafened him, numbed him, crushed him. Scalding heat swept through his body, blazing down into his bones. And the curse, that cruelest of gifts from the cruelest of queens, cinched tight around Vex's heart.

All at once, the magic dissipated.

Vex staggered and sucked in a harsh breath. Echoes of agony pulsed through him, a stinging, burning, permeating ache, but it did not compare to the cold, icy grip on his heart.

He'd endured such agony hundreds of times in his attempts to cross over, many of those occurrences just over the past seven months. But this time...

He fell onto his knees, barely feeling the jolt of the impact, and roared. All his suffering, all his helplessness, and all his longing emerged in the sound, which became broken and hoarse as he collapsed.

Forehead to the ground, he clawed at the moss and earth beneath him. Clawed at it and wept. He'd cursed the queen for dooming his mate, but this was his doing. This was his choice. And despite it, Kinsley had held on. She'd endured. She'd remained.

But he'd lost her anyway. Just when *soon* had been its closest, he'd lost her, and he could do nothing to find her, nothing to help her, nothing but love her from so damned far away and hope she and their child were safe.

The tears falling from his eyes were hotter than the curse's grasp, but there was nothing to dam their flow.

A flicker of magic brushed against Vex's senses when the wisps came to him. With gentle touches and soft voices, they soothed him, comforted him, supported him, just as they had for untold years. Yet in that moment, he was a broken creature. Naught could assuage his agony. His mate, his life, was beyond the barrier, and he could not get through. His love was not enough to tear down the wall.

Vex pressed his forehead against the ground as tears dripped off his nose. "Kinsley..."

Whatever strength had remained in him drained slowly, and he sagged down, wings falling over him limply.

That huge, consuming ache in his heart overpowered all else. He'd failed her. Failed them. He had succumbed to despair in two days, after his mate had kept faith, had clung to hope, for months.

Something stirred. Not Vex, not the wisps, not the standing stones or the tree. Something beyond all that but somehow part of everything, something unfathomably immense but infinitely delicate and tiny, something woven into all existence and wrapped around it.

A shiver stole through Vex. The movement of that barely perceivable, incomprehensible force rippled into him. If it was magic, it was unlike any he'd ever felt. It was terrible yet comforting, ominous yet filled with promise.

The curse's venom seeped into his veins as though in response, spreading fire through him. The cords of that net sizzled inside him, drawing tight, coiling like a serpent. He exhaled.

Vex's chest seized. His heart stopped, and his lungs refused to draw breath. The wisps' frantic, concerned voices washed over him, their words lost to his understanding. He scarcely felt their touches as that stirring within the fabric of creation intensified and radiated into him.

The pain receded against a slow, refreshing tide. The threads of the curse, the links of the chains the queen had forged out of pride, greed, and spite so long ago, unraveled as that force engulfed them.

Vex's heart thumped. He sucked in a sudden, shuddering breath and pushed himself up on trembling arms.

With the same unhurried inevitability with which it had come, that force faded into the ether. Silence spread in its wake—the sort of silence that came only when a sound one had heard ceaselessly for as long as could be remembered suddenly fell quiet.

Fate.

That force had been fate.

Sitting back on his heels, Vex inhaled again. He couldn't recall the last time he'd breathed so deeply. He couldn't recall the last time he'd felt so...unrestrained, unshackled. So...free.

His eyes widened, and fresh tears rolled down his cheeks. "Ah, Kinsley. My moonlight."

"Magus..." Wonder and disbelief filled Flare's voice as the wisps floated in front of Vex.

Echo spread their arms. "Are these ones..."

"Free," said Shade with an uncharacteristic twirl. "These ones are free."

Vex had dreamed of this moment countless times over the centuries, had imagined it over and over in countless ways. Never once had he pictured it happening like this—quiet, subdued, profound.

Yet he had no desire to relish this here and now. The curse was broken, which meant...

Our child has been born.

Vex's heart stuttered.

That did not mean Kinsley had survived.

"We must away," Vex said hurriedly, cupping his hands around the wisps and drawing them against his chest. They pressed against him as he drew upon the ley lines.

The runes blazed with green magic, the air thrummed, and the earth sang. For the first time in so long, power flowed through him freely, uninterrupted by the curse. He shut his eyes and focused it all on one thing.

Getting to his family.

"Open the way."

CHAPTER FORTY-SIX

STILLNESS AND SILENCE ENVELOPED VEX, so complete that he was certain he'd been erased from existence. There was only...nothingness.

And then there was *her*.

His heartbeat broke the silence, kindled by his Kinsley. He sensed her presence, her lifeforce, so, so close. She lived.

But that was not enough. He needed to know she and their child were hale, needed to hold them in his arms, needed to never, *never* let go again.

He opened his eyes to a night-shrouded forest illuminated by silver shafts of moonlight. Though naught looked familiar, it felt familiar. He'd been here before, long, long ago. Magic swirled inside him, no longer restrained by the curse, no longer cut off from this land that had once been so familiar, the land from which he'd drawn so much power.

But this was not his home.

Vex released the wisps. They darted around him excitedly, their ghostfire blazing with renewed vitality, as he braced his hands on the ground, shifted onto one knee, and spread his wings. He launched himself into the air, hardly feeling the branches and leaves as he crashed through the canopy.

Countless stars twinkled in the night sky, and the moon, round and full, cast its glow on the glen and the loch below. The treetops shimmered in the moonlight, and the water sparkled. He knew this was his realm of old. All this had been his.

He cared not for any of it now.

His eyes snapped toward a source of light on the ground. A tiny cottage, standing at the edge of a meadow with its back to the forest.

There.

Wind whipped around him, blowing back his hair, as he raced toward the cottage with mighty pumps of his wings. He saw nothing else but that building and the yellowish light spilling from its windows.

An arcane wave preceded him just before he landed on the hard dirt path in front of the cottage, blasting open the door. The interior lights flickered and went dark. From somewhere within, a female shrieked.

As Vex crossed the threshold, the wisps fell into place behind him, casting their blue glow on a room where all the furnishings had been pushed against the walls. The air was perfumed by Kinsley's scent, but it was tinged with more.

Her sweat. Her blood.

Without thought, his feet carried him across the room. Each step built his anticipation. His chest swelled with it, close to bursting, as he neared an open doorway leading into another chamber. A bedchamber.

"Oh, my God," a woman breathed from within as Vex stepped into the doorway.

But he did not see the woman. His eyes fell upon the bed, and for a moment, he could do naught but stare.

His Kinsley reclined upon the bed with a blanket draped over her legs. Her skin was pale and glistening with perspiration, and her hair had been woven into a thick braid that rested over her shoulder. Kinsley's eyes, those beautiful, violet-blue eyes, locked with his.

"Vex," she rasped before breaking into sobs.

He rushed to the bedside, cupped the back of her head, leaned down, and kissed her hard. All the longing and pain of the last seven months, all his heartache and guilt, all his love, flowed into that kiss.

Kinsley slipped her fingers into his hair and grasped it. She leaned into the kiss, returning it just as fervently even as she quietly wept.

Blue light pulsed through his closed eyelids as the wisps excitedly danced over the bed.

She tightened her grip on his hair, sending a sting across his scalp sharp enough to make him hiss. "Don't you *ever* fucking send me away again."

"Never," he growled. "Never again, my moonlight."

Kinsley pressed her forehead to his. "I missed you so, so much."

The ache in his chest intensified, constricting his heart, and tears burned in his eyes. He kissed her again before drawing in a ragged breath. "I shall spend eternity earning your forgiveness, Kinsley."

Something lightly struck his chest.

Vex drew back from his mate to look down. There, wrapped in a blanket and cradled against her breast, was their babe.

The breath fled from his lungs. He'd never dared let himself hope he would find a mate. It had seemed so far out of reach. And this? This precious child, created from their love, was something he'd never truly thought possible. This feeling spreading through him, filling him, warming him, was beyond anything he could ever have imagined.

A means to an end… How could he *ever* have thought that about either Kinsley or their child?

"Our daughter," Kinsley said, lifting the baby toward him.

With all the care he could muster and more, Vex took the baby into his hands. She was so tiny, so delicate, so perfect. Green skin a few shades lighter than his own, pointed, black-tipped ears, short black hair, little claws on her fingers. He could feel small wings on her back through the blanket in which she was wrapped.

And her eyes…they were mesmerizing. Vibrant blue on black—her mother's blue, tinged with a hint of violet. He brushed the pad of his finger over her chin. Her tiny hand shifted, catching his finger, and squeezed.

Vex smiled, and the tears fell from his eyes as he whispered, "At long last, I am home."

The wisps gathered around his daughter, casting their blue glow upon her.

"Oh, magus," Flare said, running a tendril across the baby's head.

Echo's ghostfire sparked. "She is beautiful."

"And already this one sees the flame of her spirit, strong and bright," said Shade.

There was movement from the corner of Vex's eye. He turned his head to see a woman step closer to the bed. Her brown eyes were wide as she stared at Vex and the wisps, and despite their color, he could not miss their similarity to his mate's. She settled a shaky hand on Kinsley's shoulder.

Vex fought back his instinctual urge to growl in warning. The woman looked bewildered enough as it was, and she did not deserve such treatment.

"Kinsley," the woman said, "is this…"

"Vex. My mate." Despite how tired Kinsley appeared, she was radiant as she beamed up at him and placed her hand over the woman's. "And these are the wisps. Flare, Echo, and Shade."

Each wisp offered a little bow as they were introduced.

"You are Emily. Kinsley's mother." Vex bowed his head, holding his child just a little tighter. "My gratitude is yours eternally. I owe you everything."

"Of course, you don't. She's my daughter, and she"—Emily nodded to the bundle in his arms—"is my granddaughter." A nervous laugh escaped her. "I can't say that I wasn't surprised by her appearance though. Despite how Kinsley described you, I wasn't quite prepared. And you… Well, you are…"

"He's beautiful," Kinsley said.

"Yes, well, he's also big and frightening."

"You've naught to fear from me," Vex said.

His daughter let out a soft sound that was followed by a cry. That sound, so small, so sad, pierced his heart. Worried, he looked at his mate. "Have I done aught wrong?"

"No." Kinsley lifted her arms. "She's probably just hungry."

Vex passed the child to her. Kinsley cradled the baby, using one hand to open the front of her nightgown and expose her breast. She drew their daughter closer, and the babe immediately sought and latched onto Kinsley's nipple to suckle.

Awed by the sight, Vex tamped down the magic roiling within him. As he reclaimed control, the strange flameless torches that provided light to the room flickered back on. Dismissing his wings, he carefully climbed onto the bed beside Kinsley and slipped his arm around her shoulders, watching her gently brush the baby's cheeks as she fed.

To be this close to his mate again, to feel her warmth and her skin, to smell her... Vex clenched his jaw against the surge of emotion roiling within him.

The wisps floated down to hover just over the bed, also watching.

This... This was his family.

Kinsley sniffled, turned her face toward him, and pressed a lingering kiss to his cheek. "You're free."

He drew her closer against him. "I'm yours."

His mate released a shuddering breath against his neck.

Emily wiped a tear from her cheek. "What will you name her?"

Vex hummed, gently stroking the baby's dark hair. "A true name is a thing to be cherished. To be guarded. It is not something lightly bestowed."

"We can name her when we are alone." Kinsley rested her head against him and looked down at their daughter. "But what should we call her?"

The answer came to him without the need for thought. "Hope."

EPILOGUE

MADISON HELD Hope aloft and rubbed her nose back and forth across the baby's. "Who's the most beautiful baby in the world? That's right, you are. Yes, you are."

Little giggles erupted from five-month-old Hope as she wiggled her arms and flapped her little wings. She was wearing a silver dress and looked absolutely adorable with her short black hair gathered in pigtails with matching bows, making her pointed ears more prominent.

Aiden, who stood next to Emily and Cecelia in front of the Christmas tree with his arms crossed over his chest, smirked. "The most spoiled too."

Cecelia snorted and lightly swatted his arm. "You take part in that spoiling."

"Of course. It's my duty as a grandparent. And if you think she's spoiled now, just wait until Christmas morning."

Madison chuckled and pecked a kiss on Hope's forehead before setting her down on her hands and knees on the floor. "You spoiled me and Kinsley when we were kids too. It's kind of your thing."

Smiling, Kinsley hung a wooden reindeer ornament on the tree. "That's true."

"I did no such thing," their father protested.

Emily rolled her eyes. "How many times did you sneak things behind my back when I told the girls no?"

Aiden gasped, flattening a hand over his heart. "Never!"

"Lies."

"You wound me, my wife."

Emily chuckled, stood on her toes, and kissed his lips. "But I loved you for it anyway. You're such a wonderful father and grandfather."

The cottage was barely big enough to accommodate Kinsley's parents, sister, and aunt, but they filled it with such love that the lack of space never mattered. Kinsley wished everyone didn't live so far apart, but that only made her cherish these times of togetherness all the more. And this would be the first Christmas they all shared with Vex and Hope.

The baby let out a little squeal.

Kinsley knelt, the skirt of her purple dress pooling around her, and held her arms out to her daughter with a big smile. "Come to mommy!"

Hope, who'd grown so much in the past couple months, gave Kinsley a gummy grin and rocked back and forth on her hands and knees with her bum in the air. It was only a matter of time before she would get the hang of crawling, and Kinsley knew there would be no stopping her then.

She didn't even want to think about the inevitable day when her little girl learned how to fly.

"So is it official?" Cecelia asked as she sat down on the sofa, crossing her leg. She sipped her tea.

"Yep." Kinsley picked her daughter up and stood. "The cottage is mine now. Gordon and Lucy were ready to part with it. Taking care of two properties was getting to be too much for them, especially considering this one is so far out of the way."

"And they knew you'd give the place the love it needs."

The little cottage had served as a home for Vex and Kinsley after Hope's birth. Though he'd been able to cross over from the ritual chamber in his realm, he hadn't been able to do the same with the fairy ring. It simply couldn't channel the ley lines' magic well enough to open the way.

So, Vex had erected a new stone circle around the fairy ring to solidify the link between worlds. Even with his magic, it had taken him weeks to shape the stones, carve the runes, enchant them, and set them in place.

Yet even once they were able to return to Vex's realm, they'd decided to keep this cottage. Being so close to the stone circle, it allowed Kinsley easy access to means of communication with her family, and it was the perfect place to host them when they visited. It also ensured that no strangers would take residence there. Though Vex's illusions kept the stone circle shrouded, there was always a chance of it being discovered by someone wandering the woods. It was safest to keep people away.

But this world... It was not for Vex and their daughter. It might have been a long, long time ago, but it had changed too much to accommodate them.

They'd taken trips to nearby towns, and they'd even gone to Inverness once—always after sunset, and always with Vex and Hope disguised as humans by his magic. There had been unmasked wonder on Vex's face as he beheld the modern world.

He'd spoken of using magic to transport them to other parts of the Earth using existing portals. Apparently, such magic was much easier when traveling within the boundaries of a plane than when trying to cross between them. They'd decided to wait a while before attempting such journeys, allowing Vex time to research potential portal locations and Hope time to grow a little more.

The first place they planned to go, at Vex's insistence, was Kinsley's parents' house.

But no matter where they eventually journeyed, they could not escape the truth. This world would never let them openly be themselves. Not even Kinsley, who would remain young while everyone around her aged.

Their home was in Vex's in-between realm. In their own little world.

Where they'd been so, so happy.

Hope curled one of her fists in Kinsley hair. Kinsley smiled and touched her forehead to her daughter's.

Maddy plopped down beside Cecelia, whose eyes flared as she shifted her mug to keep the tea from spilling.

"Maybe I should move here. It's pretty and peaceful." Maddy

wiggled her eyebrows at Kinsley with a grin. "And who knows? Maybe I'll find my own goblin king someday."

Kinsley chuckled. "I think they might be in short supply."

Madison stuck out her bottom lip in a pout. "Not fair."

Cecelia patted her niece's knee. "There, there. We can't all have otherworldly partners, love."

Pressing the back of her hand to her forehead, Maddy sighed dramatically and slouched back. "That means I must make do with old, boring human men."

Aiden cleared his throat.

Smiling, Emily hugged him. "Not you, dear." She reached up and tugged on his short bread. "Getting a little old, maybe, but never boring."

Aiden scoffed and slipped his arms around her, burying his face against her neck and making her laugh. "Might be getting old, but I still know how to make you feel *real* good."

"Dad!" Kinsley and Madison exclaimed.

Cecelia raised her mug in the air. "To lovers who make us feel good. May Madison and I find our own someday."

"Hear, hear!" Madison chimed.

The electricity flickered, making the string lights on the tree cast erratic, colorful flashes across the room.

"Looks like we have company," Aunt Cece said with a smirk.

The front door swung open. Chilly winter air swept in, and three blue orbs followed it, swirling around Kinsley. Hope giggled as she reached for the wisps. They hovered before her, brushing ghostfire tendrils along her arms.

But Kinsley's eyes focused on the open doorway.

Vex emerged from the evening gloom beyond the threshold, stepping into the room. The door closed behind him without so much as a gesture on his part. That quickly, the electricity returned to normal. His long, dark hair shimmered in the light, and silver accents gleamed on his black tunic.

Kinsley's heart quickened, just as it always did when she saw him.

His glowing crimson eyes immediately met hers, and he grinned, flashing his white fangs as he strode toward her. Without missing a beat, he swept Kinsley into his arms and slanted his mouth over hers. His split tongue teased the seam of her lips, and she parted them, allowing that tongue to slip inside and twine around her own. His taste was sublime, and his breath bore a hint of snow and spice. Groaning, Kinsley clutched at his tunic with her free hand, needing more.

Madison released another loud sigh. "As I said, not fair."

Breaking the kiss but not lifting his head, Vex arched a brow. "What is not fair?"

Kinsley smiled and brushed the tip of her nose against his. "That you are mine."

Vex smiled. "Forever."

Hope babbled and grasped a handful of Vex's long hair, giving it a few enthusiastic yanks.

Vex gently caught Hope's wrist and, with patient delicacy, freed his hair from her hold. He leaned his head down and kissed the baby's knuckles. "Hello, my little love."

She cooed at him with the biggest smile on her face, her eyes bright and shining.

Watching their interactions always filled Kinsley with such warmth and adoration, never failing to melt her heart. Before Vex and Hope, she wouldn't have thought such love and tenderness was possible. It was so much more than she ever could've imagined. So much more than she'd ever dared hope.

And it was all hers. *They* were hers.

Vex lifted his gaze to the Christmas tree, which the wisps were circling slowly as they made little sounds of awe. "I see you've managed well enough without me."

"Once the tree is up, Kinsley and Madison can't help themselves," Aiden said.

"At least they're a little more mindful about where they put the ornaments." Emily chuckled. "When they were girls, they'd rush around the tree like little tornadoes, racing to see who could put up the most ornaments. It was…"

"Chaos," Aiden finished.

"It was *fun*," Madison said.

Emily snorted and shook her head. "What wasn't fun was having to untangle tinsel from your hair afterward. I'll never understand how you two always managed that."

"Just a little sisterly competitiveness," said Kinsley with a grin.

"Did you have time to, uh...get everything set up, Vex?" asked Aiden.

Flare zipped to the center of the room, their ghostfire nearly sizzling in their excitement. "Oh, it is—"

"Quiet," Echo said as they joined Flare.

"This one said nothing."

"Thanks only to Echo," Shade said, hovering close to Hope.

Brow furrowing, Kinsley looked at Vex. "Get what set up?"

He met her gaze and brushed the back of a claw down her cheek. "You shall see."

Vex lifted Hope out of Kinsley's arms. She reached for his hair again, but he intercepted her hand with a finger, which she grasped and tugged toward her mouth. He bent it before his claw could come anywhere near her face. "As for you, little one…"

He carried her to Kinsley's parents, staring down at her the whole way, and paused there. It seemed more words had formed behind his lips, but he did not let them out. He simply looked at their daughter with such wholehearted, unconditional love.

"Now that we've come to it, I cannot help but hesitate," he said, voice low and rough.

Kinsley walked over to him and placed a hand on his shoulder. "Come to what, Vex?"

Emily smiled. "Vex asked us to watch Hope for the night."

Eyes flaring and panic sparking in her chest, Kinsley looked between Vex and her parents. "For the night?"

"Ah, love." Her mother stepped closer and cradled Kinsley's cheeks. "It's natural to feel this way when parting from your baby, especially for the first time. But it's healthy for you and Vex to have some time to yourselves. To simply be husband and wife. Or, er...mates?"

"These ones will remain also," Echo said.

"She'll be safe." Aiden held his arms out for Hope. "We promise."

Kinsley watched as Vex passed their daughter to him. "But what if she cries?"

"We'll soothe her," Emily said, stepping back.

"What if she gets hungry?"

"You pumped plenty of milk to last her until tomorrow."

"What if—"

Vex caught Kinsley's chin, tipped her face up toward him, and slipped his other arm around her waist, drawing her body against his. "Should aught occur, the wisps will fetch us immediately."

Kinsley released a slow exhalation, trying to calm herself as she flattened her hands on his chest. "We've never been away from her before."

"Ah, my moonlight… I am just as frightened as you. Just as uncertain. But there is naught to keep us from her. No barriers, no curses. She will be doted upon here, loved and protected, and we will return for her ere dawn breaks over the glen."

She searched his crimson and black eyes. Maybe she was being overprotective, maybe she was being irrational, but she could see her worries reflected in his gaze. They'd both known such loss in their lives, had both been so ravaged by their time apart, that letting go for even a little while was hard. So, so hard.

But hadn't they weathered worse and come out stronger for it?

And she also saw yearning in Vex's gaze, the same yearning burning deep her heart, calling out for him.

"It *has* been a while since we could just be…mates," she said.

Madison scoffed. "Oh, would you two go fuck already?"

"Madison!" Emily snapped with the sort of ominous threat only mothers seemed able to evoke.

"What, mum? We're all grown adults here."

Aiden cleared his throat, nodding toward Hope.

"And one baby," Maddy muttered. "Sorry."

Vex chuckled, brought his lips to Kinsley's ear, and spoke in a deep, sensual whisper. "I do intend to fuck my mate this night."

She sucked in a sharp breath, and her core clenched. *Fuck* had been a foreign word to Vex, but whenever he used it…

I'm so done for.

Aiden turned Hope toward them and, gently holding one of her wrists, made her wave. "Say goodbye to mommy and daddy."

Moving to her daughter, Kinsley pressed several kisses on her cheeks and head. "We'll be back, love. We promise."

Though she knew they were right, and though she really, really wanted some time alone with Vex, it was still hard to let go, even for one night.

Emily shooed her. "Go on. Away with you both."

Before Kinsley could respond, Vex scooped her off her feet, cradling her against his chest. She threw her arm around his neck, and he whisked her out through the front door into the night.

He clutched her close as he leapt into the sky and soared toward the stone circle. In contrast to the biting winter wind, he was solid and warm, and his eyes were filled with fiery desire and wicked promise. She was certain that the glen was beautiful, especially after yesterday's snow, but she didn't look away from him.

Kinsley's heart sped, and her mind raced. What had he prepared? She caught her lip between her teeth, forcing her imagination to still, or else the anticipation would only fill her with restlessness.

His feet had barely touched the ground within the circle of standing stones before the world around them changed. The once disorienting journey now only roused a flutter of excitement in Kinsley—even more so than usual under the circumstances.

The ritual chamber was the same as always. Dark, mystical, thrumming with power. Vex carried her to the doors and up into the foyer. But he didn't bring her deeper into the house from there, didn't go to their bedroom or the library, didn't go to the kitchen to surprise her with a fancy dinner for two.

The cottage's front door swung open ahead of them, and when Kinsley gazed through it, her breath hitched. "Oh, Vex…"

He carried her out into a winter landscape unlike any she'd ever seen. Pure white snow covered the ground and the branches of the trees, with tiny ice crystals sparkling upon its surface like multifaceted diamonds. The trees were adorned with red and white poinsettias, and little lights, resembling countless twinkling stars, shone amidst the foliage.

And there wasn't even the slightest hint of a chill in the air.

"This is…magical." Kinsley looked up at Vex. "So this is what you were doing while we decorated our little Christmas tree? You were decorating an entire forest?"

"I suppose shaping an illusion is not unlike decorating," he replied. "This is for you, my moonlight. You alone."

Vex walked along a short path paved with carved stones, at the end of which lay a bed of ferns and moss, framed by more of those red poinsettias. It was backed by a small rock wall which was free of snow. Dozens of lit candles atop the stone created a warm, welcoming, intimate glow.

When he reached the bed, he knelt and sat her atop it. The soft ferns gave beneath her weight. She smiled at him as he drew away and sat back on his heels, tucking his wings against his back. A warm breeze lifted the strands of his hair, and as Kinsley took in his regal features, she was again reminded of just how otherworldly he was. How breathtakingly *beautiful* he was.

And he was hers. Her mate, the other half of her soul.

Kinsley reached out to tuck wayward strands of his long hair behind his ear before brushing the backs of her fingers down his cheek. "I love you."

He caught her hand and turned his face toward her palm, kissing its center. "And I you." His lips moved to her wrist, trailing small, tender kisses. "It has been too long since last I worshipped you as you deserve, my Kinsley."

She shivered as magic tingled across her skin just ahead of Vex's lips, making the sleeve of her dress disappear. He kissed along her forearm, each brush of his mouth so soft and teasing, so arousing.

"It has been too long since I've shown you what you are to me. My queen." He pressed his lips to the inside of her elbow. "My goddess." His mouth moved faster, up over her shoulder to her neck, where he rasped, "My everything."

Kinsley's breath and heart quickened with his kisses, and she closed her eyes, tilting her head to grant him access. That soothing breeze flowed over her skin, making her nipples harden, as the rest of her dress disappeared with a whisper of magic. Raising her hand, she slipped her fingers into his hair to cradle his head. "As you are mine."

Vex released her arm, and the fern bedding dipped as he planted his hand beside her and leaned closer, his knee nudging her thighs farther apart. He slipped his other arm around her, bringing his heated skin into contact with her now bared flesh, and braced her back as he trailed his lips up her throat, her jaw, and finally to her mouth, which he captured in a deep, claiming kiss.

She clenched his hair and gave over to that kiss just like she had to all the previous ones, just as she would for all the kisses to come for the eternity they would share. He was her breath, the beat of her heart, the blood in her veins. He was the force that had brought her back to life in every way imaginable.

And every kiss, every touch, every word and every glance, no matter how small, would always make her belly flutter, her chest warm, and her soul sing. With adoration, with desire, with love.

Breath ragged, Vex caught her jaw, forcing her eyes to meet his. "My mate, my heart, my love." He touched his forehead to hers. "You are all the magic I will ever need."

AUTHOR'S NOTE

We can't believe it's been five years since we wrote His Darkest Craving. We always intended to return to this world but hadn't realized how long it's actually been. Regardless, we immensely enjoyed writing Vex and Kinsley's story, and we hope you enjoyed reading it!

Will there be more stories in The Cursed Ones series? Yes! We have another one planned, so this won't be the last.

To keep up on current news from us, be sure to join our newsletter. We always share monthly updates on what we're working on as well as art, book recommendations, and more. Also consider joining our Facebook Reader Group!

And if you loved His Darkest Desire, please consider leaving a review. We'd appreciate it so much!

ALSO BY TIFFANY ROBERTS

THE INFINITE CITY
Entwined Fates

Silent Lucidity

Shielded Heart

Vengeful Heart

Untamed Hunger

Savage Desire

Tethered Souls

THE KRAKEN
Treasure of the Abyss

Jewel of the Sea

Hunter of the Tide

Heart of the Deep

Rising from the Depths

Fallen from the Stars

Lover from the Waves

THE SPIDER'S MATE TRILOGY
Ensnared

Enthralled

Bound

THE VRIX
The Weaver

The Delver

The Hunter

THE CURSED ONES
His Darkest Craving
His Darkest Desire

ALIENS AMONG US
Taken by the Alien Next Door
Stalked by the Alien Assassin
Claimed by the Alien Bodyguard

STANDALONE TITLES
Claimed by an Alien Warrior
Dustwalker
Escaping Wonderland
Yearning For Her
The Warlock's Kiss
Ice Bound: Short Story

ISLE OF THE FORGOTTEN
Make Me Burn
Make Me Hunger
Make Me Whole
Make Me Yours

VALOS OF SONHADRA COLLABORATION
Tiffany Roberts - Undying
Tiffany Roberts - Unleashed

VENYS NEEDS MEN COLLABORATION
Tiffany Roberts - To Tame a Dragon
Tiffany Roberts – To Love a Dragon

ABOUT THE AUTHOR

Tiffany Roberts is the pseudonym for Tiffany and Robert Freund, a husband and wife writing duo. Tiffany was born and bred in Idaho, and Robert was a native of New York City before moving across the country to be with her. The two have always shared a passion for reading and writing, and it was their dream to combine their mighty powers to create the sorts of books they want to read. They write character driven sci-fi and fantasy romance, creating happily-ever-afters for the alien and unknown.

Sign up for our Newsletter!
Check out our social media sites and more!

Made in United States
Orlando, FL
20 April 2024